DEAD OF SUMMER

Also by Sherry Knowlton

DEAD of AUTUMN

Diana Thomas
pass it on
Marion Coulter
and on

DEAD OF SUMMER

SHERRY KNOWLTON

Mechanicsburg, PA USA

Published by Sunbury Press, Inc.
50 West Main Street
Mechanicsburg, Pennsylvania 17055

www.sunburypress.com

NOTE: This is a work of fiction. Names, characters, places and incidents are the product of the author's imagination or are used fictitiously, and any resemblance to actual persons, living or dead, business establishments, events or locales is entirely coincidental.

For information about special discounts for bulk purchases, please contact Sunbury Press Orders Dept. at (855) 338-8359 or orders@sunburypress.com.

To request one of our authors for speaking engagements or book signings, please contact Sunbury Press Publicity Dept. at publicity@sunburypress.com.

ISBN: 978-1-62006-593-8 (Trade Paperback)
ISBN: 978-1-62006-594-5 (Mobipocket)

Library of Congress Control Number: 2015947339

FIRST SUNBURY PRESS EDITION: July 2015

Product of the United States of America
0 1 1 2 3 5 8 13 21 34 55

Set in Bookman Old Style
Designed by Crystal Devine
Cover by Amber Rendon
Edited by Jennifer Melendrez

Continue the Enlightenment!

One may smile and smile and smile and be a villain.
—Shakespeare, *Hamlet*

They say if you remember Woodstock,
you weren't really there.
—Anonymous

For Robert and Virginia Rothenberger, with love.
Mom and Dad, you're in my heart always.

CHAPTER ONE

"I'M BEAT FROM ALL THIS DRIVING. You owe me big time, Melissa. Rescuing you from jail wasn't what I had in mind today. I was meditating when you called. Scout was rolling around on the lawn. I was going to take him on a long walk."

"Go ahead, lay on the guilt. But I thought I was going to lose it, locked up in that small cell with all those other women. I'm so glad that my best friend is an attorney. Thanks to you and your pal with the political pull, I didn't have to spend the night." Melissa grimaced at the thought.

"Remember that the next time you decide to climb in a restricted zone on one of our national monuments—and then get into a pissing contest with the Park Police over it."

Melissa waved her camera. "I was just trying to find the best place for a crowd shot."

"Before they hauled you off to do hard time, did you get a chance to actually participate in the RESIST rally?"

"Absolutely. I heard several senators speak about the anti-sex-trafficking bill that RESIST is supporting. Cecily wowed the crowd, talking about international sex trafficking and how this bill could impact it. Some people from the other national anti-trafficking organizations gave speeches. Three survivors told their stories. One was practically a child. Horrible experiences that made me cry." Melissa shuddered.

Alexa pulled her ancient Land Rover into Cecily Townes' driveway. "I'm glad it's staying light longer. It would be hard to find this place in the dark." The small brick farmhouse sat a few hundred yards back from the narrow gravel road. "I've never been back here before. Nice place."

"Check out that garden." Melissa pointed to a huge cultivated area to the left of the house. Even this early in the season, there were patches of green. "Cecily loves digging in the dirt."

Alexa stopped next to Melissa's metallic red Prius. A gray passenger van, a soccer mom model, sat in the far end of the pullout. "Are you going to touch base with Cecily before you leave?"

"Yeah. I'm sure she's been worrying about me. I should have called right after you got me released. But I was so excited to be free that it slipped my mind. Then I passed out on our ride home."

"I noticed."

Melissa plowed right past Alexa's dry comment. "The RESIST march was in full swing when the cops hauled me off. Even though I traveled down there as a chaperone with Cecily and Tyrell , I couldn't ask them to hang around D.C. and worry about my arrest. They had a busload of kids to handle."

Alexa muttered beneath her breath. "Sure. No big deal. You probably told them your best friend would gladly drive ninety miles to bail you out."

Melissa ignored her and pointed at the van. "It looks like she's home. Come on in, and I'll introduce you."

"Sure, for a few minutes. I'm dying to meet this Saint Cecily."

"She is a saint. You know, she was once a Catholic nun but left the order years ago. Now she saves women all over the world." The redhead slipped out of the SUV and waited for Alexa to join her.

"Come around to the back door. No one ever uses the front."

Following Melissa onto a tidy brick walkway that wound around the corner of the house, Alexa paused for a moment to drink in the scene. Huge rolling fields of wheat rustled in the breeze. The final rays of the setting sun turned the distant mountains a dusky mauve.

"What an amazing view."

As she lingered, a dark cloud blotted out much of the fading sunset, and a gust of wind whipped the field into a frenzy. The breeze took on a hint of ozone, signaling distant thunder and lightning.

"Whoa. I think we've got a storm coming." Alexa turned toward the house when Melissa gasped.

Shards of glass covered the small porch, flickering pale orange in the fading light of the setting sun. On the windowed farmhouse door, a gaping square yawned wide where the glass had been.

"Cecily. This is Melissa. Is everything OK?" Melissa called out as she ran up the steps and onto the porch, grinding the broken glass in pops beneath the soles of her sneakers. She pounded on the door.

"Melissa. Be careful." Alexa moved cautiously up the stairs behind her friend. She winced at the loud crunch of glass at each footstep, impossible to avoid on the porch floor. "Maybe Cecily isn't home. Or there's a burglar inside right now." Alexa reached into her pocket for her cell phone but realized she had left it in the car.

Melissa abruptly stopped shouting and knocking. "Alexa, something is wrong. I'm going to check."

Alexa let out a deep sigh and tilted her head to the left, then to the right, trying to dispel the tension building between her shoulder blades. Melissa was pushing her to the limit today. With reluctance, she gave in.

"We'll both go. Does she have an alarm system?"

"I doubt it. Cecily rarely even locks the door." Melissa reached for the doorknob, which turned easily in her hand, and the two women slipped into a mudroom area.

"Cecily?" Melissa called again in a hushed voice.

Alexa grabbed Melissa's hand as they crept into the big kitchen. Following the scent of cinnamon, she noticed an uncovered plate of muffins next to the stove. The sight of a black pocketbook sitting undisturbed on the wide counter sent her pounding heart into overdrive.

"There's a living room and an office through that door," Melissa gestured, her steps slowing.

"Maybe we should go outside and call the police."

"But what if Cecily has been hurt? Let's at least check out the downstairs." Melissa squared her shoulders and marched into the hall. Alexa scanned ahead and behind, on high alert, as she followed her friend.

"I'll check in here. You look in there." Melissa disappeared through the door on the right, and Alexa turned into the room that Melissa indicated on the left. Clearly, this was the office. She could make out the shape of an old roll-top desk in the near corner.

The stormy twilight that filtered through the tall casement windows steeped the room in shadows. This whole thing was creeping Alexa out. She ran her hand along the wall next to the entry, searching for a light switch. Finding none, she took a deep breath and strode toward the silhouette of a floor lamp on the far side of the room. She flipped the switch and sighed with relief as light flooded the office.

That relief vanished when Alexa took in the roll-top desk to her right. The desk was a mess. It looked like someone had pulled papers out of the little cubbies in the back of the desk and dumped them in the center. The big drawers all stood open, and more paper littered the floor beside the desk. The computer monitor hung by a cord, facedown, perched over some files. When Alexa took a step toward the desk, the monitor shifted, hitting the table with a thump. Startled, she backed away.

A coppery smell, like new pennies baking in the sun, hung in the still air. In the silence, Alexa noticed a faint buzzing noise coming from outside the house. Beyond the reflection of lamplight, she could see hundreds of flies crawling over the wavy glass panes of the antique windows.

With dread, Alexa turned left to survey the rest of the room. She moaned and swayed when she spied a pool of blood on the floor at her feet. "Not again. This can't be happening again," she protested under her breath.

As she looked in revulsion at the blood, a thin crescent of red inched toward her like a scarlet claw. She jerked her foot away in horror before she realized that it was a lone, blood-drenched fly, staggering out of the crimson pool in a drunken stupor.

Finally, Alexa took a deep breath, rested one hand on the nearby table for support, and forced her gaze higher. Her eyes followed an obscene waterfall of red-soaked cardboard upward until they came to rest on a motionless body. The slight, gray-haired woman sprawled facedown over a pile of boxes, hands dangling toward the floor.

Alexa gagged and dashed to the doorway. "Melissa," she called into the hallway. "We need to get out of here. I think I've found Cecily . . . and it's not good." She struggled to keep it together.

Melissa emerged from the living room with a look of concern on her face. "Where is she? Is she hurt?"

"In the office. I'm pretty sure she's . . ."

"Oh no. She can't be dead. I don't think she had any health issues." Melissa burst into tears.

"Come on," Alexa grabbed Melissa's elbow. "I'll call an ambulance outside."

"Not until we make sure. Maybe she passed out." Melissa wrenched away and took a step toward the office.

Alexa sighed and reached out with both hands to halt her. "You don't need to see this, Melissa. There's a lot of blood. I'll check for a pulse."

"Blood?" Melissa repeated, tearfully, as if she didn't understand.

"Wait here." Alexa dreaded the idea of going back into that room, but another look at her best friend in shambles stiffened her resolve.

Alexa tiptoed back into the office, skirting the huge pool of congealing blood. Cecily lay completely still over the stack of boxes. Alexa bit the inside of her lip to keep from screaming and gingerly lifted a chalky wrist. No pulse. The woman's slender arm felt cool and powdery, like a child's doll. Alexa trembled as she carefully released the wrist and took a step away from the body.

When Melissa shrieked hysterically, Alexa whirled in terror, thinking the killer was still in the house. However, Melissa stood alone in the office doorway, her eyes fastened on Cecily's dead body.

Alexa gathered up her friend, steering her back through the kitchen and out of the house. "We have to get out of here and call the police, Melissa. Come on." Alexa practically carried her friend through the glass debris on the porch and guided her into the Land Rover.

The minute Alexa reached the driver's seat, she turned the key in the ignition and peeled away from the house. The wind had died, but the gathering darkness seemed to swallow the Rover's lights. She slowed just enough to dial 911 when she reached the macadam road.

"We'll meet the police at the South Middleton Park," she told the 911 operator. "We can't stay at that house. It's not safe."

CHAPTER TWO

"Alexa Williams? You're the one who called this in? Did someone from the Church of the Blessed Lamb come after you?" State Police Trooper John Taylor emerged from the unmarked car and called to Alexa through the open window of the Land Rover. When Alexa recognized the tall trooper, she climbed out of her car. Melissa seemed paralyzed by grief and stayed in the passenger seat.

"Trooper Taylor. We always meet at the worst of times," Alexa replied in a shaky voice, but just seeing the trooper calmed her.

"That's one of the unfortunate aspects of my job." He peered into the Land Rover. "Can you tell me what happened? Who's in the car?"

"That's one of my best friends, Melissa Lambert. She's the reason I'm involved in this. We went to Cecily Townes' house to pick up Melissa's car. The place is a few miles away from here. I gave 911 the name and general location. I don't know the exact address.

"Anyway, we found Cecily dead." Alexa shivered. "At least we think it is Cecily, and I'm pretty sure she was murdered. There was so much blood. And a window on the back door was shattered."

"OK. I have a lot of questions for both of you. Right now, I need you to lead me to Ms. Townes' home. Can you handle that?" he asked with concern.

When Alexa managed a nod, he continued. "Troopers were dispatched to the residence as soon as you called 911. I need to go there now, and I want you and Melissa to walk me through what happened."

"I can do that. I'm worried about Melissa, though. This has hit her pretty hard. She might need medical attention."

"There should be EMS on-site at the house by now. The paramedics can evaluate her and get her to the hospital, if necessary."

"OK." Alexa nodded again. "Follow me."

About ten minutes later, Alexa headed the Land Rover back down the narrow lane to Cecily's farmhouse. Every fiber of her being screamed to turn around and drive in the other direction. But she knew that the police needed to question Melissa and her as soon as possible.

On the brief return trip, Alexa dialed Melissa's boyfriend, Jim Kline. After filling him in on the day's events, Alexa assured him, "I'll get Melissa checked out by the ambulance crew."

She added, "I think we're going to be here for a while with the state police. Can you do me a favor and run over to my cabin to feed Scout and let him out for a few minutes? He's been there alone for hours. The key is hanging under the bench on the deck. The alarm code is 1934. I'll let you know what happens here by calling the cabin phone or your cell."

"You told Jim?" Melissa whispered. "Thanks for calling him. I think I can pull myself together now. I've never seen anything as terrible as Cecily lying there in all that blood. How could someone do that to such a wonderful woman?"

"I don't know, Melissa. I can't understand it either." Alexa pushed away the mental image of Cecily's body. "The police want to talk to each of us, probably separately. Just tell them exactly what happened. Hopefully, we'll get out of here soon."

As they rounded the bend, Alexa parked the Land Rover behind a long line of official-looking vehicles. Flashing red and blue lights gave the farmhouse the look of a carnival fun house. As she and Melissa stood by the car waiting for Trooper Taylor, Alexa blanched at the thought of reliving her discovery of the dead woman.

The paramedics gave Melissa a mild sedative but said she needed no additional treatment. With Alexa's permission, the police did a quick search of the Land Rover. Then, they waited. As the minutes ticked by, tedium whittled away at Alexa's earlier terror. By the time the troopers summoned her, she had regained her equilibrium.

Trooper Taylor and another plainclothes investigator, Trooper Matt Cannon, questioned Alexa, then Melissa, at a table on the tidy brick patio. When introduced, Alexa couldn't hold back a wry smile at the aptness of the partner's name. Cannon looked like one of those no-neck guys who spent most of their waking hours in a gym. The excess muscle and buzz cut made his sport coat and slacks look like they belonged to someone else. But his questions showed sensitivity to the shock that she and Melissa had experienced.

When the troopers finished with their questions about the discovery of Cecily's body, Taylor asked Alexa and Melissa to return to the car. He wanted them to stick around in case there were additional questions.

About fifteen minutes passed, but it seemed like hours. Alexa leaned against the Land Rover's bumper for support. She glanced at Melissa, sitting in the SUV with her feet dangling out the open doorway. She could see that, even with the sedative, her friend was hanging on by a thread.

Alexa pushed onto her feet when the two troopers approached. Melissa climbed out of the vehicle to join her.

Trooper Taylor addressed his remarks to both Alexa and Melissa. "We'll want you to come into the station to go over this again and make a complete statement. I'll call you both tomorrow to arrange times. Thanks for your cooperation tonight. I can only imagine how difficult this has been.

"Ms. Lambert, I just have two additional questions for you right now. Do you know if Ms. Townes has any relatives that we should contact? Or is there someone who knows her family situation?"

Tears filled Melissa's eyes as she answered. "I think she has a brother in Colorado; he lives in one of those little ski towns. Not Aspen. Maybe Telluride? I want to say his name is Richard, Richard Townes. Cecily talked a lot about him and his family when we were in Thailand this winter. Maria Santiago, Cecily's assistant at RESIST, would probably know more than me."

"Resist?" the trooper asked.

"R.E.S.I.S.T., Resolve to Stop Illegal Sex Trafficking. That is, I mean was, Cecily's work; her whole life really. The office is on Louther Street in Carlisle, near the college."

Trooper Cannon wrote in a little notebook as Melissa talked.

Alexa stepped in. "You had another question, Trooper?"

"Yes. When was the last time you saw Ms. Townes alive?" He directed the question at Melissa.

"A little before noon today in Washington."

"Washington, D.C.?" The two troopers exchanged a glance, clearly interested in this development.

"Yes, we were there for a RESIST march. I got separated from Cecily and the rest of our group when I got arrested."

"A minor issue with the Park Police. The charges were dropped," Alexa jumped in, but Melissa continued to babble about the arrest.

"I swear; I have the utmost respect for President Lincoln. I would never hurt his memorial. I just stood up there because it gave me enough height for a good photo. But those bastards tried to take my camera. I mean, those officers." Melissa looked abashed at her gaffe.

Alexa glared at her friend, trying to will her into silence. "I drove down to D.C. to arrange for Melissa to be released from custody. We came straight here upon our return to pick up Melissa's car."

"What were the charges?" Trooper Taylor's tone took on greater authority.

"There was some discussion of defacing a national monument and resisting arrest. But a friend in D.C. government assisted Melissa. No charges were filed."

"Who would we contact to verify this?"

"She was held at the Park Police Central District Station."

Trooper Cannon jotted down another note and took up the questioning.

"And, Ms. Williams, when was the last time you saw Ms. Townes alive?"

"Never. I never saw Cecily Townes before tonight when I found her dead in her office. I went into the house with Melissa so I could meet her." Alexa shuddered at the memory.

Trooper Taylor stepped back a pace. "I think that's enough for now. Ms. Lambert, I'm so sorry for the loss of your friend."

Trooper Cannon asked, "Can you get home on your own or do you need someone to drive you?"

Melissa exclaimed, "My car. That's why we were here in the first place. But I'm not sure I should drive tonight."

"We're not ready to let you have the Prius tonight, Ms. Lambert. The technicians will want to go over the car tomorrow since it has become part of the crime scene. Ms. Williams, you are free to take your SUV."

"Melissa, we'll figure out your car tomorrow. Come on, I'll drive us both to my place. Jim is waiting for you there." Alexa hustled Melissa into the Land Rover before her friend collapsed.

On the long, dark ride home to Alexa's cabin, Melissa fell immediately into a restless sleep. Alone with her thoughts, Alexa couldn't erase the grisly image of Cecily Townes' body collapsed over those boxes like a bloody, broken doll.

What could have precipitated the murder? Melissa wasn't a person who praised easily, yet she had called Cecily a saint. Could this just be a burglary that turned violent? If not, who would kill a saint? Then, Alexa remembered: One of the downsides of sainthood is that martyrdom is often part of the package.

CHAPTER THREE

ALEXA COULDN'T ESCAPE THE DREAM. It was always the same. Reverend Browne, a giant of a man in a towering rage, chased Alexa across the living room of her cabin. His hands reached for Alexa's throat but paused when his wife rushed into the cabin screaming. Alexa picked up the loaded shotgun.

"I will not hesitate to shoot."

When the fanatical minister leapt toward Alexa, she pulled the trigger. Mrs. Browne's wails filled the air as Alexa stared helplessly at the woman's husband, dead and bleeding all over her mother's favorite oriental rug.

But this time the dream changed. Reverend Browne's body morphed into a feminine form, and Alexa was staring at Cecily Townes, bleeding on the cabin floor. Mrs. Browne had vanished along with her husband, but another woman was screaming.

"Melissa?" Alexa jerked awake and bolted upright in bed. Beside her, Scout raised his big head, on alert as if he had heard the voices in her dream. In the glimmering predawn light, Alexa tried to determine if she was awake or still dreaming. Her heart leapt into her throat at the sound of a low moan and footsteps down the hall.

"I am awake," she whispered aloud.

The noises came from Melissa and Jim, who had spent the night in one of the guest rooms down the hall. Last evening's discovery of Cecily Townes' body came back in a rush.

Alexa couldn't deal with that terrible experience yet. She collapsed back onto the pillows. "Let's go back to sleep, buddy," Alexa murmured to the English mastiff. "I am so exhausted."

Scout inched closer to Alexa and nudged her arm with his nose.

"OK. Just a few more hours." Alexa threw an arm over the big dog and closed her eyes.

When Alexa woke again, soft sunlight streamed through the windows. At the same level as the budding green leaves, the second floor bedroom felt like a tree house. Downstairs she could hear someone clattering pans in the kitchen, and the tantalizing smell of brewing coffee wafted through the open door.

Scout hopped off the bed and made for the steps. Alexa figured that Jim or Melissa would let him outside, so she headed for a quick shower. She needed to wash the cobwebs of bad dreams from her head.

As she tugged a wide brush through wet honey-brown curls streaked with blonde, Alexa studied her image. The woman in the mirror looked no different today than yesterday. Same medium height and medium weight. Same hazel eyes clouded with self-reproach. Despite the calm exterior, Alexa felt like an Alice who had fallen down a second rabbit hole. The first time she found a dead body, her life had changed forever. The experience had wrecked her ability to trust, gotten a young mother killed, and ultimately cost Alexa a man she had come to love. Yet, here she was again, confronted with another dead woman. Bad news in oh so many ways.

Stop it; she broke off the torrent of self-recrimination. This situation is totally different. You have no connection to Cecily Townes other than Melissa. So that makes your link to Cecily more like one of those six-degrees-of-Kevin Bacon things. Last night was horrible. But, after you give your statement to Trooper Taylor, you can walk away from this. It's tragic that a good woman has been killed. But this is not the same as finding Elizabeth Nelson dead in the woods.

Alexa swept her unruly hair into a clip. Before she left her room, she threw a lightweight fleece over her t-shirt and jeans. Even in early May, the cabin held onto the night's chill well into the morning.

On the way downstairs, Alexa glanced into the second guest bedroom at the big bed. Melissa still slept, curled into a small ball with her auburn hair spread across the pillow. Alexa pulled the door shut and headed for the kitchen. Melissa needed the rest.

Jim had taken his coffee outside to the deck. Alexa smiled to see the tall, burly forest ranger rubbing Scout's ears. The happy dog thumped his tail a few times when Alexa shuffled out the cabin door, too content with Jim's ministrations to rise.

"I hope you don't mind, but I rummaged through your cabinets and fridge for some cereal and yogurt."

"Of course." Alexa sat down beside him. "I'm glad you found the coffee maker. Do you want anything more? I think I have some English muffins. A good hostess would have been up at the crack of dawn to make you pancakes or something."

"I'm good. Scout has been keeping me company. Actually, I tried to be quiet so you and Melissa could sleep in."

"Thanks. I needed a few extra hours. Melissa was still sound asleep when I came down. I'm worried about her."

"I didn't want to press for too many details last night. I could tell you were both wiped out. Can you tell me everything that happened?"

"Give me a minute to get a cup of tea and something to eat. Then I'll fill you in on the entire mess." Alexa strode into the kitchen, trying to boost her mood with brisk action.

"So she didn't even tell you about the arrest in Washington?" Alexa took another sip of tea as she watched Jim process this new chapter in yesterday's saga.

"No. We didn't talk about anything last night except Cecily's murder. When Melissa and I went up to bed, she fell asleep almost immediately."

"You're right. I guess we focused so much on Cecily's death that we never mentioned Melissa getting hauled off to jail. She only had one phone call, so she contacted me—the lawyer." While she tackled her breakfast, Alexa brought Jim up to speed on Melissa's brush with the law and finding Cecily's body.

Jim became so engrossed in the conversation that he stopped petting the fawn-colored mastiff, so Scout padded down the stairs onto the lawn.

"Wait," he said when Alexa recounted their entry into Cecily's house. "The window's broken. Nobody answers your calls. But the two of you just barrel into the house? My God. Why didn't you back off and call the police?"

"That idea did come up. But Melissa worried that Cecily might be hurt. I probably could have stopped her, but neither of us thought it through. In retrospect, I wish we had stayed outside. It's going to be a long time before I'll be able to get past the sight of Cecily's body and all the blood." Alexa couldn't believe how stupid she had been to let Melissa lead them into that house.

Alexa rubbed her temples, which were beginning to throb. "I tried to keep Melissa out of the room. But she wouldn't stay in the hall. I've never seen her like that. She got hysterical and went practically catatonic in the car when we hightailed out of there. Although they gave her a mild sedative, the EMS guys didn't think she needed any further treatment. But I think we need to keep an eye on her."

"This whole thing sucks. What a traumatic experience. But you know Melissa. She lives life at full speed. Her enthusiasm keeps her on a natural high most of the time." Jim dropped his voice and frowned. "But something like this could devastate her. Especially since she'd gotten so close to Cecily. You know that she's been involved in this RESIST group for months now. She and Cecily became real friends during that ministry trip to India and Thailand. She basically tagged along on one of Cecily's routine checks on the network that RESIST has established to rescue women from the sex trade. She told Melissa that watching her photograph the women was a gift."

Jim leaned forward. "I worried that the trip could be dangerous. But Melissa arrived home with thousands of photographs and a huge amount of respect for what Cecily did for those women."

Alexa shredded her English Muffin. "Yeah. I knew about India and Thailand. That's pretty much all Melissa's talked about since she came back. Isn't her photo exhibit opening next week?"

"Next Saturday."

"I've been too preoccupied with my own issues. I should have paid more attention to Melissa's new cause." Alexa felt a twinge of guilt for tuning out Melissa's constant prattle about RESIST and the ministry trip.

"Look, I know that you've been struggling ever since you shot Reverend Browne." Jim punctuated each word with a rap on the wooden table as he continued. "It. Was. Self. Defense. Period. If you hadn't pulled the trigger, he would have killed you. The man was a maniac."

"Intellectually, I understand that. But it's more than the shooting. It's my lack of judgment in getting involved with Caleb. It's Emily Baxter dying in my place. It's been hard, but I've been way too self-absorbed. Reese couldn't take it anymore; I drove him away." Alexa cringed that she still became so upset about all of this. Scout sensed Alexa's distress and returned to the deck to rest his big head on her knee.

"Reese thought it best to give you some space. When his friend, John Lucas, called with a job on the predator research project in Kenya, he leapt at it. That decision wasn't just about you, Alexa. I could tell that the park ranger job bored him at times. Besides, the way he talked about Africa, you could just tell that his first stint there claimed a piece of his heart."

Jim had shared a house with his fellow forest ranger, Reese Michaels, so Alexa respected his insight into her ex-boyfriend's point of view.

"It was the right thing for Reese, and probably the right thing for me. We left things open. Maybe we'll find our way back to each other. Maybe not. Neither of us made any promises. But, damn." Alexa slammed her empty tea mug down onto the table. "Just when I'm finally getting my act together, it's déjà vu all over again. Here I am, minding my own business, and I find someone else who has been murdered."

"The whole thing is pretty damn freaky. I'd like to see the statistical odds of someone coming across two dead bodies." Jim winced. "Ruling out war zones, of course."

Jim's eyes shifted to a point behind Alexa's shoulder. He smiled and jumped up to greet his girlfriend.

"It's my sweet Melissa. How are you feeling?" he asked as he folded her into his arms.

"Much better. Thanks to both of you. Is there more of that coffee somewhere?" Melissa wore sweats that Alexa had loaned her last night. The pants looked more like capris on her tall body. Against her auburn hair, still damp from the shower, Melissa's wan face appeared paler than chalk.

"Sure, let me get you a cup. Sugar, but no milk, right? How about some cereal or toast?" Alexa gave Melissa a quick hug and headed for the kitchen.

"Toast would be good."

When Alexa brought Melissa breakfast, Jim asked, "What's the time? I have a shift that starts at noon. I can try to get someone to cover if you need me, but I have to let them know."

Alexa glanced at her watch. "It's almost ten-thirty. I expect to get a call from the state police soon. They want Melissa and me to come in and give a formal statement today."

"Do you think you can handle that, darlin'?" Jim asked Melissa with a frown.

"Yes. I'm feeling much better." Melissa bit her lip. "I lost it yesterday. First, spending a few hours in jail. Then, finding poor Cecily lying in a pool of blood. It was just too much. Those EMS guys gave me some potent stuff. Not only did I sleep like a log, but I feel like I can deal with Cecily's death. The police interview. Whatever I can do to help." Her voice became plaintive. "What kind of sick bastard would kill a woman whose only goal in life was to help others?"

Alexa could see through Melissa's struggle to put on a brave front. Clearly, she hadn't fully recovered. But her BFF had to find her own way. Alexa knew from experience that recovering from violence was a personal journey. Still, a little encouragement couldn't hurt.

"Trooper Taylor will track the killer down. I have a lot of faith in him." Alexa stood up. "You two can discuss Jim's work schedule. I'll call Graham to let him know what happened. Melissa, I'd feel better if he goes along to your police interview." With Scout on her heels, Alexa headed inside the cabin to phone her brother. She knew that Graham, the managing partner in their family law firm, would agree to sit in on the interviews.

On the way to police headquarters, Alexa swung by Melissa's little stone cottage on the outskirts of town. She lounged on the front porch swing while her friend went inside to change into fresh clothes.

Melissa emerged a short time later dressed in one of her trademark hippie dresses. It seemed like the redhead had recovered much of her equilibrium with the change of clothes. Although Alexa had upgraded her own outfit to a nice shirt and jeans, Melissa's transformation left Alexa feeling a tad underdressed.

Graham met them at police headquarters. Alexa, glad to see her big brother, felt like the reinforcements had arrived.

He leaned down to put an arm around Alexa's shoulders in an awkward hug, a look of concern creasing his face. "Lexie, are you OK? I can't believe you're involved in something like this again. Melissa, I'm so sorry. I understand that Cecily Townes was a good friend. I didn't know her well, but Kate and I have attended a number of RESIST fundraisers. With her energy and dedication, Cecily was a force of nature. It's hard to believe she's gone."

Trooper Taylor, dressed in his trademark sports jacket and khakis, ushered all three of them into a small conference room. "Thanks for coming in. I know that last night was rough. Probably the last thing you want to do is relive it. But it is important that we go through everything that happened once again. It's possible that you have remembered something new—something that you forgot to mention in the stress of the moment. We'll need to speak to each of you separately."

Trooper Cannon appeared in the doorway and said, "Ms. Lambert. We'd like to start with you. We're hoping you can supply some additional background on the victim."

Alexa got the message and rose. “I’ll be out in the waiting area. Just call when you’re ready for me.”

Sitting in the tiny waiting area, Alexa tried to keep busy by checking emails on her phone. She had trouble concentrating on anything but images of Cecily Townes’ body and that blood-soaked room.

Graham sat in on Alexa’s interview as well. The troopers covered the same ground as the night before, often asking the same question in several ways. They kept honing in on the moment when Alexa found Cecily’s body.

“You say that the blood looked like it was still running across the floor. Did you hear any sound of liquid dripping?” Trooper Taylor continued with the questions.

“That’s an awful thought.” Alexa shivered. “No. The room was silent, except for the sounds coming from outside. The sound of thunder and flies. It had started to thunder just before we went inside the house. And the flies covered the outside of the windows. There were so many; I could almost feel the low hum of their buzzing.” Alexa twisted her hands.

“I don’t think that the blood actually trickled toward me. There was a fly crawling around through the blood. It could have been an optical illusion. I could hardly breathe when I realized that I was looking at a huge pool of blood on the floor.”

“You say that you approached the victim and grasped her wrist. Which one? Did you touch any other part of her body?”

“I had no doubt that she was dead. The body lay completely still. I couldn’t see her breathing. But Melissa thought we should check for a pulse. So, I walked along the wall, away from the blood, and picked up her right wrist. I couldn’t detect a pulse, so I let go of her arm. At that point, Melissa walked into the room and panicked. So I rushed her out of the house.”

“Did you hear any movement anywhere in the house? Any sounds at all? Or see anyone?”

“No. But someone could have been upstairs or hiding somewhere else in the house. I didn’t want to take a chance. I just wanted to get out of there.”

Trooper Cannon spoke up. “Did you try to ascertain the nature of Ms. Townes’ wounds? Did you try to render any assistance?”

“No. I didn’t touch anything but her right wrist. I saw some blood on her upper back, but it appeared that she had a big wound on the front side of her body. It was hidden by the way she fell forward over the boxes, but I could see a column of blood on the boxes, like it had gushed down the side and pooled on the floor.” Alexa shuddered at the memory.

"Do you own a gun, Ms. Williams?"

"My family owns a shotgun that I keep at my home."

"Is that the same weapon used in the shooting incident that resulted in the death of Jebediah Browne last December?"

"Yes." Tears filled Alexa's eyes as she glanced at Trooper Taylor in dismay. She felt like she had been punched in the gut. The events of last fall still haunted Alexa. Anti-abortion extremists killing several young women. Being terrorized by the religious group. Being forced to kill their leader, Reverend Jebediah Browne, in self-defense. Trooper Taylor had been the lead investigator on the case. He knew that she had been cleared of any wrongdoing.

"Alexa, I'm sorry, but you know we have to ask all of these questions for the record." Trooper Taylor reached across the table toward her but pulled back abruptly and picked up a clipboard. "Do you own any other guns?"

Graham interjected. "Can you be more specific? Is there a particular type of gun that you are interested in? Was Ms. Townes' cause of death a gunshot wound?" Alexa silently thanked her big brother for giving her a minute to collect herself.

"We're not prepared to discuss any particular weapon or other details relating to cause of death at this time. Alexa, do you own or have access to any additional firearms?"

"No. The last thing I would want is a gun."

Trooper Cannon shot a hard look at his fellow trooper and picked up the questioning. "Is there anything else you want to mention about last evening? Something that we haven't covered but that may have struck you as odd or out of place?"

"I had never been to that house before last night, so it would be difficult for me to judge whether anything was out of place—other than the dead body. Obviously, the mess on the desk in the office and the broken panes of glass on the door didn't seem right. Other than that, I couldn't say."

"Well, thank you for your cooperation. We'll be in touch if we need anything more."

As they rose from the conference table, Trooper Taylor came around to Alexa and clasped her hand. "I'm sorry that you stumbled into this ugly incident. I doubt that we'll need anything more from you."

"How is Corporal Branche?" She had hoped to say hello to the older policeman who had worked with Taylor on the case last fall.

"He's been assigned to a special task force, so they paired me with Cannon on this investigation. He's a stand up guy. Say hello to Ranger Michaels."

"Reese has gone to Africa on a long-term research project. I'll mention that you asked about him in my next email."

Trooper Taylor finally released Alexa's hand as he murmured, "Africa. You're on your own then?"

"Yes, I am, Trooper. Yes, I am." Alexa realized that Trooper Taylor had more than a professional interest, but she couldn't deal with that now. She just pushed open the door and left the room.

CHAPTER FOUR

"I'M EXHAUSTED. By the time those troopers finished, I felt like I'd done something wrong. I'm so glad Graham came with me. Please tell him how much I appreciated his help." Melissa collapsed into the seat and closed her eyes.

"He would have freaked out if I hadn't asked him to come along to these interviews," Alexa replied. She turned the ignition and shifted the Land Rover into gear, navigating her way through parked state police cruisers. Graham had already left, trying to catch a hockey playoff game on TV.

"Can you drive me out to Mom and Dad's? I need to tell them about all of this. Plus, the cops are going to keep my car for another couple of days. I'll borrow some wheels from them. I think Dad is up to about six old sports cars at this point. I'm sure he can spare one of them for a few days . . . maybe the Triumph."

"Sure. It's always nice to see your mom and dad. They'll be so proud that you were arrested at a protest."

"You're right. I'm just keeping up the family tradition. Although I think my parents spent more time talking about the revolution than actually participating in it."

"Surprisingly, my mom was arrested back during the Vietnam anti-war protests. I'll have to ask her about it, but I seem to recall something about a march on D.C. and being detained in a football field. Looking at her now, it's hard to believe."

"I'm not so sure about that. Your mom likes to traipse around the world to exotic places. She's always been involved in social causes. I can still see a bit of rebel buried beneath the surface."

Alexa shrugged and pulled into Tagg and Fiona Lambert's home. The place looked deserted. Two black labs came running from a small outbuilding to greet the car, but no one emerged from the huge cedar house. Two lines of Tibetan prayer flags, strung between the house and the barn, fluttered listlessly in the anemic breeze. A chicken wandered across the lawn, stopping periodically to peck at the ground.

The Lamberts lived in a sixties time warp and had raised Melissa and her brothers to live in the moment. They named Melissa after one of their favorite Allman Brothers songs. Other beloved musicians served as inspiration for her brothers' names, Jefferson and Donovan.

"Looks like nobody's home," Alexa observed.

Melissa slipped out of the Land Rover. "That's OK. I'll go inside and hang out until they come back. I need some time alone to deal with Cecily's death." Tears came to her eyes. "I just can't believe she's gone."

"Let me know if you need anything. Yesterday was tough for me, and I didn't even know Cecily. So I know you're hurting. Call me if you need to talk." Melissa shut the car door, and Alexa headed home, anxious for time to just chill.

When she walked into the law firm on Monday morning, her assistant, Melinda, followed Alexa into her office. "Mrs. Bertolino called and said it's urgent that she see you this morning. So I moved some things around to give her a nine-thirty appointment. She sounded pretty upset."

"OK. Can you pull her file for me? I wonder what this is about. The adoption is on track as far as I know. I hope there isn't a problem. I can't handle any drama this morning."

"Don't put the cart before the horse. You don't know what Mrs. Bertolino wants. Let me get you a cup of tea before she gets here."

Alexa groaned at another one of Melinda's pithy quotes, but the brief exchange with her irrepressible assistant had lifted her spirits. Mondays seemed to always be one of the busiest days at Williams, Williams, and O'Donnell. So Alexa needed to push past any preoccupation with her weekend experience and get ready to face the busy day.

Alexa loved her job as a junior attorney at the family law firm. Her semi-retired father, Norris, carried a light caseload. Dad wasn't quite ready to quit the firm altogether, but he and Alexa's mother spent several months each year traveling. Her older brother, Graham, managed the firm. The third partner, Pat O'Donnell, planned to retire soon. At that point, Alexa expected to become a partner, although the other junior attorney, Brian Stewart, had his own hopes for advancement.

After graduating from Columbia Law School, Alexa had taken a brief ride on the fast track at one of the big New York City law firms. Soon realizing that she wanted more out of life than sixty-hour workweeks and daily internecine warfare, Alexa came home to the family practice. She had never regretted the move.

By the time Melinda returned with tea, Alexa had finished scanning the Bertolino file. She put it aside and turned to the morning newspaper. The lead story trumpeted Cecily Townes' murder.

Alexa studied Cecily's photo, hoping to replace the image of her dead body with one of the living woman. A handsome woman in her late sixties stared serenely from the page. Her graying hair and plain jacket conveyed a simple elegance. The half-smile on her lips hinted at some secret knowledge. So, this was Saint Cecily. Alexa regretted that she hadn't gotten a chance to know the woman.

The newspaper article didn't mention who had found Cecily's body. The police still had no leads. Most of the story concentrated on Cecily's life history and her many charitable activities. Even though Alexa had heard a lot about RESIST from Melissa, she hadn't fully appreciated the scope of the organization and its international reach. Cecily had won a slew of humanitarian awards, and the list of donors to her advocacy organization included some heavy hitters from around the world.

Although RESIST had been Cecily's main focus, she had been involved in other similar efforts. Alexa noted her role on the board of Children of Light, a local organization that ran a foster care program and worked with juvenile delinquents.

Following a quick knock on the door, Melinda stepped into Alexa's office to announce Mrs. Bertolino's arrival. She whispered, "She's got some guy with her. Not Mr. B."

Alexa rose to greet her client. "Hello, Mrs. Bertolino. How can I help you today? Melinda told me that it was urgent?"

A small woman with curly dark hair, Toni Bertolino was usually a ball of fire. Today, she faltered, each step an effort, until she crumpled into the loveseat.

"It is urgent. Alexa, this is Tyrell Jenkins. He's a social worker for County Children and Youth Services and leads our church youth group. I thought he might be able to help."

Tyrell Jenkins towered over both Toni and Alexa as he struck a pose. His spiraled dreadlocks were parted down the center and cut short enough to frame a face the shade of burnt umber. Moving forward to shake his hand, she had to remind herself to breathe. This man was gorgeous—and he left no doubt that he knew it.

"Nice to meet you, Ms. Williams. I've heard a lot about you." The social worker took a seat next to Toni.

Alexa turned to her client. "Is there a problem? I expect the adoption papers to be signed in the next few weeks. As I told you, the process usually goes smoothly in a case like this, when a foster family is adopting and the parents have willingly terminated their parental rights. We've filed the Notice of Intent to Adopt. The placement supervision period will be finished soon. I don't expect any issues with finalizing the adoption. In little more than a month, Meg will become an official member of the Bertolino family."

"It's not about the adoption. We don't know what to do. Meg has disappeared!"

"Disappeared? What do you mean?" Alexa leaned forward in alarm.

"We haven't seen her since Thursday. She went to school like always. Then, she went to Tyrell's youth group meeting after classes ended. But she never came home. Ed and I were pretty upset when she didn't show up for dinner at six. That's one of our rules. We always sit down together for a family dinner. We called her cell and sent her some texts. But she never answered.

"By nine o'clock, Ed got pretty steamed. He threatened to ground Meg for a month. But I was frantic. By ten, we had called all of her friends. No one had seen her since youth group ended. Then we called Tyrell."

"Meg did attend Thursday's session." Tyrell took up the narrative. "It's the youth group at the Letort Methodist Church. That was an important meeting because we reviewed our plans to participate in a march on Saturday in Washington. I handed out permission slips and went over all the details. Meg signed up for the event. She seemed to be pretty psyched about marching in support of RESIST."

Alexa jerked forward at the news that Meg had been involved with RESIST but didn't interrupt the social worker's story.

"Nothing seemed out of the ordinary with Meg. Like always, she was one of the most active members, asking questions and buzzing around with her friends.

"After I heard from the Bertolinos that night, I immediately called all the kids who had attended that afternoon's meeting. Two of her good friends, Lynn and Amira, told me that Meg left the church annex with them, but they went their separate ways. Meg told them that she wanted to get home and try to finish her homework before dinner."

"Toni, I hope you called the police."

"Yes, for all the good it did. They promised to look into it. But I'm afraid that when they found out that she's a foster child they decided that she ran away. And I understand that, to some extent. They probably see a lot of foster kids go on the run. But that's not our Meg." Toni cried, and Tyrell reached for her hand in comfort.

"I know that the police are often reluctant to launch a full-fledged search in the early hours of a disappearance, especially with teens," Alexa said. "They don't call out the bloodhounds unless the circumstances point to foul play. But what are they doing now? Have they listed her as missing?"

"Yes. They started an investigation. They came and searched through her room but haven't come up with anything as far as we know. I gave them Meg's school picture." Toni drew a photo from her jacket pocket and handed it to Alexa.

Meg was a beautiful girl. The fourteen-year old in the photo had long blonde hair and a wide smile. Alexa found her even more stunning in person, with the tall, slender frame of a dancer and a sunny disposition.

Meg had lost her father to an automobile accident and her mother to an oxycodone habit that morphed into heroin addiction. Meg's only living relative, her father's aunt, had a serious medical condition. The woman wasn't in a position to take responsibility for Meg's care. After five years in foster care with the Bertolinos, the childless couple asked her to become their daughter. When Meg's mother agreed to relinquish parental rights, Alexa had helped them through every step of the adoption process.

"I am so sorry. You and Ed must be frantic."

"We are. I just know something bad has happened to Meg. She would not run away."

"I agree that seems unlikely. Meg is a level-headed girl, and she has seemed so excited about the adoption."

Tyrell nodded in agreement. "I work with a lot of kids in the foster care system. That's part of my job at Children and Youth Services. I can usually spot the ones who are going to run or the ones who are going to end up in juvie. Meg has been one of the success stories–a child who has coped with the trauma of losing her parents and entering the system. She lucked out . . . to be placed with Toni and Ed from day one, and to be welcomed into their family–even luckier that she was placed with foster parents who wanted to adopt a teenager."

Alexa turned to Toni. "What can I do to help?"

"Can you go to the police for us and find out what they're doing? You're a lawyer. Maybe the damn cops will tell you what they are doing to find our little girl."

"You have Children and Youth involved already, right? Are they in contact with the police?"

"Yes. We've gone through the official channels. One of Tyrell's colleagues has spoken to the police. But you're my lawyer. I'd feel better if you would help."

"I'll try, Toni. It's the borough police, right? I'll go over there this morning and check on the status of the investigation." Alexa turned to Tyrell. "I have a question for you, Mr. Jenkins."

"Tyrell, please. Mr. Jenkins is my father."

"OK . . . Tyrell. Did Meg know Cecily Townes? You mentioned that your church group went to Saturday's march in Washington in support of RESIST?"

"I just found out about Cecily this morning. The newspaper says she was killed in her home on Saturday. I can't believe it. I was with her most of the day on Saturday. My kids and I rode to and from Washington on the bus that RESIST had chartered. I sat with Cecily on the ride home." Tyrell hung his head. "Then I found out she was dead. Gone in an instant. She was one of my heroes. The world has lost a special person. I so admired Cecily."

Alexa almost regretted raising the topic of Cecily's death. Tyrell seemed genuinely distraught. She asked again, gently. "And Meg's involvement with RESIST?"

"To answer your specific question, Meg had some limited contact with Cecily. Our group began our project to support RESIST after Cecily spoke at one of our meetings. We held a car wash and a bake sale to raise money for RESIST. I'm pretty sure that Meg participated in all those activities, so she certainly met Cecily once or twice. However, I don't think any of my kids had more than a passing acquaintance with Cecily. They were pretty much in awe of her. Most of them were too tongue-tied in her presence to have any meaningful interaction."

Toni dabbed at her eyes with a tissue. "Meg attended Ms. Townes' talk and helped out at the car wash. She came home from that first meeting pretty impressed by Ms. Townes and anxious to help girls her age from being sold into sex slavery."

"I know I'm out of touch with the life of teenage girls in this day and age. My niece and nephew are still children. But isn't the sex trade a little R-rated for this age group?"

Tyrell laughed. "You'd be surprised at how knowledgeable teenagers are today. They watch all these movies and television shows that leave little to the imagination. Some of them are sexting and God knows what else. But most of these kids are more naïve and vulnerable than they realize. We emphasize the slavery part of the issue and find that the kids relate to girls and boys their age or younger who are being taken from their families and sold or coerced into slavery. We don't gloss over the sexual victimization aspect, but we don't spend a lot of time dwelling on the details."

"My Meg is quite a crusader. She's not interested in boys yet, not that Ed would let her date anyway. But the plight of these young kids Ms. Townes told them about—that just touched my girl's heart." Toni broke into sobs. "Now you have me worried, Alexa. What if the same people who killed Ms. Townes hurt my little girl?"

"I was just surprised when you mentioned RESIST. I can't imagine that there is any connection to Cecily Townes. Hopefully, Meg will turn up safe and sound." Alexa stood. "Has she expressed any anxiety about the adoption? Maybe she's trying to track down her mother?"

"I hope it's something like that. Ed and I are so worried."

Alexa ushered the distraught woman to the door. "I'll be in touch after I speak to the police." Alexa hoped that the cops had some good news. No wonder the Bertolinos were frantic.

Tyrell handed Alexa his card as he swaggered out the door. "If I can help at all, just give me a call."

"I will. One more thing: I suggest you call State Police Trooper John Taylor to tell him about your last contact with Cecily Townes."

CHAPTER FIVE

June 10, 1969

Make love, not war.

"Check out this concert. An Aquarian Exposition with Three Days of Peace and Music. Far out." Sukie bounded from her bed, long blonde braids swinging. The bells on her ankle bracelet tinkled as she hit the floor and slammed the Sunday newspaper section into her best friend's chest.

Nina lounged in a butterfly chair in the corner, her bare feet propped on a stack of record albums. Enveloped in the mellow strains of Jefferson Airplane's "Embryonic Journey," she barely moved.

"Look at the paper," Sukie commanded, bouncing with excitement as she hovered over Nina.

Finally, her friend opened her eyes and read the ad. "Where's Wallkill, New York?"

"What difference does it make? It can't be that far away. My dad got a Road Atlas from the Esso station. We can look it up." Sukie sank back onto the bed with a dreamy look on her face.

"It's a groovy idea. We'd need a ride." Nina plopped down next to Sukie and spread the paper across the paisley bedspread.

"I'll talk to Ben. How cool if he could come with us. And maybe some of his friends. That guy Robbie's a square, but his parents gave him that big green van."

"Sukie, is this about the music or Ben?"

"Both. Lancaster isn't that far, but I've only seen him once this summer. A whole weekend together would be unreal. How about Phil?"

"Maybe. I don't think he's into me anymore. He really digs that tramp, Marie." Nina twisted a dark curl around her finger. "But maybe I can get him back. What the hell. I'll ask him. I know he likes some of those bands in the ad: Canned Heat, the Airplane, the Grateful Dead."

"We should buy tickets before they sell out." Sukie grabbed a pen and notebook from her nightstand. "We need a list. Sleeping bags, food, drinks, a tent. Everybody could chip in for the food. Don't you have a Coleman stove?"

"Yeah. It's like planning a camping trip."

"What else?" Sukie looked up from her notebook.

"You and your lists. Mark this at the top: get permission from parents." Nina's expression turned bleak.

"They let us drive to Maine to visit your cousins last summer. And now we're juniors. And we went to that anti-war march in Washington." Sukie knew that Nina's concern about parental permission was spot on, but they had to at least try.

"You and me driving to Maine or taking a college bus to a protest is not the same as taking off for a weekend with a van-load of boys."

"Don't freak out yet." Sukie's voice took on an optimistic lilt. "Your mom and dad are pretty cool. If you can get them to say yes, mine will go along."

"I'll try." Nina rolled onto her back and examined the tips of her curls for split ends.

Sukie bristled at Nina's halfhearted tone. "Have faith. I will be so bummed if we can't go. If I don't get out of here soon—even for a few days—I'm going to freak."

On the portable stereo, the song "White Rabbit" reached a crescendo, with Grace Slick belting out advice from the dormouse.

Everything clicked into place for Sukie. She knew that she had to go to Woodstock. She resolved, "That's it. I have to expand my mind."

With an elated expression on her face, she declared to Nina, "I think this concert will be a transcendental experience that changes our lives."

Nina shot Sukie a mocking look and rolled off the bed onto the floor. "You've been reading too much Timothy O'Leary. Who cares about transcendental?" Her eyes sparkled as she looked up at Sukie and grinned. "I think this concert will be a blast, especially if Phil comes along. The only experience I'm looking for is to get laid."

CHAPTER SIX

ALEXA SKIPPED OUT OF WORK a little early and headed to her parents' house. Always the snitch, Graham had told them about her role in finding Cecily Townes' body. She knew that Mom and Dad would be concerned about her.

"Sweetheart." Her mom swept Alexa into her arms the instant she walked through the kitchen door. "I can't believe this happened to you again. You've just begun to recover from that whole experience with Caleb and his crazy father. Now you find another woman who has been murdered. Your father and I have been so worried since Graham called yesterday morning."

Alexa remained close to her parents. Susan and Norris Williams were in their mid-sixties and quite active. Her willowy mother could have modeled for a magazine catering to trendy baby-boomers. The blunt cut of her short, ash-blonde hair looked like it came from a posh New York City salon. As always, the simple white blouse and blue jeans she wore could pass for an outfit in *Vogue*. Alexa had long ago come to terms with the fact that she could never compete with her mother's beauty and innate sense of style.

The women sat on stools at the kitchen counter. "I'll admit that finding Cecily Townes was brutal. It was like reliving a nightmare. As horrible as it was, I'm dealing with it. I didn't know the woman. There's no way that this one will suck me in like the last time." Alexa sighed. "The whole thing hit Melissa hard. She and Cecily were good friends. I wish she hadn't seen the body. It was gruesome."

"What a tragedy. Cecily Townes was such a good woman," Susan Williams declared. "Even though she left the convent in her late twenties, she still had the soul of a nun. I think she felt that the structure of the Church was too confining for her brand of hands-on activism. But she remained dedicated to doing good. Her entire life revolved around that organization she founded."

"I didn't realize that you knew Cecily."

"I first met Cecily when I went to Dickinson Law, shortly after she relocated to this area. We were both involved in environmental issues with the Sierra Club. Then Cecily began to concentrate on children's issues. I ran into her from time to time when I did staff work for the legislature. She testified in front of committees, that sort of thing."

"You sound like you knew her pretty well."

"Perhaps. In retrospect, our relationship at its core was mainly networking between two women with drive and a certain degree of power. We often had lunch when I was a county commissioner. Then I retired. Dad and I started to travel a lot, and Cecily spent more and more time overseas on her anti-trafficking work. So, we lost touch . . . as people do." Her voice faltered. "It has to be over a year since I last saw Cecily. I think it was at a fundraiser for her charity. What a horrible thing to happen."

After a few moments of silence, Mom looked searchingly at Alexa. "Let's talk about you. Graham says that you're working longer hours than necessary. You've lost weight. Frank Crowe tells us that you've cut back your volunteer time at the Women's Clinic. Then there's Reese. I'm not entirely sure what happened there. You two seemed pretty tight, and then overnight, he leaves the country."

Alexa sighed. She gathered some loose change from the counter and stacked it into columns of quarters, nickels, and dimes.

Susan leaned closer to her daughter. "In the last few weeks, I thought I'd seen some signs that you were finally getting past all the trauma from last fall. And from Grandma Williams' death. I know that both you and Graham are still grieving for her. But, now this."

"Mom, I'll be OK." Alexa didn't look up from the counter as she arranged the pennies into a circle. "It's taken me awhile to process everything that happened. Believe it or not, I've struggled more with being so blind to Caleb's true character than with killing Reverend Browne. Shooting the reverend was self-defense, but I dated Caleb for months and never really knew him. Then Grandma Williams died when I was still reeling from everything else. But she never recovered from the stroke. We knew it was coming."

Alexa toppled the neat stacks of change and faced her mother. "Don't worry so much. I'm getting better. I'm eating well. I'm doing extra yoga sessions with Isabella. I miss Reese, but he left for a great job offer. That's all there is to it." Alexa took a few steps toward the refrigerator and fished around for a bottle of water.

"Anything to drink, Mom?"

"No thank you, dear. Don't try to distract me. I think this African safari is going to be just what you need. It will get you away from here for a few weeks. Give you time to clear your head and see some amazing wildlife."

"Mom, your answer to everything is a trip; the more exotic, the better. But I'm excited about the safari. And I've decided to tack a few days on to the end and visit Reese. You and Dad just head on to Namibia like you planned. Instead of flying home from Nairobi, I'll get a flight to Samburu."

"I think that's an excellent idea, dear. I'm sure Reese will be happy to see you. I know our trip is over a month away, but it will be here before you know it."

On the drive home, Alexa thought about her earlier conversation with the Carlisle police regarding Toni Bertolino's missing foster daughter, Meg Wilson. Alexa had spoken to Detective Hiram Miller, a policeman she trusted from past experience. It turned out that the police had made a thorough effort to retrace Meg's steps and talk to her friends.

"At this point, we're well into the investigation," the detective explained. "We've talked to Meg's friends. We've searched her room and computer to look for clues about a possible motive for running or a potential sexual predator. She and Mrs. Bertolino had an argument the night before Meg disappeared, but it seems like a typical parent-teen disagreement. Nothing unusual. The York police tracked her birth mother down. Found her in a homeless shelter. She hadn't seen or heard from Megan in years.

"We pinged the girl's cell phone, but it's either turned off or the battery died or has been removed. A few years ago that may have been cause for suspicion, but now cell phone pinging information is all over the Internet and television. A kid who wants to disappear could do the research.

"Her disappearance doesn't meet the Amber Alert criteria. Even though she's been missing for nearly four days, nobody saw her snatched off the street. We've followed all the protocols. We alerted all the local police jurisdictions that Meg was missing. We talked to the FBI office in Harrisburg about her. An announcement went in the Pennsylvania Crime Information Center's Daily Bulletin. We posted the information on Crime Watch, which generates Facebook notifications. From there, I think all of the local news outlets carried a story. There's a new federal law that requires missing foster care children to be reported to the FBI, the National Crime Information Center, and the National Center for Missing and Exploited Children. We followed that procedure." The detective paused for breath.

Alexa looked up from taking notes. "I don't know her that well, but Meg seems to be well behaved. I've discussed the upcoming adoption with her several times, and she appears to be genuinely excited about becoming an official Bertolino. Children and Youth monitors all the kids in foster care and those in pre-adoption placement every thirty days. If she was having some crisis or change of heart, they would have picked up on that."

"I hear you." Miller leaned forward. "We're treating this seriously. But she's a foster kid. She's fourteen years old. And her girlfriends say that Meg has hinted around about a secret boyfriend. They don't know his name, but both of them got the idea that he was older than Meg, and she was hiding the relationship from her parents. Those factors all point to this girl being a runaway."

"Look, there's got to be something more you can do, right? My clients are frantic with worry. What if you're wrong and this child is the victim of foul play? It may be a coincidence, but she disappeared right before she was scheduled to go on a trip to Washington with Cecily Townes. And we both know what happened to Cecily."

"The way I heard it, a whole busload of kids went on that trip. I can't see any connection between the murder of Carlisle's own Mother Theresa and a teenage girl. But I feel for the parents." Detective Miller tipped his chair back. "Tell you what. I'll try to get the local news to give the story some more coverage. We'll continue to use social media as well. I suggest that her parents put out some fliers in town. Post something of their own on Facebook. Between the two efforts, maybe we'll turn up a lead."

"Thanks. At least that's a step forward. I'll talk to the Bertolinos right away. Will you keep us informed?" Alexa rose from her chair.

"Of course. And we'll chase down any leads that we might get. With any luck, she'll come back home on her own after a fight with that boyfriend."

Alexa had nothing concrete to refute Detective Miller's certainty that Meg had left home on her own. Still, that scenario just didn't feel right. *The Sentinel* and two of the Harrisburg TV stations had agreed to run an additional story on the missing teen. Alexa couldn't help thinking that posting fliers was something that you did when a dog was lost, not a child. But the task of producing and distributing fliers had given the Bertolinos a focus and a sense action.

As Alexa coasted the Land Rover to a stop in front of her cabin, she pushed aside thoughts of both young Meg and the late Cecily Townes. She needed to clear her mind.

"Scout," she yelled as she walked into the house. "We've still got some light. Let me change and we'll go for a walk."

The big mastiff zipped through the open door, and Alexa ran upstairs for her jeans and sneakers.

CHAPTER SEVEN

ARIEL, OWNER OF THE OM CAFÉ, looked up when the three women walked in the door. She started preparing three cups of chai tea latte. "The usual, I assume?"

Alexa nodded. She, Melissa, and their childhood friend, Haley, had turned these post-yoga get-togethers into a weekly ritual. They headed toward their favorite table.

"Wasn't class great tonight? I love Half-moon Pose." Haley adjusted her Lululemon yoga top.

"You must be crazy. I'd be happy doing nothing but spinal twists for the whole hour." Melissa stirred the big cup of chai that Ariel had delivered.

Alexa inhaled the spicy fragrance, took a long sip of the tea, and listened to her two friends chatter. For at least the thousandth time, she marveled that the three of them had remained such good friends.

Haley was a tall, slender brunette who handled media relations for the Chamber of Commerce. Always exquisitely dressed, Haley had grown more conservative over the years—not surprising given the conventional bent of her husband, Blair, an investment broker. Alexa sometimes pondered the chicken and the egg question with Haley. Did her conservatism come from the husband and her job at the Chamber, or was Haley's natural reserve as a child an early indicator of her traditional nature?

Melissa seemed to have recovered from the trauma of the weekend. The humidity and yoga had turned her long tresses into an auburn halo that danced each time she laughed at one of Haley's jokes.

Alexa leaned toward Melissa with a concerned expression. "How are you doing?"

"Yes," Haley chimed in. "Alexa told me about Saturday—jail and finding Cecily Townes murdered. It must have been terrible."

"You could say that. I hope they find the bastard who killed her and lock him away for life."

"The news reports don't say anything about the police identifying a suspect." Alexa took a quick look at the news feed on her cell phone.

Haley shivered. "I swear that Carlisle isn't safe anymore. We're starting to get concerned down at the Chamber. First, that business last fall you were involved in, Alexa. Two women dead. Dr. Crowe wounded. Armed men chasing you through the forest . . . and now this. One of the most respected women in town. One with an international reputation for her accomplishments. Murdered in her home." Haley shook her head. "Blair is upgrading our security system. He called the company yesterday morning."

Melissa sighed. "Haley, the last thing on my mind is the impact that Cecily's death might have on tourism. I just found out that her brother is planning a big memorial service, but not until next Saturday—Memorial Day weekend. I hear that people are coming in from Thailand and India along with a whole contingent of muckety-mucks from Washington. I think it's going to be at St. Agnes."

Alexa pretended not to notice Haley calculating the impact that all these visitors would have on the local economy. Instead, she asked Melissa, "Can you get me the details? After finding her like that, I feel like I should pay my respects. Maybe my mom will go along. Apparently, she knew Cecily pretty well."

"Sure. I have a related announcement about my exhibit. I've decided that the best way to honor Cecily is to go ahead with my new show. The photos are ones that I took on my RESIST trip to Thailand and India. I want to let everyone see the people she was trying to help."

"That's this Saturday, right? Do you need a hand?" Alexa looked at Melissa. Melissa made her living running a small arts gallery, often showing her own photography along with other local artists' work.

"I'll let you know. Right now I think I've got it covered. Pete Costello is helping me print some of the oversize photos. Of course, Schuyler will help me hang everything and set up. I need both of you to be at the opening though. You might be the only ones who show up." Melissa's tone was pleading.

"Blair and I have the opening on our calendar. And I put it in the Chamber News so the whole business community knows about your big event."

"Of course I'll be there, too. After hearing all those stories about your trip I need to see the pictures. I don't have a date though. Can I bring Scout?"

Her friends chuckled as Alexa reached for her purse. "Speaking of my big baby, I need to leave. He's been alone all day."

On the drive home, Alexa considered Melissa's news about all the people who were coming to pay their respects at Cecily's memorial service. This woman had traveled all over the world in her efforts to stop human trafficking. Although many revered Cecily for her work, she must have made enemies among the unsavory element who profited from the sex trade.

Would it even be possible for the police to track down her killer if the murder was payback for Cecily's interference in an international trafficking ring?

At noon on Wednesday, Alexa left the office and hurried to her half-day stint at the Women's Clinic. She had negotiated time for this volunteer commitment with her father when she joined the family firm.

Alexa breezed through the front door and into a packed waiting room. Wednesday afternoons were always busy. She smiled at the cheery yellow walls of the newly renovated space. Several toddlers squabbled over a plastic building set in a corner play area. Their mothers chatted with each other, casting occasional glances at their kids if the noise volume rose too high.

Teenagers hovered over their cell phones, texting, tweeting, and checking Instagram. A few of the more mature women leafed through dog-eared magazines. The glazed look in their eyes suggested that they'd read the same editions on their last visits.

Alexa stifled a grin as she noticed that every single one of the waiting patients sat bolt upright in the same uncomfortable-looking posture. Tanisha had picked out straight-backed, utilitarian chairs with only the slightest suggestion of padding. Judging from the women's ramrod backs, the only thing these chairs had going for them was that they didn't creak and totter like the old ones.

The one positive outcome that had emerged from the clinic violence last autumn was this renovation. Abortion rights extremists had smashed the front window, shot the lead physician, Dr. Frank Crowe, and killed Emily Baxter, the clinic's young accountant. After the extremists were arrested, the board had launched a fund drive to pay for repairs and a full-time security company contract. In a wave of support, the community had been so generous that there was enough money left for a substantial refurbishment of the facilities.

"Child, I am so glad to see you." Tanisha's gray cornrowed braids bounced as she rose to greet Alexa. "Barb called in sick today, and I have to finish a big supply order before the end of the day. Can you manage intake for an hour or so?"

"Sure. Where are we on the schedule?"

Tanisha brought up the schedule on the computer screen at the reception desk. "Here. Tammy Sanders and Rajika Rideout just finished their paperwork. Carmen Foster is next. I'll back you up on the phones."

With that, Alexa plunged into a whirlwind afternoon. She enjoyed her time at the clinic and the interaction with a wide variety of people and situations. Most of the services provided fell into the preventive care, annual GYN checkups, and early obstetrical care categories.

However, Cumberland Clinic was one of the few clinics in the area that still provided abortions, a distinction that had drawn the wrath of the militant anti-abortion group the previous year. Alexa didn't miss the weekly protests that had targeted the clinic in the past. A series of arrests, followed by the death of their leader at Alexa's hand, had put a damper on the group's public activism—at least for now.

Tanisha surfaced from her computer around three o'clock. "You doing OK?"

"I think so. The appointments are starting to thin." Alexa gestured toward the waiting room. "Those three have all been through intake."

"Having you here is a blessing."

"I have one question though. Aurora Washington didn't show up today. What do I do about that?"

"Usually, we'll call and ask if she wants to reschedule. I'll put that on Barb's list for tomorrow."

Alexa wrinkled her forehead. "Isn't Aurora Washington a high school kid? Pretty with Shirley Temple curls?"

"I don't know if I'd ever describe a sister as having Shirley Temple curls, but you've got the right girl. I heard that she might be up for homecoming queen next year. She's pretty popular, which is a miracle given her home life."

"Family problems?"

"You know I'm not one for gossip, but that girl's daddy left the picture years ago. And talk on the street says her mama has always been more interested in her next man than her two kids.

The older brother is out on his own now, but Aurora is still at home."

"What a shame."

"I'm surprised that she didn't call to cancel her appointment. That's not like Aurora." Tanisha's brow wrinkled in concern.

"Miss? I have a four o'clock appointment?"

Alexa rose to help the teenager standing at the counter, but her mind was still on Aurora Washington. Another young girl, like Meg Wilson, who'd been dealt a bad hand when they'd shuffled the parent deck. At least Meg had found the Bertolinos; but girls were just so vulnerable at this age.

CHAPTER EIGHT

AT MELISSA'S OPENING, people spilled out of the gallery and onto the sidewalk, wineglasses in hand. Alexa wormed her way through the crowd to reach the door. She paused on the doorstep and surveyed the packed gallery, thankful that she'd dressed up for the occasion. She had changed out of a more casual outfit into this classic little black dress. Her shantung sheath might be a little too New York for a Carlisle opening, but what the hell. Melissa needed her best friends to be flying the flags at full mast.

Not immediately spying Melissa, Alexa took in the photos. Done in black and white, the series of gritty portraits was haunting. Melissa had captured image after image of girls, boys, and young women in Mumbai and Bangkok. One set of photos showed prostitutes, bar girls, and bar boys at work in the sex trade. Another set showed rescued women weaving, making jewelry, or plying other artisan skills.

The seamy pictures of the people caught up in the sex trade conveyed a theme of quiet desperation. In contrast, many of the women who RESIST had helped escape that life looked much healthier and more content.

Alexa stood appalled before the photo of a Thai girl who couldn't have been more than ten years old. If not for her skimpy shorts and a tank top, the child could be mistaken for a doll perched on the beefy man's lap. The man, face obscured by shadows, was fondling the child. Melissa's photo made Alexa's skin crawl.

"Powerful, isn't it?

Alexa looked over her shoulder at the man who had spoken. "Yes. All of Melissa's work here tonight is outstanding. This is certainly one of the most compelling."

"I'm amazed at some of the shots she was able to get. She must be pretty gutsy to brave those streets of Bangkok at night."

"I'm not sure what was involved, but I do know that Melissa can be pretty single-minded when she has a camera in her hand."

"Sounds like you know Ms. Lambert well."

"We've been friends since we were kids. I'm Alexa Williams."

"Quinn Hutton." The man extended his hand. "I teach at Dickinson. English."

Alexa smiled as she took in this arresting man. Tall and slender, he wore his charcoal sports coat, heavyweight linen shirt, and black designer jeans with an air of nonchalance. His thick black hair was cut long. The guy looked impossibly hip, but his air of élan seemed unforced.

"I'm an attorney with a local law firm. And a connoisseur of fine photography, of course. It sounds as if you've been to Thailand?"

"Yes. I spent a few years there, teaching English at a school in Bangkok. It was a great way to see Southeast Asia."

"Have you been at the college long?"

"I'm just finishing my second year. Classes ended this past week. Graduation is Sunday."

A bustle of activity near the gallery entrance distracted Alexa. The crowd parted for a distinguished-looking man in a tailored suit with a muted pinstripe to make his way through the middle of the room. Although he didn't seem to be making an effort to part the crowd, this man sailed through the packed room like royalty.

As Alexa turned back to her conversation with Quinn Hutton, the young professor murmured, "Excuse me. I see someone I must speak to."

Before Alexa could respond, Quinn melted into the crowd.

"Alexa. I am so glad you came. So far, the opening is fantastic." Melissa popped out from behind a pillar. Exuberant in a flowing espresso-colored dress, the star of the evening looked like a chic gypsy.

"As it should be. You've outdone yourself, Melissa. Your work is wonderful."

"Can you come with me? Jim isn't here yet, and I need some moral support for my little speech." Melissa didn't wait for a response before seizing Alexa's elbow and steering her toward a small platform area at the back of the gallery.

When they reached the platform, Melissa released her iron grasp on Alexa's arm and stepped onto the small stage. Schuyler, the anemic-looking gallery assistant, used a wooden hammer to tap on a Tibetan temple bell. A series of warm, mellow chimes rang through the gallery. After a few minutes and few more chimes, the crowd quieted.

"Hello. I'm Melissa Lambert. I want to thank you all for coming to tonight's opening. This exhibit will remain on display for the next several weeks, so please feel free to return or tell your friends to stop by."

Melissa's voice quavered. "I stand here tonight with mixed emotions. These photographs have been a labor of love because the fight against sex trafficking has become a personal cause for me. Each of the people in these portraits that you see here has a story. Many of those stories are terrifying and dehumanizing. Others reflect a different experience: tales of hope and a journey toward independence. I hope that these works can give you a glimpse into their lives.

"Of course the issue is much larger and affects many more people than you see in my photographs." Melissa spoke with mounting passion. "Human trafficking is essentially modern-day slavery. As many of you know, RESIST, an organization in which I'm involved, is dedicated to the eradication of sex trafficking in particular. Because trafficking operates primarily in dark corners and underground, the actual statistics are hard to pin down. Some recent reports estimate that over twenty million people worldwide have been forced into sexual servitude or forced labor. UNICEF states that about two million children are exploited every year in the global commercial sex trade.

"It's easy to think of sex trafficking as a third world problem. But it's not. It's clear from the varying estimates that thousands of people, often children, fall prey to sex trafficking in the United States. According to the Polaris Project, the average victim may be forced to have sex twenty to forty-eight times a day. Often, victims are kept in line through brainwashing, psychological intimidation, physical beating, and drug addiction.

"Sex trafficking is a nasty, degrading business that preys on the innocent and vulnerable. It must be stopped."

Melissa's voice softened, and her eyes grew moist. "I owe a debt of gratitude to the remarkable woman who allowed me to travel with her to Thailand and India to capture these images. However, Cecily Townes died last weekend, killed in a brutal and senseless attack. All of us who knew and loved Cecily are inconsolable at her loss. I want you to hear about the organization that was so dear to her heart. The same organization that rescued many of the people you see in these photos.

"Jack Nash, a board member of RESIST, is going to say a few words about Cecily's organization."

Alexa recognized Jack Nash as the one who had arrived with considerable drama just a short while ago. He reminded her of the managing partner at her old New York City law firm: self-assured and totally confident as the center of attention.

Nash smoothed his steel gray hair and tugged at each monogrammed cuff before he spoke. "Thank you, Melissa. And thanks to all of you. I will be brief so you can return to your enjoyment of this impressive photography exhibit. Cecily Townes' untimely passing leaves a void that cannot easily be filled. She dedicated her life to creating and sustaining an international network aimed at ending human trafficking and rescuing the victims of sexual slavery. Each year, RESIST helps thousands of women and children in India, Southeast Asia, and on the African continent."

Alexa tuned out Nash after a few minutes and studied the packed room. Haley and Blair stood near Melissa's parents. She was surprised to see Graham and his wife, Kate, next to Mom and Dad. She recognized many other local faces, including Tyrell Jenkins and Trooper John Taylor.

She returned her attention to the speaker when Nash's voice rose.

"One last important item. Melissa has generously pledged fifty percent of all sales from this exhibit to RESIST. Her work certainly speaks for itself, and I'm sure that many of you need no incentive to purchase Melissa's photographs. However, knowing that the subjects of these photos, and many others like them, will benefit from your purchase may inspire you to consider additional works for your collection. Thank you for your attention."

As the crowd returned to the party, Melissa approached Alexa with Jack Nash in tow. "I wanted you to meet Mr. Nash. This is Alexa Williams, one of my best friends."

"Nice to meet you, Alexa. Williams? You wouldn't be related to Norris and Susan Williams, would you?"

"Why, yes. They are my parents. I practice law with Dad and my brother, Graham, in the family firm. And how do you know my parents, Mr. Nash?"

"Call me Jack. I have known your mother since our days at Dickinson. Of course, I've met your father over the years at parties and the like."

"You run Children of Light?" Alexa moved sideways to let a couple squeeze past and raised her voice above the din. "I understand that Cecily Townes was also involved with your organization?"

"Yes. Although our missions differ, both RESIST and Children of Light exist to help people in need. Children of Light focuses more on foster children. We run group homes and other services for both abused and neglected children as well as juvenile delinquents. Our adoption arm used to work more closely with RESIST on placements of foreign children. However, many countries are closing their doors to the United States adoption market."

Alexa smiled. "Some of my clients have adopted children in placement with Children of Light. Your staff has always been professional and caring."

"Thank you. I'll pass that on to my management staff." Jack nodded his head at Alexa and turned away. "Melissa, I don't want to monopolize your time." He patted the photographer on the arm. "I'll let you and Alexa get back to your guests."

As Nash moved away, Melissa whispered to Alexa. "That guy has a shitload of money. He lives in a huge mansion out at the foot of the South Mountain. You can't see any of the buildings from the road, but I hear it's an enormous complex. Fences around the entire property."

Melissa broke off her enthusiastic description and looked past Alexa with a delighted smile on her face. Her voice rose in greeting. "Tyrell. I have been meaning to call you, but everything has just been too sad and too hectic." She threw her arms around the tall social worker in a hug.

"Alexa, have you met Tyrell Jenkins?"

"Hello, Ms. Williams." Tyrell spoke before Alexa could respond. "We met earlier this week." He turned to Melissa. "I'm glad to see that you're out of jail, girl. When those park service cops carted you away, I thought you were bound to Leavenworth for at least ten years."

"Alexa and her friend came to my rescue, and the charges were dropped. I definitely learned my lesson about obeying the rules when visiting national monuments." Melissa made a lame attempt at looking abashed.

Tyrell put his arm around Melissa's shoulders in another quick hug. "How are you handling this whole thing with Cecily? I can't believe she's gone."

"Me too. It's senseless and tragic." Although Melissa teared up, neither she nor Alexa spoke about their role in finding Cecily's body.

Tyrell winced. "I may be the last person who saw her alive. I mean, other than her killer. At least that's what the police think. Two dudes wearing suits and packing heat questioned me for hours at the state police station. I was starting to think I was a suspect."

Alexa rolled her eyes at this ridiculous exaggeration. This guy was clearly the star in his own movie. Still, she couldn't deny the good looks. At their first meeting, she hadn't fully appreciated his startling green eyes.

"There wasn't much I could say," Tyrell continued. "We unloaded the bus at the church parking lot. All the kids left. Most of their parents were waiting for the bus to arrive. Cecily and I wrapped up a few details about the day then she drove off. I got my bicycle from inside the church annex and rode back home." Tyrell ended with a deep sigh.

Melissa put her hand on his arm in comfort. "We'll talk some more. Maybe later this week."

"Sure." He glanced at Alexa. "Ms. Williams, maybe we could have coffee on Monday or Tuesday to talk about that other issue? The family is still distraught and looking for answers."

"Of course. Just call my office, and we can find a time."

Alexa's eyes followed Tyrell as he moved away, languidly weaving through the room in his red Chuck Taylors. When she realized that she wasn't the only woman watching Tyrell's exit, Alexa turned back to Melissa.

"I agree," Melissa teased. "The man is hot with a capital H. I guess you can't tell me what you're meeting about?"

"Nope. Good ole' attorney-client privilege. Hey, I haven't eaten a thing. I'm going to get some hors d'oeuvres before they're gone. Plus, I want to track down Mom and Dad. Go be the artiste and hostess with all your guests."

Alexa filled her plate with cheese, veggies, and tiny finger sandwiches and snagged a glass of wine at the bar. Unwilling to juggle both a glass and her food, Alexa pounced on an open bench along the wall. Her seated position provided a good vantage point to survey the room. The crowd had barely thinned, and the noise level continued to rise.

Across the room, Alexa noticed Quinn Hutton and Jack Nash standing together in front of a photo, engaged in deep conversation. Even at a distance, Alexa recognized the portrait as one of the show's best. Melissa had captured a beautiful Thai girl, who looked to be about fourteen or fifteen, leaning against a rough brick wall in a shaft of sunlight. The girl's expression radiated demure warmth. Melissa had titled the photo, *As It Should Be.*

Something about Quinn and Jack's demeanor caught Alexa's attention. Clearly, the two were acquainted. Surrounded by a room full of people, they leaned close to each other, giving their conversation a furtive air.

A deep voice interrupted Alexa's blatant snooping. "Is this seat taken?" Trooper Taylor sat down without waiting for an answer.

"Is this like in the movies where they go to the funeral to see if the killer shows up? I know that this is not exactly Cecily Townes' funeral, but are you here to look for suspects?"

"Do you think I would tell you if I was?" John Taylor laughed as he leaned back against the wall. "I'll just say that I am attending tonight's event as part of our ongoing investigation."

"Fair enough." Alexa took a bite of cheese.

"Your friend Melissa is a good photographer. I'm not really into this art stuff. I couldn't afford to buy any of these pictures if I wanted to. But a lot of these photos just reach out and grab you. It's gives me a better sense of why Ms. Townes was so big into trying to stop trafficking."

"I agree. Even though Melissa told me about her trip overseas with Cecily and RESIST, these photos do so much to bring it home. I guess it's that whole picture-is-worth-a-thousand-words concept."

"Have you remembered anything more about that night?" The trooper's abrupt change of subject caught Alexa off guard.

"Not really. Have you made any progress on the case?"

"We've learned a lot about Ms. Townes. However, the more we learn, the wider the net we have to cast. This woman interacted with people all over the world on a regular basis."

"I hope you will be able to track down her killer."

"So do I, Alexa. Would you mind if I stopped out at the cabin some evening to pick your brain on this whole thing? I understand that you didn't know Cecily Townes, but you move in some of the same circles. You might be able to help me get a better sense of the big picture here."

"Any night but Tuesday is fine. Just give me a call." Alexa wondered if Trooper Taylor's visit was necessary to his investigation or if he just wanted to spend time with her.

Get over yourself, she thought. You're probably imagining that this guy is into you.

Alexa spent another hour at the gallery, mingling and talking with her family and Melissa's parents. By ten o'clock, Jim had arrived, and Alexa passed her assigned role as Melissa's chief moral support onto his broad shoulders. She left the clamor of the gallery behind and headed for home.

CHAPTER NINE

SOON AFTER SHE ARRIVED at the office on Monday, Alexa phoned Melissa. "Hi. I didn't want to call yesterday. I figured you would be exhausted. But I have to tell you that your show is fantastic. You must be pleased with the opening. The place was packed."

"I couldn't believe how many people showed up. And I sold five pieces. But I was exhausted by the end of the night. Jim and I went back to his place after the show, and we stayed there yesterday, relaxing.

"I just pulled into the lot behind the gallery right now. I shudder to think what a mess I'll have to deal with. We cleaned up all the food and trash Saturday night, but I'll need to sweep and put all the extra tables and chairs away."

"I should get to work, too. I'm happy that your show was such a success. I'll bet that you'll have even more sales over the next few weeks."

"Hold on just a minute until I get inside. There's something that I want to tell you."

Alexa could hear the car door slam and Melissa's steps on the wooden back stoop. Then, a wail. "Oh no! Who did this?"

"Melissa, what's the matter?"

"Someone destroyed my office. There are papers everywhere, and my computer is gone."

"I'll be right over. I'm hanging up the phone now. Go back outside to your car, lock the doors, and call 911." Alexa knew that her morning schedule was clear. She had planned to work on a brief.

"Melinda," Alexa said as she dashed out the door. "Melissa has an emergency situation, and I need to go over to the gallery. I'll call to let you know when to expect me back."

By the time Alexa reached the gallery, the Carlisle police had arrived. Alexa found Melissa leaning on her gleaming red Prius in the parking lot. The state police had permitted her to pick up the car last week.

"Are you OK?"

"No. I'm not at all OK. Someone trashed the office and stole my computer and one of my favorite cameras. The police are doing their thing in there now . . . looking for clues or fingerprints or whatever they do. It appears the burglars came in through that bathroom window on the side. It was jimmied open."

"You don't have an alarm system, do you?"

"I got a quote once, but it was too expensive. I guess that was penny-wise but pound-foolish." Melissa pursed her mouth in regret.

"What about your exhibit? Was anything damaged?"

"Thank God, no. After all the work I put into the show—that would have been a disaster. Most of the photos that sold on Saturday are still hanging in place. People are coming in this week to pick them up." Melissa grimaced. "What a nightmare. I hope my insurance covers everything. Luckily, my other two cameras are at home. And I've got digital backups for all the photo files on the computer—which is good since I'm selling everything on display as a limited edition series of twenty-five. So I need to reprint everything that sold. I was planning on contacting Pete and getting that underway today."

"That makes sense. You should capitalize on the buzz from the opening. I think that article in Sunday's newspaper is going to bring a lot more people into the gallery this week." Alexa looked toward the office to see what was happening. A lot of policemen were milling around.

"Maybe that newspaper article brought the burglar into the gallery. Nothing comes for free," Melissa said in disgust.

"Such a cynic. But I can relate. I was so pissed when those guys broke into my cabin last year."

The two women fell silent as they watched another police officer arrive and rush into the gallery.

Alexa remembered their unfinished phone conversation. "Hey, you said you had something to tell me?"

"Well, mainly about all the photos I sold. But there was one weird thing. Jack Nash bought one of the framed pieces on Saturday night—the one called *As It Should Be.*"

"I would hope so. He sounded like a televangelist preaching to the congregation. 'Get out your wallets and buy so RESIST can get half the proceeds.' Very generous of you, by the way."

"Thanks. The image he bought is one of my favorites. We met this young girl in the slums of Bangkok. Her name is Roongnapar Rathanapimarn. Thai names are so interesting. Her first name means breaking dawn. Her last is the name for the third level of heaven. But we called her Pa, or the English version, Dawn. Her family belongs to a Christian church that's involved with RESIST's on-the-ground effort in Thailand. Her father, Somchart, which means good to be born now, manages part of the operation." Melissa smiled. "Pa's such a beauty. To me, she embodies the way things should turn out for children everywhere—despite the poverty she had a safe place to live, a loving family. Just like her name, she was a ray of hope after I'd been exposed to two weeks of victims ensnared in lives of misery."

"I know exactly which photo you're talking about. It was one of the best in the show."

"I'm pleased that it sold. But Jack Nash acted all Lord of the Manor when he bought it. He paid me ten times the asking price on the condition that I make it a single edition. He insisted on having the only copy of the work."

"Maybe it was his way of contributing a large chunk of cash to RESIST?"

"Could be, but I got the impression that he just wanted to show that he had a lot of money to throw around. It's unlikely that I would have sold ten prints of the piece during the show, but now I can never sell it again."

"You could have told him to go screw himself."

"Funny, that's exactly what Jim said. But Jack does a lot for RESIST, and he did me a favor by speaking at the opening. I just took the deal." Melissa walked closer to her back door to peer at the activity inside. Then she came back to Alexa.

"Speaking of RESIST, I'm supposed to run over there as soon as Schuyler comes in at eleven. They want me to take some pictures of the staff. They're hoping to do some sort of photo tribute at Cecily's memorial service. I guess I'll have to postpone that appointment to later in the day. Plus, now I need to go home and get one of my cameras for the group shot."

A policeman called from the steps, "Ms. Lambert, we need you inside for a few minutes, please."

"I can run out to the house and pick up your camera. This morning is a loss anyway. Is the key still under the porch swing?" Now that Alexa had left the office, it was easy to shirk that brief that she needed to write. Besides, Melissa looked at her wit's end.

"You are such a friend. Yes, the key's in the same place. I want the Nikon D3X that's in a bag on the kitchen table. Just bring the whole bag."

Alexa dialed Melinda as she walked toward the Land Rover. "I won't be in until after lunch. I don't have any appointments, right?"

After a brief pause, Melinda replied, "No, the schedule is clear today so you could work on the Parson brief. Tyrell Jenkins called. Said you had agreed to get together?"

"That's right, but I can't do it today. Can you fit in an hour tomorrow for me to meet him for coffee? Say, at Legal Grounds? Thanks. See you later."

CHAPTER TEN

August 13, 1969

Go with the flow.

Sukie's forehead touched the van's window as she leaned forward to study the sign. She shouted, "This is it. This is where we camp."

"I hope I can make it over this bump." Robbie eased the big Ford Falcon Station Bus off the paved road and followed a makeshift dirt road through the field. Tents and cars sprouted across the grassy meadow like clumps of colorful mushrooms. The scent of newly mown grass wafted through the open windows.

"Here, Robbie, here. Let's just park and set up camp," Ben yelled over the sound of tires thudding into big clods of dirt. Sukie held onto the back of the seat to avoid sliding off.

"I was trying to get the lay of the land. I think I see toilets over there to the right." As Robbie took his hand from the wheel to gesture, the van hit a pothole and swerved into the grass. Sukie's head grazed the roof.

"Hey, man. I can see some towers over that hill to the left. That must be the stage. Right on," JJ mumbled from the back seat, stoned out of his mind.

Cheryl laid her hand on Robbie's arm and spoke into her boyfriend's ear. "Babe, that looks like a great spot to crash. Let's stop ahead."

"Yeah, man, this looks cool," Sukie encouraged. Six hours glued to this seat were about all she could take.

Robbie finally stopped the van, and the group clambered out. Sukie grabbed Ben's hands and twirled him in a circle.

"We're here. I can't believe it. This is going to be so cool."

Ben kissed Sukie and shouted toward the sky, "The Airplane, The Who, Hendrix. What a rush."

"Plus, we have days to spend together."

"Yeah. Dig it, babe." Ben dropped her hands and looked toward the towers in the distance. From here, Sukie could see huge lights fixed to the structures.

"Do you think Joplin is going to sing 'A Piece of My Heart'? That's my favorite song on the album." Ben played a silent riff on his air guitar.

Sukie bit her lip and smiled. "I want to hear Janis do 'Summertime.'" Regaining her high spirits, she danced around singing the bluesy Joplin version in a raspy voice.

When Ben melted away to talk to Robbie, Sukie paused to scope things out. The only people near their campsite were lounging around an ancient bread truck. The words "Levi Bloom and Flatbush Boulevard" were emblazoned across the side in psychedelic letters.

Wow, she thought, how radical to live in New York City. Someday, I'll visit Brooklyn and Boston and California and Paris.

Nina approached Sukie, Ben, and Robbie. "Come on, guys, we've got to set up before it gets dark." She lowered her voice. "We'd have been here an hour earlier if Eskimo had been on time."

"We've got a lot of light left. Just go with the flow and everything will work out." Sukie skipped toward the van to grab a tent.

A few hours later, Sukie sat on a blanket next to Ben, vibing on the pleasant warmth of the campfire. Ben and Nina's boyfriend, Phil, had found a little wooded area and scarfed some fallen logs. Sukie tried to place the pleasant smell of the wood smoke: maybe pine?

Totally psyched to actually be here at Woodstock, Sukie studied the group that she and Nina had cobbled together. All eight huddled in a circle around the fire.

Ben's long brown ponytail brushed Sukie's arm as he reached over to pass the joint to Robbie. "Man, thanks for driving us here. We are in your debt."

"I'm glad we came early," Robbie observed. "That traffic got pretty hairy toward the end. Although, when you think about the relationship between mass and volume, it's not surprising."

Sukie liked Ben's gangly childhood friend even though she sometimes had trouble understanding the MIT junior's train of thought. Half the time, she didn't know if he what he said was truly heavy or if he was just spacing out.

Robbie took a long hit and blew it into Cheryl's mouth. Coughing, she sputtered, "This is primo weed."

Phil pushed his wire rims back against his face. "Hey, man, don't bogart that thing." Sukie was surprised to hear him speak for the first time in hours.

Robbie handed the joint to Nina, who took a quick toke. Sukie noticed that Nina passed it on to Phil with elaborate care, caressing his hand as she cautioned, "It's getting short. Don't burn your fingers."

When the joint came to JJ, he whipped out a roach clip for the dwindling stub. Sukie was impressed by his skill in attaching the joint to the clip. Then she remembered that Ben had mentioned that JJ, his fraternity brother and a star lacrosse player, spent most of his free time getting high. She hoped he wasn't getting high in the dorms this summer, where he was acting as a proctor for junior-high-age kids attending a four-week educational program.

"The damn thing went out," Eskimo protested when he accepted the roach clip. "I guess we'll just need to light another one." He drew an enormous new joint from his shirt pocket and fired it up in a blaze of smoke.

Sukie didn't know much about Eskimo. JJ's friend, he had come down from New England just for this trip. Eskimo was a fine-looking guy with his black hair and ice blue eyes, but he looked too much like a jock for Sukie's taste. Although he dressed preppie, Eskimo had been high since the minute he climbed into the van.

"Is that weed I smell?" A loud voice boomed from the darkness beyond the campfire.

Sukie peered through the haze of wood smoke and marijuana to see a tall, reed-thin man approaching. Several girls trailed in his wake. Their entrance made Sukie think about Nana's rooster and his flock of hens. Then, three guys emerged from the darkness lagging several steps behind the girls.

The first man, maybe in his late twenties, wore striped bell-bottoms, a flowered shirt, and a fringed leather vest. His wild Afro seemed at odds with the pallor of his skin. Clad in long granny dresses, all the girls had twined braids of flowers in their hair.

"Greetings, freaks and beautiful people. I'm Levi Bloom of the band and recording artists, Levi Bloom and Flatbush Boulevard. Arabella is lead singer. These other flowers of Brooklyn are fellow travelers seeking the healing power of music and cannabis." He pointed to each of the remaining three girls, who bowed as he introduced them in turn. "Sunshine, Sophie, and the wee one is Willow."

Levi turned slightly to indicate the remainder of his followers. "These gentleman are my bandmates, Manny and Diesel." He pointed to the small, Italian-looking guy holding a ukulele. "Manny plays a mean bass guitar and ukulele, of course. Diesel is our drummer." Diesel dressed as a miniature version of Levi, with fringed vest and striped pants.

"Over there is our roadie and lyricist, Abe, a man of great strength and the soul of a poet." A muscular black man in a tight dark t-shirt and ripped jeans flashed a broad smile.

Sukie had never heard of Levi Bloom, but she was thrilled to meet these people who had recorded an album. As she looked at the girls, she wondered where she could find flowers for her hair.

Levi raised the guitar he carried and asked, "Well, brothers and sisters, what do you say? How about a song with that doobie?"

When the group around the fire made room for all the newcomers, Levi began to play his guitar, both strumming and plucking the strings with his fingers. Diesel began keeping rhythm by slapping his thigh at the same time Manny joined in with his ukulele. Levi broke into a sad, sweet melody with a folk-rock flavor.

One day, you smiled at me,
And like a fool, I fell.
One day, you looked at me.
And now my life is hell.
Your eyes so full of lovin'
Kindled in me a flame
But now I've only memories
And the whisper of your name.

On the chorus, Arabella, Sunshine, and Sophie sang a harmony that was so beautiful that it brought a tear to Sukie's eye.

It's the memories that haunt me
My nights are filled with pain
Your eyes, your smile, your touch, your kiss
And the whisper of your name, oh yeah,
The whisper of your name.

When the group finished the haunting song, they moved to the traditional folk song, "Black is the Color of My True Love's Hair."

Sukie had to pinch herself from time to time as the evening wore on. Finally, a real adventure.

Despite her determined efforts to stay awake, Sukie began to crash long before the songs and laughter ended. When the group finally broke up, the flames had faded to embers, and she had snuggled into Ben's arms for warmth. When she and Ben headed into their tent for some sleep, Sukie stumbled from exhaustion. Stretched out in her sleeping bag, she had a single thought before falling asleep:

Tomorrow could only get better.

CHAPTER ELEVEN

ALEXA SAILED THROUGH TOWN, hitting all green lights on her short trip to Melissa's tiny cottage on the outskirts of Carlisle. She thought of the place as Melissa's dollhouse. The limestone house had been built as a carriage house. Somewhere along the line, the owners had converted the place into a residence and sold it, along with an overgrown acre of pines and flowering bushes.

The scent of lilacs in full bloom hit Alexa when she climbed out of the Rover. A narrow porch spanned the entire front of Melissa's cottage. Alexa headed toward the aging green swing at the far right. Recoiling each time her hand brushed a cobweb or a flake of peeling paint, she groped beneath the low seat searching for the key. In heels and pencil skirt, Alexa couldn't bend far enough to reach the middle of the wide seat. Exasperated, she knelt on the rough plank floor, her knees cushioned by a tie-dyed pillow plucked from the swing.

As Alexa clambered to her feet, key in hand, she froze at a loud creaking noise. She held her breath and listened. The morning was quiet except for the wind sighing through the tall pines and the low hum of bees in the lilacs.

Must have been the swing, she thought.

After slipping the key into the lock, Alexa stepped through the door into the tiny foyer and headed toward the kitchen. She sniffed the unexpected smell of men's cologne just as she sensed movement in the doorway she had just passed. A violent push between the shoulder blades sent Alexa flying. High heels sliding on the polished floor, she crashed to her hands and knees. Behind her, the front door slammed and footsteps pounded across the wooden porch.

Dazed, it took Alexa a few seconds before she kicked off her heels and ran outside. As she reached the porch, she could hear a car tear out of the old farm lane at the rear of the property. A thick row of pines shielded the lane from sight, so she couldn't actually see the vehicle.

Trying to catch her breath, Alexa lowered herself to the swing and studied her battered knees. Her shredded nylons were doing nothing to stop the flow of blood. With some hesitation, she stepped back into the house. Listening for sounds of another intruder, Alexa tiptoed to the kitchen. Melissa's camera bags were open and scattered over the table.

"What's going on here? Burglars at both Melissa's gallery and home couldn't be a coincidence. What are these people looking for?" Alexa mused aloud. She reached into her jacket pocket for her cell phone and dialed 911.

Alexa heard the siren before she saw dust rising into the air on Melissa's gravel lane. The state trooper skidded into the driveway only minutes after she'd called for help. Following a few quick questions, Trooper Black rushed into the house while Alexa sat on the porch swing. He soon emerged, holstering his gun.

"I agree that any perpetrators have left the premises. Do you want me to call an ambulance for you?"

"No, thanks. I think some Neosporin and band-aids will fix me up."

"Can you tell if anything is missing?"

"I'm not the person to ask. I think I should call the owner, Melissa Lambert. I was just here to pick up a camera. There is something that you should know. Melissa owns an art gallery in Carlisle. Right now, the borough police are there, investigating a burglary that she discovered this morning."

A distraught Melissa arrived a short time later, driving her Prius. "What is happening? First, the gallery. Now, my house. Did they steal anything here?"

"Hello, miss. I'm Trooper Black. Let's walk through the house and you can tell me if anything seems to be missing."

They had just entered the house when Troopers Taylor and Cannon pulled up in an unmarked car. Alexa stood as they approached the porch.

Trooper Taylor spoke first. "We heard about the dispatch to Melissa Lambert's home and thought we'd check it out. I didn't expect to see you here."

"Those abrasions on your knees look pretty bad. Do you need medical attention?" Trooper Cannon asked.

"I'm fine. Melissa is inside with Trooper Black. I surprised someone inside the house when I came to pick up one of her cameras. He knocked me down and hightailed it out of here. This is the second break-in today for Melissa. Somebody trashed her office at the gallery and stole some stuff."

Taylor moved onto the porch. "We'd like to go inside and check it out. Will you stay here, please?"

Alexa used her phone to check emails and called to notify Melinda that her arrival in the office would be delayed again. Limping to the Land Rover, Alexa rummaged around until she found a half-opened bottle of water and a box of tissues. When she tried to clean her bloody knees, the Kleenex turned into wet blobs that stuck to the wisps of torn nylon.

In disgust, she returned to the porch swing, sitting sideways with her legs resting on the cushion. She was dying to go inside and find out what was happening. For a while, she was distracted by a carpenter bee industriously chomping its way into the porch ceiling. A fine mist of sawdust had formed a little pyramid on the porch floor by the time Melissa and two of the troopers finally emerged from the house.

"Is anything missing?" Alexa asked.

"As far as I can tell, just the memory cards from the two cameras. I'll need to test out the cameras to make sure they weren't broken," Melissa replied.

"It looks like the guy may not have been in the house too long before you arrived. Not much has been disturbed," Trooper Cannon offered.

"Can you describe your assailant? Are you sure you're not hurt?" Trooper Taylor put his hand on Alexa's shoulder.

"I might have some trouble doing yoga tomorrow night, but I'll probably survive. Melissa, do you have a washcloth and some Neosporin or something?"

"Of course. I feel so bad, Lexie. You were doing me a favor, running out here. I'm so sorry. You could have been seriously hurt. I just don't understand why all of this is happening." Melissa brushed a tear from her eye before she headed into the house.

"To answer your question, Trooper, I didn't see anything. I sensed that someone was behind me just seconds before I felt this powerful shove in the middle of my back. I fell forward onto the floor and he ran out the front door. By the time I got to the porch, a car was pulling away—down the lane in the back, beyond the pines. I never got a look at whoever pushed me."

"Did you form any impression about this person? Height? What type of sound did the shoes make on the floor? Was it a car or did it sound more like a truck? You said 'he,' but how do you know it was a man?"

"Whoa. I'm not sure about any of that." Alexa ran through the brief encounter again in her mind before she continued. "I think the person was fairly tall. I say that because I sort of felt his hand hit my back at a downward angle. I think it was a man, not a woman. He made a little 'oomph' sound when he pushed, and the footsteps had some weight behind them. When he ran across the porch, it was a solid, flat sound on the floorboards."

Alexa watched the bee float away on the breeze and caught a whiff of lilac, reminding her about the scent that had accosted her earlier. "The only thing I can say for sure is that he doesn't spend much on cologne. He was doused in something cheap, maybe Brut or AXE. He smelled like some of the young men who come into the Cumberland Clinic with their girlfriends."

Cannon was scribbling furiously into a little notebook as she spoke.

"On the vehicle, I'd say a car, not a pickup or larger truck . . . but I'm not sure."

"Thanks. That's helpful. Maybe Trooper Black will pick up some prints off a doorknob or see something in the lane out back."

"Everything I just said is only an impression. I couldn't swear to any of this since I never actually saw the person."

"Still, this could help in the investigation," Trooper Cannon replied.

Melissa came out the front door, loaded with first aid gear. "Come here and I'll fix you up, Alexa," she directed, angling Alexa's legs so she could reach her knees.

Alexa complied, turning back to the troopers while Melissa held a wet washcloth to her right knee. "What do you think is going on? Is Melissa safe here and in her office?" Alexa grimaced as Melissa swiped the washcloth across her other knee.

John Taylor fielded the question. "At this point, we don't have a good working theory. It could be that the publicity about Melissa's opening put her on some opportunist's radar screen. The guy reads about her photography show and thinks he can make a quick buck by stealing cameras and other equipment. The gallery address was in the newspaper article about the exhibit. I imagine that Melissa's home address is in the phone book and a dozen places online, right?"

Melissa nodded her agreement. As he continued, the trooper's tone grew speculative. "It could be something more though. Both of these burglaries targeted Melissa's cameras, memory cards, and computer. Maybe this is just a photography lover. But maybe Melissa has taken some photographs that someone doesn't want her to have. They left the exhibit alone, so we're probably looking at something else."

"Ms. Lambert, don't forget to put together that list of recent photo sessions that we discussed," Cannon reminded Melissa as she rose to her feet, her medical duties complete.

"How did the guy get in here? I didn't see any broken glass." Alexa frowned as the words came out of her mouth, thinking of the broken door pane at Cecily Townes' house.

"Um, I think I know how he got in. I keep a key in the gallery, hanging on the wall." Melissa looked embarrassed as she continued in a tiny voice. "It was labeled 'house,' and it's missing now."

Cannon said, "That information makes it even more likely that we've got the same perpetrator in both incidents."

Taylor continued, "There is one more thing that concerns us. This gets to your question about safety, Alexa. Melissa was close to Cecily Townes. You two found her body. We can't rule out a connection to the murder, however slim."

The trooper turned toward Melissa. "I think it would be a good idea to stay with someone for a few days while we investigate all of this. You should go about your daily business as usual, but be careful. Try not to be alone."

"I can't believe this. OK, I can go stay with my boyfriend, Jim. But I don't want to go around looking over my shoulder every minute of the day."

"Hopefully, we will get this sorted out soon." Trooper Taylor's reassurance sounded as if he was trying to convince himself as much as Melissa.

After stopping to grab a sandwich and buy new pantyhose, Alexa finally made it back to the office around three o'clock. Melinda fussed over her boss, bringing her a cup of tea and ice-filled baggies for each swollen knee.

"They say that into every life some rain must fall." Melinda had a quote for every occasion.

"Who says that exactly?" Alexa grumped.

"And of course, there's a silver lining in every cloud."

"Just let me know when you figure out the silver lining in getting whacked in the back and gouging the hell out of my knees. Until then, let me try to get some work done." Alexa grinned as Melinda scurried out of the office. She tried to push aside her worry about Melissa and these break-ins. She really did need to get some work done.

Alexa frowned when the phone buzzed, annoyed at the interruption. Melinda said, “Sorry, but a Jack Nash is on the line. I wasn’t sure if you were expecting his call?”

Intrigued, Alexa instructed, “I’ll take it. Thanks.”

“How can I help you, Mr. Nash?” she asked when the line rang through.

“Hello, Ms. Williams. I’m sorry to interrupt your workday. I know you must be quite busy. However, I have a proposition for you.”

“A proposition?”

“Yes. I believe you are aware that we now have a vacancy on the Children of Light Board of Directors due to Cecily Townes’ untimely passing. I know by your reputation that you are a fine lawyer who has worked in family law and is familiar with the world of foster care and adoption. I was hoping I could convince you to fill that slot on the board.”

Nash’s request took Alexa by surprise. This was totally out of the blue. “I’m honored that you would consider me for your board, Mr. Nash. There is no way I could hope to fill Cecily Townes’ shoes.”

“I appreciate your modesty, Ms. Williams. But, we decided to approach you based on your own merit and the value you could bring to the board.”

“I would need more information before I could make this commitment. For instance, duties, time involved, any fiduciary responsibility for the organization.”

“I understand completely. We will be happy to answer any questions you might have. Actually, I’m having a little soirée at my place on Wednesday evening. Most of the board members will be there for the dinner. Perhaps you could come, and we could grab a few minutes to go over the details? By the way, your friend Melissa Lambert will also be there. We want to recognize her generosity to RESIST.”

“This Wednesday? OK. Thank you. I’ll come to dinner, and we can discuss this further. But I still need to think about your offer.”

“I’ll see you on Wednesday. I’ll have one of my people call your office with the details.”

Alexa shook her head as she ended the call. In some ways, the idea had some appeal. From the little she knew, Children of Light did a lot for abused and neglected children. But, she was still getting back on track after last autumn’s trauma. Did she want to take on more responsibility before she had gotten her life back in order?

She turned back to the computer screen but just couldn't pick up her train of thought. Her mind whirled, and her knees throbbed. "That's it. This day has been a total loss anyway. So, screw it." She saved the document on her computer and hobbled out the door, heading for home and some time with Scout.

CHAPTER TWELVE

"THANKS FOR AGREEING TO MEET." Tyrell Jenkins unfolded his body from the chair and stood to greet Alexa.

"Sure. I hear the coffee is good here. What would you like?" Alexa gave him a professional nod, trying to ignore a frisson of excitement.

"I'm not into all these fancy drinks. Just a cup of black coffee is fine with me." He took his chair and leaned back with arms folded.

Alexa looked toward the young barista at the counter. "Jess, a black coffee and the usual for me, please." She sat down at the table and glanced around the room before her eyes came to rest on the social worker. For some reason, Tyrell's good looks threw Alexa off balance.

"Sounds like you're a regular here at Legal Grounds."

"I volunteer at the Cumberland Clinic down the street. I make a regular coffee run here for the staff. The place is pretty empty this morning."

"Cumberland Clinic? I heard about the violence over there last fall. I hope you weren't caught up in the middle of any of it."

"I was, but I'd prefer not to discuss it." Alexa was relieved to see Jess heading toward the table with their drinks.

The perky barista leaned in a little too close as she smiled at Tyrell."The black coffee must be for you, right?"

"Watch it there, girl, or I'll call you out for racial stereotyping," Tyrell barked.

The young server flushed and stammered as she tried to deny the accusation. "No. No, sir. I just meant that Alexa always orders the chai tea."

Tyrell smiled, but his eyes remained as hard as flint. "Just messing with you. The coffee is for me."

After Jess fled to the safety of the counter, Alexa said, "You couldn't have given the kid a break?"

Tyrell's smile evaporated. "Look, I get hit on all the time. When it's a young girl, I'm pretty brutal. Maybe they'll think twice before they flirt with an older man—or respond to some old dude who's trying to pick them up."

"Maybe your intentions were pure, but that was pretty harsh. Do you save your routine just for young girls or does it work for all ages? I take it you live in constant danger of women coming on to you?" Alexa pushed her chair back a few inches.

"What can I say? The ladies want me. But I don't always say no if the lady is fine." This time, Tyrell's smile lit up his green eyes as he leaned toward Alexa and took her hand.

Alexa flinched at Tyrell's touch and jerked her hand away at the surge of warmth. Unnerved, she struggled to maintain a haughty tone.

"Mr. Jenkins, as much as I'd love to spend more time talking about your difficulties in fending off women, we're here to discuss something more important."

Tyrell sat up straight. "Of course. The Bertolinos are still frantic. They've had no word from Meg. They think that she's been kidnapped or worse, but the police haven't turned up anything."

"I know. I spoke to Detective Miller earlier this morning. They still believe that it's more likely that Meg is a runaway. She's under eighteen, but there is no credible evidence that she has been abducted. No one saw her get into a stranger's car. There has been no demand for ransom. Nothing on her computer shows that she has been in contact with a child lurer. And kids in foster care often run."

"But Meg was happy, well-adjusted. No one who knows her believes she just split." Tyrell slammed his half-empty cup onto the table, coffee sloshing over the rim.

"I'm in your camp, but I can do nothing to move the police into further action. I know that they are still investigating, but they've pretty much reached a dead end. What about the family's efforts with Facebook and the posters?" Alexa felt powerless to help the family, and she hated the feeling.

"Nothing."

"One thing I could suggest is that Mr. and Mrs. Bertolino reach out to our state senator."

"Fran Dodge?"

"Yeah. She's got an office in town. Sometimes, pressure from above can move things along."

Tyrell dropped the Mr. Cool act as his voice lowered. "The strange thing is that now two of the girls from my youth group have just up and disappeared, within weeks of each other. The first to vanish, Aurora Washington, could easily be a runaway. Her home life sucks. I thought she was too smart to take off, but something could have happened with her mother that sent Aurora running. But Meg just doesn't fit that mold."

Alexa sat up at the mention of Aurora Washington—she had missed her clinic appointment, but confidentiality rules prohibited Alexa from discussing that with Tyrell.

"Please tell Ed and Toni that I'm sorry I didn't get anywhere with the police. I'd be happy to speak to them directly if they want. I can't even imagine what they are going through. We can only hope that Meg is OK and that she returns home safely."

Alexa put money on the table for the drinks and rose to her feet. "I need to get back to the office."

Tyrell stood to shake Alexa's hand. "Thanks for your help, and thanks for the coffee. I'll keep in touch about Meg."

As Alexa walked back to her office, she thought about Tyrell. Talk about mercurial. One minute he was haughty Don Juan and the next he was a concerned social worker. He might be totally hot, but this guy had Danger Zone written all over him.

Haley missed yoga class that evening, so Alexa and Melissa skipped the Om Café. Instead, they stood in the parking lot as the light faded. The cool breeze felt good against Alexa's sweaty skin.

"How are you doing, Melissa? Do the police have any suspects in either of your burglaries?"

"No. They think the same person did both. Duh! What a surprise. Other than that, no clue who. No clue why. And I can't really point the cops in a particular direction. I can understand if they just broke in to rip off a computer and some camera equipment. I guess they could get some money for that somewhere. But why steal some of my memory cards?"

"Maybe they thought that they could sell them, too?"

"Maybe, but you can get a memory card for fifteen bucks. You'd have to be an idiot about cameras to think you could get rich pawning used memory cards. Plus, while they took the camera from the gallery, they left the cameras at the house. Who would take memory cards and leave the cameras if they were after money?" Melissa looked perplexed.

"I might have scared the guy away before he could grab the cameras."

"I'm pissed about that thieving, lowlife asshole hurting you. How are your knees?"

"Yoga mudra was a little painful tonight, but I'll heal." Alexa shifted back and forth. The more she thought about her throbbing knees, the more they hurt. "Hey, Jack Nash invited me to a dinner at his house tomorrow night. He says you're going, too?"

"I think he invited me because my show raised a lot of money for RESIST. He's hoping that I'll inspire some of his rich buddies to do something similar for Children of Light."

"I'm glad you'll be there. He wants me to join the Children of Light Board of Directors."

Melissa grinned. "Board of directors? Well, la-di-da. I'll meet you at Nash's place. I'm staying with Jim until this burglary is solved, and the Nash compound isn't too far away. We should have a blast. I hear Nash's place is fucking unbelievable. Versailles on the South Mountain."

CHAPTER THIRTEEN

"DAMN, WHAT A PLACE," Alexa murmured as she pulled the Land Rover behind a line of cars queued in front of Jack Nash's mansion. The ancient SUV looked a little out of place among the tony assortment of luxury cars. She spied a Range Rover that gleamed like the rich uncle to her ne'er-do-well vehicle.

A clean-cut, young boy perspiring in a blue blazer tapped on the window. "If you give me your keys, ma'am, I'll park your car."

Alexa slid her heels on and climbed out of the Rover. She coughed at the smell of hot asphalt and idling engines before she responded to the boy. "She's a little rough between first and second."

"No problem. I'll be careful. This is a Land Rover, right?" He glanced around and lowered his voice. "Bitchin' wheels for a lady like you—begging your pardon."

Alexa grinned. "That's quite a drive up here with the winding road. It felt like I was driving through a tunnel with those tall, narrow cypress trees on both sides."

The kid laughed. "I've never been to Italy. Hel—I mean, heck—I've never been out of Pennsylvania. But I hear that the Nashes copied this house from some huge Italian-type of mansion. I forget what they're called."

"A villa?" Alexa prompted, looking at the ornate columns, stucco walls, and entryway fountain. The alley of cypress had been just a teaser for this Tuscan extravaganza; a villa on steroids.

"Yes, that's it." He lowered his voice again. "I heard the trees are fake though—some type of evergreen that looks like those Italian trees." Another car approached and the kid hopped into the Rover. "I better clear outta here."

Inside, a mousy teenager in a blue dress directed Alexa through an elaborate foyer. The wan-looking girl slumped against the wall as if trying to disappear into the gilded woodwork, but she managed enough energy to steer Alexa toward the right hall.

Feeling a bit nervous about walking into the unknown, Alexa paused on the threshold of a glass-walled room: a conservatory the size of a high school gym. More than two-dozen people clustered in small groups, chatting with wineglasses in hand.

Moving past her moment of unease, Alexa squared her shoulders and stepped into the room. A perfectly-coiffed woman in a dark plum cocktail dress drifted forward, offering Alexa a languid hand.

Alexa smoothed the skirt of her designer knockoff. Unsure whether this was a business dinner or purely social affair, she had compromised with a fine-knit, tea-length dress to hide her scabbed knees. Now she felt underdressed. Perhaps she should have gone more little black dress.

She closed the gap between them and took the proffered hand, shaking it with more care than she used in most professional situations. Alexa worried that a strong grip might snap this woman's wrist.

"You must be Alexa Williams. I'm Vivienne Nash. So glad you could join us this evening. Jack has been detained, but feel free to join our other guests."

Jack Nash's wife stood ramrod straight; one of those painfully thin society women: all skin and bones and designer dress. Her hair had been expertly tinted a champagne blonde. Alexa assumed that she wore contacts; eyes that genuinely violet had died with Elizabeth Taylor. Vivienne reminded Alexa of many of the partners' wives from her old New York law firm.

With an almost imperceptible movement of her wrist, Vivienne gestured toward the far corner of the room. "If you'd like wine, there is a bar by the french doors. Just ask the young man for whatever you want."

With the obligatory greeting completed, Vivienne moved away. The hostess seemed so insubstantial that the air barely stirred as she floated across the room.

Left to fend for herself, Alexa wandered past rows of potted orange trees trimmed into smooth-orbed topiaries. The sweet tang of citrus wafted from the miniature fruits that dotted each tree. When she reached the bar, another well-groomed teenager in a blue blazer launched a recital of wines by name and vintage.

What was with the Prussian blue uniforms? Had there been a sale at Jo-Ann Fabrics? These kids must all be part of the foster care program, Alexa speculated.

The boy seemed to struggle to remember what came next after he nailed the pronunciation of the Chateau de Beaucastel Chateauneuf-du-Pape 1993. Alexa took pity on the kid. He wasn't even old enough to drink, but they had him masquerading as a sommelier—a role that probably violated both the child labor and liquor control laws.

"Do you have a Riesling?" Alexa interrupted.

The boy sighed in relief and retrieved Alexa's drink.

Keeping a firm hold on the fragile crystal glass, Alexa strolled toward the nearest group. As she approached, a gray-haired man smiled at her. "Alexa Williams. I'm Chadwick Young. You may not remember me."

"Of course I remember you, Mr. Young. You served as a county commissioner during my mother's first term." Alexa also remembered that Young and her mother had fought about every important issue, but she stayed silent on that point.

As she circulated through the guests, Alexa relaxed. She'd attended similar social events and soon fell into the groove. It helped that she knew many of the assembled group. Most were local movers and shakers, although a few came from New York and Washington, D.C. Several identified themselves as board members for Children of Light. Others made no mention of their connection to Jack and Vivienne Nash.

Alexa had just completed her circle of the conservatory when she became trapped in an animated conversation between two guys with golf tans. When they began debating the finer points of various brands of putters, her attention drifted. Then, Quinn Hutton walked into the room.

Dressed more formally than at Melissa's opening, he still managed to stand out in the crowd. His slate gray business suit fit his lean body perfectly. She had been around enough high-powered New York City lawyers to know that a fit like that came only from excellent tailoring.

"Alexa, isn't it? What is a photography connoisseur doing with a crowd like this?"

Before she could reply, Quinn brushed his lips against her right cheek, then her left.

It was all Alexa could do to keep from touching her cheek in surprise. "How European of you, Mr. Hutton. I thought you lived in Thailand, not France."

"Quinn, please. We're old friends now, aren't we? I did spend a few years in France as well, teaching at an international school. I hope I haven't offended?"

"I'm not sure one brief conversation makes us old friends. But a kiss from a handsome man, even just on my cheek, is hardly grounds for complaint. So, what is your connection to this gathering?" Alexa leaned toward Quinn so she could better hear his low-pitched voice amidst the cocktail chatter.

"Jack and my father were childhood friends. I visited here with my family many times as a child. That's one of the reasons I jumped on the Dickinson job when I heard it was available. I had such fond memories of this area."

"Carlisle must be pretty tame after a life on the road. Living in Thailand and France sounds like a dream."

"For me, it was time to wake up from the dream. I wanted to come home to the States. To paraphrase Michael Bublé: I had my run. Baby, I was done. I had to come home."

"You relate to your students with Michael Bublé? I'm not sure he's on most college kids' playlists." Alexa choked on a bubble of laughter.

"No. I aim for connection through Yeats and Blake and Hemingway. That Bublé song was on the radio on my way here. It seemed apropos." Quinn drew back and straightened up. "Enough about me. I hear you're joining us on the board?"

"You're a board member?" Alexa raised her eyebrows.

"Yes. Jack trusts me because of the family connection. My father had a hand in the original funding of the organization, although he doesn't take a formal role in the company. Not to get too corny, but I think Children of Light is an excellent organization. I take a lot of satisfaction from my work on the board."

"I haven't agreed yet, but I'm taking the offer seriously."

Melissa's voice called out behind her. "There you are. As usual, I ran late."

When she turned toward her friend, Quinn bent to whisper in Alexa's ear, his lips brushing her hair. "Don't worry. The board doesn't have a lot of stuffy rules. There's no bylaw that says we can't become more than old friends." Before Alexa could respond, Quinn moved away, leaving her intrigued and a bit breathless.

Shortly after Melissa's arrival, Jack Nash made his entrance. He raised his hand, and the crowd fell silent. Vivienne stood like a wraith at his side, dimmed even further by her husband's confidence and vitality. With all eyes on him, Jack gave a tug to each of his cuffs and spoke.

"Members of the board, friends, welcome. Vivienne and I regard you all as our family, sisters and brothers in support of Children of Light. Armand has prepared a feast for us to enjoy. Shall we make our way to the dining room? Vivienne tells me that place cards on the table indicate where each of you will sit. My wife so loves an interesting mix at table."

The group trailed into the huge dining room where a single table easily seated the entire crowd. Young girls in dresses, of course the house shade of blue, helped guide people to their assigned places. Somehow, these youngsters knew most of the guests by sight.

An elderly gentleman with a florid complexion sat to Alexa's right. He introduced himself as Jay Goldman and immediately reached for the breadbasket. She searched for Melissa, hoping for a friendly face, but saw her friend heading toward the far end of the table. The place card for the seat on her left angled away so she couldn't make out the name. Most likely, a self-important banker or, even worse, one of the golfers. Sighing, Alexa braced herself for a boring meal. Then, she felt a hand brush her shoulder and turned to see Quinn taking the chair to her left.

"What a lovely coincidence." Alexa remarked, happy to see the intriguing professor.

"Perhaps more than that. I have an in with our hostess."

The meal proved much more pleasant than Alexa had anticipated. She enjoyed the continued banter with Quinn but found much in common with all her nearby dinner companions, even Jay Goldman. The dinner passed quickly. Moments after yet another blue-clad adolescent served an elaborate meringue dessert, Jack Nash stood to address his guests.

"Thank you again for joining Vivienne and me in our home. Nothing can compare to spending time with friends and family. I am proud to have your support for Children of Light. Without your service and financial backing, we could not continue our successful programs that reach thousands of children in need each year.

"I want to introduce our two new companions." He gestured toward Alexa. "Many of you know Alexa Williams or her parents, attorney Norris Williams and former County Commissioner Susan Williams. We have asked Alexa to become a member of the board, following the tragic loss of our friend, Cecily Townes. I hope she agrees to join our cause."

So much for giving me time to make a decision, Alexa chafed.

"The lovely and generous young woman at the far end of the table is Melissa Lambert. She is a remarkable artist whose current photography exhibit provides a vivid window into the lives of unfortunate children in Asia. Her selflessness in donating half of the proceeds from her exhibit to RESIST is even more outstanding. I urge each and every one of you to catch Melissa's exhibit in the next week."

Jack continued to talk about Children of Light's mission and annual report. Although Alexa needed to learn about the organization, her mind wandered. Glancing down the long table, she stifled a giggle. Put tiaras on the women, tuxedos on the men, and this could pass for an episode of *Downton Abbey,* she imagined.

The analogy dimmed a bit when she focused on her host. Jack Nash would never fit the refined role of a titled lord. She pictured him more as one of those brash American robber barons who made their fortunes in commerce and relaxed by filling trophy rooms with taxidermied Kodiak bears and African lions.

The conclusion of Jack's speech signaled the end of the dinner. In unison, the guests murmured their thanks for the evening and flocked for the door. Going with the flow, Alexa rose and turned toward the dining room exit.

Behind her, Quinn touched her arm. "Leaving without saying goodbye?"

"I was looking for our host."

"I saw Jack head for the conservatory. Let me take you there." When he linked an arm through Alexa's elbow, she couldn't help another *Downton Abbey* flashback.

"Jack said that he would brief me on the specifics of board membership, but we never got a chance to talk."

"Even if we track him down, don't expect too much information. Jack doesn't often deal with the details. Usually, Ralph Price takes care of all that for him, but Ralph had major surgery and will be gone for most of the summer."

When they found the conservatory empty, Quinn steered Alexa through the darkened room toward the french doors. "Maybe he's outside with a cigar. If not, you can at least get a glimpse of the grounds. Gardening keeps some of the foster kids quite busy."

Twilight bathed the landscape in a lavender haze. It took a moment for Alexa to perceive that all the large trees scattered across the huge expanse of lawn had been clipped into large, animal-shaped topiaries. She recognized a bear, a giraffe, and an elephant but couldn't identify several of the other manicured figures perched on the distant knoll. As the light darkened to purple, a breeze whipped down the slope and the huge animals seemed to prance across the lawn. Alexa shivered at the creepy image.

Alexa turned to Quinn. “No one seems to be out here.” But she hadn’t really expected to find Jack in his oversized back yard.

“Well, finding Jack was a long shot. He often disappears after these events. But I’d be happy to brief you on board duties. How about dinner on Friday?”

“A business dinner?”

Quinn took a step closer to Alexa and lifted her chin. Gazing into her eyes, his voice dropped to an intimate whisper. “I’m a big proponent of combining business and pleasure. I’d like to get to know you better, Alexa. Just you and me, without the madding crowd.”

Without hesitation, Alexa accepted. “Friday’s fine for me.” She flashed a mischievous smile. “Maybe we can start with the business part, then consider the pleasure. Right now, though, I need to get home”

She liked this guy’s style. Sophisticated. Gorgeous. And, completely without effort, he throws an offhand Thomas Hardy allusion into a dinner invitation. Who could refuse? For an instant, Tyrell Jenkins came into her mind. Another gorgeous guy she’d just met. But Tyrell had an in-your-face aggressiveness that turned her off. Quinn’s style reminded her of Cary Grant in one of those old movies: a little too sophisticated but charming nonetheless.

As they passed the entrance to the dining room, Alexa noticed a group of teens clearing the long table like a swarm of blue bees. A few guests remained in the foyer, engaged in deep discussion. Alexa approached Vivienne Nash, who was standing alone by the wall.

“Thank you for a lovely evening, Mrs. Nash. Could you pass my appreciation on to your husband as well?”

“Of course. I hope we’ll see you here again soon.”

Vivienne turned her attention to Quinn. “My dear, could you take care of a small matter for me?”

“Of course, Viv.” Quinn kissed Alexa’s cheek. “Until Friday. I’ll be in touch with the details.”

Outside, Alexa smiled to see Melissa standing at the foot of the steps. “I didn’t get to talk to you all evening.”

“Yes. They put me in purgatory with an accountant and a judge. All the while, you sat in heaven with a grown up Abercrombie and Fitch model.”

"Quinn Hutton. He teaches at Dickinson. Didn't you meet him at your opening?"

"No, but apparently you did," Melissa smirked.

The kid Alexa had met earlier got out of a Jaguar and walked over. "You're the classic Land Rover, right?" When Alexa nodded her agreement, he took a key from a box and walked away. He yelled over his shoulder to Melissa, "Oh, your Prius is on its way too, miss."

"This has been an interesting evening. And I'm not talking about Quinn Hutton." Alexa commented in a low voice.

"No kidding." Melissa giggled. "Jack Nash acts like a used car salesman with an upscale clientele. His wife is a cross between Katherine Hepburn and Morticia Addams. And this place looks like Tony Soprano's idea of Tuscany."

Alexa had to stifle her urge to whoop aloud. "Yeah. A limestone farmhouse would have been better choice for this locale. They could've even supersized it for the wow factor. But, you have to give them some credit for thinking outside the box."

"Not when the result is this tacky," Melissa sniffed.

"At least they didn't go with a cookie-cutter ranch house. Most wealthy people in this area can't see past the same square-house-in-a-development approach. They just inflate the size of the house to match the size of their wallets."

"Yeah, everyone knows that size matters." Melissa gave an exaggerated leer. "Badda bing, badda boom."

In her inimitable way, Melissa had hit the nail on the head with her silly Tony Soprano references. Obviously, the Nash place had cost a fortune, but they'd crossed that fine line between magnificent and bizarre.

Alexa was still giggling when she emerged from the end of the faux cypress tunnel. She nodded at the man in a black uniform sitting in the guard booth and turned onto Pine Road, headed for home.

CHAPTER FOURTEEN

"YOU LOOK LOVELY, ALEXA." Quinn rose as she approached the table. Bright Japanese lanterns gave the patio of La Bella Cucina a festive air.

"Good evening, Quinn." Alexa replied as he kissed her cheek. "Great choice of restaurants. It's wonderful that the weather's nice enough for outdoor dining."

"Finally. Even though I grew up in New England, I abhor cold weather."

"So, your time abroad suited you. After living in the tropics, I can imagine that even Pennsylvania winters are too much for you. My dog, Scout, is in your camp. He has been ecstatic since spring arrived."

"You have a dog?"

"Yes. A big guy—an English mastiff. Perhaps you'll get to meet someday. Are you a dog person?"

"A dog person?" Quinn seemed to consider the question carefully. "I've never owned a dog. My mother had a poodle when I was a young child, but I don't remember him well. However, I can definitely say that I find dogs entertaining."

The time with Quinn flew by. Alexa finished the last morsel of tiramisu and leaned back into her bistro chair. "Thank you, Quinn, for a lovely dinner, not to mention the briefing about the Children of Light Board. You've convinced me that serving on the board would be a good way to contribute to these kids in need. It's time for me to call it a night though. I'm attending Cecily Townes' memorial service tomorrow morning. I told Melissa that I would help her set up a photo memory board."

Quinn stood as he replied, "I may see you there. I only knew Cecily as a fellow board member, but there's no doubt that she was a force to be reckoned with."

The professor walked Alexa to her car, parked right outside the restaurant. He stopped by the car and turned to face Alexa. For an instant, the patio lanterns bathed Quinn's face in an eerie red glow. Alexa hesitated a moment as he leaned forward, but the cool restraint of his kiss swept aside her misgivings.

Quinn broke off the kiss and ran his thumb over Alexa's cheekbone. "Let's do this again."

Beguiled by his reserve, Alexa agreed. "I'd like that."

Alexa had never seen a funeral or memorial service quite like the one for Cecily Townes. She'd expected a fairly small turnout since it was Memorial Day weekend. How wrong she'd been.

When St. Agnes moved to a new location a few years back, the congregation built the largest church in town. However, today, the new church's expansive nave could not accommodate all the people who had come to pay their respects to Cecily. When Alexa saw the size of the crowd streaming in for the service, she decided to leave.

"Melissa, I'm not going to stay. We've got the photo boards set up, so you don't need me anymore. I don't want to take a space away from someone who knew Cecily."

"OK. That's a kind gesture. But come outside with me a moment and sit before you go."

Alexa and Melissa walked past the series of photo-covered foam boards that Melissa had prepared for the memorial. Shots of Cecily helping youngsters on the streets of Mumbai and Bangkok intermingled with pictures of Cecily as a child and young nun. Cecily's brother, Richard, had supplied the personal photos.

The two women avoided the television cameras stationed outside the entrance and walked past several parked limousines. They stopped in a small meditation garden at the far side of the church.

"Are you going to make it through this?" Alexa sat on a concrete bench and tugged on Melissa's elbow until she sat down, too. "I know that you and Cecily had grown close. Today is bound to bring up all those terrible memories of finding her body."

"I'll be OK. It just makes me so angry that someone would murder the most selfless woman I've ever known. I wish the police would find whoever did this." Melissa clenched her hands.

"They need time to investigate." Alexa offered optimistic words to comfort Melissa, although she wasn't convinced that the police would ever find Cecily's killer.

Melissa looked around the empty garden then grabbed Alexa's wrist. "I wanted to tell you. Last night something came back to me. I remembered a conversation with Cecily on the day of the RESIST march . . . the day she was killed. Earlier that week, Cecily had asked to look at all my pictures from the Thai leg of our trip for RESIST. She said something vague about wanting to refresh her memory. So I gave her a thumb drive with the photos from our week in Bangkok.

"When we were standing by the Lincoln Memorial, Cecily mentioned that she had discovered something quite disturbing in the photos. I think she was going to tell me more, but I asked her to hold on a minute. I wanted to take a crowd shot from up on the memorial before the march broke up.

"That's when I got arrested, so Cecily never got a chance to tell me what was so disturbing."

"You just remembered this last night?" Alexa tried to keep the impatience out of her voice. One of Melissa's most charming traits was her artsy, often unfocused, approach to life. So Alexa wasn't surprised that her friend had forgotten what could be a critical piece of information in Cecily's murder investigation. Still, some of Melissa's scatterbrained moments could be annoying.

"Yeah, it just hit me out of the blue. I can't believe I forgot something that seems so important. But a lot has been happening. I was arrested. We found Cecily dead. I had my opening—the burglaries. I just forgot all about the conversation until last night when I was sorting through the pictures for the photo boards."

"It might be important . . . it might not be. But I think you should tell the police."

"I'll call Trooper Taylor. But I've thought about what Cecily said, and I think she must have been disturbed by something going on in Thailand. That's what the pictures would have shown. I can't imagine that it's connected to her murder here in Carlisle."

Alexa looked at her watch just as strains of organ music wafted out of the church. "Melissa, the service is about to begin. You should get back inside. Call me later if you need to talk."

When Alexa arrived at her cabin, she changed into shorts and hiking boots. With Scout at her heels, she struck out into the grove of pines opposite the house. The thick carpet of pine needles muffled their footsteps as Alexa and the big mastiff wandered through the cathedral of towering evergreens. At the church, Alexa had been wiping her brow from the heat of the midday sun. Here, in the pines, the shade kept the forest cool.

Near the middle of the grove, a shaft of sunlight cut through the big pines. Alexa stopped and plunged an arm through the beam, stirring thousands of dust motes into a luminous dance. “Cecily,” she whispered. “From everything that I know about you, your energy will never fade from this world. Go in peace.”

On the way back to the cabin, Alexa wondered again why someone would want to kill a woman as beloved as Cecily Townes. She, too, hoped that the police would do exactly what Melissa had wished for: track down the bastard and lock him up forever.

CHAPTER FIFTEEN

August 14, 1969

You're either on the bus or off the bus.
—Ken Kesey

"Hey, babe. Robbie, Phil, and I thought we'd go over to the stage area and check it out. They must still be working on last minute construction. Hear all the hammering?" Ben gestured toward the nearby hill with his tin coffee mug then filled it from a pot on the Coleman stove.

Sukie looked up from her seat in the door of their tent and nodded. "The pounding woke me up."

Ben lowered his voice. "I thought it was the pounding that I gave you." He made a lewd thrusting move with his hips and laughed when Sukie blushed.

She reached for Ben's hand and pulled him down next to her. "We have a whole day before the concert starts. I thought we'd wander around together. The Levi Bloom girls told me that there are a lot of little shops in a wooded area over that way." She waved her hand toward the back of the field.

"Yeah. I want to check out the shops, too. JJ said that they're selling weed and hash over there. But why don't you spend some time with Nina and Cheryl? I know you wouldn't be interested in watching them build the stage."

"Hey, freak. Ready for our field trip?" Robbie flicked aside the canvas flap and peered into the tent.

"Ready to roll." With an exaggerated kiss, Ben pushed Sukie back into the nest of sleeping bags. "You are such a fox. I'll meet

you here later for a trip to the shops," he said as he scrambled out the door to follow Robbie.

Alone in the tent, Sukie stared up at the green canvas and surrendered to a brief moment of disappointment at being abandoned. Brushing a tear from her eye, she sat up.

"Stop acting like some flake. You're at Woodstock, for God's sake," Sukie said aloud and went to find Nina.

"This place is so groovy." Willow darted around the buses covered in psychedelic paintings. On a nearby stage, two men were playing flutes while a third provided rhythm on a low, round drum.

The girl had tagged along when Sukie, Nina, and Cheryl had walked past her campsite. In the full light of day, Sukie realized that Willow was not just petite but quite young. The teenager dazzled with her blonde good looks. She reminded Sukie of a fairy or a wood sprite.

"Have you guys read "The Electric Kool-Aid Acid Test" *about Ken Kesey and his Merry Pranksters?" Met with blank stares, Sukie prodded, "You know Ken Kesey. I read his book,* One Flew Over the Cuckoo's Nest, *in Mr. Carter's Contemporary American Lit class. Anyway, that bus over there looks just like the Merry Pranksters' bus."*

"Great use of color." Nina, always the artist, pointed to the psychedelic paintings that sprawled across the side of the bus.

Willow hopped up and down. "Please. It's summer, and I don't want to think about books or school. We're here for music and fun." The teenager grabbed Nina's hands to form an arch. Sukie and Cheryl laughed and danced, one by one, beneath their friends' raised hands. Several people in the area followed them until, soon, everyone had joined in dancing and weaving their way through Willow's impromptu archway.

"My arms are killing me, kid," Nina complained and broke the connection with Willow. Without pause, another couple raised their hands to take the girls' place.

Dizzy from the dancing and laughter, Sukie dropped to the ground for a rest. Giggling, her companions joined her. Soon, the four girls lay on their backs in the grass, panting. The lilting, meandering melody of flute and drum continued in the background.

"That was so much fun." Willow sat up. "I love to dance. I wanted to take ballet lessons, but Mama said we couldn't afford it."

"Let me tell you, kid. Ballet isn't all it's cracked up to be." Nina frowned. "It took me years to convince my mother that those

Saturday morning classes were nothing but torture—and that I would never be a prima ballerina."

Willow's mouth opened wide in amazement. "I can't believe you turned down ballet lessons. One time, at Christmas, my school class went to see The Nutcracker. *It was so beautiful."*

"One of the great things about dancing is that you don't have to be trained as a ballerina. Just now, you danced like a free spirit. It was beautiful, too." Sukie rolled to a sitting position beside Willow and patted her on the hand.

"You're right. That's why I follow Levi and his band around. They play in clubs and even on the street sometimes. I hang out with them and dance in front of the stage. When I can get enough money to ride the subway into Manhattan, I go over to the Village and sneak into other shows. I saw Bob Dylan once."

"Bob Dylan? You're so lucky." Cheryl continued to braid a daisy into Sukie's silver blonde hair.

"I guess. His music is sort of hard to dance to though."

"What's this?" Nina rose to her feet and peered toward the stage.

"When did the music stop?" Sukie shielded her eyes against the sun as she looked at Nina.

"Let's go closer to the stage. Some guy's leading exercise classes."

"Exercise?" Cheryl moaned, but she followed the other girls as they tiptoed through the group of people seated in front of the stage.

A thin man with dark blonde hair that flowed to his waist told the assembled crowd that they were going to do yoga, something called the breath of fire.

The four girls squeezed into a spot to the right of the stage. Sukie followed the man's instructions, snorting rapidly, until she became dizzy. Taking a break, she stretched out on her side. She bent her elbow, propped up her head, and watched with amusement as her friends tried to keep up with the instructor.

When the exercise finished, the girls wandered through the expansive campsite.

"Peace be with you." A rosy-cheeked woman in granny glasses and braids greeted them as they approached a tent set up as a kitchen.

"Hello. What's all this? If you don't mind us asking?"

"It's copacetic, dear. We're the Hog Farm, a commune from New Mexico. We are here to help with the festival, feed people who might need a meal, and oversee the entertainment on this free stage."

"Wow." Cheryl looked at a big kettle on the counter. That's a lot of food. How many people are coming? We got here yesterday, and there were a lot of cars on the road."

"I heard that a lot more people are coming than the organizers expected."

"What's a commune?" Willow peered into a kettle on the ground.

Another woman dressed in a tie-dyed halter and bell-bottoms placed another huge pot on the table. "Well, little one, a commune is a family—a family we choose to join. We live together; we love together; we plant together; and we harvest together."

"Far out." Willow's eyes were wide. "I wanted to be a groupie, but maybe I should join a commune. My mother would never miss me."

"Give it a few years, honey. You can't be much more than thirteen?"

"Fourteen."

"Spend a few more years in school, then come to New Mexico. Ask anyone. They know how to find the Hog Farm."

As they walked away, Nina asked Willow, "Kid, do you know what a groupie is?"

"Sure. Groupies are pretty girls who travel with bands. They dance to the music and hang out with the guys in the band."

"Honey, there's a little more involved than that . . ."

"Like what?"

Sukie let Nina handle this on her own. After all, she'd started the conversation."

"Like sex."

Willow looked at the ground and didn't respond.

Sukie thought the tips of the girl's ears looked a little pink.

Nina plowed ahead. "Do you know what sex is?"

After a few more seconds of silence, Willow finally replied. "Yeah, I know about sex. My mother spends most of her time balling some guy or another." Her voice trailed to a whisper, "But I've never . . ."

Cheryl jumped in like a mother hen. "I would hope not. Fourteen is entirely too young to be going all the way with a guy. Honey, you should save it at least until you're in college."

"So maybe I should wait to be a groupie until I'm older," Willow offered.

"Or stick with the commune idea," Cheryl counseled.

Willow hugged Cheryl around the waist and skipped a few steps ahead.

Sukie snorted. "As if that wouldn't involve sex? Aren't communes about free love and all that?"

Willow was racing across the meadow toward a small pond by that point, so she never heard Sukie's question.

CHAPTER SIXTEEN

ENJOYING THE COOL EVENING on one of her deck chairs, Alexa listened to the chorus of peepers from the nearby pond—one of her favorite signs of early summer. She looked up in surprise at the sound of gravel crunching on the lane. Scout managed a single woof at the unfamiliar car but didn't leave her side.

Trooper Taylor pulled up in front of her cabin and climbed out, leaving his sport coat in the unmarked police cruiser. He trudged up the steps to join Alexa on the deck, pausing to scratch Scout's head.

"Hey, guy. It's been awhile. You're such a good dog. Yes, you are."

The lanky trooper asked Alexa, "Has he gotten bigger? This dog is enormous."

"I think he's finished growing. It's just been awhile since you've seen Scout."

"And awhile since I've been out here. I'd forgotten how peaceful these woods are. How old is this place?" The trooper gestured toward the rustic log cabin.

"The original cabin is about one hundred years old. The bedroom wing over there was built as an addition." Alexa pointed to the raised section of the house. "You know this belongs to my parents, right? I'm thinking about asking them if I can buy it instead of renting, but I'm not sure they'll give it up."

The trooper flashed a smile. "Sorry I didn't call ahead. Do you have a few minutes to talk?"

"Sure. Do you want a Coke or something? Are soft drinks permitted on the job?"

"Technically, I'm off duty. But a Coke would be great."

"Have you eaten? I was just about to put a burger on the grill."

"You are a wonderful woman, Alexa Williams. Offering a weary man caffeine and food. I would love a burger."

Over dinner at the table on the deck, the trooper plunged into the purpose of his visit. "I was hoping you could help me with background on all these social service agencies and Cecily Townes' local relationships."

"You realize I never knew Cecily, right?"

"Yes, but you know the connections between a lot of these agencies and people. And I know that your friend Melissa was pretty tight with Ms. Townes."

"You can't possibly think that Melissa had anything to do with Cecily's death?"

"No," the trooper smiled. "Being in jail in our nation's capital at the time of the murder is a pretty airtight alibi."

"Did Melissa tell you about the conversation she had with Cecily on that day at the demonstration?"

"Yes. We're still in the midst of our investigation, but that conversation has added some fuel to a lead we're pursuing. One of the national agencies provided us with information about two Thai citizens who entered the country about a week before Ms. Townes was killed. The men have been identified as suspected kingpins in a human trafficking operation based in Bangkok."

"The type of people Cecily and RESIST were trying to stop."

"Exactly. We've asked Melissa to give us a file with all those pictures of Thailand. Apparently, the burglars didn't get her back-up photo files when they broke into her studio and home. So we'll see if we can establish a connection between those two foreign nationals and Cecily's last trip to Thailand.

"Of course, we are also looking at Cecily's life in this country. That's where I could use your help with an overview of these organizations and the local people who are involved in these types of causes."

"Trooper, I think you may be stereotyping a bit." Alexa raised an eyebrow. "Are you saying that only the country-club set gets involved in social causes? In fact, all types of people become passionate about causes: the environment, women's rights, dog rescue."

The trooper looked a bit abashed. "I thought we had gotten to John and Alexa by now? I don't mean to stereotype, but I need your insight into that social set here in Carlisle. Admit it. You're part of it. A lawyer whose father is also an attorney and whose mother was a county commissioner. I'm not making value judgments here. Just recognizing that I don't have a good feel for these types of people.

"Plus, I didn't grow up in Carlisle. I've only been stationed here for a few years. My family owns a small farm up near State College. They stick pretty close to home. Heck, I was the first Taylor to go to college." He curled his mouth into a self-deprecating smile. "So I need some technical assistance."

"I'm not sure I can help, John, but I'll give it a try."

For the next half hour, Alexa tried her best to answer John's questions. By the time she ran out of information, the sun had slipped behind the grove of huge pines in front of the cabin. The spring peepers celebrated nightfall with a boisterous refrain.

"It's getting cold. Let's go inside." She spotted her mastiff, half asleep in the small yard. "Scout, come."

John helped Alexa load the dishwasher and wandered into the living room while she fed Scout. When Alexa joined him, she asked, "Do you think those break-ins at Melissa's could be connected to Cecily's death? Maybe those two Thai men were looking for the picture that Cecily called disturbing. Maybe she unknowingly took a compromising picture of those guys while she was with Cecily."

"We don't know at this point. Your theory could be right, but it's much too early to tell if this connection with the two Thai men will amount to anything. We have no evidence that identifies the perpetrators of the burglaries at either Melissa's studio or her home. They could be connected to Ms. Townes' murder. Or the burglar could simply be some local punk who read about Melissa's exhibit and figured that she'd have some valuable equipment. As we say, it's still under investigation." He got up and began to pace the rug.

"John, have you been working too hard? I'd swear that baby face of yours has aged."

"Damn, I'll never get away from the fact that I look so young. My mom says it's a family trait. You know I'm thirty-two, right?"

"Most people would be happy to look younger. Me included."

"Well, this face can be a real liability when I'm on the job. Or when I want a woman my age to take me seriously." When John sat back on the couch and gazed soulfully into Alexa's eyes, she blushed.

Sidestepping John's advance, Alexa persisted, "Are you as tired as you look?"

"Maybe more. Corporal Branche is still on special assignment. So Cannon and I are up to our ears. We're working a lot more than just this Townes case. We're investigating several women who have gone missing over the last few months. To top it all off, someone is killing dogs and hanging them from trees all over the county."

Alexa shuddered. "What kind of whacko would hang dead dogs from trees?" She hugged Scout, who was sitting by her chair.

"I don't think you have to worry about Scout. Whoever is doing this seems to prefer small, manageable breeds. Cannon thinks it's a gang of teenagers. I'm not so sure."

"And what's this about missing women? I haven't read anything about that in the paper."

"It's not one of those stories that gets a lot of press because most of these women are ones who live on the margins: homeless women, prostitutes, petty criminals. Hell, most of these women we're investigating live such transient lives, we're not totally certain that any of them actually are missing. But enough about my work. I'm off duty. How are you doing, Alexa? I heard that you were having some trouble coping after the incident with Reverend Browne."

Alexa couldn't keep from glancing at the spot on the floor where Jebediah Browne had died. She could see the deranged minister lying there in a widening pool of blood, his wife sobbing at his side.

"I don't know, John. I've had a hard time dealing with the finality of taking a man's life. I know that I had no choice. He would have killed me if I hadn't fired that shotgun. But I just can't seem to completely shake it. I think I'm getting better every day. What's the saying? Time heals all wounds."

"If you need someone to talk to, just call me. I don't mean to take advantage of your pain, but I would like to get to know you better."

Alexa nodded and the trooper stood. As she ushered John to the door, Scout padded along behind. At the door, John folded Alexa's hand between his palms and said, "Remember, I'm here if you need me."

Alexa stood in the open doorway watching John's taillights until they faded into the darkness. She thought about the warmth of John's concern as she settled into bed and managed to sleep an entire night undisturbed by violent dreams.

"Namaste." Isabella opened the door of her yoga studio.

"Namaste. Thanks for setting aside some time with me again." Alexa sat down in a cross-legged position in front of her teacher.

"How is your practice progressing?"

"Much better. I'm not as distracted during meditation. I believe I'm regaining my focus. But I still want to perfect those advanced poses, and I need your help on that tonight."

Recognizing that Alexa was struggling emotionally last winter, Isabella had suggested that she devote more time to her yoga practice. Her teacher also suggested some more advanced poses for Alexa to incorporate into her practice, choosing a few difficult poses that both demanded pure concentration and helped alleviate anxiety and depression.

"Let's start with the wheel asana." Tall, lithe Isabella guided Alexa through a vinyasa flow that culminated in the circular backbend known as the Wheel Pose. After a few minutes of rest in savasana, she began a new asana of inverted poses.

When Alexa unfurled her legs in a vertical line above her head, she held the pose for thirty seconds or so. Then, she lost her focus as her mind wandered. Her legs tottered over that invisible plane integral to maintaining balance, and they came crashing to the floor.

"Let's try that again." Isabella led her through the asana sequence one more time. This time, Isabella helped steady Alexa in the headstand. "Now, lower your legs into Scorpion while I'm here to guide you."

Alexa settled into her elbows and arched her back, slowly bringing her feet closer to the floor in front of her. Her body formed the arc that formed the foundation of Scorpion, but Alexa doubted that she'd ever be flexible enough to touch her head with her feet.

"Just continue to get the feel of it. Your body is already there, Alexa. You just need to center your mind and you'll be able to hold this pose. Remember, it's not a contest. When you are able to find the focus that you need, the pose will come."

Alexa and Isabella meditated for ten minutes at the end of the session. She floated out of the yoga studio in a sea of calm and home to Scout, waiting for his dinner.

CHAPTER SEVENTEEN

GRAHAM SPRINTED INTO THE courthouse with Alexa trailing a few steps behind. Although struggling to keep up in her high heels, Alexa's fear of Judge Burns' judicial wrath far surpassed any fear of a broken ankle.

"Damn you, Graham. Next time we appear in court together, you get your ass in gear. Burns hates it when counsel is late."

Just before she entered the courtroom, Alexa noticed a couple standing together down the hall. Tyrell Williams loomed over a teenaged girl, his hands resting on the wall above her head. Alexa hesitated on the threshold, vaguely disturbed by the scene. When the purple-haired girl shook her head at something Tyrell said, he seized her by both shoulders. The teenager began sobbing and slid down the wall until she sat on the floor, her tight skirt sliding up to her hips. She looked like a broken doll: Purple-haired Hooker Barbie.

Tyrell turned and caught Alexa staring. At the same time Graham whispered urgently, "Lexie. Get in here now. Burns will be coming at any minute."

"And whose fault is it that we're late?" Alexa spluttered. She followed Graham into the courtroom, shrugging off the scene in the corridor to focus on the hearing.

Taking another sip of her chai tea, Haley looked at Alexa and Melissa. "I lost my balance in Tree Pose thinking about this. Spill. Now."

"About what?" Melissa asked with a deadpan face.

"I'm worried about your lack of concentration," Alexa replied with mock concern and extended her arms above her head. "For Tree Pose, you must empty your mind."

"Will you two stop pulling my chain? Dinner at the Nash mansion." Haley leaned forward. "Everybody at the Chamber thinks Nash is a real mover and shaker. I've heard the house is huge?"

Alexa finally stopped laughing. "You could say that. It's probably bigger than the shopping mall."

Melissa snickered. "Haley, you would eat the place up, but it was a little too gaudy for my taste."

"What? Are you accusing me of bad taste?"

"No, no. Your house is a ten on the scale of typical Carlisle traditional décor. I just meant that you would get a kick out of the place. A lane bordered with trees that look like Italian cypress. A dining room big enough to feed the entire Carlisle Barracks. And there's that whole faux Tuscan drama that the Nashes have going."

Haley turned to Alexa. "Did she just insult my decorating style?"

"Don't get me into the middle of this. But, Haley, you have to admit that your house is a more expensive and tasteful version of practically every home in the county."

"I won't apologize for my taste in homes. I prefer traditional and so does Blair. But I'd love to see the Nash Tuscan Villa."

Alexa asked Melissa, "Did you think it was a little creepy, all those kids in uniforms acting as an army of servants?"

"Not really. Remember that I worked as a waitress in high school. I figured that the kids were getting valuable experience."

"They seemed a bit like Stepford kids to me. Almost no affect. But I bet Vivienne Nash would make anyone who worked in that house toe the line."

"I think they must be kids who are living in the Children of Light residential facilities up there. I was told that some of the kids are housed while they are waiting for foster care placement or adoption. Plus, they have a specialized facility for 'problem' teens, whatever that means. Why am I the one telling you this? Aren't you the new board member?"

"Quinn Hutton briefed me about the board, but I guess I have a lot to learn about the organization."

"Quinn Hutton? Is he that gorgeous Dickinson professor I met at Melissa's opening?" Haley gushed.

"Yes. We went to dinner on Friday."

"Well, I'm glad to hear that you are finally moving on. Reese has been gone since April. It's time you started dating again." Melissa patted her arm.

Haley agreed. "Yes, honey. I know that these past months have been difficult for you. That whole situation with Caleb and his father was totally gruesome. Reese leaving was tough. But spending time with a tall, dark, and handsome college professor could be therapeutic."

"We'll see. I'm pretty sure that we'll be going out again. But I'm not going to rush into anything."

Melissa sighed. "Is this where we're going to hear about your miserable track record with men?" She looked at Haley, eyebrow raised.

"Why don't we save you the trouble since we've heard it all so many times before," Haley chimed in, and her friends launched a tag team assault on Alexa. They'd done it before under the guise of tough love. She knew they meant well, but it never helped.

"Let's see." Haley tilted her head as if trying to remember. "There was Carl Hudson in high school. The brooding rebel without a cause. How long did it take you to discover that he lacked not only a cause but any redeemable qualities?"

Melissa took up the narrative. "We'll skip over the many minor mistakes of your college years and go right to law school. The love of your life, Trent, who turned your hopes and dreams into ashes when he bolted for a Hollywood law firm."

"Caleb Browne might be your worst mistake," Haley grimaced. "Religious extremist, member of some whacko right-wing militia group, and all around party boy. But I've got to admit that he kept his less desirable traits well-hidden until the end."

Melissa softened her tone. "Honey, you're not the only girl who's dated some real losers. A lot of us are drawn in by that bad boy vibe. But you've picked some good ones, too. Reese Michaels could have been a keeper. The guy you dated senior year, that exchange student, Paulo, was a real sweetheart."

"And what about Timmy Wise? I hear that he's doing some groundbreaking work with disease molecules or some science thing at the CDC."

Alexa threw her napkin into the air. "Enough, already. My God, you're digging deep. Timmy Wise had a crush on me in sixth grade. We sat together at the chorus concert and kissed once on the playground. Face it. No amount of polish can put a shine on my record with men. I almost always pick the bad ones. And when I have a chance with a good guy, I tend to throw it away."

Alexa stopped and composed herself. "So I am taking it slow with Quinn Hutton or any man who wanders into my orbit."

"You go, girl." Melissa pumped her fist into the air, and the three friends broke into uncontrollable giggles.

CHAPTER EIGHTEEN

WHEN ALEXA OPENED THE DOOR, Scout bolted toward her father for a dog biscuit. Norris Williams kept a jar of Milk Bones on the kitchen counter just for Scout's visits.

"Am I early?" It was Friday pizza night, a Williams tradition.

Mom hugged her and said, "You're fine. Graham and Kate are running late. They called and said something about picking up Courtney from a play date. They'll be here soon."

Dad looked up from scratching Scout's ears. "Since we have a little time, let's go over some details for our safari. You've finished all your shots, right?"

"Yeah. I went to the travel clinic over a month ago. They gave me a prescription for malaria pills that I filled last week."

"I know your mother gave you a packing list. Do you have all of that squared away?"

"The only thing I'm missing is binoculars. We've got an old pair at the cabin, but they're almost shot. Can you tell me what kind to buy?"

"Norris, don't we have another pair of binocs up in the attic? When you bought those new Leicas, I think we stored your old ones up there. Wouldn't they work for Lexie?"

"You're right. I'll go up there tomorrow and find them."

"I'll run up right now so I can take them with me. Mom, do you remember exactly where you put them?"

"I think they are in that chest of drawers in the front of the attic. Maybe the top drawer?"

Alexa grabbed a flashlight from a cupboard and dashed up the stairs to the second floor. She opened the attic door in the corner of the spare bedroom and switched on the dim light. A wave of heat from the airless space made her hesitate. Bracing herself, she ascended the narrow stairs, deliberate in placing each foot to avoid tripping on one of the boxes that lined the passage.

When she reached the main attic, Alexa headed directly to an old maple bureau, its surface layered in dust. The top drawer resisted her first attempt to slide it open. On the second try, she positioned her legs in a Warrior Pose and used both hands to yank the brass pulls. With a loud creak of protest, the drawer popped halfway out. Alexa flicked on the flashlight so she could see into the dim space.

"No binoculars here," she muttered. "Maybe in that box." Lifting out a square metal box covered in paisley designs, Alexa sat on a nearby wooden trunk to open it. Instead of binoculars, the box held a single rectangular book: a small scrapbook. A flowing script on the cover said WOODSTOCK.

Intrigued, Alexa lifted the book and set the box on the floor. Her mother rarely discussed her Woodstock experience. When they were teenagers, Graham and Alexa had watched the movie and had asked all sorts of questions. But Mom played her Woodstock cards close to the vest. Alexa had always assumed that her mother was avoiding any conversations in which Susan Williams, hippie festival, and marijuana could appear in the same sentence.

Considering her mother's reticence on the subject, Alexa hesitated for a moment. Should she pry into Mom's stuff without permission? Driven by curiosity, she rationalized that the box hadn't been hidden. It was right there in plain sight in the drawer. Alexa opened the cover and leafed through the pages.

The opening pages of the book contained a newspaper ad for Woodstock, some pages torn from a program, and several yellowing news articles about the concert. A few pages in, two pristine Woodstock concert tickets were affixed to the thick sheet of paper by little triangle-shaped photo corners.

"I bet these are worth a small fortune on eBay. Original, unused tickets from Woodstock," Alexa speculated to the empty room.

Except for a few small items—a crumbling pressed flower and two tear-off tickets that said Food for Love—the rest of the book was devoted to photos. The dim attic light made it difficult for Alexa to make out the details. Most were four-inch by five-inch black and white snapshots.

On the last page, there was a larger photo that had been shot with an excellent camera. A group of kids posed in front of an old van. They looked like all the pictures of hippies that Alexa had ever seen: long hair on both the girls and guys; round, wire-rim glasses on one of the guys; and wide smiles on every face. One small girl with white-blonde hair looked like a child.

She aimed the flashlight at the page to study the photo more closely. There, in the center, with a wreath of flowers in her flowing ash blonde hair, was her mother. Alexa caught her breath at how beautiful and free her mom looked in her bell-bottoms and peasant blouse. Two boys flanked her. Alexa didn't recognize the one with brown hair in a long ponytail who was holding her mother's hand. However, the guy on the right looked familiar in some way. Alexa scanned the rest of the picture, but the only person she could identify was one of her mother's closest girlfriends.

Alexa had closed the scrapbook when it hit her. The guy on the right was Jack Nash! She took a second look at the picture to confirm her conclusion before placing the book back in the box and closing the drawer.

When she tried the second drawer, it opened easily to reveal the binoculars she sought. As Alexa made her way downstairs, she wondered why her mother had never mentioned the Woodstock connection when they discussed Jack Nash.

"Aunt Alexa."

"Look, she's here!"

Courtney and Jamie squealed in delight and ran to Alexa when she entered the kitchen. As usual, Courtney beat her petite older brother in the race to greet their aunt.

"Hey, munchkins. Let me put down these binoculars before I drop them." She deposited the binocular case on the counter before she crouched down to hug her seven-year-old niece and eight-year-old nephew. "Are you guys ready for pizza?"

"Yes. I'm hungry, but Grams said we had to wait for you," Courtney sniped with a shake of her honey blonde curls.

Kate intervened. "That's enough, miss. We've only been here a few minutes, and we're the ones who are late."

It continued to amuse Alexa that petite Kate acted as disciplinarian with the kids. Perhaps Graham was so exhausted by managing the law firm and keeping the staff in line that, at home, he was happy to cede the role of the heavy to his wife.

Alexa's dad picked up two giant flat boxes from the kitchen island and sang out, "Pizza time, boys and girls. I want the entire Williams clan around this table right now."

There was an immediate flurry of activity. The kids climbed into their chairs. Graham handed them napkins. Kate poured milk into two plastic cups. Alexa's mom grabbed a stack of plates from the counter and whisked them to the table. And Scout managed to get in everyone's way until he stationed himself at the kids' end of the table.

Alexa waited for the furor to abate before grabbing a Coke from the fridge. "Does anyone need a drink?"

"I think everyone is set," Graham mumbled. "If you don't sit down soon, the pepperoni will be gone."

"You found the binoculars?" Dad asked Alexa after the meal. He sat at the table with Graham and Alexa. The kids were watching a movie in the family room while Kate and Mom kept an eye on them.

"Yep. I think that's the last thing I need for safari. I am so looking forward to it."

"Me too," Graham whined. "You'll be out stalking lions and communing with elephants while I'm slaving away in the office."

"Give me a break. It's only three weeks. What about all that work-life balance stuff you're always promoting at staff meetings?"

"Behave, children." Their father barked with mock severity.

Graham looked at Alexa. "Speaking of work, let's run that Children of Light Board appointment by Dad. I talked to Pat about it. We agree that sitting on the board is consistent with the firm's policy to encourage participation in the community. There appears to be no conflict; if we take on any legal work that would involve Children of Light, someone else in the firm could handle the case. But I think Jack Nash uses some big Washington mega-firm for his legal work."

"This is the first I've heard about a board appointment, but I don't see any issues. I assume that your time commitment will be minimal?" Norris directed his question to Alexa.

"I don't think it will be a major burden. Monthly meetings. They might want me to sit on a subcommittee of some sort. Since I've cut down my Wednesday afternoons at the clinic to every other week, I'll have time. I would be filling Cecily Townes' vacant seat, so it's an interim appointment. I can always walk away next year if it ends up becoming a problem for either the firm or me. And it's a worthwhile organization. I've read their annual report and some additional material. They do a lot of good for children in need."

Alexa's mother had entered the kitchen in time to hear most of the conversation about Children of Light. "So you'll be working with Jack Nash," she stated in a flat voice.

"Yes. He's chairman of the board. I don't expect to see much of him except at the meetings. He mentioned that you were friends in college, Mom. And you went to Woodstock together?" Alexa sidestepped how she had learned about the Woodstock connection.

"I'd hardly characterize him as a friend, but he was part of our group that went up to Woodstock." Susan crossed her arms in a disapproving posture that Alexa knew well. "If you're going to take this board position with Jack Nash, honey, just be careful."

A crash sounded from the living room, followed by loud sobbing. "Mommy, it hurts," Jamie screamed.

All the adults rushed into the family room to find Kate cradling Jamie in her arms with Scout looking on in concern. Courtney, eyes glued to a cartoon on the television screen, ignored the commotion.

"He's fine." Kate wiped Jamie's face with a Kleenex. "He just tipped his chair over. I think it startled him, but I don't see any damage."

The slight, strawberry blonde boy made an attempt to pull himself together when he saw his father and the others enter the room. He pushed Kate away. "I'm OK, Mom."

Alexa noticed Graham's reaction, knowing that he worried about Kate coddling his son.

Her brother scowled. "It's time to get them home to bed anyway. Courtney, we're leaving."

"But, Daddy, the movie's not over yet."

"You've already seen that one a hundred times. Isn't that *Frozen*?" Graham lifted his daughter into his arms and switched off the television.

"Scout and I will head out, too." Alexa picked up her purse and the binoculars. "It's been a long week. Let's do one of these pizza nights out at the cabin soon. We can have a picnic on the deck. Maybe when we get back from Africa."

On the drive home, Alexa pondered her mother's surprising reaction to Jack Nash. She had been downright frosty. "What did you think about that warning, Scout? Maybe Mom and Jack had a romance during college, and he dumped her or something. She sounded pretty down on the guy."

Scout moved forward to listen, hanging his head over the front seat. Alexa laughed and patted his neck before she shifted into fourth gear on the empty road.

CHAPTER NINETEEN

"HELLO," ALEXA GRABBED the phone like a lifeline. She nudged aside a small pile of clothing to perch on the bed. Stacks of clothes obscured the rest of the bed's surface.

"Hey. What are you up to?" Melissa asked.

"I've spent the morning sorting through clothes for safari, looking for items in khaki. I've got khaki brown, khaki green, khaki tan. How the hell can they call all of these different colors the same thing?"

"Don't ask me." Melissa snorted.

"And there is no way I can fit all of these clothes into one little duffel bag."

"I got a lot of that quick dry stuff for my trip to Asia with Cecily. It really does work. Try one of the big sporting goods or outdoor stores, but you better get on the stick. Isn't your trip right around the corner?"

"In two weeks. Are you still OK to stay here at the cabin with Scout?"

"Yep. I've been spending a lot of time at Jim's. I stayed at my place a few nights, but I'm just not comfortable there since the break-in, even though I changed the locks. I wish they'd catch the fucker." Melissa's tone was savage. "So I will be only too glad to hang out at the cabin with gigundo dog for a couple weeks."

"Great. Anything new on Cecily? I heard you talked to the cops about what she said at the march," Alexa prompted.

"Yeah. Not sure what good it will do. I have no clue what she found so disturbing. If I hadn't been such an asshole with those Park Police, they probably wouldn't have arrested me. Then I would have gone home on the bus with Cecily and found out what had her so freaked. Maybe if I'd gone home with her to pick up my car, she'd be alive . . ."

"Maybe, maybe, maybe. Don't go down that path of regret and guilt. Maybe whoever killed Cecily would have killed you, too. Only one thing is certain, Melissa: you are not responsible for Cecily's death."

"I know, but it's hard not to obsess." Melissa's tone brightened. "Did I tell you that I talked to her brother, Richard, at the memorial service? Lovely man. Strong resemblance to his sister. He plans to come back to Carlisle in July to sort through Cecily's things and put the house on the market. I told him that I would help if he needs an extra pair of hands."

"Will you be OK going back into that house?"

"I think so. I owe it to Cecily to help her brother."

Alexa threw a helpless look at the unfinished packing on the bed. "So, did you call for any particular reason?"

"Oh, that's right. I called to tell you that *Susquehanna Beautiful* is doing an article on my exhibit. It will be out in a few weeks, so I'm thinking of extending the show for another month. Traffic to the gallery is still pretty high, but I might get another bump out of the magazine feature. The more I sell, the more I can contribute to RESIST."

"That's wonderful news. You'll be going national soon."

"Not likely, but a nice dream."

Alexa slipped on her shoes. "I better hang up. I'm going to run down to Harrisburg for safari clothes."

The next morning, Alexa tested out her new quick-dry khakis on an early morning hike with Scout. They wandered down a trail that led from the cabin to a nearby pond, Scout taking frequent detours to investigate intriguing forest smells. When they reached Weaver's Pond, Alexa sat on a log to rest. Scout nosed along the edge of the pond causing an undulating wave of tiny explosions as alarmed frogs hurtled toward the water. When he startled a big bullfrog, the creature's leap created a sizable splash that drenched Scout's face. Shaking his head to dry, the dog meandered back to find a spot at Alexa's feet.

His owner tilted her face to the sun, soaking in the forest. The deep staccato of a pileated woodpecker in the distance provided a bass counterpoint to the medley of small birdsong around her. A few swallowtail butterflies flitted among the dragonflies at the edge of the reeds. Alexa reveled in the peaceful morning with a lovely sense of drowsiness.

Without conscious effort, she soon found herself thinking about Cecily Townes' homicide. Just like Elizabeth Nelson and Emily Baxter from last autumn, another innocent woman had been murdered while simply living her life as best as she knew how.

Alexa's recent experience had turned her into a cynic. She now pictured death as a jealous bastard, who welcomed vibrant women with open arms while holding the evil motherfuckers of the world at bay as long as possible. She just hoped that Melissa didn't catch the bastard's eye.

CHAPTER TWENTY

QUINN TOOK ALEXA TO A RARE Monday evening concert in Harrisburg. She had suggested that they meet at Dickinson, not yet ready for an evening that ended at her cabin. When she pulled into the parking lot behind the Holland Union Building, Quinn was lounging against a wall.

"Good evening. You look wonderful, as always." Quinn managed to be disarming rather than loutish as he ran an appraising eye over Alexa's summer sundress. She had taken care in selecting her outfit and was flattered that she'd hit the right note.

He was wearing his trademark jeans and a slubby natural linen jacket over a charcoal silk tee. Alexa was almost disappointed to note the absence of a European-style scarf.

"Thank you. I'm looking forward to this concert. I can't believe you're familiar with Andreas Vollenweider. Most people have never heard of him, but my parents followed his music so I grew up with him."

"I first heard him in Switzerland. I was in Zurich on holiday from my teaching job in Paris. Lucky that another professor mentioned that Andreas was coming to the Whitaker Center."

As they talked, Alexa followed Quinn past a row of parked cars. They stopped in front of a low-slung black convertible with running boards.

Alexa's first thought was, damn, this car is over the top.

She tried to conceal her reaction from Quinn. She had to admit though: The sports car's blend of outrageous elegance and quirky uniqueness hit her as the perfect expression of the image that Quinn tried to project. But was this guy for real?

"Wow. Sweet wheels. What is this car?"

Quinn closed Alexa's door and walked around to the driver's side. When he settled into the leather seat, he plucked a scarf from his pocket and handed it to her. "You may want to cover your hair. It's a great evening for a ride with the top down. This is a classic car—a Mercedes 500K roadster."

Alexa tied the scarf under her chin in the style of a glamorous actress from the fifties. "I'm ready to face the wind if you're ready for a date with slightly tangled hair."

"I'm sure you will be just as lovely with windblown tresses."

Quinn chose back roads and avoided the highways. Still, the roar of the motor, the hum of tires on pavement, and the whistle of wind through the open cab made conversation difficult. After a few attempts at chatter, Alexa gave herself up to the pleasure of the ride.

She got a kick out of the stares that the vintage car drew from people on the street and in cars they passed. But Alexa had mixed feelings about the driver. There was something a bit off about this guy's act, although she couldn't put her finger on what bothered her. No harm in just going with the flow for now, she decided.

The forty-minute drive ended too soon when Quinn pulled the long, low-slung vehicle into an open parking spot in front of the Hilton. A parking attendant approached immediately.

Alexa stood aside and rolled her eyes at Quinn's interaction with the parking guy. Like the headscarf at his fingertips, this exchange played out like a scene from *The Philadelphia Story* or another one of those old black and white movies.

"Mr. Hutton? We'll take care of this baby for you. We've arranged to park it right over there. Someone will be outside here to keep an eye on it all evening."

"Thank you. We should be about four hours or so." Quinn paused to look at the name tag on the attendant's shirt. "I will make it worth your while if you keep a close watch on the car, Jamal."

"Yes, sir," the young man assured Quinn. "She's a beauty. I'll take care of it for you."

As they sat down for a light dinner at the trendy Café Fresco, Alexa tried to ignore all the women staring at Quinn and searched for something to talk about. In a burst of inspiration, she settled on the obvious: Quinn's extraordinary car. "The parking guy was right. Your car is beautiful, but isn't it a little impractical for everyday driving?"

"I have a pickup that I drive most of the time. I live on a farm out toward Plainfield that has a big garage. I keep the roadster there and bring her out in good weather for special occasions."

"It's a pretty extravagant car." Alexa's voice constricted as she choked out this understatement. Apparently, Quinn heard only admiration.

"I enjoy the grand gesture. What does Sara Teasdale say, 'Spend all you have for loveliness? Buy it and never count the cost . . .'" Quinn laughed. "In this case, I didn't spend anything for all that Mercedes loveliness. My dad bought it for me at an auction. We're very close. The minute he saw the 500K, he knew it was the car for me."

Quinn's offhand statement confirmed Alexa's suspicion that he came from money, but she didn't want to seem rude by inquiring further. She changed the subject as she nibbled at her quiche.

"So, you live on a farm?" Alexa glanced at his manicured hands. "I don't picture you as the gentleman farmer. Do you actually work the land?"

"No. This place is one of those quintessential Cumberland County farmettes. A two-story with assorted outbuildings. The last owners did some renovations, so I've got all the modern conveniences. I was looking for privacy, and it sits in the middle of thirty acres. A real farmer who owns one of the adjoining farms plants maybe ten acres in corn. The rest is woods and overgrown fields. It's only a short drive to the college but far enough away for seclusion. The place suits me." A fleeting smile crossed Quinn's face, almost as if he were enjoying a private joke.

If Alexa hadn't been so absorbed in the conversation, she may not have noticed Quinn's brief moment of distraction. Before she could reflect on why that smile made her uneasy, Quinn moved to another topic.

"Tell me. How is your photographer friend, Melissa, doing with her show? The first night was quite a success."

Alexa smiled. "She's had an excellent response. As you saw, she's a wonderful photographer. And people seem to be drawn to the images in this exhibit. She's planning to extend the exhibit for another month. Jack Nash bought one of her best photos. You may remember the one of a beautiful young Thai girl. Melissa titled it, *As It Should Be*, to celebrate the families who hold their kids close to avoid being trafficked."

Quinn shook his head. "Can't say that I remember the photo, but Jack has good taste in art. I expect he chose the finest one in the show."

"I think it was one of Melissa's best." Alexa wondered why he wouldn't remember that particular photo. At Melissa's opening, she had watched Quinn and Jack stand right in front of it for several minutes while they spoke. "Did you know that she had a burglary at her gallery the day after the opening?"

"No. Were any of the photos stolen? Ms. Lambert is quite good, but I wouldn't think that there is a market for her photography at this point. I mean an illegal market."

"They didn't touch the photography. Just stole some computers and one of her cameras. Still, it was a hassle for her."

For some reason, Alexa hesitated to mention the second burglary at Melissa's home. She wasn't sure that Melissa would want a stranger to know about that invasion of her personal space. And, even to Alexa, Quinn was pretty much still a stranger.

Quinn glanced at his watch and said, "If we're going to make the concert, we should leave."

Alexa loved the Andreas Vollenweider concert. Hearing all the familiar melodies, a unique blend of harp and other unconventional instruments, soothed her soul.

On the short walk to collect Quinn's car, Alexa said, "Wasn't the concert amazing? And getting a chance to meet Andreas was an added bonus. I can't believe it, but I think I've become a New Age groupie."

Quinn nodded. "One of real pleasures is seeing how the band creates all those sounds—and that it comes together in such a wonderful way. It must take them hours of rehearsal to get just the right mix."

"Yeah. Andreas says, 'I think we need to rattle a piece of sheet metal at the beginning of the chorus . . .' And one of the other guys asks 'before or after the wind chimes?'" Alexa bubbled with enthusiasm.

"This small venue suited the concert well. When I saw the band perform in Zurich, it was a much larger concert hall."

"Being Swiss, I imagine that Andreas has a quite a following with the hometown crowd."

When they reached the Hilton, Jamal materialized out of the shadows near Quinn's extravagant car. He had pulled the Mercedes into one of a few parking spots near the main entrance of the hotel.

"Just one minute and I'll bring your car up, sir. You need to pay in the lobby."

Quinn walked inside to settle the bill while Alexa stood on the corner and watched Harrisburg's evening street traffic. Groups of chic twenty-somethings strutted down Second Street to begin a night of partying. An exodus of well-dressed older couples, probably diners at the better restaurants, headed home for bed. In rapt conversation with someone only he could see, a homeless man shuffled an overflowing shopping cart across Market Street.

When Quinn emerged from the hotel, he opened the passenger door for Alexa. She watched him hand a substantial tip to Jamal. The young attendant pulled himself up tall and saluted Quinn.

"Thank you, sir. Ask for me anytime you park here."

In the driver's seat, Quinn paused before he drove away. "Top down or up?"

"Down. I slipped this sweater on, so I should be fine." Alexa tied the scarf under her chin as Quinn pulled out of the hotel drive and headed for Carlisle.

Quinn slid the long sports car into a parking slot in the still empty lot. The Land Rover sat among only a few other cars. When he opened the driver door, Alexa clambered out her side of the car. All this door opening, while charming, made her a little uncomfortable.

"I need to check in at my office, so I'm going to put up the top. People can't contain their curiosity if I leave it down." Quinn's voice tightened. "I learned that lesson one night when I discovered five frat bozos squeezed into the open car, each with his own growler of Molly Pitcher Ale."

Alexa took off the headscarf and smoothed her hair while Quinn ran through a series of maneuvers to lock the canvas top in place. At the end of the process, he walked to Alexa and took her hand in his.

"It's a lovely evening on campus. Will you join me on a stroll over to my office? It's in East on the John Dickinson Campus."

"What's this? A professor's version of would you like to see my etchings?"

Quinn laughed. "I could say that my intentions are entirely honorable, but I wouldn't want to lie. However, my office certainly doesn't lend itself to much romance." He turned on the charm. "Come on. How long has it been since you've strolled across a college campus, hand-in-hand with a man who appreciates your grace and beauty?"

"You realize, of course, that you have a way of making the most blatant bullshit sound like poetry?" Alexa couldn't help but be charmed by this outrageous flattery.

"Hence, my chosen profession." Quinn leaned so close to Alexa that his lips brushed her cheek. His voice dropped. "Does this mean you are accepting my invitation to a stroll?"

"Yes. A stroll." Alexa tried to still the flutter in her chest. When Quinn kissed her with cool lips, she tensed slightly as he pressed her body against the car. Unbidden, Reese had entered her mind.

He pulled away abruptly and seized her hand, tucking it beneath the crook of his elbow. "So, let's take that walk."

It had been awhile since Alexa had been on campus even though she passed by the college frequently. With classes finished for the semester, the place seemed deserted. They passed a security guard making his rounds as they entered the East building.

"Evening, Professor Hutton," the beefy man said as he exited through the door.

"You don't mind taking the stairs?" Quinn's question seemed rhetorical as he headed for the stairwell. Alexa followed behind as they climbed to the fourth floor, glad she was wearing sandals.

"I think this building used to be a dorm at one time. My mom is a Dickinson alum, and she mentioned something once about a boyfriend who lived in this building."

"That's before my time," Quinn said as he unlocked the office door. "It would have been a great dorm to live in. Look at the view of the campus." He motioned to Alexa to join him at the window.

He brushed aside Alexa's hair to whisper into her ear. "My version of etchings." He pulled her closer and placed a trail of kisses from her neck to her cheek.

Alexa turned to face Quinn as his mouth found hers. She gave into the sensation, warmth flooding her body as Quinn's hard kisses became more insistent. Soon, she was returning the intensity, Reese forgotten.

Quinn pulled away for an instant, his blues eyes darkening to gray. Alexa noticed the long couch against the far wall. In that moment, she knew that she wasn't ready to tumble into bed—or couch—with this guy.

Quinn seemed hesitant as well.

"We've strolled as far down this path as I'm ready to go for tonight." Alexa slipped away from Quinn. "But I'd like to see you again."

"That's encouraging," Quinn responded with a faint smile.

Alexa spoke into the awkward moment that followed. "Why don't you come out to my house for dinner on Friday? I'm leaving for vacation the next day, but Melissa and her boyfriend will be coming to dinner. Will you join us?"

"I'm sorry to hear that you're going away, but I would be glad to accept your dinner invitation. You can give me all the details at the board meeting on Thursday." Quinn grabbed a briefcase from behind his desk.

"See, it wasn't all about the etchings. I did have another purpose in coming here." He shot Alexa an oblique glance.

As they walked toward the door, Alexa did a quick survey of the room. She'd barely taken in the surroundings when they first arrived, too bemused by Quinn. Other than the shelves crammed with books, the room was surprisingly spare. Quinn's walls were bare, except for an institutional-looking round clock hanging above the beige couch.

The only personal item on his desk was an ornate little wooden house that looked vaguely oriental. Alexa would never have guessed that this office belonged to someone as distinctive as Quinn. It looked as if he had just moved in—or was getting ready to move out.

"What's that? An architectural model of some sort?" Alexa pointed to the little wooden structure.

Quinn lit up. "No, that's a tiny version of a spirit house. In many Southeast Asian countries, people place larger versions of these houses outside their homes so that the displaced spirits will have a place to live. Usually, they place offerings in the houses to keep the spirits happy."

Alexa grinned. "Yours looks empty."

"Of course, this is just a memento of my time in Thailand. It's not the real thing." Quinn's voice became serious. "Any spirits displaced by this building left many years ago."

As they walked back to their cars, Alexa looked around. "This campus is so different than Columbia. Of course, I wanted to go to school somewhere away from Carlisle. Maybe that factored into my choosing a university in the middle of New York City. But I've always loved this old campus. The limestone buildings and the old stone walls. The huge trees. It has a comforting sense of history."

Quinn responded in a relaxed tone. "I was a bit wary of how things would work out for me here, coming back into the country after so many years abroad. But I've been pleasantly surprised. Dickinson is more academically rigorous than the other places I've taught, so it's a nice challenge. And the area has much to offer outside the classroom."

As they approached the middle of the campus, Alexa imagined that the all the lights dimmed for a moment, and she shivered. "Did you see that?"

"See what?"

"Never mind. Just my imagination."

When they reached Alexa's Land Rover, Quinn planted a chaste kiss on Alexa's lips. The light from the street lamps bounced off the windows of the science center across the street, bathing the parking lot in a feeble glow. The flickering light washed Quinn's face with a ghostly pallor.

"Thank you for this evening. The concert was unbelievable. And I enjoyed those etchings." Alexa tried to keep their parting light.

"Perhaps you'll show me yours next week?" Quinn's response seemed half-hearted to Alexa; he'd become withdrawn or distracted.

"We'll see." Alexa still wasn't ready to make any commitments. She needed time to get to know this bewildering guy better. Although he was powerfully attractive, her bullshit radar signaled caution. Alexa hoisted herself into the Land Rover and headed for home.

CHAPTER TWENTY-ONE

August 14, 1969

The New York Thruway is closed, man.
—Arlo Guthrie

"You should see the size of the towers with the lights and the speakers. They are going to put out a righteous sound." Ben took another bite of his peanut butter and jelly sandwich.

Phil paced in front of Sukie, Cheryl, and Nina. "There's a huge hill that people will sit on for the concert. It will make it easy to see the stage."

"Plus, at the top, there are all sorts of booths where people are selling food," Robbie weighed in.

"Food?" Nina scowled at her sandwich. "Do they have hamburgers? I know we brought a ton of food, but I'm not sure I can do five days of peanut butter and canned beans."

"I saw hamburgers and french fries, too. The prices were sort of high." Phil looked at Nina. "But we could have lunch there tomorrow before the concert starts."

"It starts at four tomorrow afternoon, right? I can look at the ticket to make sure." Sukie drifted toward her tent.

"You're right. It's four o'clock." Ben nodded toward Robbie and Phil. "We were talking. If we want to get a good seat, we should take our blankets and cooler and head down there around noon or one o'clock."

"Yeah. There are a shitload of people here, and more are still pouring in." Phil waved his hand toward the main road.

Sukie could see a steady stream of people walking down the road and across the fields. At this distance they looked almost like ants. "The cars don't seem to be moving too fast."

"We heard that it's a huge traffic jam." Robbie smirked. "It was a good idea to come yesterday."

"Yes, Robbie." Ben bowed to Robbie as if he was saluting some Indian pasha. The rest of the group chimed in.

"You're so smart, Robbie."

"Our hero."

"Fearless leader."

"Thank you, dear."

Sukie shouted and threw up her hands. "My God, I'm at Woodstock with four Eddie Haskells."

Phil and Ben scampered around the group.

"Wally."

"Beav."

"That dress looks lovely, Mrs. Cleaver."

"Why, thank you, Eddie."

Nina yelled to be heard above the laughter. "Are we going to go shopping or not?"

"I've never seen anything like this," Sukie whispered to Ben. She clutched his hand as they strolled down the path in the woods.

Salesmen called out to their group from the small tents and wooden shacks that lined the path. The strong scent of patchouli oil and incense filled the air.

"Hash."

"I've got acid—as many tabs as you want."

An older, wizened man in a fringed vest and striped pants grabbed Ben's arm. "Mescaline. Magic mushrooms. You gotta expand your mind, man."

"Look, there's a candle shop. I want to get something to take home." Sukie gravitated toward a tent where a young woman was making candles in a pot over a fire. Nina followed her.

"I'm going to buy this pair." Sukie lifted the elaborate hand-layered candles so Nina could smell them.

"Mmm. Cranberry, right?"

"I think so. Didn't you want to buy a pocketbook? I saw some block-print bags from India at that shop over there."

"I'm going to go look," Nina called over her shoulder as she exited. "Come across after you pay for the candles."

Ben stuck his head into the candle tent. "Sukie, we're going to keep going. Robbie's looking for the best place to pick up some hash. Find me when you're done. OK, babe?"

Sukie turned. "Sure. After I go . . ." She broke off when she realized that Ben had already vanished.

"There's Ben." Sukie caught sight of her boyfriend and his buddies clustered just beyond a big tree in the distance. This section of the forest path seemed empty. The shops had petered out a little while ago.

"It's no man's land out here," she muttered to Nina.

"And it feels like an oven." Nina swept her damp curls off her face and twisted her hair into ponytail.

A guy wearing a top hat, shorts, and Converse sneakers sat under the tree on a blanket. "I've got some blue acid that will take you on the trip of a lifetime."

"We'll pass," Nina told the bare-chested acid dealer. She inclined her head toward Sukie. "The American system of enterprise at work."

"We wondered where you two were." Ben approached them and put an arm around Sukie's shoulders. He guided her to the far side of the tree. "Look who we found."

JJ and Eskimo perched side by side on the exposed roots of a big tree. Both wore blue button-down shirts and khaki pants. They looked like a pair of preppie leprechauns.

"Hello." Sukie nodded at them. "You two are early birds. Gone before the rest of us had breakfast."

Eskimo ignored Sukie with an expressionless stare. JJ snickered. "We stayed with friends."

Sukie hadn't noticed the small figure crouching near the trunk of the big oak until the girl spoke.

"Sukie. I'm glad you're here. I tried to explain communes to JJ and Eskimo, but I got a little confused. Can you help?" Willow's face creased into a frown as she pushed a strand of pale blonde hair off her forehead.

"Maybe later tonight, Willow. We're heading back to camp. Do you want to come along?"

"Not now." Willow walked over to JJ and Eskimo and settled onto the root between them. "I'm hanging with these guys for a while."

Eskimo passed the girl a hash pipe. With the ghost of a smile on his lips, he watched Willow take deep hit. Then he looked directly at Sukie, his eyes glacial. "Yeah. Willow can hang with JJ and me. We're going to talk some more about communes."

As her friends turned to make their way back to the campsite, Sukie couldn't shake a feeling of unease. Willow was too young to be getting high with JJ and Eskimo. But, hey, everyone was entitled to do their own thing.

"Babe, I missed you." Ben drew Sukie off the path and kissed her.

Sukie melted into his kiss as Ben hands traveled higher beneath her peasant blouse and fondled her breasts, unencumbered by a bra.

"I think we should spend a little time alone when we get back," Ben whispered in her ear.

Giggling in anticipation, Sukie took his hand, and they hurried to catch up with their friends.

CHAPTER TWENTY-TWO

LATE TUESDAY AFTERNOON, Alexa was immersed in preparing notes for Brian Stewart, who would cover for her during her vacation. Melinda buzzed the intercom. “I’ve got Mr. Tyrell Jenkins out here. He’s asking for a few minutes. I’m pretty sure he’s the guy who came in with Mrs. Bertolino a few weeks ago. He’s pretty hard to forget.”

Alexa sighed. She hadn’t checked with the Bertolinos recently. “Send him in.”

Tyrell strutted in and took a chair without speaking. He leaned back with folded arms.

“Mr. Jenkins. What can I do for you? Is there news about Meg?”

“That’s what I was hoping you could tell me. The Bertolinos haven’t given up hope, but they’re at the end of their rope. I understand that Toni has resorted to medication just to be able to sleep at night.”

Tyrell sat forward with a frown. “Not only that, but I’ve been dealing with a bunch of kids at the church group who are afraid to walk on the street alone. They’ve seen Meg disappear. Aurora Washington, a popular student, vanished. And I heard a preteen from Big Spring Middle School has just gone missing. Her cousin brought her to our youth group once.”

Alexa kept a neutral tone. “This is the first I’ve heard about this middle school student. But I’m going to be away for a few weeks, so I touched base with Detective Miller earlier today. He had nothing. The police still think Meg ran away. Their investigation hasn’t turned up any evidence to dispute that conclusion. The detective did make an offhand reference to another runaway girl. I assumed he was talking about Aurora.”

"Like the cops did any real investigation. They made up their minds from the get go that she bailed on the whole adoption thing." Tyrell's voice rose as he railed against the police.

Alexa felt no need to defend the police, but Tyrell wasn't being fair. It was more complicated than he acknowledged. And, she thought, Tyrell might be projecting some of his own issues with cops.

"Look, I know you are concerned. I am, too. And it's tough to do nothing. But I don't see what either of us can do to locate Meg at this point. The only thing I can think of is to find out if any of her friends are holding back information about this secret boyfriend. By now, you would think that they would have come forward with whatever information they had that could help. But teenage girls are a mysterious tribe, especially when a hint of romance is involved."

"What's this about a boyfriend?" Tyrell sounded surprised.

"I thought you knew. I'm sure that Detective Miller discussed this with Toni and Ed. Supposedly, Meg had a secret boyfriend—maybe an older boy. These kids trust you. Maybe you can find out something that they wouldn't tell the police."

"I'll try." Tyrell stood and moved to the door. Before he left, he turned and said, "Have a good trip, counselor. I'll miss seeing you in the courthouse." Alexa couldn't tell if he was serious or if it was just another sneer.

Later that afternoon, Alexa ran into Brian Stewart in the office kitchen. She and Brian would never be the best of friends, but they both had toned down the caustic remarks. Today, Brian seemed to struggle to remember their truce.

"Was that Tyrell Jenkins in your office?"

"Why do you ask?"

"Just wondered what he was doing here again."

"You keeping tabs on me, Stewart? Not that I feel compelled to share this information with you, but Mr. Jenkins is a social worker. He's acting as an intermediary for one of our clients on an adoption-related issue. Ed and Toni Bertolino are the clients whose foster daughter has disappeared. Obviously, the adoption will not be completed until the child is located. It's all in the case summary I'm preparing for you."

"Glad to hear his frequent visits aren't personal in nature. I went to high school with the guy and he had a reputation as a real horndog. I was going to warn you, but it appears that any cautionary advice is unnecessary."

"Yeah. Totally unnecessary, but it's good to know you're looking out for me." Alexa took her cup of tea and left the room, debating whether to be pissed or touched by Brian's remarks.

Alexa brought up the subject of Tyrell Jenkins with Melissa during their post-yoga get-together at the Om Café. Haley had a Chamber event that evening so they were alone.

"So, what is with this guy?" Alexa asked. "I can't tell you the details, but I have had ongoing contact with Tyrell in regard to some missing children. I want to like him, maybe because he's so frigging handsome. But I just can't figure him out."

"What's to figure out?" Melissa scowled. "He's a totally caring person. He's a social worker for Christ's sake. He runs this youth group on his own time. He's knee deep in RESIST. Tyrell's a sweetheart."

"Well, I'd say he has some anger issues."

"OK, a sweetheart with anger issues. He had a rough time growing up, and I've seen him get pretty worked up about what he sees as injustice. But no one's perfect."

Alexa leaned closer to Melissa. "The strange thing here . . . Tyrell knew all three of the young girls who are missing. Maybe a coincidence, but maybe not. One of the girls supposedly has a secret older boyfriend, and he fits that bill. And I saw an odd confrontation between Tyrell and a young girl at the courthouse—she looked very distraught. Now that I think of it, he was also the last one to see Cecily alive. Maybe she was on to his thing for young girls . . . and Tyrell killed her."

"Listen to yourself, Alexa!" Melissa threw up her hands. "You've been watching too many crime shows. Whether you like him or not, you have to agree that Tyrell is not a stupid man."

"You're right. There's no doubt that he's intelligent."

"So would a man that smart shit in his own backyard? Hell, if he wanted to snatch little girls, he wouldn't pick them out of his own youth group. Get a grip, Alexa."

When Melissa put it like that, Alexa realized that she had let a few uncomfortable interactions with this guy boomerang into a crime fantasy. Thinking that he could be responsible for these disappearances and even Cecily's murder was too pat an explanation. Long on imagination but short on substance.

"You're right. Just because the guy makes me uneasy doesn't mean he's a criminal." Alexa took a sip of tea.

Still, a little voice in her head said, But it doesn't mean that he's not.

CHAPTER TWENTY-THREE

THROUGH INTERMITTENT GAPS in the narrow evergreens, Alexa glimpsed acres of field under cultivation. As she drove upward, an expanse of forest appeared beyond the tops of the slender imitation cypress trees. On her way to her first board meeting at the Nash estate, Alexa was trying to ignore the butterflies. It was just like her first day in court on a new case: butterflies every time.

The board assembled in an ornate room in what Jack's assistant called the Business Wing. Although the décor struck Alexa as a little excessive, the meeting was conducted professionally.

Alexa recognized several of her fellow board members from last week's dinner. Quinn Hutton gave her a cool nod from the far end of the big conference table. Most surprising, Vivienne Nash sat on the board and served as secretary. Vivienne gave Alexa the barest hint of a smile as she took her seat at the table.

Expecting to need a thorough understanding of all the agenda items, Alexa had studied the briefing packet prior to the meeting. However, two presentations took up the first half hour of the meeting. A bright young manager provided an overview of the new facility for troubled youth.

For what seemed liked an interminable time, the chief financial officer reviewed in great detail the glowing financial status of the organization. Alexa remained alert for the entire report thanks to an arctic wind blowing from a duct directly overhead. She considered interrupting the financial report with a suggestion to lower electric costs by shutting down the air conditioning system. Finally, the CFO finished his report with a self-satisfied smile.

Next, Jack asked for a vote on a series of items before he launched into new business. "Last year, we briefly discussed the possibility of expanding our overseas adoption operations. I have directed the program development office to begin a feasibility study on such an expansion. I wanted to mention it today with the expectation that we'll have something definitive to discuss at the next meeting."

Fred DiGrassi raised his hand like a schoolboy. "What countries are you proposing to expand into?" Alexa recognized him as one of the golfers from the reception.

"Well, that will be part of the feasibility study." Jack tugged at each of his french cuffs. "Of course, several governments have stopped permitting their children to be adopted in the United States. But others are still working with U.S. agencies. There are many families here with a lot of love to give to a child adopted from overseas. Having on-the-ground staff in place to work with foreign authorities would almost certainly help smooth adoptions for Children of Light."

When the meeting adjourned, Vivienne Nash invited the board for light refreshments in the conservatory. Like a flock of blue swallows, a group of teens immediately flew through the room, swooping in with their trays to offer hors d'oeuvres to the guests.

After standing and making nice with fellow board members, Alexa's feet were killing her. Damn, she thought. I shouldn't have tried to impress this group by dragging my Christian Louboutins down from the top shelf of the closet.

She took baby steps toward an unoccupied group of chairs in the corner, sinking gratefully onto a Bergere upholstered in moss-green toile. Her moment of respite lasted only seconds before one of the swallows swooped in to offer cucumber and watercress sandwiches. Alexa initially refused the hors d'oeuvre, but the look of disappointment on the young girl's face persuaded her to take one. The young server had a striking, delicate beauty that reminded Alexa of a painting by Botticelli or Vermeer. She looked so sad that Alexa couldn't refuse the finger food, despite her distaste of cucumbers.

As she sat there pondering the unwanted canapé in her hand, Jack Nash sailed over and settled into the loveseat across from Alexa.

"I want to thank you for your quick agreement to join to board. The circumstances were tragic, but Cecily would have been the first to advocate action when it comes to helping children in need."

Alexa continued to cradle the tiny sandwich as she spoke, "Agreeing that it would be an interim appointment made it easier to accept."

"Only fair under the circumstances."

"So, how did you become interested in children's issues, Mr. Nash?"

Jack leaned back and adjusted the cuffs on his shirt. "Well, dear, I was a foster child myself."

"I didn't know." Alexa took a reluctant nibble of watercress and cucumber.

"Of course not, child. It's not a secret, but I don't advertise my past either. I was one of the lucky ones." He paused to nod at Quinn as the professor sat down beside him.

"When I was twelve, the Nashes adopted me and took me to live with them in Newport. It was a fairy tale for a kid who had spent years shuffling from one dreadful foster home to the next."

Quinn interrupted. "That's when you met my dad, right?"

"Your father's family lived in the mansion next door. From the day I arrived, he took me under his wing and treated me as an equal. To your dad, I was a Nash and I belonged in Newport."

Alexa trod lightly with her question. "So, Children of Light is your way of giving back?"

"You could say that. After college, I saw that there was enormous opportunity to improve lives by starting a business to find new placements for children. So, I invested some of my trust fund and got additional financial backing from some friends. My life has been dedicated to righting the wrongs that I experienced as a child."

"From what I've seen so far, Children of Light is a testimony to that vision."

"Thank you. I must touch base with some of the other board members. Alexa, I leave you in Quinn's good hands."

Quinn raised an eyebrow at Jack's departing back. "And where you would like those good hands?"

Under his amused gaze, Alexa felt warmth suffuse her cheeks. She became even more embarrassed when she realized that she was blushing.

"Get rid of that half-eaten abomination Viv calls food, and let's take a stroll through the grounds."

"Sounds great, but you've got to give me a few minutes while I run to the ladies'." Alexa hid the bedraggled mini sandwich in a napkin and placed it on a side table. Leaving the conservatory, she stood in the empty hallway, trying to remember whether the powder room was to the right or left.

Choosing left, she walked past several closed doors before she reached an alcove and realized that she should have gone the other way. Just as she turned to go back, a plaintive voice whispered from the alcove.

"Miss. Can you help me?"

Startled, Alexa recognized the exquisite server hiding in the shadows. She stepped closer. "How can I help you? Is there a problem?"

"Can you sneak me out of here in your car when you leave? You're new, and you look like a kind person. I've got to get out of here tonight." The girl whimpered, tears spilling onto her cheeks.

"I don't understand. Why must you leave?" Alexa looked up and down the hall for assistance. She was quite concerned. These grounds housed kids who had committed juvenile offenses. And she was sure that the foster care group settings also housed children who chafed at their custody arrangements. But she couldn't encourage or, even worse, facilitate a runaway. Among other considerations, she was an officer of the court.

"I heard they're going to ship me off. I've seen it happen to other girls, and I'm terrified. I've got to get out of here."

Quinn strode down the hall. "There you are, Alexa. I was going to send out a search party . . ." He broke off when he noticed the girl huddled in the alcove.

"What's this? Aren't you on duty? I would think that Mrs. Nash needs you to be helping with the guests." Quinn's tone took on a nasty edge. "Or do I need to call a counselor?"

Without another word, the girl fled toward the conservatory, wiping at her wet face with a blue sleeve.

"What was that about?" Quinn asked in a tight voice.

"She wanted me to help her leave the grounds. She said that she had to get away. She seemed genuinely distraught."

"It can't be surprising to find that many of these youngsters, especially the teens, are restless. Some of them want to find their families, despite the broken situations that brought them here in the first place."

"Of course. I imagine that few of these kids choose to be in a child custody arrangement. Still, you can't discount the emotional pain, at that age especially. Remember your teenage years?"

"Excellent point."

As they strolled back down the hall, Alexa couldn't help thinking about the girl. Her distress had seemed real. And where would Children of Light be 'shipping her off' to? Another foster care placement, probably. Unsettled, Alexa felt Quinn's harsh tone was uncalled for.

When they reached the spot where the passageways intersected, Alexa turned to Quinn. “Pleasant as it sounds, I think I’m going to pass on that stroll. I’m tired. I’m going find the powder room and call it a day. I’ll see you tomorrow evening?”

“Absolutely.”

Driving home, Alexa couldn’t shake the melancholy mood that enveloped her. She wished that she had been able to help that young girl in some way, short of driving her out of the Nash property. But in their brief encounter, she hadn’t even had a chance to take a stab at consoling the girl. Life in the foster care system must be hard, no matter how good the agency and counselors, Alexa mused. She felt lucky that she’d lived her entire childhood in an intact and loving family.

She’d been a bit taken aback by Quinn’s interaction with the youngster. She still didn’t known him well but had assumed that his participation on the Children of Light Board would have indicated a little more compassion for the foster children in the company’s care.

CHAPTER TWENTY-FOUR

"What was I thinking?" Alexa moaned to Melissa as she ran to check the oven. The rich, cheesy smell of au gratin potatoes enveloped the kitchen when she opened the oven door. "Tomorrow, I leave for my first vacation in over a year, and I decide to host a dinner party tonight."

Melissa sat at the counter husking ears of corn. "Jim and I can find somewhere else to eat if you want."

"I'm not talking about you. My God, you're doing me a huge favor by staying here with my fur ball for almost three weeks. I'm talking about Quinn. We've only gone out a few times. He's never been to the cabin before. Why would I pick tonight to invite him to dinner?"

"Don't look at me." Melissa pried a strand of silk from the yellow ear in her hand. Then she looked up at Alexa with an impish smile. "Although I could offer a theory."

"Really?"

"On this African trip, you're going to see Reese for the first time in months. You're not sure whether you want to make a move to reconcile. Plus, he may have no interest in getting back together. In the meantime, you've met this good looking new guy. I think you want to take one last look at the back-up plan before you step on that plane."

"Listen to Dr. Freud. Tonight has nothing to do with Reese. I was in a romantic daze on Monday, and the invitation just sort of slipped out. I want to get to know Quinn better, but the jury's still out on whether he's boyfriend material."

Alexa grabbed a stack of plates from the cupboard and hustled out to the deck to give them to Jim, leaving Melissa with the corn.

With everything prepped, Alexa and Melissa joined Jim and Scout on the deck. A slight breeze kept the mosquitoes and gnats away. Alexa mentally reviewed her final to do list for the next day's trip while her friends chatted. Jim had volunteered to do the steaks and had already fired up the gas grill. Aware that anything cooked on the grill usually meant a tidbit for him, Scout stuck close to the grill master. They all looked up in unison at the sound of a vehicle coming down the lane.

Quinn drove his pick-up truck, a black model with matching cap covering the bed. Alexa had told him that his fancy vintage car was no match for her bumpy gravel lane. The minute Quinn stopped, Scout ran toward the pick-up growling. Puzzled, Alexa hurried down the steps as the big dog circled the truck, hair standing on end.

"Scout, come here," Alexa commanded and grabbed his collar.

Quinn eased out of the car and walked toward her and the mastiff. He stopped about two yards away, his hand gripping the neck of wine bottle in his hand like a club. "That dog is enormous. Is he friendly?"

"Usually. Something about your pick-up seems to have set him off."

"Strange. I ran by my tenant farmer's house to pick up the rent check before I came here. Maybe I drove through some smelly farm effluvia."

Jim called to Scout from the deck. "Come here, boy. Watch me grill these steaks and leave that truck alone." When Alexa released her grip on the mastiff's collar, he trotted up the steps toward the park ranger.

"Sorry about that. Maybe the sight of my suitcases has Scout on edge."

"No need to apologize. Here, I've brought some wine. From that smell of sizzling beef, it's good I chose a red."

"Come and meet my friends." Alexa led Quinn onto the deck. She was glad that he had dressed down in jeans and a crisp cotton shirt with the cuffs turned back. She and Melissa wore capris and nice tops. Jim had traded his park uniform for khakis and a polo shirt.

"I don't know if you actually met Melissa Lambert at her opening? Melissa, this is Quinn Hutton."

"It was pretty crazy that night, but we met briefly at the Nash dinner party." Melissa stood to shake Quinn's hand.

"Of course. Your work is compelling."

"And this is Jim Kline. He's a park ranger at Pine Grove Furnace State Park."

Jim nodded from his station by the grill. "Nice to meet you, Hutton. How do you like your steak?"

"Rare is good for me."

Jim waved a wooden-handled fork in Alexa's direction. "Hey, these babies should be done in no time. You might want to go in and organize everything else."

"Sure. Quinn, could you open the wine?"

"My Porsche is a 2009, and I wouldn't trade it for the world. But I'd love to take a spin in your 500K. Those cars are practically legend." Jim's enthusiasm was palpable as the dinner conversation continued.

With Quinn and Jim deep in discussion about Le Mans, Alexa rose to clear the table. Melissa pushed her chair back to help, but Alexa waved her off. "No, just sit. I'll clean this up." She collected the dirty dishes and took them to the dishwasher.

Breathing a sigh of relief, Alexa concluded that the informal dinner party had been a success. Like a chameleon, Quinn had dialed back his erudite professor persona and assumed a folksy, small-town demeanor this evening. At this point she wouldn't bat an eyelash if he and Jim dashed out the door to rebuild the truck's engine. Alexa was happy that Quinn had meshed so well with her friends, but it felt like he was putting on a performance.

Taking some scraps of steak, Alexa stepped outside to give Scout a treat. Surprised that the mastiff wasn't in his usual spot by the door, she called, "Come, Scout. It's not everyday that you get porterhouse."

The only response was a brief yelp from the yard in front of the deck.

Puzzled, Alexa moved to the railing. Scout sat by the parking area, his attention fixed on Quinn's pick-up.

"What is it with you and the truck? Come and get this steak. It's your last chance."

The dog fell out of position and padded onto the deck. Alexa laughed as Scout snuffled each tiny piece of steak into his huge mouth. "Good boy. Now, come into the house and be sociable. I won't see you for weeks." Alexa held the door open and Scout headed for his water bowl.

Alexa looked at her three guests, still lounging around the dining room table. "Dessert, anyone? Melissa brought an assortment of gourmet cupcakes from Leila's Cupcake Palace. They look scrumptious."

Jim called out. "Cupcakes from Leila's? I have dibs on the Salty Caramel."

"Coffee or tea, anyone. Or more wine?"

"I'll have more wine along with one of those Merlot Madness cupcakes." Melissa poured some wine into her glass as Alexa placed the pink box of cakes in the middle of the table.

"Nothing for me, thanks," Quinn demurred.

Alexa plucked a cupcake out of the box and peeled away one side of the pink wrapper. Carrot cake was one of her favorites. Before taking a bite, she announced, "Thanks so much for joining us for dinner tonight, Quinn. I'm glad that you've met these two. Melissa and Jim, thanks in advance for taking care of Scout while I'm gone. I don't mean to be rude, but after you finish your cupcakes, I have to call this a night. I'm meeting Mom and Dad at five tomorrow morning for the to drive to Dulles."

Quinn stood and walked to the door. "Given your schedule, I'll take my leave now. Thank you for dinner. Alexa, have a wonderful trip. I'll look forward to your return."

"Nice to meet you," Melissa called.

"Like to see that car sometime," Jim mumbled through a mouthful of cupcake.

Alexa followed Quinn onto the deck. "Drive safely. I'll see you when I get back?"

"Absolutely." Quinn reached for her with both hands and gently traced the outline of her face from temples to cheeks. When he reached her chin, he tilted her head back and brought his lips to Alexa's mouth in a gentle kiss, soft as mist. Without speaking another word, he released her and sauntered to his truck.

Alexa raised her fingers to her lips. They were cool to the touch. Quinn's kisses didn't leave her burning with passion. But they had an intriguing allure, like a cool breeze on a summer's day.

When she walked back inside the house, Melissa shouted, "Africa. You're going on safari. I am so jealous."

CHAPTER TWENTY-FIVE

"I CAN'T BELIEVE ALL THE WILDLIFE we saw today." Alexa took a spoonful of the pumpkin soup that the server had just placed in front of her.

"We knew that you would love the Ngorongoro Crater." Her father, an old hand at African safaris, sounded nearly as excited as Alexa.

Her mom leaned a bit to the side to avoid the blazing candelabra that blocked her line of sight to Alexa. "The crater gets pretty crowded. You saw that today when we stopped to watch the lions take down the zebra. There must have been eight other vehicles. But the sheer concentration of animals makes coping with the other vehicles worth it."

"I loved the little lion cubs. I am so glad you talked me into this trip. What's this? Our fifth day on safari, or is it the sixth? I think I've finally stopped squealing at every giraffe and elephant, but I'm loving this whole experience. I can't believe we're seeing all these exotic animals up close."

The Williams family had joined a tour group of nine other Americans. The group had stayed in a tented camp and a lodge on the rim of the Ngorongoro Crater. Now they had arrived at a lovely old coffee plantation, where the staff provided impeccable service.

"I can't wait until we get to the mobile tented camp."

"The accommodations will be less luxurious, but your mother and I enjoy being right in the middle of the Serengeti. Last time, we sat right outside our tent and watched a herd of elephants for hours."

"The tented camp feels very *Out of Africa.*" Her mom laughed. "Wait until you take a bucket shower."

Alexa and her mom must have watched *Out of Africa* together at least twenty times. Alexa tilted her head and studied her father, a mischievous smile on her face. "Dad, I can see you as the dashing Robert Redford—white hunter type. And I can picture Meryl Streep living in this house—before it became a hotel, I mean.

"But, I don't see any romance under African skies for me this week." Alexa giggled as she swept her eyes down the long table at the tour group. The only other traveler under sixty was Ellen Descartes' fourteen-year-old grandson.

"You'll be seeing Reese soon enough. Who knows what that might bring?"

"We'll see, Mom. We'll see."

The mid-morning sun bathed the vast plain with golden light. Alexa stood on the rear seat of the Toyota Land Cruiser, head and shoulders rising above the roof line, hair streaming behind her. The roof's retractable panels had been thrown open to the sky. Dry African heat filled her lungs.

Alexa braced her back against the frame for balance as their guide steered the sturdy vehicle over the bumpy track. Yusef hoped to find the pride of lions that frequented a distant kopje of rocks somewhere out on the vast plain. Looking ahead, Alexa could make out only the barest hint of a road; really just two parallel lines through the tall grass.

The Serengeti Plain. Alexa lifted her face to the wind in a burst of pure joy. The Land Cruiser rolled steadily forward, a tiny speck of green sailing on a sea of endless grass and sky. As far as Alexa could see, nothing existed except blue sky and golden plain, tall grasses undulating in the wind. No people, no animals, not even a discernible horizon.

Never had she felt so insignificant. Never had she felt so alive. The overwhelming beauty of this landscape made Alexa's heart soar at the joy of just being.

"Alexa, are you OK up there?" her mother called.

"Perfect. Couldn't be better."

During this safari, she had seen wild animals do what they must to survive. Out here in the African bush, it was kill or be killed. Finally, she accepted that she'd faced a similarly elemental situation when she killed Reverend Browne last fall. As the vehicle rolled on, Alexa let the scorching wind carry away all her guilt, self-recrimination, and despair.

Alexa returned her gaze to the golden Serengeti, knowing that Africa had healed her soul.

CHAPTER TWENTY-SIX

"THIS PLACE MAKES YOU appreciate the charms of camping, doesn't it?" Susan Williams settled deeper into her canvas chair and gestured to the herd of elephants grazing in knee-high grass. She had joined Alexa in front of her tent while Norris Williams took a siesta.

"Even though these tents are ground level and the showers are open air, I'd hardly call this your typical camping experience." Alexa scanned the stand of sausage trees to the left of the tent until she located the source of a loud noise. Several shaggy Colobus monkeys chattered noisily at the elephants. "Don't you love the coloring on those guys? Like tree skunks. They should call them skunkeys."

Her mother laughed at Alexa's lame joke. "What an awful comparison. They don't have much in common other than their black-and-white coloring. I agree that this tented camp is a step above the camping I used to do in my younger days. But the feel is the same. You take a step outside the canvas flap, and you're right in the middle of nature."

"Speaking of your younger days, Mom, there is something I've been meaning to ask. When I was up in your attic awhile back looking for binoculars, I came across a photo album labeled Woodstock. I'm pretty sure I recognized Jack Nash in one of the pictures. You two were with a group standing in front of some tents. What's the story with you and Jack and Woodstock? Were you guys, um . . ." Alexa searched for the right word. "Involved?"

The bitter edge to her mother's laugh surprised Alexa. "God, no. I never dated Jack or had any type of romantic feelings for the guy. I think I told you this already—he was just part of the group that I went with to Woodstock."

"Why don't you ever talk about Woodstock? All my friends used to think it was so cool that my mom went to Woodstock. But, other than the fact that you were there, I don't think you've ever told Graham and me anything about it."

"You're probably right. Let's just say that Woodstock was a mixed experience for me. I loved the music. It was wonderful to be swept up in the dream that, with love and peace, anything was possible. But a friend died at the festival. Her death cast a pall over the whole experience for me. It's not something that I like to remember."

"What happened? An overdose?" Alexa straightened in her seat.

"I wouldn't be surprised if drugs of some sort were involved. But I don't want to go into the details." As Susan continued, she sounded as if she were speaking to herself. She whispered, "I should have kept her safe."

"Even without knowing exactly what happened, Mom, I can't imagine that you should hold yourself responsible for your friend's death. One thing I don't understand: What's Jack Nash have to do with this? Why can't you stand the guy?"

"To be honest, I'm not completely sure. I've always had this bad feeling about Jack. I think it's mainly because I associate him with that difficult time. Everything is hazy in my mind. I suspect Jack and his friend may have given my friend drugs. I just can't remember." Susan grasped her forehead with her hand as if she could extract the memory from her temple.

"I'm sorry that I even brought this up, Mom. I had no idea that your trip to Woodstock came with all this baggage." Alexa looked at her mother in dismay. Susan's face had become pale, and her eyes brimmed with tears.

"I never smoked another joint or did another drug after Woodstock. That's why I never drink anything stronger than wine. I've always thought that, if my head had been clear, I could have saved her.

"That concert became a turning point for me. I broke up with my boyfriend, stopped hanging out with his crowd at school, and recognized that there was more to life than partying. A year later, I met your dad."

The alarm clock in Alexa's tent beeped, and she dashed inside to shut if off. When she emerged from the tent, her mother had risen to her feet.

"Time to wake your dad and get ready for our game drive. It's hard to believe that we've only got one more day left in Tanzania."

"But you guys will have another two weeks in Namibia, and I'm sure that Reese will take me out into the bush in Kenya. It's not over yet." Alexa gathered her mother in her arms for a hug.

"Sorry that my curiosity stirred up all these bad memories. We're supposed to be having the time of our lives, and my questions about Woodstock really brought you down."

"I'm glad I told you. It's not a secret. Your father knows the story, of course. But, now you'll understand why I don't talk about Woodstock. The bad vibe from that time has haunted me for years. You're my only daughter. You should know what makes your mother tick." Her mom managed a wry smile and kissed Alexa's forehead before she strode toward the adjoining tent.

CHAPTER TWENTY-SEVEN

August 15, 1969

Tune in, turn on, and drop out.

"Look at all these people," Sukie marveled to Nina as they walked down the dusty road, the morning sun beating on their backs. "I've never seen so many human beings in one place. Most of them are our age, but look—some people brought little kids." She made a three hundred and sixty-degree turn, taking it all in. The shirtless boys perched on cars by the road. The young women with babies and naked toddlers sitting on a grassy bank. A host of others in bell-bottoms, fringed vests, granny glasses, long dresses, you name it, passed by them in steady flow.

"Nuns?" Nina directed Sukie's attention to two women wearing habits.

"And that guy over there must be at least sixty." Sukie hooted with laughter. "I can't imagine my dad here."

"Who's that playing? Do you recognize him?" Nina stopped Sukie so they could listen. In the distance, on the main sound system, a man was singing. It sounded like he was warming up.

"Not really. Maybe Country Joe without the Fish? Where exactly did Brenda say their tent is?" Sukie raised an eyebrow at Nina's harebrained scheme to find a friend from college.

"When I saw her at the hamburger stand yesterday, she said it was at the top of this hill. At least, I think it's this hill."

As they walked on, Sukie noticed a chain link fence bent to the ground. "Wonder what happened there?"

Before Nina could respond, a man in a pick-up truck pulled up next to them. "Could you help me pass out these programs?" He handed a stack of booklets to each of them and pointed to the fence. "People trampled down the fence. Thousands more are coming by car and on foot. We're not going to take tickets. It's a free concert." He beeped his horn to part the crowd as the truck edged forward.

"I guess we don't need our tickets anymore," Nina groused.

"Not if it's turned into a free concert. But I'm going to keep mine as a souvenir."

"We could have saved eighteen bucks."

Sukie looked at her watch. "Nina, it's almost eleven. I don't think we can find Brenda and get back in time to leave for the concert with our group. I think we should turn around."

"You're right. I'm hungry anyway. I want another one of those yummy peanut butter and jelly sandwiches before we go to the concert."

The girls retraced their footsteps, handing out programs randomly to people they passed. "I've only got ten left. We should keep one for every person in our gang." Nina peered at the dwindling stack of programs in Sukie's hands.

"I've got eight left. Let's take these all back. We can give one to Willow and the rest to Levi's group."

Sukie shifted her position on the blanket and looked around for the hundredth time, amazed at the sea of humanity surrounding them. Because they had arrived at the concert site early, their group had snagged a great spot. They were about fifty yards from the stage with an unobstructed view. Levi Bloom, his bandmates, and their ladies sat with them. Even JJ and Eskimo had decided to stick with the group for the first day of music.

The aroma of patchouli, summer sweat, and marijuana formed a redolent cloud over the laid-back throng of hippies covering every square inch of the massive natural amphitheater. Sukie found the combination of exotic scents captivating. She took a deep breath and laughed. "We may as well save our weed for back at camp. I'm getting a contact high just sitting here."

Ben looked at a group of boys on a nearby blanket. "Ain't that the truth? Check out that bong."

Phil elbowed Ben. "I learned about this in Psych 101. They call it bong envy."

Nina ignored the boys as she stretched her arms. "OK, I am ready for this concert to get its ass in gear."

"Working on a tan and getting high aren't enough for you?" Sukie thrust her ivory-toned arm next to Nina's dark brown one and wailed. "Why don't I ever get a decent tan?"

Nina fanned her face with a flattened paper bag. "Better watch it. You know how you always get sunburned."

The voice of the announcer came across the speakers. "The brown acid that is circulating around us isn't specifically too good. It is suggested that you stay away from that."

"Enough with the fucking brown acid. When is the concert going to start?" Ben fumed.

"Someone's coming out on stage." Sukie pointed.

"Ladies and gentlemen, Richie Havens."

Nina turned to Sukie. "Did we see him at the Philadelphia Folk Festival?"

"I don't think so." Havens started to strum his guitar in a rhythmic pattern. When he began to sing, Sukie could hardly contain her excitement.

As dusk gathered, Sukie announced, "I can't hold it any longer. Does anyone want to make the trek to the port-o-potties with me?"

"Go ahead." Ben never took his eyes off the stage. "I'm digging this Incredible String Band. Can't believe I don't have one of their albums."

"I'll go." Nina rolled up onto her knees. "Let's figure out a few landmarks so we can find our way back."

"We're to the front of that big tower. And, I'd say, we're directly back from the right corner of the stage." Sukie gestured toward each marker as she spoke.

"Agree. I only hope we can find this spot again."

Sukie stood and began navigating a path between groups of people on blankets or just sitting on the ground.

"I'm coming, too." Willow grabbed a corner of Nina's skirt, following the two older girls.

Excuse me, excuse me . . . excuse me." Sukie sighed with relief when she reached the far edge of the crowd. She turned back to Nina and Willow. "What an ordeal."

Nina pointed over Sukie's shoulder. "Nothing compared to that."

Sukie's heart sank at the long lines extending out from each portable bathroom stall. She clamped her legs together and said, "The sooner we get in line, the better."

During the long wait, Nina confided to Sukie, "I don't think this is working with Phil. I've already lost him."

"But you two seem to be getting it on. Maybe you're overreacting."

"I don't think so. Sure, we're having a great time. He's digging this whole scene." Nina twisted a curl around her finger.

"So what's the problem?"

"I don't just want to be the chick he balls because I'm there. I want him to love me or at least like me. I want a relationship." Nina struggled to keep from crying.

Willow piped in. "I don't get it. You have a guy who wants to be with you right now. Who cares about tomorrow?"

Sukie raised an eyebrow at the young teenager. "When did you become such a total hippie, Willow?"

"I don't have any family except my mom—and she's always with her men friends. My dad was one of her fly-by-night romances. Sometimes she says he was a Swedish diplomat. Other times, it's a Swedish sailor. She named me Greta because Greta Garbo was the only Swedish actress she knew."

Sukie kept one eye on the progress of the line. "Greta's a nice name."

"I hate it. That's why I chose Willow. I don't want to be like my mom. But I wish I was old enough to have my own guy. I won't care if he loves me as long as he wants to be with me."

Sukie exchanged a sad glance with Nina. "Well, munchkin, I hope you find a man who loves you for a good, long time."

The girl gave a wistful sigh. "I hope he's as handsome as Eskimo."

"Eskimo's good looking, but he's a little too old for you, Willow." Above Willow's head, Sukie mouthed to Nina, "And a real jerk."

"I met another guy down at one of those shops in the woods. He's dreamy, too. Long black hair he wears in a braid. He glides like a dancer. He wants me to come over later and get high with him."

"Why don't you just stay with us today, Willow? It's the first day of the concert. Concentrate on the music." Sukie remembered being boy-crazy when she was Willow's age, but she hadn't been on her own in a sea full of strange boys and men.

Nina must have been on the same wavelength. "You're only fourteen, Willow. You've got plenty of time for boys. I'd think twice about hanging out with these older guys."

"Finally." Nina wrinkled her nose as she opened the port-o-potty door. "You go first, Willow. Make it quick."

Sukie snorted. "I can't imagine anyone spending any longer in there than necessary. I hate using these things."

"Damn. We just got back and now it's raining." Drowsy from the drone of Ravi Shankar's sitar, Sukie jolted awake when the raindrops hit her face. The first drops felt good against the sunburn. But the rain intensified, and she rummaged through her bag for her poncho. Like Sukie, the rest of the group had come equipped for a camping trip, so they all had ponchos or raincoats.

"What's with these people? A lot of them didn't bring food. Some of them didn't even bring a raincoat. Haven't they ever been camping?" Ben muttered in a low voice.

Sukie looked around to find that Ben was right. A lot of their neighbors held blankets over their heads. Others sat with no protection at all from the rain shower. Looking to the next blanket, she realized the Levi Bloom group hadn't brought raincoats either. Willow had wormed her way beneath JJ's poncho, but the rest of the group was getting soaked.

Levi shrugged at Sukie's look of concern. "We're from New York City. If it rains there, you just go inside. We've never spent a weekend outdoors."

After some commotion onstage, the music ground to a halt. Someone announced they were going to postpone the music until the rain stopped.

"Ben. Are you ready to get out of here? I'm ready for a decent night's sleep."

"Sure, babe. This Indian music is bumming me out. And I'm cool with ditching Joan Baez. Are you sure you want to miss her?"

"Yeah. I'd like to hear every single performance, but we've got another two days. I'm fading fast."

The entire group agreed to pack it in for the night. By the time they had assembled their belongings and navigated their way across the wet mass of people, the rain had ended.

"Finally." Sukie rejoiced when she spied Levi Bloom's bread truck. "Slogging across this wet field is no picnic."

Robbie announced, "I am going to crash the minute I hit my tent."

Eskimo scoffed. "Crash? No way, man. The night is still young. JJ and I are going to do buttons of peyote we bought off a cat from New Mexico. He said he got it from a shaman and that this shit will blow your mind."

JJ nodded in excitement. "A real spiritual experience. That's what the dude promised. We have some extra if anyone wants to fly with us."

"Not for me."

"Thanks, but I'm already too wasted."

One by one the rest of the group begged off.

"I'll try some." Willow, bedraggled from the rain, sidled up to Eskimo with a hopeful expression on her face.

"Why not?" Eskimo shrugged his shoulders.

"No way, little one." Levi grabbed Willow's arm and steered her toward his truck. "You need to get some sleep with the rest of my ladies."

Sukie and Ben both headed immediately for their sleeping bags when they hit camp.

"Today was a real blast, except for the rain . . ." Ben's voice trailed off into sleep.

Sukie lay awake for a few minutes, reviewing the exciting day. The campsite had fallen silent. In the stillness, a brief snatch of conversation leaked from one of the other tents. It sounded like JJ and Eskimo.

"How many did you take?"

"Two."

"Give me two buttons."

"We would have had enough for Willow."

"Get her tripping out and . . . that little . . ."

Sukie strained to hear but couldn't catch any more of JJ and Eskimo's conversation. As she drifted off to sleep, Sukie couldn't shake a feeling of unease about Eskimo's interest in young Willow.

CHAPTER TWENTY-EIGHT

WITH HER NEW KENYAN VISA in hand, Alexa stood at the baggage claim waiting for her single bag to slide down the chute. She had parted company with her parents at the Kilimanjaro Airport and hopped an hour-long flight to Nairobi.

"There it is," she exclaimed and wormed her way through the sweaty crowd just in time to pluck her bright green duffel from the belt before it passed. Hoisting the strap over her shoulder, Alexa adjusted her small backpack and headed out the door.

"I'm Alexa Williams," she called, making her way toward a slight young man holding a sign with her name. He wore fashionable blue jeans and a crisp white shirt with a logo on the chest pocket.

"Jambo, miss. I am Daniel Mututho from Mara Safaris. Let me take your bag. I hope your flight was pleasant, miss?"

Alexa nodded, shook his outstretched hand, and handed over her duffel. "Nice to meet you, Daniel."

"The car is waiting outside. Did you want to stop for a small bite to eat or should we take you directly to Wilson?"

"Wilson is the other airport, right? How long will it take to get there?"

"We will see, miss. Perhaps an hour in this traffic, but we have time to stop if you are hungry."

"No, I'm fine. I have a snack in my backpack." Alexa followed Daniel through the crowded airport. She recalled that there had been a fire here a year or so ago. Now all flights were going through the domestic terminal. Daniel came to a halt in a lobby area to let a large group of emaciated people shuffle by. The long line of men, women, and children all toted white bags with a big blue logo that said OIM above the small typed words: Organization for Immigrant Migration. Some also carried rectangular blue plaid plastic bags as suitcases.

"Daniel, who are those people?"

"Miss, they be refugees. Maybe from Somalia."

"They all look like they could use a good meal. I hope they are headed to safe new homes."

Daniel continued toward the exit doors after the refugees passed by. "Yes, miss. They be the lucky ones. They're getting out of the camps."

Settled in the van, Alexa watched Nairobi flow by outside the car window. The streets teemed with vendors and shoppers. She was surprised by the walls topped with barbed wire and shards of glass in the residential neighborhoods. Daniel kept up a running commentary, pointing out landmarks and discussing life in the city.

Alexa only listened with half an ear as she fought the butterflies in her stomach. She silently acknowledged, I am so looking forward to seeing Reese. But does he truly want to see me?

"Miss, you have traveled far to see your friend in Samburu. He must be *yako mpenzi*—your boyfriend?"

"We'll see, Daniel. We'll see."

The small plane began its descent into the Samburu airport in Northern Kenya. Alexa noticed that the terrain below looked sandy and dry. She looked up in consternation when the plane banked and gained more altitude.

"Standard procedure," the sun-weathered man across the aisle spoke. "They do a pass to make sure the runway is clear of animals before they land. Colliding with an elephant wouldn't be good for the elephant or for us."

"Makes sense." Alexa tried to place his accent, which seemed British but not quite. The idea of elephants on the runway secretly delighted Alexa.

"Would you be Reese Michaels' friend?" The khaki-clad stranger asked as the plane taxied down the dirt runway.

"Yes. I'm Alexa Williams. How did you know I'm visiting Reese?"

"Process of elimination." His sardonic gaze swept up and down the aisle at the other passengers: two African men in guayabera type shirts and two French couples who wore their safari clothes with effortless chic. "Sorry. I'm Anthony Kent. I manage Archer's, one of the tented camps up here in the Reserve. Reese had mentioned you might take this flight."

"Nice to meet you." Alexa looped her backpack over her right shoulder and moved toward the exit. A wall of dry heat brought her to a brief halt when she stepped outside. As she reached the bottom of the steps, she spotted lanky Reese walking across the dirt runway toward the plane. Brown curls burnished by the sun, he towered above the others gathered to meet the plane, Westerners and Africans alike. At the sight of Reese, Alexa's heart soared.

Alexa hurried toward this man she had once loved—and maybe still did. For a moment, she hesitated, unexpectedly shy at confronting Reese after several months apart.

Reese ducked around the four French travelers, who seemed to be struggling to maintain their *sang froid* in the face of several persistent tribal women hawking beaded necklaces. When he spotted Alexa, Reese's face broke into a wide smile, and he rushed toward her.

"Hey." Alexa's throat was so constricted that her greeting came out in a hoarse whisper.

"Hey, yourself." Reese scooped Alexa into his arms and lifted her into the air, backpack and all. "It is unbelievably wonderful to see you. Here. In Kenya."

When he deposited her back on the rough track, Alexa responded. "I've missed you, Reese. Look at you, all tan and handsome. You've got a real Indiana Jones vibe going. The khaki, the bandana, the sun-streaked hair. I like it."

"I always knew you'd come walking back through that plane door and down those steps, Marion."

Alexa cracked up at Reese's mangled imitation of Indiana Jones' famous line to his old flame from *The Raiders of the Lost Ark.* She and Reese had watched every single Indiana Jones movie at least twice during their time together. In an instant, her nervousness disappeared.

"Let me grab your bag." Reese gestured toward the remaining bag sitting next to the empty plane. "If we leave now, we might be able to get in a research drive before sundown. This week, my team is tracking a pride of lions on the far side of the Reserve."

They drove thirty minutes over a sand track, moving farther into the wild with each kilometer. The landscape was dry and dusty, a mix of plains and small hills. A lonely acacia tree silhouetted against the far horizon reminded Alexa of the classic photos she'd seen of Africa. Still, Samburu's stark beauty sustained wildlife. They'd passed herds of elephants and gazelle, warthogs, and too many beautiful birds to count.

Reese slowed the Land Rover and waved his hand at the scrub brush ahead, shouting over the engine noise. "The camp is just ahead. You'll be bunking with Elsa Schumacher from Germany. I share a tent with John Lucas. We've got communal baths, dining area, research tent. There are about fourteen staff on board at the present."

Alexa's heart sank. She hadn't expected to arrive here in Samburu and immediately climb back into Reese's bed. But a summer camp atmosphere didn't bode well for alone time with her friend and former lover.

Reese brought the vehicle to a complete stop, turned to Alexa, and took her hand. "I'm not sure why you're here. Hell, I'm not even sure why I want you here. But I'm hoping you'll agree to spend a few days together—just you and me. Starting on Sunday, a friend has offered us a tent at Archer's Camp in the Reserve, if you're interested."

"That sounds wonderful. I'm not sure where this is going either, Reese. Maybe nowhere. But I've never felt right about the way I pushed you away . . . the way you left for Africa, practically overnight. I'm glad we'll have some time together to resolve things, if we can."

"So, it's Archer's for a few days, then." Reese said, his expression suddenly changing. He dropped Alexa's hand and said softly, "Slowly, to your right."

Alexa followed the direction of his gaze. Several small tan, antelope-like creatures had wandered into the acacia bushes next to the Land Rover. As she watched, a male with two curved antlers rose onto his hind legs, extended his long slender neck and began nibbling at the thorny branches.

"That's amazing." Alexa whispered.

"Gerenuk. It's type of gazelle—one of the five species endemic to the Samburu area." Reese started the engine and headed into camp.

Alexa couldn't stop smiling at the wonders of Samburu; an antelope that stood on its hind legs like a human and her own mini-safari with Reese at Archer's.

Alexa stepped through the tent flap and gasped. "I thought the tented camps in Tanzania were amazing, but this place is totally outrageous. Look at that bathtub. It's practically Victorian."

"Archer's is the best camp up here in the Samburu. We're lucky Tony Kent had a last-minute cancellation and gave us the gift of a three-day stay."

"Kent? I think I met him on the plane. A rangy, weathered guy with a British accent?"

"That's him. But the accent is Kenyan. His family has been here for more than a century."

The soaring ceiling of the tent was lined with kente cloth. A campaign chest, a leather camp chair, and a huge oriental rug gave the interior an exotic air. Alexa stood on the threshold and contemplated the huge four-poster bed dominating the center of the room.

As if he read her thoughts, Reese turned to face Alexa and wound a hand through her hair. "It's time," he murmured as he tilted her head back and brought his mouth to hers.

Alexa sighed with contentment as she sank into Reese's kiss. The soft terrain of his lips felt like familiar territory—as if Alexa had been in exile and returned home to where she belonged.

"We have hours before the next game drive. I've wanted to make love to you since the moment you stepped off the lane," Reese whispered. He pulled away for a moment, seeking assent.

Alexa began unbuttoning his shirt as she giggled. "Well, then . . ."

Soon, a trail of hiking boots and khaki clothing marked an erratic path to the four-poster bed. Throwing the exquisite quilt aside, Alexa and Reese came together in a rush of longing and passion. Alexa tattooed his muscular chest in pinprick kisses until, gasping with pleasure, she arched her body upward to meld into the thrusting curve of his hips. Oblivious to the roar of a nearby lion, Alexa lost herself in ecstatic reunion with Reese.

"Wow." Reese gathered Alexa into his arms.

"Exactly." Alexa snuggled deeper into his embrace. "I think I'll give Archer's Camp five stars."

"So, it's just the camp you like?"

"Well, I guess it could be the personal guide." Alexa ran her hand down his chest, heading downward.

Reese caught her wrist. "Enough of that, miss. We need to get dressed for the game drive. You've seen a gerenuk, but you have to see the rest of the Samburu Five: the reticulated giraffe, Grevy's zebra, the Somali ostrich, and the Beisa oryx."

"Really?"

"Yes, really. Up and at 'em, sunshine. The bush awaits." Reese planted a kiss on Alexa's forehead and slid out of bed. He looked down at her and feigned a leer. "I'll see you back here—right here—later."

"I'll count on it."

Alexa and Reese ate their last dinner at Archer's Camp on the deck of their tent. Several lanterns sputtered in the middle of the table, scenting the hot night with the smoky tang of burning kerosene. Alexa rested her elbows on the table as she confided in Reese.

"Africa has healed my soul. You know better than anyone how killing Reverend Browne shattered me. At first, I pretended nothing was wrong. I just tried to tough it out. Without your support, it would have been even worse. But I was so screwed up, I drove even you away. I'm sorry." Alexa took a shaky sip of wine and gave Reese a beseeching look.

Reese reached for her hand. "Alexa, you don't need to apologize. Elizabeth Nelson's death brought us together. But building a relationship on tragedy is like building a house on shifting sands. In different circumstances, we could have been good together. But you were trying to deal with a lot of trauma. And I needed to get away from my own mess from Roaring Falls State Park."

"My short time here has been a healing experience. Watching all these animals living each day as if it's their last. The whole life and death drama of kill or be killed. The vast open spaces. It's helped me realize that I need to get over myself. I killed a man, but I did it in self-defense. I think I'm finally ready to move on." Alexa released Reese's hand and leaned back against the leather camp chair. "Did I tell you I found another dead body?"

Reese gasped as Alexa continued.

"One of Melissa's friends. She was a real saint and saved women from sex trafficking. But, this time, I haven't let myself become swept up in the situation." Alexa curled her lip in a sardonic smile. "I'm maintaining my perspective."

"Glad to hear you're doing better. It's so bizarre—you finding the body of another dead woman. But you sound like you're maintaining a healthy distance from the situation." Reese's smile grew wistful. "It's been wonderful to see you, Lexie. Too bad you couldn't bring Scout along."

"That dog misses you so much. I won't mention your name in front of him when I get back. He would be totally pissed to find out that I didn't bring him along to see his favorite forest ranger."

Reese ran a hand through his thick brown hair and swallowed hard. "So, this is goodbye? This gig in Samburu is perfect for me. I might not stay forever, but that saying about Africa getting in your blood—it's true. I'm in no hurry to leave." Reese wrapped his hands around Alexa's.

"How about, goodbye for now?" Alexa managed a wan smile. Aching sadness pressed against her inner breastbone like a balloon filled to the breaking point. "You're free to go your way. I'm free to go mine. I suspect a life together is never going to be in the cards for us. But I'd like to think that maybe, someday, somewhere . . ."

"Let's leave the possibility floating out there in the universe for now. There's an African proverb: 'Love never gets lost; it's only kept.' Even if we never meet again, Lexie, I'll always keep you in my heart."

Long after she and Reese had made slow, tender love in the four-poster bed, Alexa lay awake in the dark tent. She was at peace with leaving Reese. They had reached the best decision. Still, she could not halt the stream of silent tears wetting her pillow as she listened to the bellow of hippos, feeding in the river below.

CHAPTER TWENTY-NINE

"THANK YOU, MISS. You have several hours before your flight leaves. There is a lounge at gate five for premier class travelers if you want to wait there."

Alexa shouldered her backpack and headed through the crowd at the airport check-in desks. Tourists in safari togs stood elbow to elbow with men in brilliant white dishdasha dress and kufi hats. Women in colorful kanga cloth fluttered like bright birds around other locals wearing more subdued Western suits and dresses. A steady hum of voices and activity filled the big hall.

In no real hurry, Alexa cleared security and meandered down the long corridor to explore the airport. Searching the sign overhead for directions, Alexa nearly ran into a young woman ahead of her. The woman seemed to be part of a large group that had come to a complete halt in front of a gate waiting area.

Noticing the Java House opposite the gate, Alexa dashed across the corridor.

"At last, a place that might serve chai tea. I can't imagine they'll have chai in the lounge," Alexa mumbled.

Alexa took a seat at a small table and settled in to enjoy her drink. Java House wasn't up to Om Café standards, but three weeks without chai called for desperate measures.

The group across the way still milled around, somewhat lethargically. Alexa noted that they were all carrying white bags with blue markings like the refugees she had seen when she arrived here on the flight from Tanzania. But these bags said OAM.

Hadn't the other group been carrying bags that said OIM?

Yes. I'm sure it was Organization for International Migration, she recalled. Daniel said they worked closely with many governments and the United Nations. This must be some related outfit.

As she looked at their faces, Alexa registered another difference from the earlier group. These refugees were practically all young women and teenage girls, some little more than children. A handful of boys clustered together in the far corner. And these girls and boys were all strikingly beautiful. Although dressed in mismatched clothes and painfully thin, any one of the group could be groomed for a Vogue photo shoot and appear on the cover.

Maybe OAM stands for Organization for Awesome Minors? I guess I'll never know the answer to this mystery, Alexa mused as she finished the last of her chai.

Leaning over to lift her backpack from the floor, Alexa was shocked to hear a familiar voice across the corridor.

"Get them moving. The plane's starting to board. I've had just about enough of your fucking incompetence."

Alexa couldn't believe it. Jack Nash stood no more than thirty feet away from her, chewing out a rough-looking man with a scraggly gray ponytail. If it hadn't been for his voice, she might not have recognized Jack in his designer safari outfit complete with bandana at the neck. For reasons she couldn't immediately explain, Alexa dropped her backpack and slid her seat back a few inches until she was partially shielded by an artificial palm tree. Traffic had thinned in the corridor, and she could hear Jack clearly.

"Now," he bellowed.

"Hey, mate, you've got to get a grip. Amin will keep them in line. You're going to draw attention if you don't put a sock in it." Unfazed, the man in the khaki jacket and jeans dismissed Jack's anger."

Then a third person appeared, a reedy, brown-skinned man who could have been Indian or Arabic or both. His black uniform looked military, but Alexa couldn't see any markings to identify its country of origin. He moved up and down the line of young women and men barking, "*Uu hore u socdo. Uu hore socdo. Deg deg ah.*"

Alexa had no idea what he was saying, but his words ignited action. In unison, the group shuffled toward the boarding gate clutching their white OAM bags. As she watched the scene, Alexa began to feel a little silly about hiding from Jack. Clearly, this group of refugees must somehow be part of Children of Light's philanthropic efforts. As a new board member, she still wasn't up to date on all of their projects. She concluded that the polite thing to do, when encountering an acquaintance halfway across the world, was to say hello—not cower behind a potted plant.

She grabbed her backpack and jumped to her feet. Just as Alexa exited the Java House, a flood of people coursed down the corridor. By the time Alexa made her way across to the gate, boarding had nearly finished. She caught a glimpse of Jack's back as he disappeared through the boarding gate.

Behind the check-in desk, a woman clad in dark blue spoke into a microphone. "Last call for Flight 920 to Cairo and Toronto, now boarding at gate two."

"That's that," Alexa muttered, somewhat chagrined at her ridiculous behavior. She slipped her backpack over both shoulders and set off to find the lounge.

During a layover in Amsterdam, Alexa extracted her iPad from the recesses of her backpack and took advantage of the free Wi-Fi. During the trip she had only used her iPad for downloading photos, but now she had to prepare for the real world again. With a sigh, she opened up her personal email, avoiding the work account for now.

Hundreds of emails loaded almost instantly, and Alexa began to wade through them. She deleted all the retail offers and requests for donations before she turned to notes from her friends.

Just two days ago, Melissa had written that the police had detained someone in conjunction with Cecily Townes' murder. She attached the newspaper article. The man, a registered sex offender named Clyde Kahn, had a run-in with Cecily not long before her death. State police were also questioning Kahn about the disappearance of several Carlisle area women.

Good news, Alexa thought. Maybe when I get home, I'll find out that Meg Wilson has returned to the Bertolinos as well.

She curled up in the big chair and ruminated. This trip to Africa had been revelatory. She'd had a wonderful time on safari. Plus, she truly believed that she had come to terms with taking Reverend Browne's life. She and Reese had reached a good place with their relationship—one that allowed both of them to move on without regret. Alexa thought about the new men in her life. She couldn't honestly say Quinn Hutton was going to be the move-on guy. Or John Taylor . . . and definitely not Tyrell Jenkins. Regardless, she was anxious to get home, see Scout, and get her life back on track.

CHAPTER THIRTY

"HEY, BUDDY, I'VE MISSED you, too." After a quick nuzzle, Scout's joy at Alexa's arrival home sent him into a frenzy. He leapt off the ground and rotated his giant body in the air in a series of three hundred and sixty-degree turns.

"Enough, Scout. You're going to hurt yourself." Alexa admonished.

"I'm glad I didn't bring the kids along. He might have crushed them both. How would I explain that to Kate?" Graham observed in a sardonic tone.

"Hey, big brother. I appreciate the lift from the airport, but that doesn't entitle you to dis my dog. He's just happy to see me."

"You think?" Melissa drawled. "I could tell he missed you, but things were fine while you were away. I took enough mastiff pictures to do a whole new exhibit."

"Let me get my duffel into the house. I've been traveling for almost twenty-four hours." Alexa inhaled the pine-scented night air and savored it, glad to be home.

"And you're going to tell us all about Africa, right? How's Reese?" Melissa bounced up the steps with her arm around Alexa. Scout darted into the house behind them, leaving Graham to carry Alexa's duffel and backpack.

"No. Let me carry your bags, Alexa," her brother muttered as he climbed onto the deck. The screen door slammed behind Graham as he dumped her bags onto the dining room floor.

"Thanks." Alexa noticed her brother sweating from the effort. "You need to start working out more. Those bags aren't that heavy. Have a beer before you leave, Graham."

"That's an offer I can't refuse."

Melissa headed to the refrigerator. "Jim has some Tröegs Sunshine Pils in here. Might be the last batch of the summer."

They all sat at the big dining room table, drinks in hand. After giving Melissa and Graham a snapshot version of the Tanzanian leg of her trip, Alexa's expression turned serious. "Bring me up to date on what's been going on here. Melissa, I read the article you sent me about an arrest in Cecily's murder."

"I want to hear about Reese."

Graham intervened. "No way. I am not going to sit around and listen to you two talk romance. Lexie, you're right. The police did take this guy, Clyde Kahn, in for questioning. But I don't think they had enough to make the charges stick. I understand he's been released."

Alexa frowned. "Because he didn't do it or because they don't have enough evidence?"

"I'm not sure. Word around the courthouse is that this guy is a real piece of work. Most people know him by his nickname, Boomer."

"Boomer Kahn. Of course. Isn't he the one from Mt. Holly who was luring all the neighborhood girls into his house to play My Little Pony? That was back when we were in high school, right?"

"Eeck. What a loser." Melissa grimaced in disgust.

"Yeah." Graham took a sip of beer. "He went away for a long time on that one. Then he went back in for another stretch for something similar. He's been out of jail for a few years. Apparently, Cecily Townes read him the riot act not long before she was killed. One of her staff remembers that she called Boomer out for hanging around the RESIST office when they were having some sort of training session for young girls."

Melissa brightened. "Oh, the self-image sessions for preteens. Cecily mentioned she'd gotten grant funding to study whether bolstering a positive self-image for at-risk preteen girls could help them avoid falling into trafficking traps."

"What a slime ball. I hope Cecily reported him to the police." Alexa hugged Scout, who was still sitting on her feet.

"I don't think she did." Graham shook his head in concern. "But her staff mentioned it to the police investigating Cecily's death. And I think that social worker—is Jenkins his name? He knew about Kahn hanging around RESIST, too."

"What about these other women? Trooper Taylor mentioned he was working on something related to missing women in the area. But he didn't tell me that the police had connected those incidents to Cecily's murder."

"I don't know much about that aspect. Maybe they just figured someone with Kahn's history could be involved in that, too."

Alexa rubbed her eyes in exhaustion. “But Kahn’s history doesn’t seem to indicate any attraction to grown women.”

“Yeah,” Melissa chimed in. “Sounds like it’s only the little girls who light up his life.”

“Well, that’s everything I’ve heard through the grapevine. And now I have to get home to help Kate put the kids to bed.” Graham downed the last of his beer. “You’re taking tomorrow off, Lexie?”

“You dweeb.” Alexa jabbed her brother’s arm with her index finger. “I’ve been away, but I know tomorrow is the Fourth of July. I need to sleep for at least a day—maybe the whole weekend. But I’ll be back in on Monday. Thanks for the chauffeur service.” Alexa rose to walk her brother to the door, Scout trailing a step behind.

When Graham’s car vanished down the lane, Alexa turned to Melissa, stifling a yawn. “Thanks so much for staying here and taking care of the beast. Did he behave?”

“He was a perfect angel, except for some moping because you were gone. Jim loved spending time with the big guy. I’m trying to talk him into getting his own dog.”

“Are you staying here tonight?”

“Yeah. I figured you’d be pretty out of it because of the travel and time zone changes. So I planned on staying until tomorrow or Saturday. I’ve got some chicken corn soup going in the Crock Pot. Why don’t we have a bowl before you go to bed?”

“It’s nice to be home.” Alexa sighed between spoonfuls of soup. “And what could be better comfort food than chicken corn soup?” The two friends sat on the deck in the waning light. The persistent hum of crickets rose and fell in symphonic waves welcoming Alexa to full summer.

“I made a ton so Jim could take some home. He’s jammed up on early shifts this week, so he’s bunking at his place—especially now that you’re back.”

“Hey, with all the talk of police, I wanted to ask: Have they made any progress on your burglaries? It’s been almost two months.”

“Nope. I’ve checked with both the Carlisle police and the state police. Neither have any leads. The Carlisle cops still think I was targeted because of the publicity around the exhibit. The state police think that’s as good a theory as any.”

“So they’ve ruled out any connection to Cecily’s death?”

“Yeah. I don’t think the cops ever gave more than a passing thought to that idea. And I can’t disagree. Someone who rips off a computer and some camera equipment doesn’t seem to play in the same league as someone who commits cold-blooded murder. I still feel bad about that jackass hurting you at my house."

Scout rose from his nap near the open door and burrowed beneath the table at Alexa's feet. "Please, Melissa. My knees suffered no lasting harm. They've been completely healed for ages."

"At least the insurance came through to cover all but my deductible. And I broke down and got a security system installed at the gallery. I should have had one all along. I'd never forgive myself if one of my artists' original works was stolen because I didn't have enough security."

"What about your house? Did you get a security system there, too?"

An impish smile flitted across Melissa's face. "No. It would be foolish to sink a lot of money into the house when I'm thinking of moving."

"Moving? I thought you loved that house."

"I do, but Jim and I are looking for a place together. And we decided to start out with a blank slate instead of my house or his house. We're already looking at places."

"Wow. That's great. I go away for a few weeks and all of a sudden you're settling down." Alexa's broad smile belied her hurt tone.

"You know, I still haven't come to terms with Cecily's death. But I think it has taught me one important lesson." Melissa raised her water glass in a mock toast. "Carpe fucking diem, baby."

By the end of the workweek, Alexa felt like she'd never been away. Although Brian Stewart had covered her cases while she was on vacation, she was still inundated with work.

At noon on Friday, Melinda popped her head in Alexa's doorway and announced, "I know you told me no calls. All the work-related calls can wait, but you've gotten some personal calls this morning . . ."

"OK, you have my attention. Who called?"

"Your friend, Melissa, called. Twice. That one's a real pistol. Says she must speak with you on an urgent matter. A Quinn Hutton called. He must be one of your New York friends. Sounds like one of those WASP lawyers you used to work with."

"Actually, he lives here in Carlisle and teaches at Dickinson."

"No kidding? One of those academic types?"

"You said several?"

"What? Oh, the other calls. Jack Nash's secretary called. She's going to send you the minutes of the board meeting you missed.

And Children of Light is having a thirtieth anniversary celebration on July 24th. Since you're a board member, Jack asked that you attend. The final call might be more work-related. Tyrell Jenkins wants to meet and discuss Megan Wilson."

Alexa felt terrible that she hadn't checked on the status of Meg's disappearance. "Try to find some time early next week for Mr. Jenkins. Put the Children of Light thing on my calendar. I'll contact Melissa and Quinn myself."

Melinda beamed at her boss. "So should I move this Quinn fellow to my priority call list?"

"Not yet. But I'll let you know if anything changes. We've gone out a few times. I'm not sure it's headed anywhere."

"And Reese . . .?"

"Is in Africa and not planning to return to the States for a good, long time."

The ample redhead sighed. "I've been telling George that you need to get a man in your life. But I guess you can't cross that bridge until you come to it."

As always, Melinda's goofy Pennsylvania Dutch sayings made Alexa laugh. "Enough already. I better call Melissa since she says it's urgent."

Before her assistant made it back out the door, Alexa dialed Melissa's number. "What's so urgent?" she asked without preamble when her friend answered the phone.

"I forgot to tell you. Cecily's brother, Richard, will be in town this weekend to start packing up the house. I told him I would help. He said Maria and some people from RESIST are going to come. And I was hoping you could spend a few hours there with me tomorrow."

"I didn't even know Cecily. I'm not sure how much help I'd be in sorting through her things."

"Lexie, it's more for moral support. For me. I haven't been in that house since the day we found Cecily's body. Richard had all that cleaned up by professionals, but I still need someone to hold my hand. Maybe revisiting the scene of the crime will be cathartic for both of us."

"Cathartic. My God, you've been watching too much Oprah and Dr. Phil."

"You know what I mean. Will you come along—even if it's just for the morning?"

"OK." If it hadn't been for the plaintive note of dread in Melissa's tone, Alexa would have said no. She had no desire to walk into that house again. But, if Melissa needed her support,

Alexa couldn't refuse. "I'll meet you at her house in the morning. What time?"

Alexa couldn't reach Quinn Hutton, so she left a brief message: "Hi. As you gathered, I'm back in town. Sorry I missed you. Maybe we can get together for lunch, and you can fill me in on what I missed at the board meeting. Give me a call."

As she put down the receiver, Alexa reflected that seeing Reese had dimmed Quinn's luster a bit. Not that she was still pining for Reese. Their relationship was over for now—maybe forever.

She and Quinn had never moved beyond a mild flirtation; basically, a couple of dates and a few vaguely interesting kisses. Still, she wasn't quite ready to write him off. But his carefully constructed brand of cool didn't appeal as much to the new Alexa, fresh from Africa's healing juju, as it had to the damaged woman she'd been.

"Maybe that's why I suggested lunch?" Alexa giggled as she returned to the stack of work on her desk.

CHAPTER THIRTY-ONE

"HEY, BUDDY. I AM SO sorry to leave you alone on my first real Saturday home. Last Saturday doesn't count since I slept through most of it. But I'll be home by late afternoon and we can hike over to Weaver's Pond." Alexa hugged Scout and gathered up her work gloves from the table.

On the drive to Cecily's, Alexa practiced deep breathing between each upshift of the Land Rover's gears. By the time she reached the parking area, she felt calm enough to walk into the house. Then a ray of sun reflecting off the glass drew her attention to one of the windows. Suddenly, all Alexa could see was a vision of that same window covered with buzzing flies.

A knock on the hood of the car broke Alexa's dark reverie. Melissa, clothed in bib overalls, yelled, "I'm so glad you came. I couldn't go in by myself."

Alexa eased out of the car before she replied. "Nice outfit. Lambert's Cleaning Service?"

"I got these overalls for a Halloween costume a few years back. Seemed like the perfect thing to wear."

"Now, maybe. What about this afternoon? It's supposed to hit 95 degrees."

"I have shorts in the car."

"Standing out here babbling to each other isn't going to make it any easier, you know." Alexa took Melissa by the arm and strode toward the back door—the one that, last time, had been marred by a shattered window.

Before they could knock, an outdoorsy-looking man in a polo shirt and chinos opened the door. Despite his gray hair, the man looked extremely fit for his age. "Melissa, thank you for coming. And who's this?"

"Hi. I'm Melissa's friend, Alexa."

"Welcome, Alexa. I'm Richard Townes, Cecily's brother. My daughters are inside. I'm expecting Maria Santiago and a few other volunteers from RESIST in a little while."

"So, how can we best help?" Melissa asked as they stepped into the kitchen. Alexa hardly recognized the room. A cheerless staging area of cardboard boxes and stacked dishes had replaced the copper warmth. The artificial smell of pine cleaning products hung over the room as if a tacky Christmas had arrived six months early.

"As you can see, the twins and I made real headway with the kitchen yesterday. I'm tackling Cecily's office right now. The girls took the bedrooms. Maybe you can go upstairs and help with that?"

Alexa breathed a silent sigh of relief; she didn't have to face the office where she had found Cecily's dead body. Melissa seemed equally pleased as she jumped at Richard's words.

"Sure thing. We'll head up there now."

Alexa sneezed at the top of the steps. Stuffy from summer heat, the second floor smelled of dust and the musty detritus of abandonment. Moving through the center hall, Alexa and Melissa followed the sound of young voices coming from a back bedroom. Alexa rapped on the door frame and stepped into the room, Melissa a few steps behind. "Are you the twins? Your dad sent us . . ." Alexa stopped when the two college-age girls looked up.

One girl dressed in barely-there shorts, a midriff top, and combat boots had Asian features, although her purple-streaked spiky hairstyle overpowered her delicate face. The second girl, dressed in running shorts and a quick-dry t-shirt, was compact and athletic. Although her liquid brown eyes, creamy tan skin, and black ponytail hinted at Indian ancestry, the red bindi in the center of her forehead helped confirm Alexa's initial impression.

The two girls registered the confused look on Alexa's face and broke into peals of laughter. The Indian girl spoke first. "Dad always does that to people. He just doesn't think to explain."

The Asian girl interrupted. "I'm Deidre Townes. This is my sister, Sydney."

"Hi, I'm Melissa Lambert. We met at your aunt's memorial service, but I know that was a tough day for your family. This is my friend, Alexa Williams. We're here to help clear out the house."

Alexa regained her voice. "Hi. Sorry, but when your dad said twins—"

"The short version of the story," Deidre replied. "Dad and Mom were unable to have children of their own. So, in their late thirties, they asked Aunt Cecily to find them a family. Through

RESIST, she located two baby girls who were available for adoption at the same time. I came from Thailand and Sydney from Mumbai. Since Cecily brought us to our parents on the same day, they've always called us the twins. They even celebrate our birthdays on the same day."

Sydney lifted a stack of lace from the bed. "I'm so glad you're here. We have no clue what to do with all of this stuff. Are these tablecloths?"

"Yeah," Deidre chimed in. "We decided to start in here . . . sort of work our way up to dealing with Auntie C's clothes. But we're not sure whether this stuff has any real value."

"Well, let's just start to sort through it." Alexa picked up the stack of lace.

Within the hour, the group had worked their way through two of the bedrooms. Alexa had been surprised at how austerely Cecily had lived. With the exception of a few family heirlooms, like the antique furniture and froth of ivory lace tablecloths, Cecily's belongings consisted primarily of bed linens and household supplies. An entire room stored clothing and supplies clearly intended for RESIST's beneficiaries. They left the room with RESIST items for Maria to deal with and tackled the rest, developing a to-be-donated pile and a family keepsake pile.

"Mom couldn't come because she was on-call at the hospital. But we'll talk to her and Dad about some of this family stuff." Sydney pointed to the smaller collection of items.

"I'm going to ask Dad for one of these beds." Deidre laid a hand on an intricately carved headboard. "Remember when we used to stay here in the summer and Auntie C would read us bedtime stories?"

Sydney laughed and told Alexa and Melissa, "Her bedtime stories were not what you might expect. When we were six, she read us the Hindu epic, *Ramayana*. The next year, she chose *The Odyssey*."

The four moved into the central hall connecting the bedrooms and the single bath. "Do you want to take a break? Or are you ready to tackle your aunt's personal things?" Alexa asked.

Sydney and Deidre exchanged a look before Deidre answered, "Let's do it."

Even Cecily's bedroom seemed utilitarian. A cross above the double bed dominated the room's decor. A collection of personal photos hung in a cluster on another wall. In one, a smiling Richard, Deidre, and Sydney posed in a studio portrait with a handsome woman, who must be their mother. An older photo showed Richard and Cecily with their parents. And a triptych showed three groups of people standing in front of RESIST clinics. Alexa recognized the Carlisle site.

Melissa pointed to the other two and identified them. "That's the office in Mumbai; this one is Bangkok."

The one anomaly in the cloister-like cell was the exquisite marble carving ensconced on the dresser. "Oh, the Quan Yin!" Melissa stroked the creamy white statue with her hand. "One of RESIST's most important financial backers gave this to Cecily when we were in Bangkok. She is a Bodhisattva, the Goddess of Mercy and Compassion. Her role in Buddhism is somewhat akin to that of the Mother Mary in Christianity. I looked all over Bangkok to find one just like it. But everything paled in comparison to this beauty."

When the twins found out that Melissa had accompanied Cecily on a RESIST trip, they pummeled her for information. "Auntie C said she would take us both on a RESIST trip when we graduated from college," Sydney offered.

Her expression became downcast when her sister sighed, "Now, that will never happen."

Alexa could see that Melissa was trying to lift their spirits as she regaled them with stories about their aunt in Mumbai and Bangkok. As she listened, Alexa had to admit that Melissa's description of Cecily as a saint was not off the mark.

Soon, nearly everything in the bedroom had been sorted. Alexa reached into the recesses of the long narrow closet and pulled out a large hanging bag. "This looks interesting."

"Do you think she saved her habit from when she was a nun?" Sydney speculated.

Alexa laid the bag on the bed and stepped aside. "One of you girls should open this intriguing package."

Deidre zipped open the old-fashioned clothing bag and drew out three dresses. All four women gasped as she held the first one in the air. It was an exquisite silvery confection of lace and crystal.

"It's beautiful," Sydney bubbled. "It looks like something a flapper would have worn in the nineteen twenties. Maybe it belonged to Grandmére Deidre, your namesake." She confided in Melissa and Alexa, "The Townes are an old aristocratic family. Auntie renounced all that when she entered the convent. Daddy was never interested in all those blue blood trappings either. Look at us—we hardly fit into that mold." She giggled.

Deidre chimed in. "Yes, Daddy inherited all the family money, but he went west and built ski resorts. I guess Auntie C inherited some of the antique furniture and these outrageous dresses." She pulled out a second flapper-style dress with long black fringe and gossamer sleeves.

"I've got dibs on this one, Syd."

"That's fine. I want the silver one." Sydney elbowed her sister aside and plucked the final dress from the bag. When she held it in the air, both girls frowned in disappointment.

"Blah."

"Blah, blah. Nothing special about this one."

Sydney tossed the dress on the bed with a dismissive gesture. Alexa, however, had been struck by the elegant simplicity of this gorgeous black dress. She picked it up.

"No . . . this is lovely. It's a slightly larger size and from a later era. Maybe this one belonged to Cecily when she was young." Looking for the size, she located the label and breathed, "Chanel. It's Chanel."

"I would never think of Cecily and Chanel in the same sentence," Melissa commented.

"Designer labels are just a trapping of the endless cycle of consumerism. Plus the dress is deadly dull," Deidre pronounced.

"Yep." Sydney agreed with her sister. "The dress is too small for our mom. Since you're so crazy about it, Alexa, why don't you take it?"

"I'll admit I'm tempted." Alexa nodded drily toward Deidre. "Despite the whole dangerous cycle of consumerism. But it may be valuable."

"We'll ask Dad, but I'm sure he'll be fine."

Richard Townes appeared in the doorway just as Sydney mentioned his name.

"Of course you should have the dress . . . I remembered why the name Alexa Williams sounded so familiar. You were the one who found Cecily, right?" His voice broke for a moment and the twins looked at Alexa with sad expressions.

Richard recovered then turned to Melissa. "May I speak with you downstairs for a moment?"

Alexa and the girls completed a quick sweep of Cecily's bathroom, throwing out everything but a few unopened toiletries. Finished, they headed downstairs for a break. They took some cheese, crackers, and sodas outside to the table where Melissa and Richard were sitting.

Nibbling on a Triscuit with Brie, Alexa felt the hot sun beat down from directly overhead. She glanced at her watch. Nearly noon. She had hoped to finish her contribution to the packing effort by now and be on her way home. Just then, a van and a pick-up truck pulled into the driveway, and six people spilled out.

A Latino woman dressed in a ratty t-shirt and bright orange headscarf led the group toward the house. She called out cheerfully, "RESIST is in the house."

Richard stood and welcomed the newcomers. "Thanks for helping out. We've got a lot of things packed up that can go to your warehouse. And we can certainly use some help with the attic and basement."

As he turned to lead the group into the house, Alexa caught his attention. "Richard, since the second shift has arrived, I'm going to leave in a few minutes. I've got some things to take care of this afternoon."

He leaned over the picnic table to shake Alexa's hand. "Thanks so much for your help today. I know it wasn't easy to come back to this house after finding my sister's body. If you ever come to Telluride, you've got a place to stay." He took a few steps and turned. "And be sure to take that dress. Cecily wore it to my mother's annual New Year's Eve party the day before she announced she was entering the convent. And, Melissa, I want you to have the Quan Yin as a remembrance of the trip you took with Cecily. The twins told me about its special meaning to you.

"Girls, let's get back to work. That snack should tide you over for a while. We can call to have some pizzas delivered in an hour or so."

After the flurry of activity, the patio seemed silent with just Melissa and Alexa at the table. Alexa noticed that the dark green wheat rippling in the languid breeze had reached its full growth. Harvest would not be far away.

"You have to see this." Melissa interrupted Alexa's reverie by pushing a Kraft envelope across the table. Melissa's name was scrawled in black Sharpie across the front of the big rectangular envelope.

"What is it?"

"Richard found this in Cecily's office. It was at the bottom of a stack of papers and knitting in the big tote she carried to the office.

"Is it something the police should see? Maybe I shouldn't touch it."

"I'm going to call Trooper Taylor. But, hell, Richard opened it. I've touched it. I'll just tell them that you looked at it, too."

Alexa's curiosity won out over better judgment. She wiped her hands on her jeans before opening the flap to find a thumb drive and a piece of paper.

"Remember I told you about Cecily asking for a thumb drive of all the pictures I took in Thailand? She needed to refresh her memory about something? Then, that day at the march in Washington, she wanted to tell me about something disturbing related to the pictures?"

"Yeah. And you managed to get yourself arrested before she could give you any details."

"This note helps shed a little more light on the mystery."

Alexa read the note out loud.

"Dear Melissa,

Thank you for allowing me to review these photos. Several shots in particular helped confirm a terrible truth. About two weeks ago, during an event I attended in Washington, I found a young Thai girl with an important politician in suspicious and disturbing circumstances. I stumbled upon the scene by accident, and my glimpse of the incident was fleeting before I was whisked away.

At first I thought I had misinterpreted what I had seen. Although I thought I recognized this young girl, I was sure she was safe with her family in Bangkok—that I must be wrong. Plus, a man whom I've trusted implicitly hosted the event. I was certain he would never condone the trafficking of young girls for sex.

But, your photos have confirmed my worst fears. The girl is exactly who I thought she was that night at the Willard.

I plan to fill you in during Saturday's march. I know you will be distraught to find that this angel has fallen prey to a trafficking network. Her family must be out of their minds with worry. Next week, I'm planning to call a contact in the FBI to discuss this incident.

In Christ,
Cecily."

"What a fuck up I've been." Melissa moaned. "If I hadn't gotten arrested, Cecily would have told me everything. And maybe she would still be alive."

"Or, like I said before, maybe you'd be dead, too. Do you have any idea what girl she's talking about?"

"No. I took pictures of literally hundreds of young girls and women during the trip."

"What about this reception?"

Melissa rose from the picnic table and began pacing. "No. No idea what reception Cecily attended. She was always going to dinners and receptions to raise funds for RESIST or to speak at events for charities with a similar cause. Sometimes she got awards. A lot of those were in Washington. I guess the police could get a copy of her schedule from Maria."

"Let's go ask Maria now. Afterward, you should call Trooper Taylor about this note."

They found Maria in a second floor bedroom, taping boxes.

"Whew, it's hot in here." Alexa tried to open a window but couldn't get the old wooden frame to budge. She joined the conversation in time to hear Maria respond.

"I would have to check my calendar at the office. But Cecily liked to manage her own schedule for the big events. She usually paid for all her own travel and made the arrangements." Maria scrunched her face in concentration. "Earlier this summer, she went to Washington and Baltimore for a series of events. She got an award from the National Anti-Trafficking Network at some hotel in the Inner Harbor. On another trip, she went to a fundraiser in Washington—maybe for a rape crisis organization . . ." Her voice trailed off. "Or maybe for Children of Light? I can't remember."

Maria set the tape dispenser on the floor beside her and scratched her head. "The Stilson Family Trust held a small dinner with some of RESIST's heaviest contributors. And she met with some people who wanted her help on a documentary. Often, Cecily would sandwich in private lunches or dinners or even breakfasts with senators or congressmen or key staff people—anyone who could help RESIST and the cause. She worked hard when she was in the capital."

"Sounds like it," Melissa agreed, but her tone held a hint of disappointment.

"The state police may have some follow-up questions for you about this, Maria."

"No problem. Perhaps I have more information at the office. Of course, Cecily's calendar would have all the details. She kept everything on her computer so she would have it on her smartphone."

Alexa's heart sank as she remembered the damaged computer in Cecily's office, steps away from her dead body. But perhaps the hard drive had not been compromised.

Back outside, Alexa waited until Melissa had left a message for Trooper Taylor. She picked up her new dress and told her friend, "I'm out of here. Let me know what the police say. This felt like a breakthrough that could help them find Cecily's killer." Though, now, she wasn't so sure.

CHAPTER THIRTY-TWO

TWO COEDS IN THE CORNER carefully placed their coffee cups on the table and stopped chattering so they wouldn't miss a single step of Tyrell Jenkins' glide across the floor. Alexa rose to shake his hand.

"Mr. Jenkins."

"Damn, Alexa. I thought we were past that. Please call me Tyrell."

Alexa smiled, ignoring his comment. "I've been away for a few weeks and was hoping for good news about Meg when I returned."

"No such luck. As far as the Bertolinos know, the police don't have a lead. Personally, I think they've stopped looking. They always thought she was a runaway. Nothing has surfaced to refute that theory. I think they've all but closed the case."

"What about this guy they questioned about Cecily Townes' murder? I heard he has a record as a sex offender."

"It was the state cops who nabbed that pervert, Boomer Kahn. Tell you how fucked up things can be. The Bertolinos actually had a flicker of hope when they heard that sicko had been arrested." Tyrell sighed. "Hope that a suspected killer might have information about their girl. If he did, I doubt it would be good news. But I don't think the Carlisle cops ever questioned him about Megan or Aurora. I hear he's back out on the street now. In-suf-fic-ient ev-ee-dence." He drew out the words in disdain. "Seems like the only time the cops have sufficient evidence is when a brother is the one in the handcuffs."

"So there is no news about Meg?"

"No. Ed tells me that Toni sits alone in her room for hours. They won't say it out loud, but I know they think she's dead."

"I can't imagine what they're going through. The only thing I can do is reach out to Detective Miller once again. From what you've told me, I don't expect to learn anything new. I'm sure he would inform the Bertolinos the minute he got any information about Meg's disappearance."

"Thanks. He'll be straight with you."

Alexa lifted her cup of chai and took a sip. The tea was still quite hot.

Unbidden, the thought popped into her mind: Like Tyrell. Disgusted that she was acting like those two silly college girls in the corner, she straightened in her seat and pushed the thought away.

"How are things at Children and Youth?" She searched for a neutral topic.

"Nothing ever changes. Too many cases. Not enough money or staff. I hear there's a move to try to privatize part of the foster care placement program. Children of Light is pushing for a bigger piece of the action." Tyrell's cup clinked as he plunked it onto his saucer. "That's right. I hear they sweet-talked you into joining the Children of Light Board. What were you thinking?"

"What's your problem with Children of Light? Isn't it one of the key agencies that you folks use for foster care and juvenile delinquency placements?"

"There's no doubt that we need their services. The non-profits don't have enough capacity. But Children of Light doesn't give jack shit about the kids. They're in it for the almighty dollar."

"That's not how I see it. It might be for-profit, but everyone on the board seems quite sincere in their dedication to the clients' welfare." Even to Alexa's ears, her defense of Children of Light sounded a little priggish.

"Girl, Jack Nash could sell snow to Eskimos. It sounds like you bought the snow and the igloo, too."

Even though Alexa was having some doubts about Jack Nash since her trip to Africa, her immediate instinct was to protest anything Tyrell said.

"I agreed to serve on the board and intend to do a good job. Children of Light is about much more than Jack Nash."

"Right . . ."

"If we're finished here, I need to get back to the office." Alexa gulped down her chai and picked up her purse.

"Sure." Tyrell leaned forward. "Hey, I hear there might be a new lead in Cecily's murder. Something about a meeting in Washington."

Alexa was surprised that Tyrell knew about this. News sure traveled fast. "Where'd you hear this?"

"The police questioned Maria about Cecily's schedule."

Alexa refused to acknowledge that she was already aware of this lead. It appeared that Tyrell knew nothing about Cecily's note to Melissa. "I hope this means the police are making progress."

"Me too." Tyrell gestured to the barista for a refill. "I'm going to hang out here for a while. Thanks for meeting."

Alexa rose to her feet. "I'll let you and the Bertolinos know if Detective Miller has any new insight on Meg."

As she walked out the door, Alexa speculated again about Tyrell Jenkins. Was his interest in Meg's disappearance sincere, or was he involved? Striking that he also seemed to be on top of every move the police made in the Cecily Townes investigation. Tyrell was a complex guy. She wondered about all those unresolved issues simmering beneath his dazzling façade.

"I understand you handled the note, so I need to interview you," Trooper Taylor had said when he arranged the meeting. So Alexa was expecting him when the unmarked police car crested the hill. Scout woofed a few times but switched to wagging his tail when the state policeman stepped out of the vehicle.

"Let's sit on the deck," Alexa called. "It's too nice to be inside on an evening like this. Do you want a Coke or iced tea?"

"A Coke sounds good. Do you mind if I take off my jacket?"

Alexa laughed. "Why don't you go all out and loosen the tie, too?" When she returned with two soft drinks, the trooper had settled into one of the deck chairs—jacket off, but tie still in place.

"This place is so peaceful. It must be a great place to live."

"Obviously, I like it. Even home invasion and attempted murder couldn't drive me away. Where do you live?" Alexa perched on a chair at the outdoor table so she could face the trooper. Scout immediately curled up by her feet.

"One of those condos east of Carlisle. When I was first stationed here, I needed to find a place fast so I took what was available. Three years later, I'm still there. I guess inertia set in. At least it's low maintenance. I work a lot of hours and don't have much time for yard work."

"You said you're from State College, right?"

"Yeah, near State College. I went to college in Philadelphia at Penn. After I graduated from the State Police Academy, they stationed me in Wilkes-Barre. They transferred me here a few years later." The trooper straightened in his seat. "But, I'm not here to share my life story. Like I said on the phone, I need to interview you about the note Melissa received. I hear that you handled both the envelope and the paper?" he asked with a disapproving look.

"I know I shouldn't have picked it up, but Melissa and I got carried away. It's like a movie where the victim communicates from beyond the grave with a letter she left behind."

"Not quite like the movies. This note didn't reveal the name of the murderer. It certainly points us in a new direction, but it's not a smoking gun. Can you tell me where you touched the envelope and the letter, your involvement in questioning Maria Santiago, and anything else that is relevant?"

Alexa walked through the entire discovery of the envelope and her handling of the documents. After answering several of the trooper's follow-up questions, she frowned. "Melissa said that Richard found the envelope in a tote bag. I don't remember seeing anything like that when I found Cecily's body."

"It was there, stashed in the corner of the room. It looked like a bag of knitting, and we missed it when we searched the place. Big mistake."

"Have you figured out which meeting Cecily went to at the Willard? That's a pretty high-end hotel."

"Yes. I've learned that it's one of the premier hotels in our nation's capital—a favorite of the political elite. Not my kind of place." The trooper frowned. "I wish I could tell you that we've narrowed down the event Ms. Townes referenced in the note, but we're not there yet. Apparently, the assistant didn't keep Ms. Townes' calendar for out-of-town events. Only the RESIST office meetings. Ms. Townes took care of all that herself. Strange setup, if you ask me."

John shrugged. "Since Ms. Townes' hard drive was stolen the night she was killed, we don't have her calendar. Her cell phone is missing, too. We're trying to trace her meetings through the Willard, but they only track events booked through the hotel.

"Ms. Townes attended two of those, but staff remember that she also took several meals in the Willard restaurant. Since there are no reservations in her name, we have to assume she dined with another party. But she could have walked in on her own, without a reservation. Not to mention they have afternoon tea and a cocktail lounge. It could take awhile to reconstruct those few days she spent in Washington." The trooper sighed.

"I heard that you arrested some guy while I was in Africa . . . that you thought he was the one who killed Cecily." When he sat up at the sound of her voice, Alexa stroked Scout's fur.

"Detained for questioning. We had some evidence to suggest he had threatened Cecily. We also wanted to explore any connection he might have to the disappearances of women in the Carlisle area. Another one went missing last month."

"But you let him go?"

"Yes. As the newspaper reported, Clyde Kahn is a registered sex offender, and someone who bears watching. But we couldn't establish a firm connection to either Cecily's death or the case involving the other women. In fact, we still aren't sure if the missing women are the victims of foul play or just five women who all moved or disappeared on their own."

"That's unlikely, isn't it? Just like those young girls all running away is a pretty big coincidence."

"Young girls?"

"Meg Wilson. Aurora Washington. I don't know the other girl's name. They're teenagers from the Carlisle area. I was assisting Meg Wilson's foster parents with her adoption before she disappeared."

"I know Troop H gets reports of missing children from all the local jurisdictions. I'll have to look into this."

"The Carlisle police have investigated Meg Wilson's disappearance. At this point, I think they've exhausted any leads and think she's probably a runaway. Talk to Detective Hiram Miller." Alexa continued to pump the trooper for information. "At one point, you mentioned that two Thai criminals could be suspects in killing Cecily. Were they cleared?"

"Not exactly. We've confirmed that their organization has a beef with RESIST—although it's not clear that RESIST does enough damage to their trafficking networks to precipitate an assassination of Ms. Townes. But both men have left the country, so it's not possible to question them. Even though the U.S. has an extradition treaty with Thailand, we'd have to build a solid case first. And we just don't have any evidence that they stepped foot in Pennsylvania, let alone killed Cecily. That's still just a theory."

"What a mess."

John's voice became resolute. "It can take a long time to investigate and build enough evidence to make an arrest. But we're not going to give up."

The trooper sat forward in his chair, an earnest expression on his boyish face. Scout wandered over and placed his chin on the trooper's knee, happy when John reached forward to scratch his ears.

"Do you want another Coke?"

"No thanks. You've answered my questions, and I should leave. But," the trooper started, hesitantly. "I wondered about your trip to Africa."

"It was wonderful. Everybody should go on safari at least once in their lives. I haven't organized my pictures yet, but I'll show them to you when I finish. I got some great lions and a sweet shot of a leopard in a tree."

John dropped his voice so Alexa had to strain to hear the question. "And, Reese?"

"I did spend a few days with Reese. It was wonderful to see him."

"Is he coming back to the States soon?"

"Maybe someday, but I think he's in Africa for the long haul. He loves Kenya and is totally excited about the big cat project he's working on."

"So . . . you two are over?"

Alexa gave the trooper an arch look. "Is this going into your report?"

John blushed and stammered as he responded. "You know why I'm asking. It's strictly personal."

Alexa stopped playing games. "Yes. Reese and I are over."

John rose from his chair and crossed the deck to where Alexa sat at the table. He grasped her shoulders and gently drew Alexa to her feet. She was surprised at the ease with which the lean policeman lifted her from her seat.

"So will you go out with me when this case is finished?" His brown eyes gazed down at Alexa with compelling force. "You know I can't date you now. You're a key witness."

"I'm not going to make a binding commitment. It could be months—or years—before you close this case."

"Spoken like a lawyer." John took a step back. "Never a straight answer."

Alexa rested her hand on his chest. "But, hypothetically speaking, I can state that I have no objection to going out to dinner or the movies some night."

John peeled Alexa's hand from his chest and moved closer. "Hypothetically speaking, if I was free to date you, this is what I might suggest after that dinner or movie."

He lowered his lips to Alexa's mouth and kissed her with passionate intensity. After a moment's hesitation, Alexa found herself rising to her tiptoes to meet John's kiss with fervor. As if that first kiss had ignited a fuse, their passion exploded in crescendo of deeper, more satisfying kisses. Alexa melded her body into John's, and he drew her closer still with the insistent pressure of his encircling arms. Finally, she broke away, breathless with surprise at the excitement coursing through her body.

John's eyes darkened with desire; arousal transformed his boyish features into those of a confident, sexy man. Alexa couldn't believe she'd failed to notice how obviously hot this guy was.

“Hypothetically, this kiss never happened,” John whispered in a voice still rough at the edges.

“Hypothetically, this kiss will keep me awake tonight. It will remain between the two of us, but I sure as hell can’t pretend it didn’t happen.”

“Good.” John gave Alexa a crooked smile. “So, it’s a date? Time and place to be determined.”

“It’s a date,” Alexa confirmed as the trooper picked up his jacket and, boyish again, bounded down the stairs toward his car.

When the gray car melted into the gathering dusk, Alexa sat on the deck still reeling from what had just happened. She closed her eyes for a moment and touched her lips. They still burned from John’s kisses.

“Scout, what is it with me and men? Reese and I finally bring closure to our relationship, and two weeks later, I’m jumping into another man’s arms—a state cop, no less. And where does Quinn Hutton fit into this picture?” She thought about that last restrained kiss with Quinn, just before she left for Africa. It hadn’t rung any bells or curled her toes.

Before Tanzania and Kenya, that detached, arm’s-length type of companionship held a measure of appeal. But the sizzling kiss with John tonight obliterated the charm of a merely companionable relationship. Alexa moved Quinn Hutton firmly into the just friends category.

CHAPTER THIRTY-THREE

August 16, 1969

If it feels good, do it.

"I heard the concert is going to start early." Robbie raced headlong into camp.

"Coffee?" At Robbie's nod, Phil poured a cup from the pot on the Coleman stove.

"Who told you that?" Sukie looked up from her little box of cold cereal. "I thought it was scheduled for four this afternoon."

"Some guy. He had on one of those shirts with the guitar and dove—a concert guy. It's got something to do with the weather. Now, the first band is going to play at one o'clock."

Sukie looked at the Timex on her wrist. "That's only two hours away. If we're going to be there at the start, we need to make sandwiches and stuff."

"We've got to stay for the whole concert today, rain or shine. Janis Joplin and the Airplane are both scheduled." Ben leapt to his feet and strummed an air guitar. In a high-pitched falsetto, he sang an off-key chorus from "Piece of My Heart."

Phil and Nina groaned. "Look, we're going to see the real thing today. Don't ruin Janis for me, please," Phil pleaded.

"I was just joking around. I love Janis." Ben stopped screeching his imitation of the rock legend.

Robbie's voice became dreamy. "I love Grace Slick. That woman is pure perfection."

Sukie swallowed a laugh when she saw the glare Cheryl aimed at her boyfriend. She knew from his immediate about-face that Robbie must have caught the look.

"I mean rock and roll perfection, of course. Not like I would want to date her or anything."

The entire group howled at Robbie's lame attempt to dig out of the hole he'd created with Cheryl.

Sukie took pity on the guy. "So where are the peyote twins this morning? Still in the sack?"

"Nope. I looked in their tent when I got up, and they weren't there." Phil twisted the corner of his mouth in a half-grin. "Maybe they're off trying to locate that shaman dude from New Mexico."

"What band is this?" Sukie leapt to her feet next to Nina and began to weave to the sultry rhythm.

"Santana, I think he said. Never heard of them before."

"This music is so cool. Like Latin music and rock all blended into one." Sukie leaned her head back and gave herself up to the music.

When the final Santana song ended, Sukie collapsed next to Ben on their muddy blanket. He flashed her a smile then took a long hit on a joint.

Coughing a little, he held out the roach. "Want a toke, babe?"

"Not right now. I'm high on the music."

"Those guys are far out. I hope they have an album. I'm going to look for one at the record store when we get back home."

After a rambling speech, a folk singer named John Sebastian sang on stage. With the electric excitement of Santana still coursing through her veins, Sukie couldn't quite warm to Sebastian.

Bored, she took a drink from her canteen and reached into the cooler. "I'm tired of sandwiches—especially Lebanon bologna."

"At least we brought food. I heard they're almost out of food up at the top of the hill. Soon, the Hog Farm is going to be feeding half of this crowd." Nina accepted half of Sukie's sandwich.

Several hours and another rainstorm later, darkness had fallen and the crowds had thinned considerably. Robbie suggested the group move closer to the stage. "We've seen a ton of people leave. There's got to be some space down front now."

With Phil and Ben dragging their muddy blanket and cooler, the group made their way through the crowd, inching closer and closer to the stage. Sukie followed, several steps behind, fighting a pounding headache. The level of moisture in the air dampened her clothes and plastered her braids against her neck.

"Up there." Robbie pointed to a space just in front of the stage.

When they sat down, Sukie couldn't believe the fantastic spot. "I feel like I could reach out and touch the Creedence Clearwater Revival. Far out."

When Phil passed around a bowl of hash, Sukie took several hits, hoping the high would erase her worsening headache. A short time later, floating, she tried to read her watch in the light streaming from the stage. "My God, it's past one in the morning," she mumbled. The rest of the group was grooving to "Proud Mary" and ignored her.

In her excitement, Sukie almost forgot her aching head when Janis Joplin took the stage. She was so close Sukie could read the Southern Comfort label on the bottle Janis swigged from between songs. When Janis broke into "Summertime," Sukie closed her eyes for a moment. "This must be a dream," she muttered. But when she opened her eyes, Janis was gripping the microphone only a few yards away, giving every note of the classic song her bluesy, gravelly nuance.

Several songs later, Janis sang Ben's favorite, "A Piece of My Heart." He reached out and hugged Sukie with a huge smile.

A few more songs, and Janis was gone. During the long break before the next act, Sukie's headache roared back in full force. "Hey, guys. I need to get back to camp for some aspirin. I really, really want to hear the Airplane, but I don't think I can make it that long. My head is killing me."

Ben looked concerned. "I'll take you back, babe."

Robbie spoke to Ben. "I'll go with you. We can come back here after she's in the tent."

"No. I can make it back on my own. The Airplane could come on after the next band. I can't ask any of you to miss them for me."

Ben looked up the hill with a worried expression. "That's a hell of a climb if you're sick."

"I have an idea." Robbie looked toward the stage.

A few minutes later, supported by Ben and Robbie, Sukie approached a door in the wall below the stage. Robbie pounded on the door until it opened. Two guys wearing Woodstock t-shirts stood there.

"What do you want? This space is off limits."

"We don't know what to do. My girlfriend is sick." Ben's tone verged on panic. "I think she needs some air. Maybe she's dehydrated or something."

"Did she drop acid?"

"I don't think so."

Sukie got into the spirit of things and sagged toward the ground. Rob and Ben struggled to hold her upright.

"OK," the security guy said. "Give her to us. We'll make sure she gets help." He pushed the boys back out the door and into the crowd.

The man with a long braid guided Sukie to a chair and brought her a glass of water. "Drink this. I'll get someone to take you to the medical tent. Can you walk?"

Sukie downed the whole glass of water before she nodded. "I can walk. I think it's just a terrible migraine. I've got medicine in my tent. I'll be OK."

"I get that you want to do your own thing, but are you sure?" The kind guard looked doubtful. "You seem pretty wasted."

Sukie wondered just how bad she must look. She hadn't seen a real mirror in days. "I'm sure. Can you get me to the road? Thanks for your help. I just need aspirin and some sleep."

Sukie didn't remember much of the walk back to the campsite. Although the water had helped settle her stomach, the pounding in her head had only increased. Sukie knew from experience that the intermittent flashes of light in the corner of one eye only boded more intense pain. Stoned from the hash, she felt like her body was drifting in slow, undulating waves of pain. She nearly tripped several times as she crossed the rough fields.

Surprised when she stumbled into the circle of tents, Sukie sighed in relief. She massaged her temple as the aura from her migraine increased. Then she realized that the light was coming from JJ and Eskimo's tent; it wasn't flashes from the migraine. In a daze, she peered through their open tent flap.

"Willow? What are you doing here?" Sukie stepped inside to talk to the young girl, who was lying on a sleeping bag, gossamer hair fanned around her head like a halo.

Sukie stopped when she caught sight of JJ and Eskimo stretched out on either side of Willow. The thick haze of kerosene and weed created a sulfurous stench that made Sukie cough in the airless tent. "Oh . . . I didn't see you."

A burning joint dangled from Eskimo's mouth. "Where are Ben and the rest of the gang?" Eskimo asked as he passed the joint to JJ. The lantern cast Eskimo in an unsettling red glow as the preppie sat up. Since he hadn't used his hands to push off the ground, it seemed like he'd levitated into a sitting position.

For a moment, Sukie thought he had floated right off the ground. She lurched against the side of the tent.

"Are you alone?" Eskimo raised his voice. In the dim red light, his eyes appeared eerie in their intensity.

"What? Alone? Um, yes. They stayed to watch the Airplane. But I have a terrible migraine, so I came back on my own."

Sukie tried to focus on the conversation but could only think about getting to her own tent for an aspirin. She started to sway on her feet; the tent walls felt like they were closing in.

Eskimo jumped up. "You don't look so good. Hey, I've got something here that works great for migraines. My doctor says it's the best thing to cure a headache. It will help you sleep." He held out two large white pills.

"JJ, toss me that canteen." JJ threw a canteen, and Eskimo snagged in it midair. "Here. You swallow these pills with some water and get a good night's sleep. You'll be right as rain."

"This isn't acid or mescaline, is it?" Sukie knew that both Eskimo and JJ were flying high on some drug, not just grass.

"Absolutely not. Just medicine for your migraine." Eskimo assured her.

The pounding in her temples made it hard to concentrate. Sukie swallowed one pill and took a long drink of water. She was so thirsty.

"I'm going to bed now." Sukie started to back out of the tent, but something made her hesitate. " Is something wrong, Willow?" The girl's eyes were glassy.

JJ prodded the teenager, who shook her head left, then right, almost like a mechanical doll.

Eskimo steered Sukie toward the door. Behind them, she heard Willow's plaintive voice, "Do you want to hang out with us?"

A wave of dizziness struck Sukie, and Eskimo steadied her. By the time they reached her tent, Sukie could barely stand. Eskimo unfastened the tent flap for her. Oblivious to the blast of stale heat that rushed out, Sukie sank to her knees and crawled like a baby toward her sleeping bag. As her eyes drooped closed, she still saw red shadows on the inside of her eyelids. Sukie tried to focus. But all she could muster was a vague sense of apprehension before she passed out, dead to the world.

CHAPTER THIRTY-FOUR

"DETECTIVE MILLER ON THE phone for you," Melinda announced when she buzzed Alexa.

"Oh, good. I was going to call him today. Send the call through, please."

"Ms. Williams, I have some bad news for you about Meg Wilson. Her body was found today near one of the truck stops out at the Middlesex interchange." The detective's tone was grim as he got right to the point.

"Meg is dead? What happened?" Alexa's hand flew to her mouth.

"Middlesex Township Police have taken jurisdiction of the case now, but cause of death is unclear. There are no signs of trauma. The coroner suspects a possible drug overdose."

"Meg didn't use drugs."

"Maybe she didn't . . . maybe the parents just didn't know about it."

Her parents. Alexa cringed to think about the painful impact that Meg's death would have on Ed and Toni. What a tragedy. "Has the family been informed?"

"First thing after Middlesex identified the body. Needless to say, they're devastated. We informed Children and Youth, too."

"Any idea how she ended up at a truck stop months after she vanished?" As the news sank in, Alexa became angry.

"The working theory is she was hooking at the truck stops. Maybe for drug money. Or maybe someone was trafficking her. There's a group out of Ohio that pimps out young girls along the truck stops on the I-81 corridor. There's an interstate task force trying to shut them down—but so far no luck."

"So she wasn't a runaway?" Alexa knew this was why Miller hadn't come to the office to share this awful news.

His tone was defensive. "Maybe not. But she could have run away and gotten swept up by these traffickers when she needed money. I hope the Middlesex police's investigation can get to the bottom of this. But we pursued all the leads we had—and, you may remember, we didn't have a whole hell of a lot to go on."

"Perhaps Meg's death will spur your department to take a more aggressive approach to missing kids in the future. Unfortunately, it's too late for anything to save Megan. Thanks for informing me of her death."

Alexa slammed down the phone and buried her face in her hands. What a fucked up mess. This vibrant teenager—with so much promise and a chance to become a permanent part of a loving family—tricked out to truckers and dead of an overdose.

She wouldn't intrude on the Bertolinos' grief. She would wait until at least tomorrow to contact them. With a sigh, she remembered Tyrell. She buzzed her assistant.

"Melinda, could you call Tyrell Jenkins and find out if I can walk over to Children and Youth to speak to him for a few minutes? Or if he can come here? I need to see him as soon as possible. Tell him it's about Meg Wilson."

Ten minutes later, Tyrell sat in her office with tears running down his face. He'd already heard about Meg's death from his supervisor. Seeing his genuine distress, Alexa now had no doubt that Tyrell's interest in Meg's disappearance and his support for the Bertolino family had been sincere. Still, the depth of his emotion shook Alexa.

He raised his head and accepted the box of tissues Alexa offered. "Some days in this job are glorious—when a child is saved from harm or you see the pure joy on an adoptive family's face when they hold their child for the first time. But there are just too many days like this. All too often, working in child welfare makes me feel like that dude, Sisyphus? You know, the one who pushes the rock up the hill day after day after day."

He wiped his eyes again. "I so wanted to hope that Meg just ran away. And that someday soon she would come back to Ed and Toni, tail between her legs and no worse for the experience. But, damn, that's just not the way the world works. I knew that the longer she was gone the sadder the ending was going to be. I think the Bertolinos knew it, too."

Tyrell placed the Kleenex box back on Alexa's desk and rose to his feet. "I better go alert Reverend Mayne and see what I can do for Ed and Toni."

He looked directly into Alexa's eyes and spoke with barely contained fury. "There is so much evil in the world. Sometimes, I wonder why I continue to put my faith in the Lord and that rock. But I keep hoping. If I can move the rock just a few inches, maybe it will roll right over a posse of those evil motherfuckers and crush them into oblivion."

With those words, Tyrell walked out the door, leaving Alexa standing in the middle of her office, shocked. She felt as if she'd finally met the real Tyrell Jenkins and glimpsed why he'd chosen a career in social work.

Still struggling with the news about Meg, Alexa couldn't muster much enthusiasm for her noon lunch with Quinn. But she shied away from canceling. Unless she counted voice messages, she hadn't spoken to him directly since she'd returned from safari.

Quinn rose from his chair as Alexa made her way through the tightly-spaced tables on the outdoor terrace of Caffe 101. In deference to the hot July day, he'd rolled back the sleeves of his creamy linen shirt in sharply-creased folds. A lightweight sports coat draped over the back of his chair.

Alexa felt the heat, even in her sleeveless sheath dress. Bowing to summer, she'd left her jacket at the office.

"Finally," he said as his lips brushed Alexa's cheek. "I must apologize that it's taken so long for us to get together. I went home for a short visit. When I returned, I became immersed in planning for the upcoming semester. Classes begin in late August."

"And I've been slammed with work. Although my trip to Africa was wonderful, the work piled up while I was away."

Over chicken salad for Alexa and gazpacho for Quinn, they chatted aimlessly. Alexa described some of the high points of her safari. Quinn talked about the lesson plan he was constructing for a new course he was teaching for the fall semester.

"I'm calling it 'Elegies and Eternity: Death and Dying in Western Literature.'"

"Hmm. Do you think a lot of kids will be interested in the course?" Alexa had her doubts.

"Absolutely. When you search for the theme of death in poetry and fiction, it's everywhere. My biggest problem has been deciding which pieces to discard and which pieces to teach. Of course, I'm doing Gray's *Elegy Written in a Country Churchyard* and Thomas Mann's *Death in Venice*. I've settled on Hemingway's *A Farewell to Arms* for the death-in-war text, although I debated about Stephen Crane's *The Red Badge of Courage*. Of course, Crane is so prep school. I'd love to do a semester on death in Eastern literature.

Compare and contrast, all that sort of thing. But my department head is not enthusiastic enough about Eastern literature to go for something so specialized."

"Perhaps today's not the best day for me to appreciate a course with a death theme." Alexa took advantage of a brief pause in Quinn's enthusiastic monologue to steer the conversation in another direction. "Two of my clients lost a child today. Her death is weighing on my mind."

"I had no idea. Of course, let's talk about something else. Shall I fill you in on the board meeting you missed?" Quinn became solicitous.

"Yes. Were there any major decisions that I should know about?"

"I did bring you the materials." Quinn passed her a small binder. "Actually, the meeting was totally uneventful. One of the division managers gave a dull report about the juvenile delinquency program, chock full of statistics and performance outcomes. Ralph Price has come back to work on light duty after his surgery. He gave a report on the planned expansion of overseas adoptions."

"Ralph Price?"

"Oh, yes. I suppose you've not met him. Ralph is actually Jack's right hand man—an Iago to Jack's Othello, if you will. As I mentioned at Jack's dinner party, Ralph was injured in late spring; a car accident, I believe. Needed some serious surgery and recuperation. So Jack has had to take on much of Ralph's work for the past few months."

Alexa almost snorted aloud at Quinn's analogy. She doubted either Ralph or Jack would want to be compared to Shakespeare's legendary shyster Iago and the homicidal Moor, Othello. Despite his air of hip and effortless erudition, it was clear that Quinn worked hard to pepper his conversation with these literary allusions. Today, he was clearly off his game.

"Speaking of Jack, he missed the meeting as well. I can't recall him ever missing a board meeting before. But he was attending an international adoption conference in Brussels."

"Brussels?"

"Yes. I believe he was in Europe for a week or more."

With a side-trip to Africa . . . Alexa kept that thought quiet. Her chance sighting of Jack in Nairobi still made Alexa uneasy. She wasn't ready to discuss the incident with Quinn.

"Quinn, it's been lovely to catch up, but I need to get back to the office. I have several meetings this afternoon."

"Of course. I must run, too. I'm working on this new course and have a lot to do. We must get together again soon. Perhaps another dinner in Harrisburg?"

"It sounds like we're both pretty busy. Maybe in a few weeks? You'll be at the Children of Light anniversary event, right?"

"Oh, yes. Is that next week?"

"Next Thursday."

"I'll see you then."

Because it was such a fine day, Alexa had parked on the other side of the lovely Children's Lake. She gave her reflection in the still water a goofy thumbs up, pleased at her success in sidestepping another date with Quinn. Actually, Quinn's suggestion of dinner had seemed pretty half-hearted. Maybe they could just drift apart without affecting their work together with Children of Light.

CHAPTER THIRTY-FIVE

"Tell me about Namibia. Was it as wonderful as Tanzania?" Alexa's parents had arrived home yesterday and insisted on a Friday pizza night with the entire clan.

Dad looked up from feeding Scout his obligatory biscuit and answered, "Very different landscape. Wonderful animals, and a fascinating tribe—the Himba. We'll tell you all about it over dinner."

"And you can tell us about Kenya . . . and Reese," her mother demanded.

"Gran, when will the pizza be here? I'm so hungry." Jamie tugged at Susan's arm.

Alexa laughed, glad to be together with the family. "You say that every Friday, Jamie."

"Because it's true, Aunt Alexa. I'm absolutely starved for pizza. Pepperoni with lots of cheese."

An hour later, the Williams clan had worked their way through most of three pizzas. Courtney and Jamie huddled on the floor around a game involving dice in a dome that made loud popping sounds when pressed. "Ooh, Scout, you're getting the board wet," Courtney squealed as she tried to shove the dog's big head off the game board.

"Scout, come here," Alexa instructed as Kate went to wipe the board with a paper towel. "Leave them alone."

"It's not like he can hurt the game. I think that one belonged to Graham when he was a kid." Norris consoled Scout by scratching the dog's ears.

"So, it's over with Reese?" her mom asked Alexa again. Clearly, she was hoping for a different answer this time.

"It was wonderful to see him. I think we'll always have a connection, and we were able to get closure, as they say, to our relationship. But it's over. And I'm OK with that."

"Such a wonderful man, Reese."

"Enough, Mom," Graham insisted. "We all liked Reese, including Lexie. But she told you that the relationship is over. If she's moved on, I think you can do the same."

"Spoken like a man." Kate rolled her eyes.

"Speaking of manly pursuits, I think the Phillies are on. Only Africa could make me miss four weeks of baseball." Norris headed for the family room with Graham close behind.

Kate watched her husband leave the room. "Looks like we're here for a while. Susan, can I give the kids a bath and put their PJs on? That way, I can pop them both into bed when we get home."

"Of course, dear. Do you need help?"

"Nope. I've got this. Come on, kiddos. It's bath time." Holding Courtney and Jamie by the hand, she push-pulled the children toward the stairs. As usual, the smaller of the two put up the biggest fight. "Noooo," Jamie whined. "Mommy, we need to finish the game."

Courtney threw a prissy look over her shoulder at Alexa and her grandmother as if to say, "What a baby," even though she was a year younger than her brother.

In the ensuing quiet, Alexa said to her mother, "I'm trying not to be influenced by your story about Woodstock, but I'm starting to have some doubts about Jack Nash. Something weird happened before I left Kenya." Alexa described what she had seen in the Nairobi airport.

"There may be a reasonable explanation, dear. After all, Children of Light has a program for couples who want to adopt children from overseas, right?"

"Correct, but these children were older than the typical adoption age. Mostly teenagers."

"Or maybe Jack's helping out with something for RESIST. I'm sure they're scrambling with Cecily gone."

"Maybe, but the whole thing seemed shady, somehow. And another board member told me that Jack had been at a conference in Brussels—at the same time I saw him in Nairobi. It's just weird."

"Well, don't jump to conclusions unless you have all the facts."

"Yes, Mom." Alexa had heard this same advice from her mother many times over the years. Why hadn't her friends included her in their night at the movies? Why hadn't dreamy

Julio Rodriquez called for a second date? Why hadn't Yale Law sent an acceptance letter? It was Susan Williams' mantra: Don't jump to conclusions unless you have all the facts.

"You know Jack Nash well enough to help me get the facts. I don't want to be involved with Children of Light if the chairman of the board has something to hide."

"Lexie, I told you. I've spent as little time as possible with Jack since Woodstock, even during our last years at Dickinson. My God, that was more than forty years ago. I barely know him anymore."

"There's a big anniversary celebration for Children of Light next Thursday at the Nash estate. Come with me. I want to ask Jack if he was in Africa and see what he says."

Her mother's expression was dubious. "I'm not sure that's the best course of action, Lexie. You've always been a little too fond of the direct approach. My years in politics have taught me that a subtler path usually leads to greater success."

Alexa's face fell in disappointment.

Susan pondered for a moment and continued. "Tell you what. I'll grit my teeth and walk into that man's house if you agree to a more measured approach. We can talk more about it before we enter the lion's den."

CHAPTER THIRTY-SIX

"WON'T YOU MISS THIS PLACE?" Alexa parked the Land Rover in front of Melissa's dollhouse cottage. When she climbed out of the SUV, the hum of bees and the scent of old-fashioned climbing roses brought a smile to her face.

"I will miss it. This place has been perfect for me, living on my own. But it's not big enough for Jim and me. His head practically scrapes those low ceilings in the living room. And we need to start our official life together in a new home."

Alexa opened the back door of the Rover for Scout, but he was fast asleep. "Boy, our little hike knocked this guy out. I'll leave the door open. I have no doubt he'll make a beeline for the porch if he wakes up while we're here." Scout had been to Melissa's many times and knew she kept special, giant dog cookies in the kitchen.

"I got some great shots of the Stony Creek. Can you hold this?" Melissa handed her camera to Alexa and used both hands to turn the key and the knob simultaneously on the old door. "I won't miss this damn door," she muttered as she stepped into the house.

Alexa turned to glance at the car. Scout was still sleeping. She left the front door hanging halfway open so Scout could join them if he woke. Alexa deposited Melissa's camera on a small table inside the door and called, "Melissa. I desperately need something cool to drink. Do you have iced tea or lemonade?"

When she heard no response, Alexa figured Melissa was in the bathroom. It had been a long drive from their hike in the Stony Creek Valley. As she glanced to the left, she noticed the chaos in Melissa's living room. It looked as if it had been ransacked. In alarm, Alexa turned, poised to race out the front door and grab her cell phone. She gasped at the beefy man in a black ski mask blocking her way.

Alexa struggled to remain calm, but panic nibbled at her mind: What was going on here?

"This way," the man muttered as he grabbed Alexa's shoulder and forced her down the hallway, reinforcing his message with a few painful jabs from the ugly pistol in his hand. When Alexa smelled cheap aftershave, she knew she'd met this man once before—in this same hallway.

Alexa gasped when they entered the kitchen. Pans and broken dishes littered the floor. An overturned chair rested on a haphazard pile of books. Alexa recognized the broken spine of the teal fleur-de-lis-flocked volume of Julia Child's *Mastering the Art of French Cooking.* She'd given it to Melissa as a gift last Christmas.

With a flutter of terror, she finally focused on Melissa, sitting in a chair by the kitchen table. Another man in a shapeless charcoal sweatsuit stood behind her friend, a gun trained at her head. This man had made no attempt to conceal his Asian features behind a mask. Although his lank black hair lacked the traditional topknot, he looked like a Sumo wrestler who'd lost a few pounds. He was a massive man.

With a sinking feeling, Alexa realized that Melissa was about to lose it. Although the free-spirited photographer had a sunny disposition, every once in a while something would set her off. And that old saw about redheads with a temper proved accurate with Melissa. When her face flushed scarlet and her eyes flashed, Melissa's anger could be a thing to behold. But a rash action right now could get them both killed.

Alexa caught Melissa's eye, gave an almost imperceptible shake of her head, and mouthed a silent no. But Melissa only widened her eyes in disagreement.

"What's going on here?" Alexa blustered, trying to calm the situation. "What do you want?"

"We'd hoped to find it in the house," the Asian man replied without taking his eyes off Melissa. He waved his gun in Melissa's face. "But it looks like Red here is the only one who can help us find what we're looking for."

"What's this about?" Alexa moderated her tone.

"Cecily Townes."

"Screw you," Melissa hissed and snapped her head around to look at the burly man. "Are you the ones who killed Cecily?"

"Didn't have the pleasure. We were just hired for clean up."

Alexa went cold at the confirmation that these men were professional criminals. Maybe they were from the Thai trafficking syndicate that John Taylor had mentioned. She and Melissa were caught up in something they didn't fully comprehend. But it was clearly dangerous and getting worse.

Sumo man unleashed an evil-looking smile at Alexa. "Now you, honey, are a gift. You might be the wild card that gets this little hellcat to talk."

He nodded at the silent man behind Alexa. Alexa turned enough to see her assailant holster his gun and pull a huge folding knife from his pocket. She gasped a ragged breath, tensing for the coming slice of the knife.

At that moment, the soft click, click, click of dog toenails on wood approached down the hallway. Scout was awake and had entered the house.

She caught Melissa's eye and hoped her friend would understand as she mouthed the word "Scout" and inclined her head toward the hall. Then, everything exploded.

Screaming like a banshee, Alexa chopped the thug's wrist. The unopened knife clattered to the floor as Alexa leapt toward her friend.

Melissa catapulted her chair backward into her captor's midsection and ducked beneath the big farmhouse table. Caught off balance, the huge man grabbed at a large hutch to keep from falling.

"You bitch," the man in the ski mask roared as he tried to seize Alexa.

"Get off me!" Alexa yanked away and shrieked again, eyes searching for the fallen knife.

Gentle Scout reacted to the panicked tone of his mistress' voice and dashed from the hallway to charge her attacker. The terrified man scuttled like a crab across the kitchen floor with Scout in pursuit. His gun dropped out of its holster and skittered under the stove. Scout bit into the man's thick calf, shaking his head back and forth like he was playing tug with his rope.

"Get this fucking animal off me," he pleaded to his partner.

"Off, you goddamn monster." The Asian spokesman recovered from Melissa's shove, scrambled back onto his feet, and took aim at Scout.

Alexa picked up a glass pitcher from the table and hurled it in Sumo man's direction. "Scout, come," she commanded, trying to get the dog out of harm's way.

The man ducked the pitcher, but the distraction gave Scout just enough time to ignore Alexa and launch an attack at the Asian man's crotch. Cursing, he again turned his gun at Scout.

"No!" Alexa protested just as Melissa popped up from beneath the table and slammed the blade of the open knife into the man's gun arm. His pistol dropped to the floor, and Melissa scooped it up. Across the kitchen, the guy in the ski mask was moaning and trying to sit up.

Both men were injured and bleeding, but Alexa didn't think either one was out of commission for long. "Let's get out of here," Alexa yelled. "Scout, come."

Melissa clambered out from beneath the table, gripping the pistol. This time the dog obeyed Alexa's command, and all three raced out of the house, slamming the door behind them. The minute Scout jumped into the back of the Land Rover, Alexa pushed the tailgate shut. She gunned the engine as soon as Melissa plopped into the passenger seat and took the quickest route to the road, driving straight over the lawn.

Out on the road, Alexa floored the gas. "Call the police," she gasped at Melissa. "My phone's in the console."

Five miles down the road, Alexa turned into the Sheetz gas station and convenience store, crowded as always. She closed her eyes for a moment and tried to control her breathing.

"The police are on their way." Melissa burst into tears, the confiscated pistol still clutched carefully in her hand. "Did you see what those bastards did to my house? Liars. They probably are the animals who killed Cecily. What do they want from me? Why does this keep happening?"

Alexa patted Melissa's shoulder until a cold nose lifted her arm. Scout had a bewildered expression on his face. "Oh, baby dog. Thank you for saving us. I wasn't sure you had it in you, but you gave those two assholes a run for their money." Alexa turned and hugged the mastiff.

"Good boy," Melissa kissed the bridge of Scout's nose. "You lived up to your mastiff heritage. Didn't they use ancient mastiffs to fight gladiators and elephants—or was it bears?"

"All three, I think. But this guy has never hurt a flea. I guess his protective instinct kicked in. Lucky for us." Alexa shuddered. "I hate to think what could have happened without him."

Melissa said in a flat voice, "That does it. I'm going to pack up what I need and leave. I'll pay someone to come in and clean up the mess and sell the house as soon as I can. I'll never spend another night in that place. I'll stay at Jim's until we find a new house."

After another round with the police, Alexa and Scout finally made their way home. Alexa stopped at the foot of the South Mountain at Keck's store for a sandwich. While she waited for the turkey sub, she walked the worn wooden floors, cruising the shelves for junk food. She barely had enough energy to exchange the usual pleasantries with the store's proprietor.

"Thanks, Doris. Scout and I have had a long day. He's out in the car waiting. This sandwich will be perfect. I'm too tired to even think about cooking. "

The aftermath of the melee at Melissa's house didn't fully hit Alexa until she walked into the cabin and started to shake. But when she noticed Scout hunched over with his tail between his legs, concern for the dog took over.

"You don't know whether you did a good thing or a bad thing in attacking those men, do you? You were a good dog, buddy. A hero dog who saved the day." She collapsed onto the couch and snuggled under an afghan for warmth. She was cold despite the ninety-degree day.

"Come here." Alexa patted the rug beside the couch. When Scout sidled toward the couch and lowered his big body onto the floor, Alexa hugged his head and continued to try to soothe him with a stream of soft words.

"You did save us. You were a good dog to bite them because they were bad men. The police took them away and will lock them up for a long time. Melissa is safe and sound at Jim's house. We all survived with nothing but scrapes and bruises. Grandma Williams used to say 'You'll be black and blue tomorrow.' I imagine we'll both have some aches and pains tomorrow. I should probably have Dr. Buck check you out, just in case you broke a tooth or something." Alexa grabbed the dog's snout and looked into his mouth. "I don't see anything, but I think I'll take you in . . ."

Alexa fell asleep in the middle of the sentence. When she woke, dusk had fallen and Scout was snoring, still lying on the rug beside her. She called her parents in case they saw something on the news about the afternoon's ordeal.

"I'm fine, Dad. Melissa's not hurt, but she's shattered at the way they trashed her house. I'm afraid for her. Whoever killed Cecily seems to think Melissa knows or has something relating to Cecily's death. I don't think she'll be safe until the police figure out what's going on."

Norris suggested, "Maybe these two brutes will talk now that they're in jail."

"Not that I've had a lot of experience with this type of thing, but they seemed like professionals to me. One guy could have been Thai."

"Which makes me wonder, what has Melissa gotten herself mixed up in?"

"I know, Dad. I'm worried about her safety."

"And I'm worried about yours. I'm losing count of the number of times you've been interviewed by the police. This is the second time you've been assaulted in a little over a month."

"It's like the other time at her house. They weren't after me. Melissa is clearly their target."

"You still need to be careful. Why don't your mother and I come out to the cabin tomorrow. We'll bring lunch. I'm sure she's going to want to see for herself that you're OK."

"That sounds good, Dad. I'll see you tomorrow."

CHAPTER THIRTY-SEVEN

Brian Stewart walked into the break room where Alexa was making herself a cup of tea. "Williams. I just heard Melinda searching for you over at my end of the office. Something about a policeman looking for you." He smirked. "That offer about legal representation still stands. With the parade of local law enforcement in and out of your office, it's only a matter of time before they charge you with something."

Alexa's heart flip-flopped when she saw John Taylor standing in her office. She couldn't help but remember both the scorching kiss and their agreement to treat it as 'hypothetical.'

"Trooper." She offered her hand.

"Ms. Williams. I'm here to follow up on the incident at Ms. Lambert's home on Saturday. I am assisting Trooper Cannon and investigating ties between that incident and Cecily Townes' death."

They sat side by side in front of Alexa's desk. After walking Alexa through everything that had happened once again, Taylor commented, "You and Melissa did a real number on those guys. Scout did enough damage to slow both of them down. I hear the one guy's leg was pretty ugly. Judging from the toothmarks on his inner thigh, the other one dodged an even uglier fate. They hadn't even made it to their car when the troopers arrived. I'm glad Cannon caught the assignment on Saturday. I don't know what I would have done, seeing those bastards on the scene and knowing what they tried to do to you. Are you OK?" He touched Alexa's wrist.

"I'm fine. I really am," she reassured him, hastily withdrawing her hand as Graham burst into the room with a perfunctory knock on the closed door.

"Trooper Taylor." Graham nodded and threw a peeved look at his sister.

"I thought I should be present if Alexa is being questioned." Rather than taking a seat, Graham stood, hovering over Alexa and the trooper.

"This is just a routine follow-up to Saturday's incident." John pushed his chair back to look at both Alexa and Graham as he spoke. "Sometimes victims remember additional details in the aftermath of a crime."

"We're nearly finished." She looked at the trooper. "Right?"

"Yes. I do want to advise you to exercise extreme caution. There is no specific reason to believe that these men were targeting you. It appears that their interest is in Ms. Lambert. However, Alexa, you have been present at three incidents that may relate to Cecily Townes' death. You were with Melissa when you found the body. You were assaulted during the first break-in at Melissa's home, and you narrowly escaped harm on Saturday."

Graham's expression was grim. "If Scout hadn't been there, you and Melissa might both be dead."

"But we're not. We trounced their asses."

Graham raised a skeptical eyebrow. "Who exactly trounced their asses?"

Alexa's voice faltered. "Mostly, it was Scout."

"Right."

John's look of concern had not wavered during the brother-sister exchange. "Was the dog injured?"

"No. The vet checked him out first thing yesterday morning. Opened up the office on a Sunday. Scout is fine."

"Glad to hear that. We understand that Ms. Lambert has left the country for a week or so."

"Yeah, Jim took her to the Greek islands. They moved up their scheduled trip a few weeks. His boss was quite understanding about taking time off even though this is peak season for the park."

"I'm not suggesting that you need to leave the country. But, until we can get our suspects to cooperate or make further progress in our investigation, you need exercise caution at all times."

Graham gave Alexa another pointed look.

"Message received, guys. I sure don't want a repeat of Saturday or anything close to it. The cabin has a security system —plus Scout. I promise not to go wandering off on my own while this is still up in the air. I will be careful. John, I hope you catch whoever is behind all of this. Soon."

"Yes. Let me walk you to the door, Trooper." Graham hustled the policeman out of the office, leaving Alexa alone to consider the question: Was she in danger?

CHAPTER THIRTY-EIGHT

August 17, 1969

There's always a little heaven in a disaster area.
—Wavy Gravy

Raised voices outside the tent woke Sukie. She rubbed her eyes and tried to separate her parched lips. The air in the tent was stale and warm.

"I'm so thirsty." She flailed about for her canteen but couldn't locate it. So she decided to go outside and see what all the commotion was about.

She rolled out of her sleeping bag and realized she was fully dressed.

"You must have been totally wasted when you went to bed last night," she exclaimed to the empty tent. As she untangled her braids and ran a hasty brush through her hair, Sukie tried to remember the night before but was drawing a big blank. She climbed out of the tent, hoping some fresh air would clear the cobwebs from her head. And she needed water.

In the middle of the campsite, Robbie stood toe-to-toe with Levi Bloom. His bandmates, Manny and Diesel, flanked the singer. Robbie's tone was belligerent. "I told you, man. The five of us just left the concert. We stayed up there until the Airplane finished. We were eating breakfast until you guys showed up. None of us have seen Willow.

Phil hurried over to stand by Robbie. "Wasn't she with you?"

"No. She stayed back while we went to the concert. I told her not to wander around alone at night, but we thought she might have come over here."

Ben looked up at the sky. "News bulletin: it's morning now. I'm not sure why you're so freaked out. The kid probably woke up and headed to the Hog Farm for breakfast. Have you checked over there for her?"

"What's going on?" Sukie asked. The group had been so involved in their conversation, no one seemed to notice her emerge from the tent.

Nina responded. "Willow's missing. Levi and his group are worried."

"Can I get some coffee? My head's so fuzzy that I can't think. You say Willow's gone?"

"Babe, how's the headache?" Ben rushed over and kissed her forehead. "You still look a little rough around the edges."

"Smooth, Ben. What a way to hand out the compliments." Cheryl handed Sukie a cup. "Coffee, but there's no more milk."

"Thanks." She turned back to Ben. "The headache's gone." Like seeing shadowy forms in the dim light of a tunnel, she recalled snatches of the night before. She remembered leaving the concert area and trekking back to camp. Seeing a lighted tent.

"Oh, that's right. Eskimo gave me a pill that knocked me out. It was pretty strong, but no more migraine."

"When did you see Eskimo?" Ben asked.

"It must have been when I got back here. I can't really remember much. I think JJ was with him."

Levi looked at her. "Did you see Willow?"

Sukie turned to the tall musician. "I don't think so . . . Or maybe she was there, too, with JJ and Eskimo? Yes, I think I saw her?" Sukie shook her head. "Wow, I can't believe that everything is such a blur."

"This is important," Levi barked."Maybe she's still with those two." He addressed the group. "Have you seen them this morning?"

"No, but they'll show up eventually." Phil rolled his eyes.

Nina looked at Sukie before she turned to Levi. "Did you check out the shops in the woods? Willow was telling Sukie and me about a guy there who invited her to get high."

"Yeah. She said the guy was older with a black braid. She didn't give us a name. Hey, I'm sorry that I can't remember what happened. My brain is still fried." It scared Sukie that she was blanking on several hours of her life.

Robbie spread his hands out in a conciliatory gesture. "Why don't you guys sleep for a while? That's our plan. By the time you wake up, Willow will probably be back."

"OK, people." Levi sank back into his usual laid-back persona. "We're tired. Maybe we overreacted. But I feel responsible for the

kid. She didn't even tell her mother she was leaving the city. We'll check in later." He led his group back to the bread truck.

"That was strange." Robbie dug into a carton of dry Kix cereal.

"I'm not sure why they're concerned now. The kid's been floating around on her own for most of three days." Nina poured the dregs of her coffee into the fire pit. "She's probably at the Hog Farm learning more about communes."

Cheryl laughed. "It wouldn't surprise me if Willow has already booked a seat on the Hog Farm bus when it leaves here."

Ben drew Sukie aside. "Are you sure you're OK? I feel guilty that I let you leave on your own last night."

"I must have been pretty convincing when you shoved me through the door in the stage. A security guy tried to take me to the medical tent. But I talked him out of it and made it back here fine. Then Eskimo gave me this pill that completely knocked me out."

"What kind of pill?"

"He said it was for migraines. He gave me two, but I just took one." Sukie dug into her front pocket. "Here's the other one."

Ben examined the pill. "That preppie fucker. This isn't headache medicine. He gave you Ludes."

"What?"

"Quaaludes. They're a pretty strong sedative. People take them to come down from uppers or sometimes just for a mellow high. It's good you didn't take the second one. You would still be out cold."

"I should never have trusted him. There's something about the guy that's a little off."

Ben rubbed his red-rimmed eyes. "I'm dead on my feet, babe. I've got to get some sleep. Wake me up in a couple of hours, and we can go back to the concert."

Sukie followed Ben into the tent. "I'm still feeling pretty fuzzy. Maybe a few more hours' sleep would help me, too."

When Sukie and Ben rolled out of the tent around one o'clock, Nina and Phil were lounging by the van. The skies had turned gray again; the earlier sunshine was gone.

"Good afternoon, sleepyheads," Nina chirped. "Is your migraine all better, Sukie?"

"Yes. And, I don't feel fuzzy anymore from that pill I took last night."

Ben made a beeline for the boxes of food in the van. "What's left to eat?"

"Not a whole lot." Phil joined him and began rifling through a box. "We've still got some Hershey bars. Lots of baked beans."

"Bonanza. Ham." Ben waved a tin in the air. "Can we open this up or should we wait for dinner? There are two more cans left."

"Let's go for lunch. We might be up at the concert at suppertime. Here's some bread to go with it. And some canned peas."

The two boys lit the Coleman stove. Next, they peeled the cans open with the built-in keys and began carving chunks of ham into a frying pan.

"Do we have enough food to make it through tomorrow? The concert should be over tonight. We originally talked about staying here tonight and leaving tomorrow morning." Sukie walked to the van and peered into the boxes.

"We should probably have a group pow-wow to figure out what we're going to do. A lot depends on when Robbie wants to try to drive out of here. The roads could be crazy tomorrow morning."

"Robbie and Cheryl are still asleep. Big surprise, JJ and Eskimo aren't around." Nina assembled some paper plates and silverware.

"Did someone call my name? Or maybe it was the smell of frying ham." Robbie bounded out of the tent. Cheryl trailed behind.

"We were talking about leaving." Ben flipped the ham slices.

"Not until I hear Hendrix. 'Foxy Lady.'" Robbie twirled around and kissed Cheryl on the cheek.

"Of course. But he should end around midnight or so. The question is: Do we hit the road early or do we wait for some of the traffic to clear?"

"Just in time for lunch," JJ exclaimed as he and Eskimo appeared from behind the van. "I could eat a whole ham by myself."

Phil grabbed the other cans from the box and opened them. Nina assembled more plates and silverware.

"Feeling better, Sukie?" Eskimo bent over and peered directly into her face. Without waiting for an answer, he stood and addressed the group. "You should have seen this chick last night. She had one serious hurt going on."

Ben turned from the stove. "And you gave her Quaaludes, you bastard. She thought you gave her aspirin."

"Back off, bro. There's nothing wrong with dropping a few Ludes to take the edge off. I was doing the sister a favor."

JJ jumped in. "Seems to have worked. No harm, no foul, right?"

Sukie rose to her feet. "Levi Bloom was over here looking for Willow this morning. Do you guys know where she is? Was she with you last night?"

Eskimo shot her a strange look. "Don't you remember?"

"Everything's sort of a blur."

He shrugged his shoulders. "She was here for a few minutes, but we haven't seen her since she left our tent. It wasn't long after you stopped by for your medicine."

"Did you see her anywhere today?"

"Fuck. Do we look like babysitters to you, Sukie?" JJ snarled. "We haven't seen the kid since last night."

Robbie asked, "Are we sure she's still missing?" He looked at his wristwatch. "Levi was here hours ago. She's surely back with them by now."

"You're right. I'll check later." Sukie tilted her head at a distant sound. "Is that music?"

"The concert's starting." Ben stepped away from the stove to listen. "I'm not sure who's playing."

"After lunch, we can get things together and head over." Phil looked at Nina.

"Let's pack plenty of sandwiches and water," she suggested.

As the group finished lunch, Robbie stood. "So we need to agree on a plan for tomorrow. I say we sleep in and let the crowd get out of here. Maybe we pack up the tents in late morning and get on the road a little after noon?"

Sukie gathered up the empty plates and silverware. "That's fine with me. I don't have to be back at work until Wednesday."

All around her, the rest of the group nodded in agreement with Robbie's plan.

JJ cleared his throat and looked at Robbie. "Hey, man, Eskimo and I won't be going back with you all. We're leaving today."

"We ran into some friends, and we're going to catch a ride back to my house with them," Eskimo offered. "They're guys who JJ and I went to prep school with. It'll be a blast to spend some time with them on the road."

JJ plucked at a daub of mud on his jeans. "I haven't seen my parents all summer, so it seemed like a good chance to drop in on them. I borrowed the tent from Ben. We'll tear it down before we leave."

Sukie raised her eyes to the heavens in a gesture of thanks. She would be so glad to get rid of these two jerks. Plus, it meant more room in the van for the trip home.

Eskimo stood and looked at JJ. "We'll get started now. Our friends are leaving in an hour or so."

As they washed the silverware, Sukie whispered to Nina. "I'll be glad to see those two go."

"There's something they're not telling us. Eskimo and JJ just ran into these friends who offered them a ride? More likely, they

got a deal on mescaline with that shaman, and they're actually going out West."

Sukie giggled. "Or they were getting high with Edgar Winter and he offered them space on the helicopter out of here after his set."

Then she sobered. "I don't think I've heard Eskimo say that many words at one time since we got here . . . almost like he was nervous or something. There is something fishy about this whole thing."

"Or stupid. Who passes up a chance to see Hendrix play live?" Nina dropped the skillet into the dishpan with a splash.

JJ and Eskimo packed and left in lightning time. As she watched them rush toward the road, Sukie turned to Ben. "Outta sight. Outta mind. Those two are a drag."

"JJ's a pretty solid guy, but I can't figure out why he's friends with Eskimo. That bastard treats JJ like some flunky."

Sukie tossed her head back and declared, "Enough of JJ and Eskimo." She grabbed Ben's hand and pulled him toward their tent. "Let's get ready for some music. We already missed the first act."

They were just steps from the tent when the skies let loose. Rain streamed down in torrents, and thunder rolled across the meadow. Sukie and Ben dove into the tent to escape the storm.

"So much for the music." Ben fumed.

Sukie crawled to the tent flap and looked out. Lightning flashed in the distance, and the downpour had increased in intensity. When she looked toward the van, she caught movement in the corner of her eye.

She gestured to Ben. "Come here. You've got to see this."

Robbie, dressed only in his boxers, was walking around in circles, quacking like a duck. When he saw his friend, Ben stripped down to his jockey shorts and jumped out to join Robbie. Laughing hysterically, Sukie pulled off her jeans and tumbled out of the tent in her cotton peasant blouse and panties. Minutes later, Nina, totally naked, and Phil, wearing only his glasses, joined the rain parade.

Sukie tilted her head back so the water streamed over her face and hair. "This feels so wonderful to wash off all the dust and mud."

Nina broke into song. "It's raining, it's pouring . . ." Soon, the whole group was chanting the old nursery rhyme.

"That's enough." Sukie shook her head. "I'm getting cold." She ran back to the tent with Ben on her heels. Inside, Sukie peeled off

her wet clothes and tossed them in a corner. Ben pushed her back onto the nest of sleeping bags and grabbed a towel. Moving the towel from her face to her hair to her arms, he began drying Sukie.

When he reached her torso, Sukie tugged the towel from his hand. Heart pounding, she slipped Ben's wet jockeys down his hips and over his feet. With the towel, she traced the route northward from Ben's feet, skimming his legs until she reached his erect penis.

When Ben tossed the towel aside and pressed her back onto the sleeping bag, Sukie's breath caught in anticipation. Then she plunged into a whirl of passion, wet flesh, and the staccato beat of rain on canvas.

"Wow." Ben sprawled onto his back. "That was fantastic, babe."

Sukie snuggled closer and rested her head on his outstretched arm. "Better than listening to another band."

"Totally." He paused. "Except for Hendrix."

Hurt, Sukie sat up so she could see his expression. "A joke, right?"

"Hey, babe." Ben caressed her hand with his thumb. "Since you're sitting up, could you toss me that pouch of weed over there?"

Sukie sighed and fished Ben's stash from his backpack.

CHAPTER THIRTY-NINE

"YOU LOOK LOVELY, DEAR," Alexa's mom remarked as she stepped up onto the deck. "Good idea to take one car to this gala event." She grimaced. "Maybe a glass of wine before I have to face Jack Nash?"

"Mother, you act like this is the biggest ordeal of your life. How many boring political dinners have you attended? Countless hours in rooms full of windbags and hangers on? You can survive a brief encounter with Jack."

Susan walked into the cabin and came back with a brimming glass of white wine. She waited until she was seated before she took a sip from her glass. "The heat and humidity struck with a vengeance today. It's even warm out here in the mountains."

Alexa finished her glass of iced tea and set it on the table with a thunk. "I appreciate you coming with me, Mom. Whatever Jack was doing in Kenya looked sketchy. And I don't want to stay with Children of Light if they're involved in illegal adoptions or something worse."

"I'm still not clear how you expect me to help. It's not exactly like Jack's nose is going to grow if he's lying. Besides, my clutch is too small for a tape measure." Susan waved her small purse at her daughter.

"You know it's a sign that you're spending too much time with the grandkids when you start using Disney movies as a frame of reference."

Susan shrugged. "But you get my point. I've avoided Jack's company for more than forty years. Woodstock was the only extended time I ever spent with him. I'm probably the last person on earth to know if the man's lying."

Alexa rolled her eyes and jumped to her feet. "Just watch his expression when I ask him about Africa. Then we can compare notes. Are you ready?"

Susan gave Alexa a mock salute with her empty wineglass. "Scout, get in the house. We're leaving."

Alexa stopped the Land Rover at the little guardhouse and handed the unsmiling security guard her invitation.

"Name?"

"Alexa and Susan Williams. I'm a board member."

He slid a nasty-looking gun aside to uncover a piece of paper. He ran his finger down the sheet, stopping near the bottom. Handing back the invitation, his voice officious, the guard finally said, "OK, Miss Williams. You may proceed. Enjoy the party."

His dour expression made Alexa doubt the sincerity of those last words. When she'd been here before, the guards on duty at least seemed human.

"Isn't this a bit elaborate for rural Cumberland County?" her mother sniped as they drove through the open gate.

"The AK-47 or Uzi or whatever that gun was does seem a bit over the top. But some of the Children of Light facilities up here are for juvenile offenders. It's not a youth development center, but who knows what some of those kids might have been involved in before they came here. So they've got this guard post. You saw the fences when we drove by on Pine Road. I understand the entire hundred-plus acres is fenced."

"Seems excessive to me. Why not just enclose the secure facilities?"

Alexa shot her mother a smart-alecky smile. "They probably got a county grant. Economic development money or something."

A bevy of young boys in the Prussian blue jackets were parking cars. Alexa didn't see the breezy attendant from the last event. A polite new kid took her keys. Alexa winced as the boy ground the Land Rover's gears when he pulled away.

"Well, well," Mom observed as she took in the Italianate villa.

"Wait until you see the rest," Alexa answered with amusement.

The moment they entered the foyer, a teen in a blue dress assigned them to a tour group. "We're asking all the guests to take a brief tour before joining the reception. Children of Light is proud of the campus and wants our guests to get a glimpse of the work we do." The girl recited the lines as if she'd practiced them for hours.

Alexa sighed. She was focused on finding Jack Nash, not wasting time on some public relations tour.

"I'm glad I wore flats." Susan looked down at her black ballerina slippers. She confided, "I figured we'd be doing a lot of standing, and these have secret Nike air technology."

"I don't have the benefit of all that high-tech padding, but I'm right there with you." Alexa lifted her foot, clad in a fashionable Mary Jane with a substantial sole. "These are all the rage this year."

As they shuffled along the hillside in a group of twelve, Alexa became engaged in the tour despite her original objections. When she had joined the board, she'd only received an abbreviated introduction to Children of Light's physical plant.

A reedy teenage boy with terrible acne and a blazer in the standard blue walked the group through one of several small, homey-looking buildings, which he described as foster care group homes. Back outside, he brought the tour to a halt and gestured at three large buildings. "The first building to your left is the boys' transitional dorm. The second is for the girls." He pointed to a smaller building surrounded by a high wall. "That's the secure facility for juvenile offenders."

Alexa noticed that beyond the secure building, the paved road ended but a dirt road continued up the mountain. "Where does that road go?"

"I believe it's just a fire access road, ma'am. But it's off limits to the residents." He turned and led the group onto a stone path that skirted the upper lawn.

A nudge to her side interrupted Alexa's attempt to come to terms with the fact that she'd just been called ma'am. She looked at Susan strolling beside her on the walkway.

Her mother nodded at the menagerie of topiaries below them. "Even more bizarre," she murmured to Alexa.

Finally, the boy turned back toward the house. As they descended a set of broad stairs, he stopped at a small stone patio that offered a sweeping view over the valley. "Down there is our community farm. A number of teen residents live in the farmhouse group home and participate in a farming work-study program. A few others learn mechanical and equipment-related trades. The farm gardens supply organic food for the kitchens."

Alexa couldn't see the farmhouse. All she could see were expansive fields of what looked like wheat and corn. She turned to her mother. "There's more here than I knew about. The scope of this operation is pretty impressive."

"It is. They appear to help a lot of children," her mother agreed. "Where do they house the younger children?" she asked their guide.

"I believe they try to place all the younger kids in a home setting with foster parents. The harder-to-place teens end up here."

"At last." The minute the group reached the back lawn, her mother headed toward the bar. Alexa followed, searching the crowd for Jack Nash. A few minutes later, the two women were sitting at a table with drinks and plates of tiny sandwiches. Classical music, played by a string quartet positioned near the house, wafted on the air.

"It's finally getting cooler." Alexa put on the lightweight linen cardigan she'd been carrying over her arm.

"Another New York find?" her mother asked.

"Yep. I bought the whole outfit, slacks, shell, and cardigan at Bloomies. But I like your look tonight, Mom. Is your jacket silk?"

"I picked this up in Jaipur, but the slacks are from the mall."

"The dark blue looks great on you." As she spoke, Alexa continued to scan the crowd for Jack Nash. She hadn't seen Quinn Hutton yet either.

Impatient, Alexa rose. "Let's mingle and look for Jack. Have you ever met his wife, Vivienne?"

Susan stood, sighing as she lifted her clutch from the table. As Alexa and her mother moved through the crowd, a number of people stopped them, mostly to say hello to Susan. In the midst of the crowd, they bumped into Quinn.

"Mom, this is Quinn Hutton, another board member," Alexa said as Quinn turned to greet them.

"And an ardent admirer of your daughter, I might add." Quinn extended his hand.

"Mr. Hutton." As Susan shook Quinn's hand, a peculiar look fleeted across her mother's face. "Have we met before, Mr. Hutton?"

"I don't believe I've had the pleasure."

"Perhaps not. But you look like someone I used to know long ago."

When Quinn looked a bit taken aback, Alexa stifled a chuckle. She was certain Quinn thought of himself as totally unique. "Have you seen Jack and Vivienne? We haven't had a chance to say hello to our hosts yet."

"Yes. These tours have thrown the reception line into disarray. You'll find them by the conservatory door. I'd take you to them, but Vivienne asked me to get a message to the string quartet."

"No problem. Maybe we'll catch up later." Alexa made a beeline toward the reception line, marshaling her forces for the upcoming confrontation with Jack Nash. Susan trailed in her daughter's determined wake.

Jack and Vivienne turned to welcome Alexa and her mother as they approached. Behind the hosts, Alexa recognized the broad back of Chadwick Young. He and another man faced the house, chatting with a couple who had just emerged from the conservatory.

Jack Nash's greeting was effusive. "Alexa, I'm so glad you could make it. Vivienne, do you know Susan Williams, Alexa's mother? Susan and I are old friends from my Dickinson years."

Vivienne managed a bored smile and extended a languid hand to Susan. "That must seem like so many, many years ago."

Susan deflected the jibe with her tongue-in-cheek reply. "This is quite a place you have here. The décor is truly unique."

Alexa plunged right into her mission for the night. "I'm sorry I missed the last board meeting, but I was on safari in Tanzania with my parents." She took a breath. "Mom and Dad went on to Namibia, but I spent some time in Kenya."

Jack tensed when she mentioned Kenya. He glanced over his shoulder toward the man who still had his back turned then wrenched his attention back to Alexa. He flashed a tight smile, straightening the cuffs of his perfectly-tailored shirt.

She plowed ahead. "It's funny, Jack. When I was in the Nairobi airport, I thought I saw you from a distance. Were you in Africa, too?"

"Africa?" Vivienne looked like she'd eaten something sour. "How ridiculous. Jack was in Brussels to accept the Queen's International Children's Advocacy award."

Alexa wanted to swat this skinny, violet-eyed fly away as she kept all her attention focused on the husband.

After a long pause, Jack broke his silence. "Perhaps I have a doppelganger out there, my dear. I haven't been to Africa for years. As Vivienne says, I also missed the board meeting due to the conference in Brussels. I was so honored to receive the queen's award. Was this your first safari?" He directed the question at Susan.

"No. Norris and I have been on several trips to Africa, but this was the first for Alexa."

"Oh, I don't believe in doppelgangers. I could swear that it was you, Jack." Alexa's attempt to press further was interrupted when the tall, silver-haired man next to Chadwick Young turned to join the conversation. Alexa did a double take. This man looked exactly like an older, heavier Quinn. Even his eyes were that same shade of blue—the one that reminded Alexa of glacial lakes.

Jack laughed and clapped the newcomer on the back. "Quinn, look who we've got here. You remember Susan from Woodstock? And this is her daughter, Alexa Williams."

The tall man spoke with a pronounced upper-crust New England accent. "Susan, I'm sorry . . ." He appeared to be at a loss. After a moment his expression cleared, and he flashed an enigmatic smile. "Of course! Sukie, isn't it? Ahhhh." His plummy voice became nostalgic. "Peace and love. Those were the days, weren't they?"

Her face frozen in shock, Susan stood there as if rooted to the ground, pressing her clutch to her chest. Finally, in a strangled voice, she croaked, "Eskimo?"

While intrigued to finally meet someone from her mom's Woodstock days, Alexa was concerned that Susan looked so terribly pale and distraught.

Jack and this older Quinn exchanged a delighted glance. Jack cried in a jovial tone, "You got it, Sukie. Quinn, the mighty Eskimo. It's been ages since anyone called him that."

"So," Alexa interjected. "I take it you are my friend Quinn's father?" She edged closer to her mother, who seemed close to collapse.

"He probably never mentioned that he's Quinn the fourth. I'm Quinn the third. Although, when your mother knew me, I went by Eskimo. That nickname absolutely appalled my parents, which was probably part of the motivation."

Vivienne, who had paid little attention to the conversation, put a petulant hand on Jack's arm. "I hate to interrupt this reunion, but we have other guests waiting."

"Of course, dear." He turned to Alexa and Susan. "Perhaps we can talk more later. Nice to see you both."

Jostled aside by another group of guests, Alexa gritted her teeth at the abrupt end to any chance to further quiz Jack on Africa. But she had to attend to her mother, who looked on the verge of fainting. Alexa grabbed her mother by the elbow and steered her toward the house. "Mom, are you OK?"

Behind them, Quinn's father called, "Peace out, Sukie. That's a lovely daughter you've got there. She's yar."

"Did he just say yar, like Katherine Hepburn in *The Philadelphia Story*? Who says that?" Alexa snorted.

Her mother asked in a choked voice, "Where is the ladies' room?"

Alexa glanced over her shoulder before they entered the villa. A few yards away from the reception line, Jack and Quinn the Eskimo were deep in conversation with a stocky man in a gray suit and a uniformed security guard.

CHAPTER FORTY

WHEN SUSAN STUMBLED INTO the empty powder room, Alexa yanked a chair from the vanity in the anteroom and eased her mother into the seat.

"Mom, I'm seriously worried here. Are you sick? What's wrong?" She fished through her purse for a cell phone to call 911.

Susan closed her eyes and whispered. "I remembered. They killed her."

Alexa abandoned the search for her cell and strained to hear. "Killed who? Cecily?"

Her mother opened her eyes and raised her voice in anguish. "No, I have no idea who killed Cecily. I'm talking about Willow, the girl who died at Woodstock. The shock of seeing Eskimo so completely out of the blue—I remembered what happened."

"Shhh. I don't think this is the place to talk about this." Alexa looked again to make sure they were alone. "Let's use the facilities and get out of here."

Without saying their farewells, Alexa and Susan rushed out of the house. As they waited for the Land Rover, Alexa shifted her weight from foot to foot uneasy about the scene they'd just fled. She kept glancing toward the front door expecting Jack Nash or the stocky man to appear. Susan leaned against a balustrade, taking deep gulps of air, her normal color returning.

Heading down the lane, Alexa was glad to leave the villa behind even though she had unfinished business with Jack Nash.

"You're looking much better, Mom." Twilight waned, and the tall trees on both sides of the winding lane blotted out the remaining glimmer of light. Alexa drove slowly, watching for deer on the road. "There's a bottle of water in the center console."

Her mother rolled down the passenger window a few inches and took a drink. "Oh, that air feels good. I'm fine, dear. It was the shock of seeing Jack and that vile man, Eskimo, all grown up. In an instant, that night at Woodstock came flooding back."

"You remembered something?" Alexa cracked her window open, too. Cool, pine-scented air streamed through the Land Rover.

"Yes, about my friend's death. I left the concert because I was feeling terrible—a migraine on top of being high. When I got back to our campsite, Jack and Quinn were in their tent . . . with Willow, a young girl we'd taken under our wing.

"I thought the boys were acting odd, but my head hurt so much. I just wanted to go to sleep. They were stoned out of their minds. I think Willow was high, too. She was curled in a pile of sleeping bags. Jack sat next to her with a leg flung over her in a disturbing way. Eskimo lounged on her other side with a joint in his mouth. I was a little worried when I saw her there with those two. She was so young . . . only fourteen. I asked her where Levi and her friends were. She told me that they had all gone to hear the Airplane. When she woke from a nap, she'd come to Eskimo and JJ looking for food."

Susan's words continued to spill out as if she couldn't stop them. "Willow asked me. 'Do you want to hang out with us?' She sounded like she wanted me to stay. I tried to get her to leave. I said, 'I'll walk you back over to camp.' My head was pounding so hard I felt like I was going to throw up.

"But Eskimo jumped up and said, 'You don't look so good. We'll take care of Willow.' He pulled a pill out of his pocket and told me, 'Take this. It will help you sleep.' He handed me his canteen and told me they were pain pills. So I swallowed a pill and left the three of them there. I remember I turned back at the tent door. I think I was going to offer again to walk Willow back to her tent. But whatever Eskimo gave me had started to kick in. I was getting dizzy. I barely made it to my tent before I passed out. I found out later that he'd given me a Quaalude, a powerful tranquilizer."

Susan's voice choked with emotion. "They found Willow when a truck ran over her body. The police questioned me. I got the impression from what they asked that Willow had been raped and beaten before she died.

"A lot of what happened that night has always been hazy. My walk back to our campsite . . . how I got to bed. I had a vague recollection of seeing Willow with Jack and Eskimo. I had a bad feeling about those two guys, but that's all. Hell, they were such jerks that no one much liked them.

"I just couldn't put it together—until now. I remember feeling something wasn't quite right when I stumbled into their tryst with Willow. And Eskimo ensured that I would pass out by giving me a Quaalude. I just know that those two animals raped and killed that child then hid her body under those blankets." Susan's voice sounded teary as she finished her long monologue.

"That's a pretty heavy accusation, Mom. You didn't actually see them hurt Willow, did you?"

"No, but they left Woodstock early. They probably wanted to get out of there before someone discovered her body. It all adds up." Susan's voice became strident with certainty.

While appalled at what Jack and Quinn's father had done, Alexa was pleased to see her mother begin to regain her equilibrium. In unlocking the suppressed memory that had haunted her since Woodstock, her mother's demeanor had evolved from shock to melancholy relief.

Alexa took a quick glance toward Susan. "And forty years later, I see Jack with a group of young refugees in Africa, and he flat out lies about it."

"I told you, Lexie. Jack Nash is bad news."

An icy tremor skittered down Alexa's spine and she pressed down harder on the gas pedal. "And I think he knows that we're on to him."

They had descended the mountain and were onto the final flat stretch of the lane. "What's this? Is there an accident?" Alexa slowed the car. The Land Rover's headlights revealed a vehicle parked across the lane.

Soon, she could read the words Children of Light Security on the side of the SUV blocking the road. Alexa came to a complete stop well back from the vehicle. There were two security guards standing on the road.

"I don't like this," Susan said just as several strong spotlights hit the Land Rover.

Alexa used an arm to shield her eyes from the bright light. "I agree. This doesn't feel right. It's not an accident."

A disembodied voice came over a loudspeaker. "Ladies, please step out of the car."

"No way." Alexa protested to her mother.

"Alexa, I think they know I remembered about Willow."

"Or I could have hit a nerve. Maybe Jack was up to something terrible in Africa."

The loudspeaker blared again. "Alexa and Susan Williams. We must insist that you step out of the car. This is a security matter."

Alexa shoved her cell phone toward her mother. "Call 911, now." But, before Susan could dial, one of the security guards fired a gun in the air.

"What the hell?" Goosebumps blossomed down Alexa's arms as her mother exclaimed.

"They have no legal grounds for this."

"We mean business here, ladies. Step out of the car now."

Alexa and Susan exchanged a dubious glance just as both guards opened fire. A thunderous racket filled the air as the guards unleashed a round of warning gunshots. Shredded pine branches peppered the windshield.

The minute the shooting stopped, Alexa yelled, "Hold on and keep low," and engaged the Land Rover's four-wheel drive system. Heart pounding, she drove forward hoping to find a way to edge by the security vehicle. Frantically scanning the area, she spied two evergreen trees on the left that were much shorter than the rest, probably replacements for trees that had died. Alexa jerked the steering wheel and aimed for those trees. If she was right, there was just enough space for the Land Rover to break through —although she had no idea what was on the other side.

"Hold tight. Maybe I can get around these guys through the field."

When the guards realized what was happening, they began firing again—but the shots were no longer just a warning. As Alexa gunned the Land Rover, shots thudded into the heavy metal of the SUV.

Susan ducked her head and grabbed the dashboard. "Oh my God. Drive, Lexie. Drive!" she screamed.

The passenger window shattered with a loud crack as the car swerved. Alexa ignored the slivers of glass that pierced her right arm, and she plowed right over the trees, just like their guide had done on safari. She breathed a sigh of relief when they landed in a field. Shots pinged off the back of the Land Rover as she drove haphazardly across the field, angling downward toward the fence and the road. But getting back onto the lane safely looked like a long shot.

Tentacles spiraled out in multiple directions from three bullet holes in the right half of the windshield. Air whipped through the opening where the passenger side window had completely shattered. At least the tires seemed unscathed.

"Mom, I don't know how far I can take the car. We might have to get out and run." Although Alexa's actions had initially caught the security team off guard, the lights in the rearview mirror indicated that they had recovered quickly. At least two security vehicles pursued the Land Rover.

Alexa registered that her mother had not answered. “Mom?”

“Drive, Lexie. Don’t worry about me. Something hit me . . . either a bullet or a shard of glass. My side is bleeding, and it hurts like hell.”

“Shit. Shit. Shit.” Alexa pounded the steering wheel. “We’ve got to get you to a doctor.”

“First things, first. We need to get out of this place, but it’s surrounded by fences, right?” Susan gasped.

“There’s got to be more than one exit.” Alexa’s tone was grim as she tried to steer the Land Rover over the rough fields.

She spied a grove of trees to the left. Even though it was uphill, she drove toward the wooded area, hoping to use the trees to shield them from her pursuers. Out here in the open fields, dusk had not completely given way to dark. Alexa took a chance and doused the Land Rover’s lights. It was a gamble. Become less visible to the security guys, but risk driving over unknown terrain in near darkness.

Alexa drove behind the grove of trees and downshifted until she coasted to a stop to avoid flashing telltale red brake lights. She smiled when the headlights of the security vehicle veered to the right, toward the fence. Her expression quickly sobered at the sight of her mother holding a cloth, dark with blood, against her lower abdomen.

“I think we lost them for a few minutes. How are you doing?”

“I’m doing, but we need to get out of here. Is that a dirt road over there?” Her mother motioned weakly toward a faint track on the left.

“I think you’re right. I don’t know where it goes, but maybe we could make better time. And it’s headed away from the security guards. There’s got to be some sort of exit near that farmhouse the tour kid talked about.”

Alexa disengaged four-wheel drive and ramped up the speed the minute her wheels hit the dirt lane. Soon, she calculated that they had a five- to ten-minute lead on their pursuers. Of course, they were still trapped inside the fence.

Alexa noticed her mom fiddling with the cell phone. “Did you get through to 911?”

“I don’t think so. When they stared shooting, I dropped the phone. Now I can’t get it to work. And I didn’t bring mine because that damned clutch purse was too small. It’s in my car at the cabin.”

Alexa could see her mother fading. She worried about loss of blood and onset of shock. Her mind raced frantically, trying to figure out a plan. She knew it was only a matter of time before the security vehicles would be joined by reinforcements.

Peering ahead, Alexa spied a large shadow on the horizon. Bales of hay. About thirty big round bales were stacked two high and two deep. As they drove closer, Alexa could see that these bales had been around a while, perhaps since last year's harvest. She pulled up near the middle of the row.

"Mom, I'm going to get help. But, pretty soon, this car is going to become a liability. I need to be able to travel on foot. Do you have enough strength to climb up there and burrow between the bales?"

"I'll find the strength." Susan spoke through obvious pain.

Alexa took off her sweater and tied it around her mother's side, happy to note that the bleeding had slowed. Then Alexa jumped into the midst of the bales from the hood of the Land Rover. As she suspected, the old bales had deteriorated enough for her to dig a shallow tunnel in the straw between two of the upper-level bales. She dug frantically, ignoring the stalks of hay that stabbed her hands. When she had hollowed out a hiding place, Alexa returned to the SUV for her mother.

Susan's knees buckled when she slid from the car, but she gritted her teeth and hobbled forward. Alexa helped her mother make her way from the front bumper to the hood. "Come on, Mom. You can do it."

Kneeling on the hood, Susan moaned and swayed. Alexa caught her mother and leaned her against the wall of hay. Straining with effort, she pushed from beneath as her mother crawled into the bales. Groaning in pain, Susan kept going until she reached the trough that Alexa had carved in the hay. Alexa covered her mother with more hay and handed her a bottle of water.

"Try to stay away from the edge. I'll be back soon. I love you, Mom." Alexa kissed her mother's forehead.

"I love you, Lexie. Go now and get help, but please be careful." Susan closed her eyes and sank back into the hay.

As Alexa slipped off the bales, the dusty smell of freshly turned hay mingled with the metallic smell of her mother's blood. Her brimming eyes overflowed, and tears trailed down her cheeks. Was she abandoning her mother to the security guards and Jack Nash? Even worse, what if her mom died out here in this godforsaken field?

Alexa wiped her eyes and jumped back into the Land Rover. Although she was frantic about her mother, the best way to help was to find a way to escape this cage. Continuing down the lane, Alexa passed through fields planted with low-growing crops, probably wheat. But it was so dark she could barely see the road anymore. It was either turn on her vehicle's lights or risk crashing into something.

She grimaced and switched on the headlights. With the illumination, she increased her speed. However, a few minutes later, she knew her pursuers had honed in on the beams like a homing beacon. She could see the glow of a car's headlights in the distance, turning away from the fence. Her heart sank at a second pair of headlights coming toward her far ahead on the lane.

In the next moment, Alexa lost sight of both cars' lights. It took her a minute to understand she'd entered a tunnel between two cornfields. The corn plants towered over the Land Rover, but Alexa knew the sense of protection from the tall stalks was illusory. In just minutes, she would be trapped between two vehicles full of security staff with guns. She had to lead them away from her mom.

Alexa gathered her courage and took a hard right off the dirt lane. She plunged straight into the middle of the corn. Stalks whipped across the windshield as the sturdy Land Rover plowed across the field. Mature ears of corn slapped against the car like giant waves. The SUV rocked like a boat as it crested each row of plants and sank into the troughs between. Alexa clung to the wheel as she slid back and forth across the seat.

She'd gotten off the road, but a swath of broken and bent stalks marked her wild ride into the cornfield. Alexa knew she had to leave the Land Rover behind, although the thought of continuing on foot terrified her. Without the SUV she'd be totally vulnerable. She brought the Land Rover to a stop in the middle of the field, took the keys, and slipped out of the vehicle. Alexa eased the door shut and set off toward the fence bordering Pine Road.

Walking through the cornfield proved to be much harder than Alexa expected. When she and Graham were kids, they'd loved to run down the long passageways between the tall cornstalks on Nana's farm. The rows that had accommodated a child felt much narrower now that she was an adult. As she raced through the field, unyielding stalks and indifferent ears of corn pummeled her shoulders. A rich verdant smell filled her nostrils, and her eyes watered from the pollen. Her feet stumbled over the uneven field.

No more than five minutes passed until shouts erupted near the place where she'd driven off the road. She tried to ignore the commotion and pushed on.

Through her exhaustion, it hit Alexa. Surely, the pursuers would expect her to make a run for the fence and cut her off. Wiping sweat from her forehead, she turned left and away from certain detection.

She needed to get farther away from those guys on the lane. She could chance a run for the fence later.

Her new course meant Alexa had to cross through the tightly planted rows of corn. Razor-sharp leaves sliced her bare arms, raising bloody stripes. She spit out wisps of corn silk that clung to her mouth. Most worrisome, as Alexa thrashed through the corn, the tasseled stalks rippled like flags marking her progress across the field. If the security guys had a spotlight aimed in the right direction, they might be able to see the plants stirring.

As if they'd read Alexa's mind, she caught a flicker of lights in the sky to her left. She tensed but determined that the lights were aimed closer to the spot where she'd abandoned the Land Rover. Alexa pressed on, trying to slide through the stalks as stealthily as possible.

She hadn't progressed far when a row of floodlights blazed to her right, followed by the deep, clack-clack-clack-clack roar of a powerful diesel engine. Gasping in dismay, Alexa spun toward the lights and noise. She freaked out.

A phalanx of twirling spiral disks, each two feet across, tore into the corn at the far end of the row. Frenzied cornstalks and chaff flew ten feet into the air as the deadly metal blades chewed up the field. A maelstrom of chopped silage gushed behind the yellow monster, turning the air thick with dust. In the blinding light, Alexa could see the outline of the farm machine towering high above the tops of the corn. A combine. If the machine caught her in its silver-toothed maw, it would mean certain and horrible death.

Terrified, Alexa turned yet again and fled the huge combine. Coughing, she held a hand over her nose to filter the dust. Behind her, the machine advanced in an unrelenting din of grinding gears and disintegrating corn. Since she'd done a U-turn, Alexa's path took her between the rows, making her headlong flight easier.

As she approached the dirt lane, the searchlights of men on foot moved toward the wheat fields. Distance had muted the roar of the combine. She stopped at the edge of the lane, hugging the shadow of the cornfield. Seeing no activity, Alexa dashed across the dirt lane and disappeared into another cornfield. She sprinted through the new field, each step taking her farther away from the fence—and farther away from help for her mother.

CHAPTER FORTY-ONE

ALEXA'S LEGS FELT LIKE used rubber bands by the time she hit the end of the cornfields. The corn stalks trailed off into uncultivated fields, covered in weeds and bushes. Ahead, she could see the edge of the forest.

Alexa slogged uphill until she reached the tree line. Sobbing in exhaustion, she leaned against a large trunk; sweat poured off her entire body. Any adrenaline boost had long worn off, and she felt shaky and a little nauseous. Clinging to the tree trunk, she could look down over the fields below. The combine had decimated the cornfield, and she could make out the Land Rover in its blazing headlights. Two other vehicles patrolled the dirt lane with spotlights.

Her heart leapt to her throat when another SUV approached from the direction of the house. Its spotlight passed right over the bales of straw where her mother hid, but it kept on driving—headed toward the action. Apparently, they still thought Alexa and her mother were trapped somewhere in the corn.

Alexa took another minute to catch her breath and evaluate her options. Her access to the lower fence was cut off. No way would she get by that crew down there.

Maybe she could flag down a car leaving the party. Get help. Get a phone to call 911. Drawing a breath, Alexa pushed through her physical discomfort and headed back toward the lion's den.

As she slipped along the edge of the forest, just inside the tree line, Alexa watched the strobe effect of one car after another traveling down the winding lane away from the house: brief flashes of light angling through gaps in the faux cypress marked each car's progress. By the time she approached the grounds, the flicker of lights had slowed to a trickle.

Alexa had climbed higher on the mountain than she'd realized. She emerged from the woods near the topiary garden above the house. Breathing hard, Alexa sat down with her back against a boulder to check out the situation. From that point, she could see most of the parking area. Although all the lights in the villa were blazing, two security SUVs were the only cars left in the lot. Alexa's heart sank. All the party guests had gone home.

For a minute, exhaustion and fear got the better of Alexa. She cradled her head in her hands, slipping into despair. What was she going to do? Then, she thought about her mom, bleeding and in pain, lying in that makeshift hiding place.

"Pull yourself together, Alexa. You've got to get help."

A westerly breeze chilled Alexa in her clammy clothes. It was time to move. She used the boulder for leverage and forced her body to a standing position.

A screech of metal from down below froze Alexa in place. She crept behind the boulder for cover. Peering around the big rock, she watched a security guard and dog emerge from a door in the side of the villa.

How many guards did this place employ? Way too many for a basic foster care operation.

The guard headed around the corner, away from Alexa. When he reached the french doors leading into the conservatory, the Doberman Pinscher went nuts. The dog pulled toward the topiaries, barking furiously.

Had the dog smelled her? At this point, Alexa's body odor was a pungent mix of Coco Mademoiselle parfum, corn juice, sweat, and fear. Shivering, she tried to merge with the rock to avoid detection.

Chuckling, the guard dropped the dog's leash, and the Doberman bounded toward the bear topiary. For an instant, Alexa imagined that the bear hopped forward to confront the dog. The illusion evaporated when she heard the screams. The movement was a young boy and a young girl emerging from beneath the topiary bear. Alexa could hear them yelling.

"Stop!"

"Help!"

"Call off the dog. Please!"

The guard waited until the dog stormed to a point no more than a yard away from the kids before he commanded, "Darth, sit. Stay."

Alexa breathed a sigh of relief to see the dog instantly comply.

The man in uniform strode toward the two kids. "What are you two doing outside your dorms?"

As the kids broke into a fearful babble of explanation and pleading, Alexa took advantage of the distraction and made her move. She had reached a conclusion.

The only way out was up. They hadn't expected her to loop back toward the house, but this villa area was clearly guarded. It was too risky to try for a phone in the house. The others still seemed to be searching for her in the valley. So her best option for escape was to walk to the top of the mountain and follow Ridge Road until she found help.

Alexa stole through the woods, trying to remain quiet as she plodded upwards. Progress was slow. The woods were pitch black. Even though her eyes had made an adjustment, she kept stumbling over branches and deadfall. Her fashionable Mary Janes had not been made for extreme hiking; her feet were killing her. Alexa's legs ached as she fought collapse. But thoughts of her mother kept her moving.

Pausing to listen for pursuit, Alexa heard nothing. She took in a deep breath, filling her lungs with the familiar and comforting smells of the forest. She could barely make out the lights of the house below through the trees. The tour from earlier in the evening came to mind, and she remembered the old logging road. She could travel much faster if she could circle over to that lane above the dormitories.

Making her way in that direction, Alexa sensed, more than saw, a gap in the trees. Cautious on the open logging road, she stopped and crouched to the ground, listening. The sound of the altercation below had faded. The woods were silent and still.

Alexa nearly toppled from her crouch when an owl hooted nearby. Waiting until her heartbeat returned to a semblance of normal, she stood and eased her car keys from her pants pocket. By feel, she detached a mini-LED flashlight from the chain. She decided to chance it.

Shielding the beam so that only a pinpoint reached the ground in front of her, Alexa sped upwards. The hint of light was enough to keep her from wandering off the ancient lane. About fifteen minutes later, Alexa reached a barrier. Although she had expected a fence, when confronted with the reality, Alexa whimpered in despair. But she'd come this far; she had to find a way over.

An eight-foot steel mesh fence fanned out on both sides of the lane. Like at the front of the property, Children of Light had erected a high barrier but must have realized that barbed wire or electrification would draw unwanted attention.

Alexa studied the gate in front of her with the LED flashlight and giggled out loud. The sound echoed in the quiet night, and she immediately stifled the laugh before it turned hysterical. A tall, slatted steel gate secured the lane. In an extraordinary lapse in security for this fortress, two-inch gaps fell between each horizontal slat. Alexa's spirits soared at this lucky break.

Clearly, they didn't have much trouble with runaways heading this direction. Energized, Alexa put a foot on the second slat and scrambled over the gate.

On the other side, the lane came to a T at a wider gravel road. This was Alexa's goal. Ridge Road. This road traversed the top of the South Mountain, mostly through state land. It originated in Mt. Holly Springs to the east. This section intersected with Route 233 near Alexa's home.

She took a right, believing she was near Hammonds Rocks, a popular hangout for local teens. The rocks were covered in years of graffiti from kids who came to drink beer, get high, and indulge their hormones every weekend. Alexa hoped that on a summer Friday night, someone would be there partying.

The kids didn't hear Alexa coming until she limped into the circle by the campfire.

"Holy shit," exclaimed a boy in a motorcycle jacket holding a bong. The smell of marijuana hung in the air. In the flickering firelight, Alexa could read the words SPEED KILLS and SD LOVES FN on one of the big boulders behind him. She often complained that vandals with spray paint had ruined this once-beautiful place, but tonight graffiti was the last thing on her mind.

Two skimpily-dressed blondes screamed, and another older boy jumped to his feet. Alexa caught the glint of a heavy chain looping from his belt to his back pocket. The boy's t-shirt pictured two men with the words "Pitbull and Iglesias."

"Lady, what the hell? You scared the shit, I mean crap, out of us," he groused and peered more closely at Alexa. "Hey, are you OK? You don't look so hot."

The blonde in the pink tank top leaned forward to get a better look. "She's hurt."

The other girl yelled, "Lady, your arms are covered in blood. What happened to you?"

Alexa ran a hand over her hair and realized that these kids were the masters of understatement. She must look like she'd survived the zombie apocalypse. Dirty, ripped clothes and bloody arms. But none of that mattered.

"I need to call the police. Do you have a cell phone?"

The two girls exchanged a glance and conferred in excited murmurs. Alexa heard the words "car accident" and "rape."

The kid in the motorcycle jacket dropped the bong to the ground. "Cops?"

Alexa ignited in anger. "Look, I don't give a flying fuck about the beer or the grass. I'm not going to get you in trouble. But if you don't help me, my mother could die." With tears in her eyes, Alexa glared at the older boy, somehow sensing he was the leader of this little group.

With an abashed look, he took a phone out of his pocket and handed it to Alexa. "Here."

Alexa called 911 and reported what had happened. She asked that they send an ambulance along with the police to take care of her mother. Then she dialed John Taylor. She'd called him so many times last autumn that Alexa had memorized his number.

"Where are you?"

"At Hammonds Rocks."

"I'll come and get you."

The wiry, black-haired boy had been listening to Alexa's end of the conversation. He broke in to say, "Lady, we can drive you wherever you want to go."

"Are you sure? What's your name?"

"Angel Ruiz." He looked down at his feet and mumbled. "I been taking it easy. I'm the designated driver."

Alexa returned to the conversation with John. "Trooper Taylor, a young man named Angel Ruiz has generously offered to give me a lift. The Land Rover is sitting in the middle of a field inside the Children of Light compound, so I have no transportation. Can you pick me up at the intersection of Ridge Road and 233?"

Arguing in low voices, the four kids gathered up their beer and other paraphernalia. She could tell that the girls had reservations about helping. But Angel was insistent. The boy in the jacket fished out a bottle of water from his backpack and handed it to Alexa while the girls doused the fire. She chugged down half the water in a single gulp.

Together they walked the short distance to the parked car. Although Alexa didn't know much about cars, she thought it was an ancient Oldsmobile or Chevy. Angel opened the passenger door and steadied Alexa as she collapsed into the wide passenger seat. The other three kids piled in the back. Angel turned the ignition switch and the big car rumbled to life.

"Thank you so much." Alexa addressed the entire group. "I'm sorry I ruined your evening. But my mother needs help." As Alexa choked out those last words, her voice faded. How many hours had it been since she left her mother hidden in the hay?

She whispered, "Let Mom be alive. Please."

Her heart twisted when she realized that she had another call to make. "Can I use your phone one more time?" she asked. As they drove out of the forest, Alexa called her dad.

The three-mile trip seemed to take forever. Angel drove slowly, but the low car still bottomed out several times on the gravel road. When they finally reached the intersection with the main road, Alexa insisted that the kids leave. "This way, you won't be involved."

"But, lady, what if the cops don't come? There's bears and shit out here," the boy in the motorcycle jacket cautioned from the back seat.

"They'll be here any minute. You don't want them to take your names and call your parents, do you?"

Angel took charge. "Baby, you come up here with me in the front seat when the lady gets out." Alexa wasn't sure which blonde was his baby until the shorter one in the sparkly top climbed out the back door and shimmied into the passenger seat.

Alexa held the car door open for a second and spoke to the group inside. "Thank you so much. I'll never forget your kindness."

The rumble of the big, souped-up engine lingered in the air for a few seconds after the red glow of its taillights disappeared around the curve. For a moment, Alexa felt vulnerable standing there, alone again in the dark forest. Then John's unmarked police car turned onto Ridge Road and stopped. He spoke a few words into his radio then leapt from the car and swept Alexa into his arms. Alexa leaned into his embrace, feeling safe for the first time in hours.

"Are you OK? What the hell is going on? I've been worried sick ever since you called."

"My mom's in serious danger. The guards from Children of Light shot at us and chased us. A bullet hit Mom, so I stashed her in some haystacks. They're to the west of the villa, close to Pine Road. I abandoned the Land Rover in the middle of a cornfield and ran for it. You have to save my mom. By now, she could've bled to death." Alexa couldn't hold back the tears now that she was with a man she trusted completely. "It took me hours to climb up the mountain and find help."

Reacting to Alexa's distress, John hugged her tightly for a moment before he leapt into action. "Get in the car. Do you need medical attention?" He caressed Alexa's dirty cheek with his hand.

"No, I'm pretty beat up from running through the forest in the dark, but I'll survive."

In the car, John swung onto the main road. He picked up a handset and radioed a message. "Dispatch from Taylor. I'll be taking one white adult female into my custody, transporting to scene working on Pine Road. She has physical injury but appears to be OK. Please advise Pine Road team that another white adult female with possible serious injury is on-site there." He relayed the information about Susan Williams' location and finished with, "I am on my way to the scene. I will interview Ms. Williams on the way."

After he signed off, John turned to Alexa. "Are you sure you're OK? You're bleeding."

"It can wait. I need to get to my mom." Alexa wiped at her eyes with the tattered hem of her shell.

"Tell me what happened. Why the hell would the guards at a child welfare facility shoot at you and your mother? I thought there was a big party there tonight."

Alexa closed her eyes and sighed. "I'm not one hundred percent sure, but I worked out some things while I was trudging up the mountain. I'll tell you what I think is going on. There are two possibilities."

"Two?" John kept his eyes glued to the asphalt as they screamed down the winding mountain road.

"First possibility: My mom witnessed what she now believes to be a murder—or what led up to the murder—at Woodstock."

"Woodstock? You mean the hippie Woodstock back in the sixties?" John echoed in a tone of disbelief.

"Yes. She'd suppressed the details for more than forty years, but they came back tonight when she saw Jack Nash and Quinn Hutton together at the party."

"Quinn Hutton wasn't even born in 1968 or 1969—whenever it was."

"You're right. I'm talking about Quinn Hutton's father. Same name. Except he's the third. Quinn Hutton III." Alexa struggled to explain.

"Hmm. I can't imagine what the father would be like."

"I didn't know you knew Quinn."

"Yeah, I've met the professor." John's voice was flat. He became more animated as he considered Alexa's information.

"OK, I might buy that two killers wanted to shut your mom up. But, unless she actually saw the homicide, it would be difficult to prosecute after all these years. Even though there's no statute of limitations on murder. What's the second possibility?"

"That there's something bad going on at Children of Light. I've been noticing bits and pieces that haven't felt quite right about the organization. But I didn't connect the dots.

"A frightened girl who told me they were going to send her away. An expanded overseas adoption program when many countries are shutting down adoptions to the U.S. The most damning thing happened in Kenya. I saw Jack Nash transporting a group of African refugees, teenagers really. Somehow, the whole thing had a wrong feel to it. Tonight, when I confronted Jack about being in Africa, he denied it. I suspect he's involved in human trafficking."

"Jack Nash? Isn't he supposed to be a big philanthropist? He's the guy who spoke at Melissa's reception, right? On behalf of RESIST, which fights trafficking."

"Yes. I think he talks a good game. Hard as it is to believe, I'm convinced that Children of Light is a front for a sex trafficking operation. And I think Cecily Townes found out about it—and Jack had her killed. I wouldn't be surprised if his organization is behind the death of Meg Wilson and the disappearances of those other missing girls and women."

"Do you have any evidence?"

"Other than his guards trying to kill us? Not really, but that's your job." Alexa leaned back and closed her eyes, frantic about her mother.

When John blew by the gatehouse, the entire area was alight with emergency vehicles. It looked like every state police vehicle in the area had been dispatched to the Nash estate. Several big trucks had powerful spotlights trained on the fields. A big, panel-van-type ambulance was lurching down the dirt road toward the main lane.

"Mom," Alexa cried.

John drove toward the ambulance and brought his car to a stop at the edge of the dirt road. Evergreen trees lay toppled like fallen dominoes along the lane. John flagged down the ambulance before it turned toward the exit gate. The driver rolled down his window.

"Do you have Susan Williams in there? What's her condition?" Taylor yelled.

"Yes, Susan Williams, the county commissioner. She's lost a lot of blood and is in pretty bad shape. We need to get her into surgery, pronto."

John told the driver, "I've got her daughter, Alexa, here. She'd like to ride to the hospital with you folks."

The trooper ushered Alexa to the back of the emergency vehicle and, with a quick squeeze of her hand, helped her climb in. "We'll take care of things here. I'll check in with you later. I'll need to take a formal statement."

Alexa gasped at the sight of her mother strapped into the gurney, IV tubes attached to her arm, temporary bandages covering her wound. Susan looked so insubstantial that Alexa felt her mother might vanish into the blinding white sheets.

The ambulance turned on the siren and sped toward the hospital. Through a tiny back window, Alexa watched the kaleidoscope of red, blue, and amber lights flash behind them like distress beacons for her wounded mother. As the lights receded into the distance, Alexa held her unconscious mother's hand and whispered, "Hold on, Mom. Stay with me. We're almost at the hospital. Don't let that goddamn Jack Nash and Quinn's asshole father kill you, too."

CHAPTER FORTY-TWO

August 17, 1969

I'll let you be in my dreams if I can be in yours.

Sukie and Nina slogged their way back to camp through ankle-deep mud in the fresh glimmer of early dawn. "It's getting light. Any idea what time it is?" Sukie stopped. "Or I could look at my watch, right?"

Nina said, "I bet it's four in the morning."

"You're right. Four-fifteen. We sure aren't going to get out of here at noon. I think there are three or four more bands before Hendrix."

"At least we'll avoid the traffic if we leave later." Nina glanced around the field. "Although it looks like practically everyone left already. Most of the tents are gone."

"The Levi Bloom group is still here." Sukie pointed toward the bread truck. "Hope they found Willow."

"They never came back to look for her or talk to JJ and Eskimo. She must have turned up." Nina smiled. "That kid is a trip."

"It sounds like she has a pretty rough home life. Give her a few more years, and she might actually show up at the Hog Farm commune."

"I'm glad we came back here. Those guys can wallow in the mud for a few more hours to hear Jimi Hendrix, but I've had it." Nina held up a mud-caked poncho with a disgusted look.

"Me too. Right before we left, my poncho had sunk so deep in the muck I thought someone was going to have to dig me out. Hard to believe we decided to skip Hendrix."

"Cheryl made the right decision. She's been warm and dry all night in her tent."

"But then we would have missed that new band. What was the name, Crosby, Stills and something?"

"That song about Guinevere was beautiful." Nina's tone became wistful.

When they reached the tents, Sukie shuddered. "I'm going to get out of these clammy clothes and catch a few hours sleep."

"Good idea." Nina cocked her head in the direction of the stage. I'm not sure who's playing now, but that's not Jimi Hendrix."

Sukie could hear the music quite plainly. "I don't recognize the band." She giggled. "We can hear everything perfectly right here. Another excellent reason to come back."

As Nina headed toward her tent, she looked back over her shoulder at Sukie. "You many want to take those off before you go inside."

Glancing down at her jeans, Sukie recoiled. Thick, wet mud covered most of the pant legs starting about three inches below her knees. "Ugh." Sukie wrinkled her nose at the smell as she carefully extricated each leg and spread the dirty jeans over the top of the tent to dry.

Sukie awoke to the distinctive chords of one of her favorite Hendrix songs, "Foxy Lady." It took a moment to register that she was at Woodstock, hearing Jimi Hendrix live. She bounced up to throw on some clothes, slipping into her last mud-free pair of jeans. Then she rolled out of the empty tent.

Cheryl and Nina were sitting on the metal cooler with coffee mugs in their hands. Nina looked up. "He's magnificent, isn't he?"

"And we can hear the music plain as day." Cheryl beamed.

Sukie filled a cup with coffee and rummaged for some dry cereal. "Trix is the only thing left?" She frowned.

"The little cereals come in packs of eight. Apparently, no one likes Trix." Cheryl scooted over on the big ice chest to give Sukie some space.

The girls sat in silence and listened to Hendrix work his magic on the guitar. Sukie gasped when she recognized the first strains of "The Star Spangled Banner." By the time he had finished and segued into "Purple Haze," she was in tears.

"Damn," Nina exclaimed. "Have you ever heard anything like that?"

"That was so far out." Sukie jumped up in excitement but stopped in her tracks at Cheryl's expression.

"What's wrong?" Cheryl's look of shock reminded Sukie of a child who had heard her teacher swear.

Cheryl whispered, "Is it legal to play the national anthem like that?"

Nina rolled her eyes. "Of course. Are you afraid the police are going to arrest us for listening to a rock version of 'The Star Spangled Banner'? Seriously, Cheryl."

"If they haven't arrested us all for getting high, I think we're safe from the music cops." Sukie turned away to stifle a laugh and saw Levi Bloom making his way toward them.

"Here comes Levi. It's weird. He's alone, without the usual flock of followers." She took a few steps in his direction.

"Levi. Are you getting ready to pack up?" Nina rose to join her friend.

"When are you leaving?" Sukie asked. "I'd like to say goodbye to Willow."

Levi's grim expression alarmed Sukie. He spoke in a tight voice. "That's why I'm here—to tell you about Willow."

"Tell us what? Is she still missing? Since we didn't hear anything more, we thought she came back." Nina glanced at Sukie in consternation.

"No. We never found her. We spread out yesterday looking for her, but no luck. We even went to the hospital tent in case she'd gotten sick. She wasn't there . . . they hadn't seen her. I stopped over there again this morning." Tears rolled down Levi's face. "They told me that Willow's dead."

"Dead?" Sukie protested. "She can't be dead. She's just a kid."

Nina and Cheryl both broke into sobs. "What happened? Was it some sort of overdose or a bad trip?" Nina wiped at her eyes and put an arm around Sukie.

"A truck rolled over her sometime last evening. It happened on the far side of the woods. They brought the police in to investigate. The doctor said that they think Willow could have already been dead—before the truck. She was wrapped up in a blanket of some sort."

"Oh my God." Sukie bent her head in grief. "I can't believe such a beautiful little angel is dead."

"I hate this godforsaken festival." Cheryl startled Sukie with her wail.

Levi hung his head. "We are all so bummed out. Willow was a ray of pure light—we loved her. I should have never let her come up here with us. I feel so guilty for letting her wander around on her own."

Sukie put a hand on his arm. "That girl adored you, Levi. But it was pretty clear that she marched to her own tune. She was a free spirit."

"I have to get back to the truck. The police are doing an investigation and they're coming to talk to us. Sukie, they want to talk to you, JJ, and Eskimo. You were the last people—that I know of—who saw her."

"JJ and Eskimo left yesterday. But we'll be here for a couple hours at least. The boys still aren't back from the concert."

"You ladies have kind hearts, letting Willow tag along after you. She was happy to have you as new friends." Levi turned and took a few shuffling steps toward the bread truck.

"Levi," Sukie called after him. "What was Willow's full name? Greta what?"

"Greta Shapiro."

Sukie repeated the name, "Greta Shapiro. Our little Willow, dead at fourteen." Then, it all hit her, and she broke down. Cheryl and Nina wrapped their arms around her until the three distraught girls formed a circle of tears.

When the van pulled up in front of Sukie's house in Carlisle, it took her a few minutes to register that she was home. The last ten hours had been a blur. Tearing down the campsite. Talking to two policemen who seemed to be just going through the motions in Willow's death.

The long ride from Bethel had been mostly silent. The boys were exhausted from spending the night at the concert. The girls were devastated by the news of Willow's death.

As the miles unfolded, Sukie tried to remember if she had actually seen Willow in JJ and Eskimo's tent. Her memories of that night were still hazy, blurred by the pain of her migraine and Eskimo's helpful Quaalude cure.

"If I hadn't been so out of it, I could have helped her when she stopped by our campsite. I could have even brought her into my tent to sleep. Maybe I could have saved her." The what-ifs churned endlessly round and round her brain.

Robbie turned to address Sukie in the back seat. "This is the end of the road for you. Don't bother with the tents and all of that. We'll bring everything over next weekend. Just grab your backpack."

Ben leaned over and kissed her. "Great weekend, babe. I know it's a bummer, but don't let this Willow thing bring you down. I'll call you."

Sukie slipped out the door. "See you folks. Keep the faith." Several minutes after the van had driven away, Sukie remained on the sidewalk, drinking in the cool evening air.

"Pull yourself together," she whispered. "Mom and Dad will want to hear everything about Woodstock. They've probably been worried sick about you. And they'll totally freak out if you tell them about Willow."

Sukie raised tear-filled eyes to the starry sky and spoke aloud. "Farewell, little sprite. Knowing you was a gift."

With those words, Sukie locked Willow away in a small corner of her mind. Lifting her filthy backpack over one shoulder, she walked to her house and opened the front door.

"Honey, we were so worried about you. We knew that you kids had prepared for the concert with tents and food. But when Walter Cronkite announced on the news that Woodstock was declared a disaster area, your father and I were beside ourselves." Sukie's mother rushed to hug her.

Dad gave her an appraising look. "Clearly, you need a bath and some food. But are you OK?"

Sukie managed a wan smile. "I'm tired, but I'm fine. Sorry I worried you. It was quite an experience."

Her mother held Sukie at arm's length and asked, "Did you have a good time?"

"Three days of peace and music from some of the greatest bands in the world? How could I not have a good time?"

CHAPTER FORTY-THREE

"MOM, YOU'RE LOOKING BETTER." Alexa walked straight to the bed and kissed her mother's forehead.

"Yes. I think they're finally going to let me go home on Friday—assuming I continue to improve. We're going to have to cancel our trip to Asia though. Dr. Benson says I'll need at least two months to regain my strength."

"I'm not surprised." Alexa squeezed her mom's hand. "You were hanging on the edge when you came in here. After three weeks in the hospital, which is a long inpatient stay by today's standards, you'll be in no shape to go to the other side of the world. But, if you listen to the doctors and take it easy for a while, you'll make a full recovery. Then you and Dad can fly off to whatever remote corner of the world you want to see next."

"How are you feeling, dear? Did you go back to the doctor to get your stitches out? I see you're walking normally. Have your bruised feet healed?"

"I'm fine, Mom. I'm back in the office full time. Lucky I could work from home for a while." Alexa downplayed the after effects of her marathon flight for help in the Nash compound.

"You're here for the meeting with the state police?" Susan hit a button to raise the head of her hospital bed to an angle.

"Yeah. Trooper Taylor said that he and Trooper Cannon want to fill us in on their progress. I imagine they'll want to talk about us both giving testimony when this goes to trial. Dad and Graham should be here in a few minutes. I drove separately because I need to stop by the auto body shop. I'm still hoping they can save the Land Rover, but it's not looking good."

"So apparently I'm doing better than the car?"

"Hello, dear." Norris walked into the room and kissed his wife. Graham trailed behind him, legal pad in hand. A few minutes later, the two state police troopers joined them. Since this meeting had been cleared with the hospital, several extra chairs had been brought into Susan's private room.

John looked directly at Alexa, his warm brown eyes holding her gaze for a few seconds before he spoke. "Thanks for meeting with us. We wanted to brief you on our investigation and the charges that will be filed tomorrow. Mrs. Williams, please let us know if you begin to tire."

"I'm the only one with a bed here. I'll be just fine, Trooper."

Trooper Cannon's muscles rippled under his fitted jacket as he leaned forward in his chair with a serious expression on his face. "The investigation can be split into four parts. In the first, we'll be filing charges against Jack Nash and Quinn Hutton III and the security guards for attempted murder, assault with a deadly weapon, and numerous related offenses. Those charges stem from the attack that wounded you, Mrs. Williams, and endangered your daughter. The second set of charges are extensive and relate to sex trafficking and Meg Wilson's death."

John broke in. "Alexa, your theory was basically spot on. Children of Light does perform legitimate child welfare and juvenile delinquency services. However, the whole operation is basically a cover for a far-reaching sex trafficking scheme. They smuggled refugees into the country; they snatched kids off the street, locally and elsewhere. Although the foster care group homes, for the most part, seem on the up and up, they used those other buildings . . ." He looked at Cannon.

"Transitional housing."

"That's it. A big chunk of the transitional housing and the detention center were actually holding cells for kids awaiting a buyer. To avoid detection by state and county officials, they falsified paperwork to make it look like those kids were out-of-state placements. And, of course, they also had legitimate out-of-state kids housed there—so the smoke and mirrors were elaborate.

"The refugees were warehoused in New York and California when they first hit the United States. It's going to take the Feds awhile to unravel the entire organization. Nash and Hutton ran a sophisticated and multi-faceted sex trafficking operation on the backs of these minors."

Cannon grimaced, "Something went very wrong with Meg Wilson. We still haven't pinned down all the details, but apparently she was being held on the Nash estate while negotiations were proceeding with a wealthy oil baron in Nigeria. Because she was uncooperative, they were sedating her. But they overdosed her by mistake. To cover things up, they shot her up with heroin and dumped her near the truck stop. This is consistent with Ms. Wilson's autopsy results."

"So Meg was up at Children of Light the whole time?" Alexa gave the troopers a horrified look.

"Yes. Unfortunately, none of us in law enforcement had any reason to suspect Children of Light at that time."

Norris interrupted, "Can you tell us who will be indicted?"

John answered. "Jack Nash, Vivienne Nash, Quinn Hutton III, Ralph Price, and several key staff. As you probably know, the FBI is leading the sex trafficking investigation. So far, they've arrested more than fifty people around the country. They are also working with the authorities in a number of foreign countries."

Alexa's whistled. "So Vivienne Nash was actually involved in all of this?"

"Up to her neck. Let's just say that her position as board secretary was not an honorary title. She was deeply involved in the criminal activities of the organization."

"What about the Children of Light Board? Any other arrests there?" Graham shifted in his chair.

"At this time, we believe the board members were duped by Jack and Vivienne Nash. However, the investigation is ongoing."

"Obviously, I'm also concerned about Alexa's fiduciary responsibility as a member of the board—for this whole mess. I can just envision the lawsuits." Graham had turned a little green.

"I can't advise you on that. If I were on the board, I might consider suing Jack Nash and Quinn Hutton III. But, hey," John waved at Norris, Graham, and Alexa. "You're the lawyers here."

"Graham, we'll deal with all that. I have a liability policy. I was an interim appointment." Alexa shot her brother a look of warning. "What about Cecily Townes' murder?"

Trooper Cannon jumped up and paced around the room as he responded. "We have reason to believe that Jack Nash ordered the murder. Ms. Townes attended a fundraiser at the Willard Hotel in Washington. During the event, she apparently walked into a private meeting between Jack Nash, a senator who I will not name, and a young Thai girl. Jack spun a story about educating the senator on the foreign adoption program. It might have worked, except Cecily noticed that the girl appeared to be under duress. She realized that she had seen the young girl before but couldn't remember where."

"Melissa's photo," Alexa shouted.

"Exactly. Cecily later realized that the girl looked like Roongnapar Rathanapimarn." Cannon stumbled over the pronunciation.

"Melissa called her Pa or Dawn," Alexa offered.

"The daughter of Cecily's longtime agency manager in Bangkok."

That's why Cecily asked Melissa for the photos from their trip to Thailand. And it was what she wanted to tell her at the RESIST march."

"Yes. Cecily also contacted Pa's father, Somchart, and confirmed that his daughter was missing. Nash suspected that Cecily had not been convinced by his story. He couldn't take the chance that Cecily would blow the whole operation out of the water. So he sent Ralph Price to kill her. Apparently, the hit didn't go as smoothly as they planned. Cecily put up a fight. In the melee, Ralph Price popped a hernia. Still, he managed to clean out her computer's hard drive before he left. They thought they had stopped the threat."

"But then that asshole, Jack, walks into Melissa's opening and spies a three-foot by four-foot photo of Pa hanging on the wall." Alexa finally knew how Melissa had become a target.

"Yes. She was the girl in the photo at Ms. Lambert's exhibit called . . ." Cannon glanced at his notes. "*As It Should Be*. We've spoken to Melissa and she told us that Jack Nash bought that photo and paid her to take it off the market."

"That was why they broke into her gallery and her house—twice. They wanted to make sure they'd eliminated all the copies of this girl's photographs. Right?"

"Yes, your friend Melissa—and you—became collateral damage. Nash sent those guys to grab Melissa's computer files, her photo cards, anything with pictures of the Thai girl."

Alexa held her breath as she asked, "Have the police located Pa Rathanapimarn?"

Trooper Taylor nodded with a look of disgust. "The FBI and D.C. police located her in a property owned by the senator Cecily saw. Apparently, the sales transaction she witnessed was completed, and the senator stashed the girl in a place in the Adams Morgan district of the city. Pa is in good medical condition. I don't have details about her state of mind. The FBI is making arrangements to return her to her family in Thailand. The senator is about to be indicted. I guess his home state will need to fill a Senate seat very soon."

Susan Williams brought her bed to a fully upright position as she entered the conversation. "And what about the murder of Willow at Woodstock?"

Cannon replied, "We're sorry to tell you that the New York State Police are not going to bring charges. I know they interviewed you.

And they tracked down most of your traveling companions and Levi Bloom. But there is no hard evidence to build a conviction. The young girl who called herself Willow was identified at the time of her death. Her name was—" Cannon paused to look at his notepad. "Greta Shapiro, age fourteen. Police thought her death was due to trauma from being run over by the truck. There was some indication of sexual trauma, but it could have been consensual sex. This was Woodstock, with free love and all that.

"Her mother didn't want an autopsy, and since the cause of death seemed accidental, the police didn't insist. Remember, they were dealing with the aftermath of a disaster area: clogged roads, vehicle accidents, and calls from concerned parents. In retrospect, it might have been a bad call on their part, but the police had a lot on their plate.

"It's not clear that an autopsy at the time would have even pointed to a homicide. Any signs of physical trauma might have been attributed to the truck. And what would the evidence of drugs in her system proved? Most of the kids at the concert had drugs in their system."

"I can't believe it," Alexa's mom protested, silent tears spilling from her eyes. "What are those two bastards, Jack Nash and his twisted friend Eskimo Hutton saying?"

"About Greta Shapiro's death?" Trooper Taylor sighed. "Nothing. They know it's your word against theirs. And, as much as I'd like to see them pay for this, ma'am, you have no direct knowledge that they killed that girl. Your suspicions may well be true, but you didn't see them drug her, or rape her, or drag her out to the field. Without an eyewitness account or physical evidence, there's nothing we could do now."

Susan wiped away her tears and replied, "You're right."

"The Nashes and Hutton have hired a flock of fancy lawyers to defend them on all of these charges. I expect they believe that their high-powered legal representation and money will help them walk." John stopped as if he had just remembered his audience. "No offense. Everyone deserves legal representation, of course," he mumbled.

"Agree, but no offense taken." Norris waved his hand in dismissal.

"I guess I'll have to live with this. At least I finally remembered what happened." Susan's tears dried to be replaced by a commanding look. Alexa knew this mom-in-charge-of-the-universe look well.

"I would think that Jack Nash and Eskimo, I mean Quinn Hutton, are looking at years in jail for all these crimes. Troopers, you must develop an airtight case so that they both spend the rest of their lives behind bars. If they are going to walk on Willow's murder, the rest of it has to stick, even with the high-powered lawyers. Cecily's murder. Meg's death. And all the trafficking charges. Hell, they shot me and could have killed Lexie."

Alexa's dad walked over to his wife's bed, sat down, and folded Susan into his arms. "I'm not a criminal lawyer, but it sounds like a conviction on just half of these charges could send them to prison forever."

"But we are going to need your help, Mrs. Williams." John turned to Alexa. "And yours. There are both federal and state charges here. You may be called on to testify several times."

"Fine with me," Susan muttered. "I can't travel for months anyway. I'll be happy to help nail those bastards to the wall."

"You can count on me as well." Alexa gave him a wry smile. "Although I expect you would subpoena me anyway."

The trooper remained serious. "I'm sure the federal prosecutor prefers cooperative witnesses. The Feds allowed us the courtesy of giving your family a heads up on the various pieces of this. But all the trafficking cases are theirs now, and the FBI is all over them. They're utilizing the Human Smuggling and Trafficking Center. They're working with other international police agencies since this mess spans multiple countries."

Cannon's tone was even more somber. "The prosecution of Cecily Townes' homicide and Meg Wilson's death remain in Cumberland County. We're getting some signals that Ralph Price may roll over and take a plea deal on the Townes case. He's looking at a first-degree murder charge. Too early to tell how this will end up. Since Nash and Hutton were in charge, they're also looking at first-degree murder since one or both of them solicited Price to kill Townes. They will probably be charged with Meg Wilson's murder, too. The whole sex trafficking operation brings in conspiracy charges, RICO violations, and a slew of other charges. The FBI and Justice will be sorting all of that out."

"We'll let Mrs. Williams get some rest now. We hope you're on the mend, ma'am." John rose and Trooper Cannon followed his lead. "Thanks for your time."

Alexa stood as well. "I do have a question. Is the younger Quinn Hutton going to be charged?" She caught the look of annoyance that fleeted over John's face.

Cannon answered. "No. So far we've discovered nothing that suggests Quinn the fourth knew about the dirty little business his father and Uncle Jack were running. He claims that he thought his father managed the Hutton family inheritance and dabbled in investment banking. The son hasn't even lived in this country for most of the last decade. His lack of knowledge could be plausible."

Although Alexa had cooled on Quinn, she felt a twinge of sympathy for the man. He appeared to idolize his father, and now he had to deal with the reality that his hero was a murderer and a despicable man who trafficked children.

It's no wonder I haven't seen or heard from him since the meltdown of everything on the night of the Nashes' party, she concluded.

When Alexa walked the two policemen to the door of her mother's room, John lagged a few steps behind. "You should expect to hear from Special Agent Carter of the FBI."

"We've already met. He questioned us last week."

"I might stop by the cabin one night this week." John dropped his voice so low that Alexa had to strain to hear him.

"Sure. I'll be home. But, next week, when Mom is discharged, I'll stay with my parents to help out." As Alexa watched the troopers walk down the hall, she realized that she felt much closer to John after he had rescued her from Ridge Road and helped bring down Jack Nash and his organization. Since the Cecily Townes investigation was still Troop H's case, she wasn't certain if the ethical issues about dating still existed.

"I hope they disappear soon."

"What did you say, dear?" her dad asked.

"Nothing." Alexa smiled as she returned to the room. "Just talking to myself."

CHAPTER FORTY-FOUR

"We found the perfect house. It's just outside Mt. Holly along the mountain. Jim will be close to the park. It's only ten minutes to Carlisle and my gallery." Melissa bubbled over with her news.

"How many bedrooms?" Haley asked. "Is there room for a nursery?"

"Whoa, girl. You're getting way ahead of me. Just moving in with Jim is a major decision."

"I'm thinking there's a little bit of projection going on here," Alexa observed. "Is there anything you want to tell us, Haley? Perhaps the stork is flying a bundle of joy to the Donahue household?"

Haley's tone was wistful. "I wish. Blair and I are trying to get pregnant."

Melissa affected a look of confusion. "Wait a minute. Which one of you is going to carry the baby?"

"You know what I mean, Melissa."

Alexa sipped her chai. "So when is settlement on this dream house? I'm glad you'll still be close to Scout and me. Haley, it's a shame you live so far away."

"Mooreland is on your side of town. You just don't like town living."

"I lived in Carlisle until I left for college. It's not that I hate town, but living out in nature is better."

"For some," Haley sniffed.

"Look, there's Tyrell Jenkins." Melissa jumped up, nearly spilling her chai, and dashed across the café. A hug and a brief conversation later, she returned to the table with Tyrell trailing behind.

"Haley, do you know Tyrell?"

"I don't think so. I'm sure I would remember meeting you." Haley stopped and blushed when she realized what she'd just said.

"Join us, Tyrell," Alexa invited. "It's been awhile."

Tyrell eased into a chair and ordered a café latte from Ariel. "Yes. I'm glad you're here. I wanted to thank you for your part in exposing Jack Nash and his band of thugs. When I first heard about it, I just wanted to chuck it all in. When you work in child welfare, one of the fundamental things you rely on is the quality and commitment of the provider agencies. To find out that Children of Light was worse than a sham . . . it violated the trust of every child we placed there. Damn dogs."

He absently stirred his drink as he continued. "Our agency and the state are both taking some heat for not knowing what was going on up there on the mountain. But the state monitored Children of Light. They always passed with flying colors. Our agency routinely visited the kids in placement. None of them ever gave us any indication that there were problems. Maybe they were too scared. Few of the kids were actually affected by the trafficking operation, so maybe they didn't know what was going on. The only anomaly was a high runaway rate—but since they specialized in teens, even that had an explanation. They listed most of those kids as missing from off-campus foster home placements."

"They served a lot of kids from out of state, right?" Alexa remembered a board presentation.

"Yeah. They ran a whole paper trail on out-of-county and out-of-state kids they had trafficked. On paper, it looked like the kids were still around. Those site visits were contracted to another arm of Children of Light, so they pulled the wool over everyone's eyes. They also had a whole adoption scam going on. They had fake parents who went through the adoption process on many of the kids. Then, Children of Light got paid to monitor the fake adoptions. Meanwhile, the kids had been sold to the highest bidder. What a twisted racket."

Alexa grimaced. "I heard that the diversion of foster kids was a very small part of their business. Most of Children of Light's foster care and adoption business was legit. But they used the company and the structure as a front for the illegal trafficking that relied on kidnapping and funneling kids in from overseas."

"What kind of people do that to children?" Haley's expression was a mixture of shock and anger.

Melissa gave a bitter chuckle. "Evil people, honey. You'd be surprised how many black-hearted bastards hide behind an ordinary-looking façade. Cecily opened my eyes to the way these traffickers care about nothing except the money they make. They just chalk up the misery they cause to the cost of doing business." Melissa's voice rang with passion.

Alexa and the others sipped their drinks while lost in their individual thoughts. She remembered that group of refugees in Kenya: young people who'd already lost their homes and had then been further victimized by Jack Nash and his partners in crime.

Tyrell broke the silence. "I also wanted to thank you, Alexa, for what you did for the Bertolinos. We found out why Meg died. Toni and Ed Bertolino will never fully recover from her death, but at least they know she was taken against her will—that she didn't run away from their loving home."

Alexa demurred his praise with a shrug of her shoulders. "Last Wednesday at the clinic, Tanisha told me that the authorities located Aurora Washington as part of the FBI investigation into Children of Light. Tanisha didn't know the details of where she'd been taken other than she was alive, relatively healthy, and still in the United States. I've heard that the FBI has its victim specialists working with all the victims who have been found through this investigation."

"Just think what that poor girl has been through. And hundreds like her." Melissa ripped her napkin in half. "I'd like to do this to Jack Nash and his sanctimonious, snobby priss of a wife, Vivienne. Wonder how she'll fare in prison."

"Maybe they'll let her bring her own designer prison uniform," Alexa's scoffed.

"I imagine Aurora is going to need counseling when she comes home. She's a strong girl, but there's not much family support," Tyrell spoke like the social worker he was. "Alexa, these children owe you so much for rescuing them."

"I can't take credit for any of this, Tyrell." Alexa pictured the face of the teenager who had pleaded for help that night at the Nash villa—the one she had rebuffed.

"You warned me about Jack Nash, but I joined the Children of Light Board thinking I was doing a service for the community. Bit by bit, I stumbled on some things that didn't add up. Hell, Melissa is the one who's been in the middle of this. Cecily tried to tell her what was going on."

"Both of you were nearly killed at Melissa's house," Haley exclaimed. "And, Alexa, I can't believe what you went through, being shot at and chased by those animals. Climbing up a mountain in the dark. How were you able to get through even just the physical challenge?"

"Clean living and lots of hiking." Alexa 's attempt to lighten the mood fell flat.

"I heard your mom was hurt pretty badly. She was county commissioner when I first started in child welfare. I always respected her." Tyrell touched Alexa's arm.

"She's going to make a full recovery. It will just take some time before she's one hundred percent. But, she's a tough one, my mom."

"I wish her well. She and Cecily were friends, right? I remember seeing them lunch at that restaurant down the street from the courthouse; the one that closed last spring."

"I miss Cecily." Melissa sighed. "Who is going to run RESIST?"

Tyrell took a sip of latte. "Theresa Avignon, the head of the RESIST Washington office, is going to step in as CEO. They've asked me to take a job as her second in command. I haven't said yes, yet. I'm still thinking it through."

Alexa recognized this genuine side of Tyrell—the nice, dedicated guy Melissa had described.

"So, what brings you ladies to the Om Café on a Tuesday evening?" The social worker leaned back in his chair.

"This is our regular Tuesday night routine: yoga class followed by chai tea and gossip." Melissa flashed a broad grin.

Haley turned to Alexa. "What's this I hear? You've been doing private lessons with Isabella on advanced poses?"

"Yeah. I've made it a personal challenge to master the headstand, Scorpion, and the Wheel. I'm not quite there yet, but I'm close. I haven't been crashing to the floor as often—which is good because Scout freaks every time I wipe out."

"I can't figure out if I'm impressed or want to just write this off as another example of Alexa Williams, overachiever."

"It began more as a way to focus and distract myself from all the craziness last fall. Now, you're right. It's become a bit of a challenge to master these poses." Alexa slipped her toes into her flip flops and rose to her feet. "Well, this overachiever has to get back to the house and help Mom get ready for bed. I told Dad I'd take evening duty tonight. I think I can get back to the cabin some time next week. Mom's gaining strength every day. Scout is ready to go home, too."

"Now who's projecting? Making Scout take the rap because you're jonesing for that precious cabin." Haley rolled her eyes.

"See you two soon," Alexa told her best friends. Just before turning to the door, she rested her hand on Tyrell's shoulder. "For what it's worth, I think you should take the RESIST job. You have a lot to offer the organization, and it would be a tribute to Cecily's confidence in you."

Alexa left the office early Wednesday afternoon, excited to get back to the cabin. "Scout, it is good to be home." Alexa opened the door and immediately ran around the house, throwing all the windows open to the soft summer breeze. Scout snuffled through the cabin while Alexa unloaded her suitcase and groceries from the rental SUV.

The mastiff escaped the house during her last trip to the car and frolicked around the yard, clearly excited to be back in familiar stomping grounds. "Great idea, buddy." Alexa set the small toiletry case on the deck and stretched out in a lounge chair.

Even in the shade of the cabin, the warm August afternoon felt balmy. Alexa closed her eyes and listened to the sounds of home. A woodpecker hammered a tree in the distance. Close by, the songs of countless birds blended into a tumultuous, ecstatic chorus. The boughs of the giant pines sighed in the gentle breeze. And, beyond that, silence. Home.

Alexa wasn't sure if she'd drifted off to sleep or just a blissful daze, but the light had shifted when she opened her eyes to the sound of a car on the lane. Bright rays of sunlight bathed the pines in a golden glow. Scout leapt up to check out the intruder. His tail began to wag long before Alexa recognized John's unmarked police car.

"Hey," John greeted Alexa when he emerged from the car wearing khakis and a blue twill sport coat. "Are you busy?"

Alexa laughed. "Do I look busy?"

John mounted the steps and nodded at the last of her suitcases still parked on the deck. "Coming or going?"

Alexa sat up into a cross-legged position. "I'm finally back from helping take care of Mom. She's moving around pretty well on her own. I think both she and Dad were as happy to get the house to themselves again as I was to leave. My sister-in-law, Kate, is going to stay with her if Dad has to go into the office or something."

"Glad to hear she's recovering so well. When I saw her lying there in the ambulance that night . . . it looked pretty touch and go. But she looked much better by the time we had the meeting in the hospital."

"I'm so grateful that you got me down the mountain so I could go to the hospital with her. Me being at the ER also helped with explaining to Dad and Graham what had happened."

The trooper leaned against the deck railing, arms crossed. "Sorry I couldn't connect a few weeks ago. When we spoke at your mom's hospital room, I didn't realize all the follow-up work I'd be involved in with this Children of Light case."

"Even with the FBI in the lead?"

"Yeah. But now Corporal Branche has been assigned as the FBI liaison. That task force he's been working on focuses on human trafficking, so the whole thing falls right down his alley. That means I don't have to deal with the Feds anymore.

"And you probably heard that Ralph Price took a plea deal on Cecily Townes' murder. They offered him twenty-five years with the possibility of parole. He escaped life or the death penalty. Plus, he's probably hoping to avoid federal prison on the trafficking counts."

"Melissa was thrilled that Cecily's killer will be locked away for a long, long time. But it's a bittersweet celebration, isn't it? A wonderful woman is still dead."

"Price implicated Jack Nash in Cecily's death. Since Nash gave the order, the D.A. will prosecute him for first-degree murder at some point. All the federal and state cases against him, Vivienne, and Quinn Hutton the father, are competing for priority. At this point, I'm following up on the piece of the puzzle that doesn't fit. You know about the missing women, right?"

When Alexa nodded, John continued. "We can't link them to the Children of Light. And the FBI has pushed back, convinced that the women are another case entirely. They say that the women who have disappeared have little in common with the teens kidnapped by Nash's outfit. And, frankly, I agree with their observation. The adult women don't fit the mold. These ladies, mostly in their thirties or forties, are all working women. From their descriptions and photos, they all seem a little worn down from poverty or a life on the street. Not a marketable profile for the rich, sophisticated clients Nash and the elder Hutton targeted."

The trooper shook his head. "The whole case is a little ragged. One of the women who we listed as missing resurfaced last week. Turns out she met a truck driver and made a spur of the moment decision to join him for a few months on the road. Her reappearance just underscores how few solid facts we have. But I still believe something's going on. I have this gut feeling that the disappearances are real and connected in some way. I've been following up on a few theories, but nothing yet."

Alexa's neck had developed a crick from gazing up at the tall trooper as he paced back and forth in front of her. She eased out of the lounge chair and stood. "Why don't you sit down? Would you like something to drink?" She looked toward the car. "I guess that means no beer?"

"It was quicker to just leave the station and drive out here than to head back to the condo for my car. A soft drink will be fine."

"A Coke? Or I think my niece and nephew left some birch beer here."

John smiled in delight. "Birch beer would be great. The red kind or the white kind? I haven't had birch beer for years."

Amused by John's excitement, Alexa bantered. "I'm pretty sure it's the white. Is that OK?"

"Absolutely." His tone became dead serious. "White is the much rarer and, therefore, much better kind of birch beer. When we were kids, my best friend, Billie Clark, and I would ride our bikes the whole way to Posten's Store for white birch beer."

When Alexa returned to the porch with their drinks, John was seated at the table scratching Scout's ears. He looked up with a wide smile and accepted the bottle of birch beer. "Thanks." After a long swallow, he sighed and said, "Pure heaven. Of course, I should have expected that one as beautiful as you would possess the nectar of the gods." He raised the bottle in tribute to Alexa, who had taken a seat facing him.

Alexa cracked up. She was seeing a new side of this guy: slightly goofy and poetic at the same time. "Trooper, I'd hate to see you tackle alcohol if you get this giddy on soda."

"Not all soda—only white birch beer." John deadpanned.

In the ensuing silence, Alexa groped for something to say. She considered that, other than in an official capacity, she didn't know this man that well. Then she remembered that kiss.

"So what brings you—"

"I was hoping—"

Alexa stopped when her words tripped over John's.

"Sorry, you were saying?" John appeared flustered.

"No. Go ahead."

"OK." John leaned toward Alexa. "I'm here to ask you out. Would you consider having dinner with me on Saturday night?"

"You didn't need to drive the whole way out here to ask me on a date. You could have called."

John leaned closer until his lips nearly touched Alexa's. "But then I wouldn't have a chance to see you . . . or do this." He shifted forward a few inches until their lips joined.

Alexa leaned into the birch beer-infused kiss, her breathing erratic. Their seated position created a clumsy triangle, with an apex of fused lips and a base of knocking knees. Just as Alexa thought she couldn't bear the space between them, John rose and pulled her to her feet, never breaking the kiss.

Alexa melted into John's embrace with rising passion. She could feel an ardent pressure against the zipper of her jeans that left no doubt about John's fervor. In the surrounding forest, dusk's arrival unleashed the nightly clamor of summer cicadas. The electric vibration of the cicadas' hum pulsed through Alexa's core. As if her body was acting on its own volition, she rose to her toes in an effort to further meld into John's tall frame.

When John broke off the sizzling kiss, Alexa felt bereft. As if he sensed her struggle to regain equilibrium, John took her hands in his.

"So, I'm waiting for your answer." John chided.

"Answer?"

"Will you go out with me Saturday?"

"The conflict of interest thing is no longer an issue?"

"Let's just say it's less of an issue. Cecily Townes' murderer is behind bars. It could be months and months before Jack Nash is prosecuted for his role in that death. You aren't involved in the Meg Wilson case. Corporal Branche is working with the Feds now. I think I'm in the clear."

"I just need to tell you that I have a terrible track record with men and relationships."

"I'm willing to take the risk."

A neglected Scout pushed his way between John and Alexa, breaking them apart. Alexa laughed and leaned over to kiss his snout. "Poor baby, you have to be the center of attention."

She raised her eyes to meet John's hopeful gaze. "What time do you want to pick me up on Saturday?"

CHAPTER FORTY-FIVE

ALEXA STOOD IN FRONT OF the Carlisle Theater trying to ignore the sweat trickling down her spine. She slipped off her linen cardigan. With work finished for the day, she could shed the sweater that even casual Friday at the office demanded. She hoped that Quinn would get here soon so they could find somewhere cool for that drink.

She sighed with relief when Quinn pulled his vintage sports car to the curb in front of her. He left the car running and jumped out.

"Thanks for agreeing to meet. I understand this might be a bit awkward. But, we've been good friends, and I wanted to say good-bye to you before I left town." Quinn had dressed down in black designer jeans and a silky dark charcoal t-shirt. He opened the passenger door in invitation.

"I know you enjoyed our trip to Harrisburg in this old beauty, and I thought you might like a last spin."

The thought of a ride in a convertible sounded wonderful in this sweltering heat, but Alexa hesitated. "I thought we were walking over to Roussillon for a drink."

"Why don't we ride out to Chestnut Farms instead? The patio has plenty of shade, and it should be quite pleasant." Quinn glanced toward the open car door.

"Sure, why not." Alexa tossed her handbag onto the floor and settled into the low-slung seat. Chestnut Farms sounded like a good idea. They had an outside terrace and served great shoofly pie. "I didn't picture you as a fan of Pennsylvania Dutch cuisine."

"When in Rome . . ." Quinn pulled into the flow of Friday night traffic. "You'd be surprised at the taste I've developed for the local fare. Did you leave your car at the office?"

"Sure, it's just a few blocks to the theater, although something other than these ballet flats would have been better for walking." She looked down the legs of her knit pants suit. "Fridays are pretty casual at the firm in the summer."

"I apologize that I didn't call to run the change in plans by you. I could have picked you up at the law firm."

Once again, it seemed like everyone on the street was gawking at this gleaming black sports car as Quinn drove down High Street. Even in a town habituated to a constant stream of vintage and classic cars from the Carlisle car shows, this Mercedes 500K Roadster stood out from the pack.

Alexa hadn't seen Quinn since the party at Children of Light and the estate security force's harrowing assault on the Williams women. Now he was leaving town and she wanted to wish him well. Their relationship was still hard to define. They'd made a few tentative steps toward romance before they'd settled for something else. She wasn't quite sure she'd characterize it as the "good friends" that Quinn had described. But certainly more than business associates. She had enjoyed spending time with Quinn.

When she'd accepted Quinn's invitation to get together this evening, Alexa had made a conscious decision: Quinn was not responsible or involved in his father's crimes. The police investigation had absolved him. She wouldn't let the sins of the father affect her opinion of Quinn. In fact, she felt sorry for the guy.

"So you've decided to leave town, but doesn't the new semester start in a few days?" Alexa asked at the next traffic light.

"Yes. Monday. I know I'm leaving the college in the lurch. But I just can't stay here after everything that's happened. It's time to move on. The college understands my situation and has been extremely accommodating. Officially, they're calling this a sabbatical. But I'm going to take a break for a few months then begin searching for a new position."

"Your dad's arrest must have been quite a shock."

"You have no idea," Quinn muttered as he stepped on the gas. He glanced over at Alexa with a solemn expression. "I know that you and your mother went through quite an ordeal. And, apparently, my father and Uncle Jack bear some responsibility for that. I feel terrible about the whole situation."

"Quinn, you can't be held accountable for what your father and Jack Nash did. Let's leave it at that."

Alexa leaned back to enjoy the artificial breeze, while Quinn maneuvered the car through Friday evening traffic. He seemed unusually taciturn, but Alexa attributed it to the awkwardness of their situation.

When they turned onto the road toward Plainfield, Alexa turned to Quinn. "Isn't Chestnut Farm out beyond the high school, off Wagner's Gap Road?"

"You're right. But it's turned a little cool." He nodded toward the cardigan in her lap. "You've got your sweater, but the wind is cutting right through this thin shirt. Do you mind if we make a quick detour to my house so I can pick up a jacket?"

Alexa didn't bother to reply since Quinn was clearly headed home. But she was a little annoyed that he hadn't had the courtesy to explain this detour until she had asked. Quinn's polished manners and charm had worn a little rough around the edges in the aftermath of his father's arrest.

For a moment, she wondered whether this trip with Quinn was a good idea. After all, she didn't know how his father's spectacular downfall had affected him. She knew that the two had been quite close. And, in many ways, Alexa and her mom had precipitated the elder Hutton's crash and burn. But, surely, Quinn was his own man. He seemed truly upset by the actions of his father and Jack Nash.

She brushed her reservations aside. This little side trip would give her a chance to see Quinn's—What had he called it?—quintessential Cumberland County farmette. She loved all the old limestone farmhouses that dotted the valley and imagined Quinn's home as one of those.

The whole jacket thing was a bit strange, though, even for a clotheshorse like Quinn. Maybe he expected the evening to cool down, but the thermometer outside the bank they'd passed a few minutes ago had registered 97 degrees.

Quinn took a sharp right into a gravel lane hidden by an overgrown hedgerow that almost swallowed the entrance. Alexa frowned at the scruffy entry. She would have imagined stone columns or even an outrageous pair of lions from Quinn. Instead, she flinched, half expecting the briars to scratch the Mercedes as they drove through. But the opening proved just wide enough for the car to pass unscathed.

The lane wound a serpentine route through acres of wild meadows thick with tangled weeds. Alexa identified Joe Pye Weed, sumac, thistles, and even a patch of deadly nightshade as they passed. For a moment, she imagined that the gnarled and ragged fields were closing in on the car like the menacing hedge of thorns in that Disney movie. She shook her head to clear the disturbing image. She was getting as bad as her mother, applying Disney cartoons to real life.

"Didn't you say a farmer rented some of your fields? None of this looks cultivated."

"I like my privacy, so the only fields I rent out are at the far end of the farm. I've got thirty acres in total." Quinn's tone was clipped, as if he resented Alexa's prying. When she glanced at the professor, he returned her gaze with an inscrutable expression. Uneasy about the strange vibe she was getting from Quinn, Alexa wondered again if meeting him had been a mistake.

After five minutes or more of driving through the desolate fields, Alexa finally glimpsed a roof surrounded by a thicket of dense trees. She recoiled when they reached the house. No pristine limestone farmhouse here. Instead, the house looked like a Victorian gone to seed. A jumble of dormers and columns competed for attention with a round turret topped by a pointed roof. The gingerbread trim must have been beautiful once. Now, it was so stained and discolored that Alexa could barely make out the ornate details against the peeling gray walls.

She could never have imagined the always-impeccable Quinn Hutton living in a dump like this. The small barn in the rear actually looked in better shape than the house.

With surprise, Alexa noticed an exquisitely carved wooden house on a pole toward the back of the small, scraggly yard. A larger version of the little structure on Quinn's office desk. What had he called it? A spirit house? It astonished Alexa to see this spirit house filled with candles and food. Apparently, Quinn wanted to keep the spirits of this dismal old farmhouse happy. The man continued to be a puzzle.

When Quinn cut the motor, he turned to Alexa with an enigmatic expression. "If you'll just wait for a minute, I'll run in for my jacket." Leaving Alexa perplexed by his sudden air of excitement, Quinn bounded out of the car and headed toward the house.

This whole trip was getting weirder and weirder. Alexa found herself wishing that she'd just insisted on sticking with the original plan of a drink in town.

Making its descent toward sunset, the sun plunged behind the tall thicket of mature trees, leaving the courtyard murky with shadow. But the stifling heat refused to yield to the deepening shade. In the dim light, the dilapidated Victorian loomed like a haunted house.

Alexa jumped at the unexpected chirp of her cell phone. She wiped a hand across her damp brow before plucking the phone from her pocketbook, happy for a distraction from her gloomy thoughts.

Melissa had texted: “Jim’s working. Come over?”

Alexa texted back. “No. Out with Quinn. At his house now. Creepy place.”

“Ditch him. Hang out with me.”

“Not tonight.” Alexa typed. As she hit send, a flock of huge black birds broke from the trees and flew low over the car. Startled, Alexa shrieked and dropped her cell phone into a slot between the seat and the console.

“Shit.” She scrunched her body around in the tight seat to fish for the cell phone with her right hand. As Alexa bent over, she caught sight of a jacket lying on the floor behind the driver’s seat.

“What the hell? Quinn already had a jacket.” With a sense of foreboding, Alexa knew that this situation had morphed from weird to frightening. Alarm bells pealed in her mind. She had to get out of here. Now.

Quinn had left the keys in the ignition. She whispered under her breath, “Fuck it. I’m going to drive this beast out of here.”

But the gearshift prevented her from easily sliding into the driver’s seat. Sneaking a surreptitious glance at the house, Alexa eased open the car door and slipped out. She had taken a single step toward the front of the car when a hand gripped her shoulder from behind. Alexa froze, her heart pounding.

“I never let anyone drive this car,” Quinn stated in a matter of fact tone. Before Alexa could reply, he clamped a red cloth over her nose and mouth. She gagged and felt her legs buckling, then nothing . . .

CHAPTER FORTY-SIX

WHEN ALEXA REGAINED consciousness, she thought she could be dreaming. Her head felt thick and slow. The soft wool of a Persian rug cushioned her cheek. Its deep maroon tones reminded her of the one in Grandma Williams' old living room. The wall in front of her, fuzzy at first, came into focus as rough-cut lumber.

Wake up, Alexa, a voice in her mind commanded. When she tried to sit, a sharp pain bit into both wrists. The pain cleared her head, and she realized with a sinking feeling that she wasn't dreaming. This was real.

"Welcome back. I'm sorry for the brief trip to dreamland, but I was fairly certain that my charms alone wouldn't lure you into my temple." Quinn's voice came from somewhere behind Alexa.

As he spoke, she scoped out her situation, trying to control mounting panic. Her hands were bound in front of her with a rope that looped around a metal ring set low in the wall. Although the thick ropes chafed her wrists, Quinn had left some play in the length of cord between her hands. About three feet of rope separated her hands from the wall. Carefully this time, she rolled into a sitting position and shuffled backward until her back could rest against the boards.

"That's better. Would you like a drink?"

Alexa nodded; her mouth felt like dry cotton. Quinn brought a bottle of water and held it to her mouth for a few sips. "If you need to use the ladies' room, just let me know. Of course, I'll have to accompany you."

Alexa shuddered at the thought.

"What's going on, Quinn?" Although Alexa was frightened, she thought she could reason with Quinn and escape this predicament. Alexa couldn't figure out what the man was up to.

Was he lashing out in reaction to his father's arrest? Was he holding her for ransom?

The professor ignored Alexa's question and returned to the center of the room. Alexa continued to study her surroundings. She was certain that this was the small barn she'd seen when they arrived at Quinn's house.

The high ceilings were the same rough-cut lumber as the wall behind her. The air carried the faint smell of dry hay and pigeon poop—the same as Nana's barn. The cavernous space felt much cooler than outside.

When Alexa turned her attention to Quinn and the space where he stood, she rocked with a surge of icy terror. Ornately embroidered indigo fabric covered all three walls. She'd seen the cloth in catalogs, on pillows made by the Hmong and other hill tribes of Southeast Asia. But that fabric was crazy expensive and there were more yards here than she could count.

On the far wall of the shadowy room, there was an area that looked like an altar. In place of a crucifix or a Buddha, a six-foot shape that looked vaguely female stood atop a long, low pedestal. The form's arms were stretched at a slight angle from its sides, the inside honeycombed with small compartments. Most were filled with decorated wooden boxes.

In front of the altar, Quinn, still clad in black, hunched over a high table draped in blood red silk. Candles burned at the foot of the altar. But the main light supply came from an elaborate crystal chandelier suspended above the table.

Alexa took in this bizarre scene with mounting dread. A glacial weight drove the air from her lungs. Gasping, she reeled: Quinn planned to kill her. Horror pinned her to the wall. She felt helpless to resist its giddy embrace. She couldn't breathe. She couldn't move. But then Alexa pushed back, refusing to succumb to obliterating fear.

She subdued the rising terror with a silent chant: Panic means death, panic means death, panic means death . . .

Quinn broke his long silence to answer the question she'd posed earlier. "I've chosen you, Alexa, to help me complete my tribute to the Nang Ton Pho. You should be honored. See these reliquaries? The relic you're going to provide is arguably the most important piece among all the sacrifices."

Fighting to keep her breath steady, she chanced a reply. Quinn seemed calm, but she strived for a noncommittal tone that wouldn't agitate him. Her voice was hoarse. "Relics? Reliquary? Quinn, I'm not sure I understand."

"Well, you see," Quinn took on a condescending tone. "A reliquary is a box used in certain religions to house the body parts or relics of important religious figures. For example, the Shwedagon Pagoda in Burma houses hair of the Buddha. Every cathedral and second-rate monastery in France and Italy boasts the relic of some saint."

Alexa tried to force the words through her dry mouth, "Yes, I'm familiar with reliquaries. I saw the crown of thorns at Notre Dame in Paris."

"One of many relics related to Jesus; wood from the cross, his shroud, even his foreskin. If you put together all the Jesus relics scattered around the world, you'd end up with a reconstructed Jesus as big as Godzilla. A Jeszilla, if you will." Quinn emitted an urbane chuckle, clearly pleased with his little *bon mot*.

"The suspect provenance of many reliquaries aside, it pleases me that you are familiar with the concept. You are here because I respect your intellect. The long history of relics shows their powerful force. Even if the relic's connection to Buddha or Saint Whoever is dubious, the offering and worship of the object instills it with real power."

Alexa couldn't decide which was more terrifying. The suggestion that part of her body was going to end up in one of those ornate boxes or that Quinn's conversational tone was no different from when they'd chatted over a meal.

When Alexa failed to respond, Quinn continued. "But I see you are still a bit confused, so perhaps I should start at the beginning. You see, our lives became intertwined before we were even born, you and I. You're aware that your mother and my father were traveling companions to the Woodstock Festival?"

Alexa nodded, actually interested in what he had to say.

"Your mother was a nosey parker at Woodstock, who stumbled into some private business my father and Jack were into. But, I imagine that for her, Woodstock was all about the typical sex, drugs, and rock and roll." Quinn sniffed in disdain.

"For my dad, Woodstock provided the opportunity to blossom and accept his own special power. In a crowd of stoned hippies, cut off from all the social norms that had stifled him for so many years, Dad and his best friend, Jack, had the chance to experiment with something they'd only talked about. Well, I suppose they had done a bit of practice on small animals and such. But, they picked a girl, a child really, to rape and kill. It was the first time that they truly unleashed their power." Quinn smiled in admiration.

Repelled, Alexa knew he meant Willow, her mother's young friend.

"For both of them, the rush of that powerful act became a springboard for more. Dad told me that every year he and Jack would go somewhere away from Newport, usually one of the beach towns, and pick other girls to kill. He said it was easy. By the seventies, girls had a lot more freedom. Many left home to become hippies and live in communes or make their way in the big city. Hitchhiking was common.

"After college, Dad and Jack turned their hobby into a business. They figured, hell, if they were having so much fun with these young girls, there must be other men out there who'd like to have their own fun. Or women—they had to change with the times and welcome equal opportunity.

"Of course, they found that most clients seemed to prefer just the sex and not the killing. What visionaries. With just some seed money from the family fortune, my dad and Jack managed to expand their little business into a worldwide operation in a little over a decade. Just like the Rockefellers or one of the transnational oil companies."

Quinn looked to Alexa as if she should be impressed. "It certainly was a complex operation," she managed, her throat tight with fear and revulsion.

"But you'll be wondering what my role in all of this was. It's quite an absorbing tale." Quinn looked at Alexa with a self-satisfied smile. "My mother died when I was ten. Her death brought Dad and me much closer. By that time, Jack had moved here to set up the Children of Light facility. So, Dad took me under his wing to teach me about the power. Everyone was a lot more security-conscious by then, telling their daughters not to talk to strangers and all that. But, since I was a kid, older girls had no qualms about talking to me . . . or following me to see a puppy." Quinn's voice grew nostalgic.

"Of course, I was too young at first for the sex part. But Dad let me watch and we experimented with different ways to take the power." Quinn sniggered like a little boy. "Later I got to do the sex thing. Sometimes we'd do it together. I've never felt closer to my father than in those times." Quinn sat on a leather stool near the high table, clearly enjoying his reminiscence.

It was all Alexa could do to keep from throwing up as this maniac, this guy she had willingly kissed, described his childhood apprenticeship in rape and murder.

"Then the time came for me to go to college and graduate school. So, Dad and I 'would go no more a-roving,' as Lord Byron might say. After college, I wanted to see a bit of the world so I got a job in Paris. Actually, two jobs. As you know, I taught school, but I also helped out with Children of Light business, shepherding some of our young charges throughout Europe, doing recruitment in orphanages in some of the larger European cities.

"Ah, Paris, the City of Light. You've been, of course? Why yes, you mentioned Notre Dame." Quinn slid off the stool to pick up a long, curved knife and began to sharpen the blade with a whetstone. The light from the chandelier cast his distended silhouette on one wall: an enormous monster with a huge bulge at his crotch, smiling as he honed a giant machete.

Alexa tore her gaze from the terrifying shadow image and managed to nod in response. Nauseous, she recoiled at the thought of Quinn raping her. How could she have spent time with this man and not realized his depravity?

"Paris is where I came into my own. It was a wonderful environment to hone my power. So many chic women. I found that my own taste runs toward a slightly more experienced, sophisticated woman—one with a bit of *je ne sais quois*. But, eventually, I began to feel that something was missing.

"One night, I ran into a wiry, white-haired man in a rather seedy bar on the edge of the 18th Arrondissement. Almost immediately, we recognized our shared predilections . . . that we were fellow seekers of that certain power. Emile Delon was his name—although I suspect he wore names like a loose overcoat that he shrugged off when things became too hot.

"Emile helped me understand what was missing: Dad's approach to the power was crude and uncontrolled, lacking in higher meaning. The old man had found meaning by turning his power to the service of Lord Buddha and the spirits."

As Quinn's soliloquy continued, Alexa sank into a torpor. Whatever he'd used to knock her out combined with the aftermath of the subsequent adrenaline rush had drained her completely. Even this new absurdity—murder in service to one of the world's most peaceful religions—couldn't rouse more than a passing moment of incredulity. She tried to sit up a little straighter, but the ring in the wall was too low and the rope too short. She hadn't noticed Quinn lighting incense, but now a heavy exotic scent, like myrrh, filled the enclosed room. Alexa's stomach roiled at a fetid undertone in the cloying odor.

Apparently, Alexa's lack of enthusiasm didn't bother Quinn, who continued his narrative with great animation.

"Emile had spent some time in the Golden Triangle, where he came across a village that practiced a unique form of Buddhism. Some of the ancient Tantric texts from Tibet talk about the use of human sacrifice. Emile had studied those ancient texts for many years. Then he stumbled into a place that actually practiced human sacrifice. Like many of the Shan, this village's Buddhism included healthy dose of animism; they also believed in Nats."

Quinn's tone turned pedantic again, as if he were in his classroom. "Nats are spirits, usually of people who met a violent death. They can be found in trees, in water.

"Instead of some of the traditional gifts, like tobacco or liquor, this village's Guardian Nat demanded young women in sacrifice. So the thread of Tantrism and animism fused into a ritual built on sacrificial death. After visiting this village, Emile channeled his pursuit of the power into honoring both Buddha and the Nats with new female sacrifices.

"The whole idea electrified me." Quinn flashed a boyish smile at Alexa. "I found a new posting in Thailand almost immediately. Of course, I could continue to perform duties for the family business since Thailand was a major branch of the operation." Quinn finished honing the curved knife and turned to sharpening an ornate saw.

Alexa slipped deeper into a protective daze. Although she heard every single one of Quinn's vile words, it was like sitting in a room with the television volume turned low. Quinn's loathsome chatter hissed and crackled with static.

"After a few fruitless trips to the jungles of the Golden Triangle, I finally tracked down Emile's village. The head woman welcomed me and invited me to spend a few months there, studying and participating in their rituals. What a wonderful sense of belonging I had that summer. I felt like I was part of something much bigger than myself. As an honored guest, I got my pick of women to sacrifice at each full moon, and I could choose how.

"I went a little wild with the freedom. I used an elephant to crush my first sacrifice. Although it was exciting to see what applied pressure can do to the human body, the end result was quite messy. I feared that I had offended the Nat. So I studied the use of Shan weaponry." He nodded toward the curved knife, a dreamy smile flitting over his face. "I find the personal interaction suits me better.

"So, now, I use my power in service to Lord Buddha and the village Nat, called Nang Ton Pho. Using reliquaries has been my own unique twist. I collect a bone from each sacrifice to complete an entire body for the Nat."

When Quinn walked to the female outline sitting on the altar, Alexa stirred to attention.

As if Quinn were teaching one of his classes, he lifted out each gilded wooden box for illustration. "This is a hand. And this. Here are the two leg boxes. And the feet. Of course, the breast is simply tissue—so odd that such an iconic part of the female form dissolves so quickly into dust. But I've captured a piece of the breastbone, here."

Alexa couldn't help but listen with a nauseous fascination to Quinn's twisted lecture . . . or notice that there were two empty compartments in the form.

"I'll confess, it took me awhile to develop the necessary discipline. There for a while I got bored between the full moons, so I sacrificed dogs—just to give me a little *amuse bouche* between the main courses, so to speak." Quinn looked a bit embarrassed at this admission.

Alexa remembered the chilly reception that her mastiff had given Quinn that night at the cabin. No wonder. His hypersensitive canine nose must have detected the smell of other dead dogs. If only I'd heeded Scout's warning, Alexa lamented silently.

"But now I've developed discipline. I've been fortunate in finding sacrifices each month. But all of them were disposable women that few would miss: whores, lower class drudges—women with no real intellectual capacity. Truthfully, taking the women was easier than capturing some of those little yappy dogs.

Alexa slowly pieced it together: the missing women, the hanged dogs—it had all been part of Quinn's twisted and malicious plan.

"I'd been fretting about where I could find someone worthy to sacrifice for the skull relic. I was worried that Nang Ton Pho would be angry if I offered her the skull of one of those vacuous sluts."

Quinn finished sharpening the handsaw. He rose to place the saw and the knife in a long, gilded box. Locking the box and pocketing the key, he returned to his seat on the leather stool. A candle by the altar sputtered into darkness as Quinn hunched forward, his feverish gaze boring into Alexa's eyes.

"Things started looking up when Jack asked me to cozy up to you. When they found out that you'd discovered Cecily Townes' body, he thought you might have learned something that could connect him to her death. As I got to know you, I began to like you. You are attractive, come from a respectable family. And you are very, very smart.

"I've had you in mind for the skull almost since the day we first met. But, I must confess, I developed some qualms because we had become such friends. I found myself choosing other pieces for my boxes; a foot, a hand." Quinn's voice hardened to steel. "But when you and your bitch mother brought down my father, all bets were off."

Alexa could barely breathe. In her heart, she had known what Quinn had in store for her—or at least the general idea—from the moment she opened her eyes and took in this creepy psycho temple. But now he'd said it. He was going to kill her and put her skull in a box to honor some spirit that lived in a tree in Thailand. Alexa swallowed a bubble of hysterical laughter with a sob.

Quinn noticed Alexa's distress and crouched down in front of her. His eyes glittered hard as ice, but he used a soothing tone. "Don't worry. I'll be quick and clean. You won't feel a thing."

Alexa forced herself to look him in the eye but couldn't speak.

He patted her shoulder as if comforting a worried toddler; then he rose. "Oh, of course. I should mention that you don't have to worry about sexual violation. Emile taught me that a sacrifice should never be traumatized with rape."

Alexa's stomach lurched as she shrank from his touch.

"My seed becomes part of the sacrifice only after she is set free. I use my sexual release to bond with the sacrifice as part of the offering." Quinn turned and sauntered toward the corner of the barn.

He spoke over his shoulder in a bright voice. "Everything is ready. I've got a light repast waiting. I'll be back when the moon has risen. I would offer you something, but I suspect you're not very hungry."

CHAPTER FORTY-SEVEN

WHEN THE DOOR CLICKED SHUT, Alexa fell onto her side and curled into a ball, whimpering. This fucking nut job was going to kill her with that wicked looking knife, screw her dead body, then cut off her head with a saw. Terror paralyzed Alexa. She couldn't move.

Like a salvation, the mantra crept into her mind: Panic means death. Panic means death. She clawed her way back from the edge and felt the floorboards beneath the carpet digging into her ribs; she smelled the musty barn beneath the cloying incense. She knew she had to fight, to try to escape.

Alexa opened her eyes and twisted so that she could examine the wall behind her. She had been so mesmerized by Quinn's little sideshow that she'd paid scant attention to the planks she'd been leaning against. On closer inspection, this wall didn't extend the whole way to the ceiling; it was more like one side of an old stable. As she ran her eyes up the half wall, Alexa noticed a rusty piece of metal dangling over the top of the stall. Perhaps a bit for a long-dead horse's mouth or a stirrup? If she could get to that, maybe she could saw through the rope.

But the top of the wall was several feet above her head. The rope that secured her was looped through a ring near the floor. There was no way she could stand to reach that length of metal.

Like a ray of clear light, it came to her. All these months of trying to master the Scorpion pose could help here. Alexa slipped off her shoes and turned to face the wall directly beneath the piece of metal. She tried to quell her panic and become calm.

After several deep breaths, Alexa positioned her arms in a V on the rug in front of her. Ironically, the rope between her wrists helped to maintain the proper arm position. On her knees, she lowered her head to a spot between her elbows then straightened her legs into a jackknife pose similar to Dolphin. She moved her legs closer to her body, and slowly and deliberately lifted her legs, one by one, until her body rose into a headstand.

It took her a few moments to attain balance before the next crucial step. She had to pick up the piece of metal with her bare feet and drop it on her side of the wall. A wrong move and it would be lost on the other side. This maneuver had to be done by touch since her eyes faced the floor.

With careful deliberation, Alexa raised her head off the floor and arched her back into a C-shape to begin the inverted backbend known as Scorpion Pose. In the full pose, the feet would be lowered close to the head, mimicking the position in which scorpions carry their stingers, looped forward toward their heads. But Alexa wouldn't need to go that far into the pose. Muscles trembling, legs parallel to her head, she sent her feet toward the wall. This was where she usually crashed to the floor.

Alexa concentrated with every fiber of her body. Straining to maintain balance, she felt her toes brush the top of the wall. With painstaking control, she brought her feet toward each other until . . . there! Her right toe touched the metal. Inch by inch, she brought her left toe to the other side of the metal and lifted.

The metal didn't budge.

She fought off despair as sweat trickled off her forehead and onto the carpet. For a second, Alexa lost concentration and felt as if she would topple. With sheer force of will, she focused on her breathing to regain concentration.

After several deep breaths, Alexa again used her toes to clasp the chain. This time, she brought her toes beneath the chain to pry it from the wood. And, in an instant, it was free.

Too heavy to hold with her feet, the metal piece slipped from her toes and plummeted to the floor, slicing painfully into her left hand. The thick carpet and her hand muffled the sound.

Alexa ignored the pain and slowly unfolded from her pose. When she reached the rug, she shook from the combined effects of tension and exhaustion.

Wiping her forehead with the hem of her blouse, Alexa pulled herself together. She had no idea how long it would be until moonrise. Quinn could return to the barn any minute. Alexa looked at the blood trickling from the gash on her left hand and grinned. At least this metal thing was sharp.

She immediately tested it by hacking at the single rope that connected her to the metal ring in the wall. The play in the cord between her wrists gave her enough mobility to saw the taut rope. Alexa hewed frantically with an ear cocked for Quinn's arrival.

Seconds ticked away until a strand of rope frayed, and then another and another until the whole thing separated.

Alexa slipped into her shoes and grabbed the metal bit. She would cut the cord between her hands later. When she first stood, she rocked in a wave of dizziness. Spots danced before her eyes. Alexa wobbled but steadied herself against the wooden wall. When the dizziness passed, Alexa rushed toward the altar and tried to open the golden box containing the knife and saw.

The lock wouldn't budge.

Leave it, she thought. There's no time.

Following Quinn's path, she rushed to escape the building. In a well-lit outer room, she found the exit.

Just as she was about to unlatch the wooden door, Alexa heard movement on the other side. Quinn was coming. She ducked behind some moldering bales of hay.

Quinn entered the barn dressed in a loose-fitting black tunic and pants. On his head was a scarf tied in a fashion that looked vaguely Asian. Or like the Dread Pirate Roberts in *The Princess Bride*.

Jesus, Alexa, she thought. This is not a time for jokes or random thoughts. You have to focus.

Quinn walked by Alexa's hiding place, oblivious to her presence. Clearly, he expected to find Alexa right where he had left her. As he entered the temple room, Alexa dashed out the door, catching it before it closed and easing it shut behind her. Emerging from the cool dry interior, she faltered for a moment as she hit a wall of humid heat.

Her earlier conclusion had been correct. Quinn had taken her to the barn behind his house. She called up every ounce of strength and sprinted past the Victorian monstrosity, hoping to find the keys still in the car. But a light shining from a front window revealed nothing but an empty courtyard. She noticed another building to the left of the house, which could have been a garage, but she couldn't chance it. The building was dark. It could be locked. He wouldn't leave car keys in the ignition.

She looked around frantically for a place to hide, though she could see nothing but an impenetrable barrier of thick dark hedges and towering black trees.

Seeing no other option, Alexa tore down the lane in the pitch dark, hoping to put as much distance as possible between her and Quinn. As she ran, she tensed for the moment Quinn would come after her. With each step, she imagined Quinn tearing apart the barn, furious to find her missing. A split second later, the barn door slammed. Quinn howled a chilling roar of loss and anger. The maniacal tone of his screams raised goosebumps over Alexa's entire body. But she didn't pause in her headlong flight to find safety.

Next, Quinn stormed through the house and garage. Alexa kept track of his movements from the sounds of breaking glass and banging doors. She measured her progress forward from the steadily receding volume of Quinn's curses. But it had taken them a long time to reach the house from the main road. She still had miles to go.

"Shit, shit, shit," Alexa muttered when that inevitable moment came. A vehicle engine roared back at the house—not the sports car; maybe the pickup truck.

She couldn't believe how fast the truck devoured each mile of her hard-won run to freedom. The pickup drove slowly, but in minutes the arc of its headlights fell only a few yards behind Alexa. Just before the headlights threatened to capture her in their snare, the truck stopped. The beam of a spotlight hit the gravel to her right. Sweat streaming down her body, she slipped into the meadow on the left. A few feet in, she became entangled in a huge blackberry bush and squatted low. The metal bit that she had been clasping like a talisman slipped from her hands into the thick underbrush.

Quinn spoke in a cajoling tone above the idle of the motor. "You may as well come out, Alexa. Clearly, I underestimated you. But that's exactly why you'll make the perfect sacrifice. I need someone as smart as you.

"But you'll never get away. It's miles to the main road. These fields are nothing but briars and brambles. There's no way you can make it out that way. I'd rather have you unscathed for the offering. Calculate the odds yourself, counselor. It's better to just accept the inevitable."

Crouched three feet off the road, Alexa couldn't dispute his description of the vegetation. This meadow was an impenetrable mass of thorns, baked brittle by the August heat. The dry smell of exploding seedpods mingled with the acrid scent of snapped stems. Alexa fought the urge to sneeze.

In just a few short feet, the brush had ripped her face and arms to shreds. With her hands still bound, she had limited opportunity to fend off the branches. Mosquitoes swarmed to the gash on her hand and the new scratches on her face. She tried to worm her way farther into the field, but the blackberry thorns had snared a clump of her hair. She crawled forward until the thorns released their hold, but the bush sprang back with a loud rustle. Alexa froze and hugged the ground.

The movement of the bush gave her away. In an instant, Quinn focused the spotlight on the spot where she lay, panting in fear.

"I know you're in there, Alexa. Just give up. Think of it as martyrdom if you want. Into the valley of death rode the smart lawyer."

Although she was cornered, it was the bastardized Tennyson quote that sent Alexa over the edge. She leapt to her feet and stalked back onto the road. "You asshole. I am not going to be your docile little sacrifice or martyr or whatever ridiculous pretext you use for your twisted murder games. And I am sick to death of your pretentious overuse of literary allusions. That shit may impress the freshman coeds, but your pathetic attempts to sound intellectual only make me laugh."

Alexa knew her chances were slim. But she wouldn't go willingly. She turned and fled down the lane.

"You bitch." Quinn's shriek hung in the air behind her as she sprinted for her life.

Quinn took his time. Alexa knew he was playing with her but didn't slow her pace. The truck door slammed. An eternity later, the pickup drove forward at a leisurely pace. Still, the sputtering crunch of gravel beneath its tires crept steadily closer.

Alexa scanned both sides of the lane as she ran, looking for an opening in the wall of brambles. All she needed was a bare stretch or even some tall grass, and she could abandon the lane. Maybe find a place to hide. Make it difficult or impossible for Quinn to follow in the truck.

But she could find no break in this endless tunnel of thorns. Alexa developed a stitch in her side and could feel her pace lag. Dimly, it registered that she had stopped sweating and dehydration might be closing in. Sharp pieces of gravel stabbed through the thin soles of her flats with every footstep. She kept pushing herself down the lane.

Exhausted to the point of collapse, Alexa had lost all sense of time as she trudged forward. Quinn's truck dogged her heels. Around her, the inky night had lightened, glowing silver over the treacherous fields. She raised her eyes to the full moon shining high in the sky and knew she had lost.

Quinn pulled up beside her and spoke through the open window. His eyes glittered in the moonlight like jagged chrome. "This has been quite amusing, Alexa. I don't think I've ever had such an entertaining experience. I believe Nan Ton Pho will be all the more pleased to receive such an excellent gift. But I think it's time to stop the games and get on with the ceremony."

Alexa finally stopped walking. Through the thin soles of the ballet flats, her feet were on fire. Head down, gasping for breath, she had to rest her roped hands on the side of Quinn's truck to remain upright. A muscle in her thigh cramped into an unbearable knot.

"Fuck you, Quinn," she whispered. When she straightened to look directly into the barrel of Quinn's pistol, she was too tired to even flinch.

"Enough, Alexa." Quinn motioned with the menacing gun. "Get into the truck."

Alexa swayed on her feet, incapable of going on. Still, from the core of her being, she refused to submit to Quinn's macabre plans for her death. She considered letting him shoot her right there in the road. Then all that knife polishing would have been for naught.

Quinn sighed and edged his door open. As his foot met the ground, Alexa stumbled backwards.

In the yawning silence, a faint sound caught Alexa's attention. She tilted her ear toward the main road and the murmur of sirens borne on the night air. Alexa shook her head to clear it. She knew that desperation must have driven her to conjure up the idea of a police rescue.

Don't lose it now, Alexa, she thought as she took another cautious step away from Quinn.

Then Alexa's heart leapt. Out of the corner of her eye, she saw a flashing line of blue and red lights. At least three police vehicles sped down the lane toward them, sirens blaring. She summoned the strength to hope.

Quinn was so focused on Alexa that it took him a moment to register the approaching police cars. When he saw the oncoming vehicles, he lunged for Alexa. She avoided his grasp and threw herself into the meadow, falling into a prickly mound of wild thistle.

The first police car screeched to a halt a short distance away from the truck. John Taylor and Trooper Cannon tumbled from the vehicle and stood behind their open doors, guns aimed at Quinn. One of them trained a spotlight on the professor.

Alexa's heart warmed to see John. But Quinn was out of control. She had to warn them.

Before she could call out, Cannon yelled. "Hutton. Drop the gun. Where is Alexa Williams?" Additional policemen in protective gear and carrying weapons fanned out on either side of John's car, slowly moving toward Quinn.

Afraid that she'd be caught in the crossfire if there was shooting, Alexa managed to wriggle farther into the field and turn to lie on her belly in the weeds. Pain from the cramp in her thigh had become unbearable. She knew that she was suffering from severe dehydration.

"Why would you think Alexa Williams is here?" Quinn asked. "I haven't seen her in weeks."

She could hear the anger in John's reply. "Don't lie to us. Earlier this evening, Alexa texted a friend that she was here with you. The friend became concerned when she couldn't get an answer to her return texts and calls. So she contacted us."

"Thank you, Melissa." Alexa whispered. The stalk of plump thistles in front of her blurred. When she opened her eyes, she could focus enough to hear John's voice but only snippets of what he was saying.

"The timing . . . confirmation from Interpol . . . women in Paris."

"I don't know what you're talking about." Quinn's haughty tones were crystal clear.

Cannon said something about "Thai Police and Bangkok."

Alexa struggled to remain fully conscious. Her head was pounding, and her body shook with chills. She needed liquids soon or she'd be in serious trouble.

John's voice penetrated through the fog. "So, Hutton, it's over for you. Things will go better if you cooperate with us. Take us to Ms. Williams. Now."

Alexa could hear Quinn's deranged contempt when he spat, "You're too late. Alexa had to die for Nan Ton Pho."

"No. I'm alive," Alexa whimpered, but no one heard.

Out on the lane, Quinn screamed at the top of his lungs, "Artists must be sacrificed to their art."

Before he'd finished his sentence, gunfire erupted. Alexa thought Quinn fired first, and the police returned fire in full force. She burrowed deeper into the meadow and covered her head. She'd come too far to be killed by a stray bullet.

When silence fell, Alexa opened her eyes and took three slow, measured breaths in an attempt to clear her head.

Ears ringing, she belly-crawled toward the road. Sticks and thorns stabbed at Alexa through her thin pantsuit. She ignored the pain and clawed through the thick brush until she reached the edge of the weeds. The pungent, smoky smell of gunfire hung in the air. Ahead of her, Quinn's body lay motionless on the lane in a pool of blood. She couldn't see any of the policemen.

She felt no sadness over Quinn's death. He had terrorized her. He had murdered countless others. She totally believed his accounts of killing many women—on his own and with his father. Even in his last moments, he'd died a pretentious asshole, shouting a self-aggrandizing quote as he committed suicide by cop. Alexa was glad the bastard was dead.

Her thoughts turned to John, worried that he'd been killed or injured by Quinn's barrage of gunfire. Alexa tried to stand but didn't have the strength to rise. She couldn't put weight on the leg with the cramp. Gasping in pain, she collapsed. Seconds later, John and another policeman walked into her narrow frame of view. The two men approached Quinn's body, guns drawn, and determined that he was dead.

"Help. Help," Alexa rasped. "I'm here. I'm not dead. I'm not dead. I'm not dead." Feebly, she grasped a stalk of sumac between her bound hands and shook it. But no one came.

A series of chills wracked Alexa's body. Dimly, she knew that if she didn't get hydrated soon, she would black out and might not be discovered. She wasn't going to let that asshole Quinn win. Gathering her last remaining shred of energy, Alexa used her bare elbows to drag her battered body onto the lane.

"Alexa. My God. I knew that bastard was lying." John rushed over and dropped to the ground, cradling her in his arms. The other cop yelled for an EMT.

"My God. You're bleeding. What did he do to you?" John's tears wet Alexa's cheeks as he cut the rope from her bound wrists. "He said you were dead."

"Another few minutes and it could have been true. I can't tell you how glad I am to see you and your posse. I need water. Water," Alexa whispered as she breathed a long sigh of relief. Two medics came running toward them with a stretcher.

"What the fuck was Hutton talking about? Nan Ton something?" John's tone held notes of anger, concern, and confusion.

Just before Alexa passed out, she mumbled, "Wait until you see the barn."

EPILOGUE

But, now I've only memories and the
whisper of your name.
—Levi Bloom

"THANKS FOR COMING WITH ME. And for driving." Susan put down her cell phone and looked at Alexa. "Your dad says he and Scout are doing just fine without us."

Alexa didn't take her eyes from the road. Even after a four-hour drive, she wasn't totally comfortable with her mother's big Range Rover. "Big surprise. Scout loves Dad like crazy. And vice versa. I think we turn here. Does this say Hurd Road?"

"Yes. Look. There's a sign for Bethel Woods Center for the Arts. This is it."

Alexa pulled into a parking lot by a big timber and glass museum. The trees on the grounds blazed bright orange and red in the October light. "Why don't they call it the Woodstock Museum?"

"Something about rights to the name." Susan climbed carefully out of the car and looked around with uncharacteristic indecision. "I'm still not sure what I'm doing here."

"I think you're looking for closure," Alexa offered as she joined her mother. Raising her eyebrows in amazement, she laughed. "Listen to me. I'm always accusing Melissa of sounding like Dr. Phil. Now here I am talking about closure."

"But you're not too far off, dear. I do think I'm looking to complete the circle that started for me here at Woodstock."

Alexa and her mother walked slowly into the museum's foyer. "We can rest whenever you want, Mom," Alexa cautioned.

"I'll be fine, dear. It's taken me awhile to recover from the bullet wound, but I'm almost fully healed. You're the one I'm concerned about, Alexa. You spent most of your summer getting knocked about in one way or the other. That whole terrifying experience with Quinn Hutton was only about six weeks ago. I will be forever grateful to Melissa for alerting the police."

"I still get nightmares, but physically I'm fine. Sometimes I can't stop thinking about all those other women who didn't make it out of Quinn's temple of horrors. What a twisted SOB. He called them 'disposable women.'"

Alexa took a deep breath. "Enough of that." She backed away from that dark memory. "Mom, today is for you. To revisit Woodstock with a fresh perspective. To lay your ghosts to rest. To remember Willow." Alexa held the interior museum door open for her mother to enter.

They spent nearly two hours wandering through exhibits about the sixties and the Woodstock Festival itself. There were quite a few videos of the actual concert, some of them little more than home movies. Susan laughed at the school bus painted in psychedelic colors. "That's a nice reminder of the Hog Farm's buses."

Susan spent a long time at the exhibit that told the tales of people like her, who had been to Woodstock. After they read a smattering of the many stories, Alexa remembered the scrapbook she'd seen in her mother's attic.

"What happened to the group you went with, Mom? Of course, I know about Jack and Quinn. And Aunt Nina is an interior decorator in Boston. What about the rest?"

"Well, Robbie fulfilled his potential. We always said he was as smart as a rocket scientist. Turned out he was exactly that smart. After getting a graduate degree at MIT, he went to work for NASA.

"I think the sixties were a little too wild for Cheryl. She married someone in Lancaster—a banker, I think—settled down, and had a bunch of kids.

"I'm not completely sure what happened to Phil. He flunked out of college and got drafted. Although he survived Vietnam, he picked up a heroin habit over there. After the war, I opened up a *Life* magazine with an article on treatment of addicted veterans. There was Phil in a full-page photo about the treatment program. I don't know if he kicked the habit or where he ended up."

"And your boyfriend, Ben?"

"I told you that we broke up not long after Woodstock. Turned out that Ben wasn't quite the guy I wanted him to be. I saw him at a class reunion sometime in the nineties. He was living in Boca

Raton, Florida selling real estate." Susan pursed her lips in disapproval. "He had one of those leather tans and dressed about ten years younger than his age. It was a little pathetic.

"And, of course, you know what course my life took after Woodstock. It seems so long ago since I was Sukie: braless and in braids, with the whole world to explore."

"Dad still calls you Sukie. And you're certainly still exploring the world. I think you've changed a lot less than you think." Alexa squeezed her mother's hand.

Near the end, they came to an exhibit honoring key figures from the festival who had died. Many on the list were musicians like Janis Joplin and Jimi Hendrix. Susan shed a tear at a name near the top of the list: Greta Shapiro, Age 14; August 16, 1969.

"Poor, poor Willow. What a tragedy that those animals killed her. I just wish that they were going to pay for her death."

"Quinn the Eskimo Hutton and Jack Nash will probably never step outside a jail again. They might not be convicted in Willow's death, but they'll serve decades on end for their many other crimes. Although Quinn's demented ramblings to me wouldn't mean a thing in a court of law, he basically confirmed that his father and Jack killed Willow."

Alexa shuddered. "Looking at all these pictures and videos about the concert and the hippies and the whole go-with-the-flow atmosphere, it's hard to believe that Woodstock also spawned the monsters that Eskimo and Jack became. Cecily Townes' homicide, Meg Wilson's death, serial murder, sex trafficking, and God knows what other foul deeds."

After a picnic lunch, they drove down a small road through the grounds that had once housed the famous Three Days of Peace and Music. Susan pointed out the general area where she thought her group had camped. When they came to a grassy slope that formed a natural bowl, she described how it looked filled with hundreds of thousands of concertgoers.

At the bottom of the hill, where the stage had been, they got out of the car. Alexa and her mom were the only two people there. They walked to a low concrete monument with a dove and a guitar that said, "This is the original site of the Woodstock Music and Arts Fair, held August 15, 16, 17, 1969." A list of performers was included on two plaques.

Susan placed a bunch of daisies on the monument. "Rest in peace, Willow." When tears began streaming down her mother's face, Alexa gave her some privacy and walked to the SUV.

The sky was a brilliant blue, and the autumn breeze whipped Alexa's hair into her eyes. With the photos in the museum still fresh in her mind, she tried to imagine rock music and the sound of half a million voices ringing through this quiet field.

When her mom walked away from the monument, she had regained her composure. As they drove out of the museum grounds, Susan smiled. "I'm glad I came. This place is pretty commercialized, but it's the twenty-first century. Practically everything is commercialized. The exhibits evoked some good memories though.

"I feel as if a miasma has enveloped me for all these years about Woodstock. I could never get past Willow's death, partly because I repressed so much of what happened.

"In reality, Woodstock was pretty amazing. The three days of peace and music and mud and marijuana—it was a once in a lifetime experience. Despite everything that happened with Eskimo, Jack, and Willow, I'm glad I was there. I think I can finally put Woodstock in the proper perspective. It was a glorious, untamed mess that perfectly captured the mood and the idealism of that moment in time." She turned to Alexa, her eyes brimming. "I feel like a shadow has lifted, and my hope has been restored."

Alexa left the new few seconds pass in silence in respect for her mother's emotional statement. "Thanks for asking me to come along, Mom. This visit certainly gave me new insight on Woodstock. And about you."

A few miles down the road they turned into the late afternoon sun. Squinting, Alexa asked, "Mom? Can you look in my bag for my sunglasses?"

A few seconds later, Susan handed Alexa a pair of tortoiseshell sunglasses. When Alexa put them on her face, she couldn't see through the dust. With a smile, she handed them back.

"Can you clean these for me? I keep another pair of sunglasses in the rental car. I haven't worn these since I left Africa. They're covered in Samburu dust." When her mother handed them back, Alexa pushed the sunglasses over the bridge of her nose and soared back in time to the moment of pure peace she'd felt that morning on the Serengeti. The scars from her encounter with Quinn Hutton receded with that memory of Africa.

After a few miles of companionable silence, Susan grinned and opened up the center console. "Did I tell you that I have an album by Levi Bloom and the Flatbush Boulevard? I came across it in a secondhand record store in Philadelphia sometime in the seventies."

"Was that their only album?"

"I think so. Earlier this month, I dug it out and had it transferred to CD. The group sounds a little like the Byrds, but with a heavier bass line." Susan took a CD out of the center console and popped it into the CD player.

Alexa grinned as the plaintive strains of the folk rock band filled the car.

"The whisper of your name, oh yeah,
The whisper of your name."

AFTERWORD

THIS IS A WORK OF FICTION, and my characters are drawn from my imagination. With the exception of the inestimable Doris Keck, proprietor of Keck's Store, any resemblance to actual people is purely coincidental. Of course, the artists who performed onstage at the Woodstock Festival are real.

Some of my references are based in fact. The Woodstock Festival did take place in 1969. Much of my description of those three days of peace and music is drawn from my own memories, as well as contemporaneous and later news articles. However, the story of Woodstock in this work is fictionalized.

Sex trafficking is a worldwide problem, and the statistics in the book are real. However, the organizations, networks, and story about sex trafficking in this work are fictionalized. There is no organization called RESIST. However, there are many fine agencies, both governmental and nongovernmental, that work to combat modern day slavery across the globe and to rescue the victims of human trafficking. Similarly, there are many reputable agencies, both public and private, that provide life-altering assistance to abused and neglected children.

The quotes that introduce each of the Woodstock chapters are primarily sayings that were popular among hippies during the sixties and early seventies. A few of the quotes that open those chapters (and statements in the narrative) are announcements that were made onstage during the Woodstock Festival of 1969. Levi Bloom, his folk-rock band, and his songs exist only in my imagination.

Many of the places in this novel, both in South Central Pennsylvania and Africa, are real. However, others exist only in the pages of this book. There is no child service organization in Pennsylvania named Children of Light. If you look for their headquarters on the South Mountain in Cumberland County, you will not find it.

ACKNOWLEDGMENTS

I WANT TO THANK ALL the people who helped with *Dead of Summer.* First and foremost, my husband, Mike, who not only gave me feedback on the manuscript but also continues to support the hours I spend hunched over a computer in the world of Alexa Williams. The Knowlton/Kuehn clan gave me assistance and feedback on an early draft of the book. This group includes Josh Knowlton and Laura Stevens, Steve and Pam Knowlton, Dave and Nancy Knowlton, and Denny and Coe Kuehn.

Once again, Trooper Jessica Williams of Troop H - Carlisle provided technical assistance on state police and other criminal procedure. Detective Sergeant Daniel Freedman of the Carlisle Police Department also provided clarification on procedures involving both missing children and homicide investigations.

Lorrie Deck, Director of the Statewide Adoption Network (SWAN) in the Pennsylvania Department of Human Services, brought me up to date on the latest adoption laws and other Children and Youth policies and procedures. Thanks to Lisa Roscoe for arranging the connection.

Dermot Groome, Visiting Professor of Law at The Dickinson Schools of Law, gave me an introduction to some of the criminal charges relevant to the book. He also shared his experience in fighting international human trafficking.

Petra Wirth, a wonderful teacher of yoga and life, provided me with a good foundation in yoga—and technical assistance on that critical plot point of the Scorpion pose.

Jesse and Tina Plengsri were my consultants in all things Thai. Dairy farmer Mark Fulton of Shippensburg, PA helped me on details around crop cycles and scary farm equipment. And Lelani Woods of the National Park Service provided information about police jurisdiction on the National Mall.

Thanks to all of these people, and the crew at Sunbury Press, for their generous help in making *Dead of Summer* more technically accurate. If I've misinterpreted the facts, the fault is purely mine.

ABOUT THE AUTHOR

SHERRY KNOWLTON IS THE AUTHOR of the successful Alexa Williams suspense novels, *DEAD of AUTUMN* and *DEAD of SUMMER*. Sherry (née Sherry Rothenberger) was born and raised in Chambersburg, PA, where she developed a lifelong passion for books. She was that kid who would sneak a flashlight to bed at night so she could read beneath the covers. All the local librarians knew her by name.

Sherry spent much of her early career in state government, working primarily with social and human services programs, including services for abused children, rape crisis, domestic violence, and family planning. In the 1990s, she served as the Deputy Secretary for Medical Assistance in the Commonwealth of Pennsylvania. The latter part of Sherry's career has focused on the field of Medicaid managed care. Now retired from executive positions in the health insurance industry, Sherry runs her own health care consulting business.

Sherry has a B.A. in English and psychology from Dickinson College in Carlisle, PA.

Sherry and her husband, Mike, began their journey together in the days of peace and music when they traversed the country in a hippie van. Running out of money several months into the trip, Sherry waitressed the night shift at a cowboy hangout in Jackson Hole, Wyoming, and Mike washed dishes in a bakery. Undeterred, they embraced the travel experience and continue to explore far-flung places around the globe. Sherry and Mike have one son, Josh, a craft brewer.

Sherry lives in the mountains of South Central Pennsylvania, the setting for both *DEAD of AUTUMN* and *DEAD of SUMMER.*

For more information about the author and the Alexa Williams series visit www.sherryknowlton.com.